March

Flay

Thorn

Boot

Hollow

Sanctuary

The Bladed Labyrinth

The Spire

Draun

The Spikelands

The Deeper

Forsaken Klatch

The Saga Of Ukumog

Wracked
Desecrated
Flayed

FLAYED

By Louis Puster III

Sean,

Thanks for continued to support my terrible writing habit. I hope you continue to enjoy the story.

Stay Awesome.

Louis Puster III

This is a work of fiction. All the characters and events portrayed in this book are either products of the author's imagination or are used fictitiously.

FLAYED

Copyright © 2016 by Louis Puster III

All rights reserved, including the right to reproduce this book, or portions thereof, in any form.

Edited by Morgan A. McLaughlin McFarland
Cover Art by Chandler Kennedy
Maps by Louis Puster III

First Edition
ISBN 1479239585
ISBN 978-1479239580

For Wendell, Blaine, and Allison

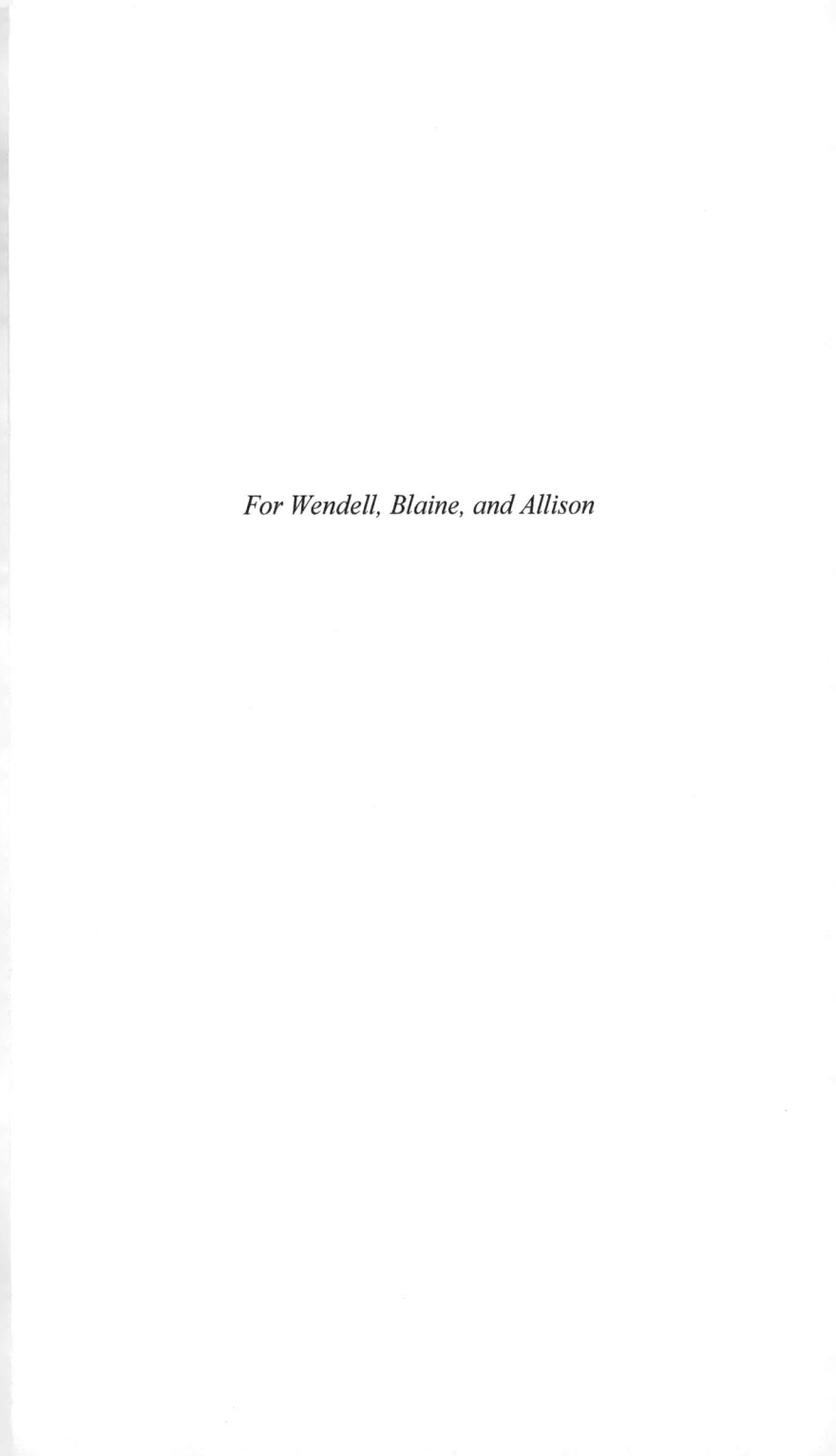

Prologue

"I need some air," I muttered to the quiet host of Hunters that lurked around me. They stared in my direction with a mixture of fear and confusion. There in the crowd, Avar's face was just as confused as the rest. Brin, on the other hand, had a sad understanding in her eyes. Her disappointment I just could not bear, and I looked away. With eyes to the floor, I gently passed through the group towards the exit of the temple. Verif stood at the entrance to the chamber. She looked at me proudly, her eyes glistened with lust. Not stopping to chat, I entered the stone hallway which led me to the surface. I did not look back at the crowd of them, the burned corpse of Tikras upon the floor, nor the empty shell of Lucien that lay upon the altar. I just kept walking until the fresh air filled my lungs.

The graveyard seemed still and quiet. Even with the few Hunters milling around a stillness loomed over the place. If I had not been present for it, I would not have known that moments ago a war raged here. It was almost disturbing, as if it were the quiet after the storm. I found myself wandering through the headstones of the graveyard, mindlessly searching through the names carved on weathered stones. On the north side of the tree and moon statue

Flayed

that marked the entrance to the temple below, I found myself surrounded by ancient stones. Some of them may have even been sculptures once, but time and wind had worn them down.

When I walked up, one of the Hunters was already there. He had a tool in his hand and was tracing the name in one of the stones. Before I could make out what he was doing, he stopped and looked up at me.

"These were some of the first Hunters." His voice was filled with reverence. "The books say they have been here for thousands of years."

"Oh yeah?" My curiosity was piqued.

He nodded. "Yeah. There are a few of us that try to keep their memory alive. The stones are so old though, hard to make out most of their names anymore."

Stepping forward, I glanced over the fragments of text that were recognizable on the various stones. A few orphaned letters here, others there. Most of the stones did not have enough definition in the markings for me to make out names.

"That was a tough fight there. And the one before it, with the armor thing…" His pause made me think he felt as if he had misspoke. "I'm Simon." He reached out his hand for me to shake.

"Hello Simon. They call me Wrack." I looked him in the eye as we shook hands. There was a proud sadness there. I found myself wondering if he saw the same sadness in my eyes.

Simon nodded at me with a knowing look. "Well, I should be getting some rest. Big cleanup will happen tomorrow. Sleep well, Wrack." And with that he walked off, towards the barracks.

Prologue

My eyes drifted back down to the stone he was carving. It was one of the very few who had a name that was complete. The carving read, MAREC. My mind reeled, combing through memories, visions, and dreams. I suddenly recalled an armored man with salt and pepper hair. A voice of reason. My guardian.

Blinking my eyes at this sudden recollection, I thought for a moment that I saw his ghostly form standing there in front of me, smiling. Stunned, I was about to speak when someone tapped me on the shoulder. It startled me so, that I almost leapt out of my skin.

"You ok?" Brin asked. Her face filled with concern.

Feeling silly about my reaction, I smiled. "Yeah. I just needed some air."

"That fight was rough." There was remorse in her voice. "I think she would have won if Tikras hadn't sacrificed himself."

"Tikras was a brave man. Someday we will have to kill that terrible monster for him." I glanced around the graveyard as I spoke. The ghost I thought I had seen was nowhere to be found.

Brin hesitated. "Did I uzk up in there?"

I was confused. "What do you mean?"

"There at the end of the fight. You started changing or something. I thought she was doing something to you. I—" Her voice trailed off.

"If you hadn't stopped me, I think was going to eat her. My jaw felt like it came unhinged."

"Yeah. You were scaring me a little bit. Like when you killed The Ghoul. But I am not sure if I should be scared by it." She let out a frustrated sigh. "I am not sure what to think."

Her green eyes darted down to the ground. A moment passed where the noise of the other people faded away and all I could hear was her. The rustling of the tiny breeze in her luscious

Flayed

dark hair, the near silent scales of her armor shifting as she breathed. I looked down her slender arm and, finding her hand empty, I gently grasped it with my own. "It isn't worth fretting over."

She squeezed my hand and looked into my eyes. The moment of relief that was on her face disappeared as quickly as it had appeared. It was replaced with a dark look. "I hate to say this... but sometimes you scare me, Wrack."

I squeezed her hand in return. "Sometimes I scare myself."

To my surprise she actually smiled and said, "Well that's something we have in common then."

My urge to consume her warmth flashed up within me. I drank in the entrancing smell of her sweat and the heat radiating from her battle-worn armor. The cold air gusted at us, and she stepped toward me. Instinctively, I wrapped an arm around her. The warmth of her hand landed on my arm. My senses were overwhelmed with ecstasy. Nothing I had experienced, up that moment, had felt so good.

Brin quickly turned her face towards me again, her velvety locks brushing my face as they passed by. Our eyes met and I heard Murks yell, "Master!"

Distracted by his exclamation, I hesitated. Brin's face started moving towards mine, and I was stunned. It took all my willpower to not lunge forward with my mouth and start to syphon away all her warmth. My soul struggled with itself. It felt like trying to hold back the tide of the ocean with a dinner plate. Her hot breath on my face eroded my willpower, but before I could act I was thrown off by a simple cough that came from nearby.

Both Brin and I seemed to wake from a trance. First we looked at each other with bewilderment, then our gaze turned to Avar, the source of the cough. "Better get some rest, you two. Tomorrow is going to be a busy and difficult day.

Prologue

Brin pushed herself away; the cold air eagerly stole the warmth of her body from me. "Yeah," she said. "See you in the morning, boys." With a quick glance of embarrassment over her shoulder towards me, Brin walked back to the barracks.

Avar didn't say anything. He just looked at me with his eyebrows up and his head tilted, then he too walked towards the barracks. I was left alone in the cold graveyard with my lust for warmth and the haunting thoughts about the headstones. It was an exceptionally long night.

Flayed

CHAPTER 1

The earliest rays of the sun revealed just how destroyed Sanctuary was. No building was left untouched. The mess hall had taken the majority of the damage, however. Its roof was completely caved in and most of the wood parts of the building had burned away. The top of the stonework chimney had collapsed, reminding me slightly of the Great Tower that lay hidden in the Forest of Shadows. A gaping hole in the side of the barracks had been covered up by a bunch of blankets to keep as much of the cold wind out as possible while the hunters slept.

The captain's house was the least damaged, but for its part the meeting room on the back side looked as if something had torn half of it off in the battle. Inside, I could see Bridain trying to preserve the artifacts that remained whole. He looked as if he were packing all of them for a long journey. I slowly walked towards the building as I watched him. When he stopped packing for a moment I asked, "Going somewhere?"

His eyes casually threw daggers in my direction and he stopped his work. With a labored grunt, he rested on a crate and took a sip from a waterskin that sat upon the table. He looked past me towards the graveyard. Following his glance, I saw what he did, a garden of death, a place filled with the stone markers of the long dead, and the still-fresh corpses of people he considered his family.

Flayed

I could not help but feel guilty for the young bodies that littered Bridain's view. I wasn't to blame for the battle that had happened, but I knew that within my blood there was a power that might have saved them, all of them. Curse me, if only I knew how to use it properly.

"Master must not blame himself. His power is great, but there is a cost..." Of course, Murks' tiny voice in my head was right. Still, I promised myself that I would not let something like this happen again if I could find a way to stop it.

"I don't know who you are, Wrack, but I know you aren't human. Maybe you never were." Bridain paused to take another gulp from his waterskin. "As much as I would like to blame you for everything that happened, truth is that we were under attack long before you showed up. Without you, Brin, and those odd northerners... Well, last night might have been the end of the Shadow Hunters." He stood up and put the waterskin back on the table. "And even though I don't understand why, Teague told me I should trust you. So, goddess help me, I'm trying."

"Teague?" I was shocked to hear the name of Brin's father so casually mentioned, especially since Avar said he had been dead for twenty-five years.

Bridain moved some crates around, but eventually grunted out a, "Yeah."

"But I thought he was—"

"Listen, kid," Bridain snapped at me, "don't go telling Brin I said anything about her father. That is the last thing I need, her thinking that her father is still alive, or worse yet, that I had something to do with his death. The old bard came here a lot when I was a boy. He used to visit with the commanders and give them information. Your name apparently came up once or twice."

Chapter 1

Now I was completely confused. When I had arrived in Sanctuary, I had been treated like a leper. Bridain himself had told Avar that I had killed Garrett. If their revered prophet had spoken about me, why was there so much doubt?

"Don't get all conflicted, kid," Bridain spoke before I could even pose a question. "The prophecies say a lot of things. Hell, old Teague was the kind of fellow who would rarely shut up. Even now it is hard to parse some of the things he said. Man certainly had a way with words." He rifled through some books and scrolls in a different crate. "With such a wealth of information, some things just get lost."

"Then why did you tell Avar that I killed Garrett?" My tone was more accusatory than I intended.

He slammed the top of the crate back on top. "Because I thought you had! By the Sundered Gate! I am trying to tell you, son. I am only human. I make mistakes. Hell, I am not sure I am doing the right thing by telling you all this. Maybe I should just keep my uzkin' trap shut for once."

There was silence between us as Bridain continued to search and pack crates. He would mutter to himself occasionally, and eventually, I thought better of trying to continue the conversation, so I walked away.

The rest of the Hunters were slowly waking. The first groups came to the graveyard and began cleaning up the corpses of their friends and enemies. I watched a few of them work to dig fresh graves in the frozen ground, a task that was not easily done.

After a time of just watching, I decided to participate. If Teague had spoken well of me to the Hunters, then perhaps I wasn't some terrible monster after all. Not something for them to

Flayed

fear, but maybe in a previous life I was their ally. My memories of Lucien and Merec would certainly seem to echo that. So I stepped forward, took a shovel, and started digging.

I dug fifteen graves before Brin came and found me that morning. She stayed only long enough to find out what I was doing, and then left me to it. By midday I had dug twenty-three graves, and by the time the sun was going down, forty dead Hunters had new homes in the frozen dirt. I wasn't tired, but I was certainly covered in earth. Looking at my handiwork, I felt proud that my supernatural strength had been put to good use. I shared a smile and a nod with the solemn Hunters that had been working with me.

During the course of the day, Bridain and some of the other Hunters had been taking crates from the commander's house and going into the temple below the graveyard. When I took a break from digging graves, I went down there to see what they were doing.

The circular room of the temple now had crates stacked along the stone wall. Tikras' burned body had been removed, but Lucien's remains still lay upon the altar, chains and all. Something about leaving him there bothered me. My thoughts flashed back to images of the bloody hammer in my hand, and I could again hear the musical clang of hammer on steel.

Before long, I was standing near the altar, staring at all the fragments of Lucien's armor. I was lost in wonder about how things could have changed from the noble soul in my memories to the twisted and empty monster that lay dead before me. Does time and power reduce us all to such immoral terrors? I refused to believe it. Some souls shine brighter than others. For some, the urge to do what is decent and good is not even a struggle. Lucien

Chapter 1

was a beacon of what humanity should be. How could I make right what happened to him? How could I wipe away the gloomy dread of The Doomed?

Without thinking, I touched a piece of the armor, and my mind was taken somewhere else.

This was not like any other vision that had haunted me before. This was more like I was looking through someone else's eyes, eyes that did not work like my own. The contrast between light and darkness had more variations than I could normally see, even with my dark sight. The air seemed to be filled with glittering particles, and towards the edges of my sight the image seemed to bend in odd ways giving me excellent peripheral vision.

Whoever owned these eyes was standing under the sky on the top of a gigantic mountain. I could see the snowy slopes that reached up from the misty clouds that seemed to be a basin from which the rock sprouted. But even as I watched, the mists would part to reveal snow covered hills below stretching as far as I could see. It was night there, and I could see tiny points of light flickering on the ground below. They were scattered and few, but there was no mistake that they were there.

The person turned, and suddenly I was looking at a great fortress, carved into the side of the mountain near its peak. Roosted all around were winged things, reptilian and black as obsidian. Braziers burned brightly inside this frozen stone palace on the mountain top, and within I could see the volcanically-blooded freth and the draconic forms of the drakkar moving about within. As if I

Flayed

needed another sign, the person who owned these eyes raised their arm, and I saw the armored fist that had fused itself to the hand of The Mistress.

As she examined it, I could see how truly her flesh and it had melted together. Her inhuman finger ran down the place where the armor joined her forearm. In the sheen of the armor, I could see Lucien's face silently screaming with torment and rage.

My fingers loosed the fragment of the armor and it clattered back to the silver altar. Somehow I knew that my ancient friend had not been entirely released from his prison. Instead, it had simply been traded for another wherein he could not act. He was locked away in a gauntlet, and some fragment of his ancient power was now at her command. I had failed him. In every way possible, I had failed him. Overwhelmed with the coursing thoughts of Lucien's torment, I wept, and my grey tears sizzled upon the cold altar that was his burial slab. I was an unholy thing.

Behind me, the Hunters who were working with the crates retreated from the temple, leaving me alone to dwell on my complete failure. Even Murks had nothing supportive to say; instead I felt him sob silently within the hidden pocket of my robes. He, too, could not bear the thought of the quiet torment of Lucien's new prison. Both of us had hoped that his twisted shackling had been redeemed in death, I felt a fool to have not realized that The Mistress's theft of his gauntlet had not transferred him to her. There was only one option: I had to finish what I started. I had to put Lucien to his deserved rest and end his tormentor. But how? When?

Chapter 1

That evening, after all the work was done, Bridain called the Hunters together for a feast around a massive bonfire. Ferrin and Avar had gone out hunting during the day, as the food supplies had been destroyed, and luck had been with them. They brought back a boar large enough to feed the twenty-something Hunters that remained.

After everyone had had a chance to get a little food in their bellies, Bridain spoke to all of them. "Brothers. Sisters. Hunters. Our victory has come at some great cost. Our home is broken, its protection shattered. So many of our family have been laid to rest with Marec and our ancestors."

At the mention of Marec, I could not help but look over my shoulder at the great graveyard, hoping to see his shape in the darkness. I did, however, catch the eye of Simon, who sat nearby whittling a piece of wood as his listened to Bridain. When our eyes met, he nodded at me and continued his carving.

Bridain continued, "Our enemy was defeated last night, but she survived. We drove her back, but this attack will not be the end. Whatever manner of creature that woman is, I doubt she will give up. She will return."

"She has what she came here for," I whispered to Brin.

Bridain stopped. "Do you have something you want to tell us, Wrack? Some mysterious secret you feel you have to keep from us?" I could not tell if he was agitated by my speaking, or if he had heard me.

Nervousness at being suddenly called out put a lump in my throat. My mind panicked at the idea of telling them that I had seen through the eyes of their enemy, but my thoughts about the torment of my ancient friend changed my mind. "She got what she came here for."

Flayed

Dumbfounded, Bridain looked at me with a bit of disdain. "And how do you know that, exactly, Wrack?" Venom dripped from the accusatory tone of my name.

"When she and I were connected and the power was shredded, I felt some of the power go into her," I half lied, for while I didn't actually feel that, I assumed it was true.

Silence fell over the crowd as everyone thought about what I had just said. The silence was followed by a cacophony of whispering. Whispers grew into murmurs, murmurs into grumbles, grumbles into shouts. Before he knew what hit him, Bridain was besieged by an assault of suggestions, comments, and accusations.

"Alright! Alright!" Bridain tried to silence the angry group, but to no avail. Mustering the scolding yet fatherly voice all battle commanders had to possess, he finally bellowed, "SILENCE!"

The Hunters went quiet instantly, many of them suddenly looking ashamed at their fear, their anger, their discord. A Hunter lost to fear or anger was a dead Hunter, and a Hunter without the rest of them…

"For the love of the Lady, I can only listen to you one at a time!" Bridain shouted at them with angry concern, then his tone softened. "Simon, you speak first."

The same fellow I had seen the night before in the graveyard stepped forward. Before he spoke, he ran his thumb and forefinger over both halves his mustache as if to align it properly. "I think we should go after her, Commander. Perhaps leave a few of us behind to make sure that the sacred ground here is not disturbed, but we can go north to hunt her."

Chapter 1

The crowd grumbled in agreement with Simon, and wisely, Bridain waited for the grumbling to taper off. "Wise words, Simon. Going into the lair of the beast will be dangerous. No doubt she has an army of drakkar and freth at her disposal. How will we few take on another army?"

The crowd grumbled again, but then one of the other Hunters stepped forward, a young boy with long brown hair who had spent most of the day digging graves with me. He loudly said, "What about the northmen? If she is in the North, surely she torments the people of Winterland. Perhaps we can help each other."

Bridain nodded. "More wisdom, Benjamin. Thank you."

I smiled. Bridain was a smart leader. He was letting them work out their own path together, but remaining as the shepherd to give them guidance. It was working. I could feel the morale of the Hunters improving. With a bonfire, some food, and a chance to decide their fate, Bridain had saved the Shadow Hunters from breaking under the terrible losses of the night before. Again, they were steeled against the future after he said, "I think our purpose is decided. Tomorrow we leave Sanctuary to find allies among the northmen, and then we kill the dragon woman."

A cheer came from the crowd, and many of the Hunters raised their fists in celebration. Simon was the one exception. Instead he threw the piece of wood he had been whittling into the fire. On the fire, I finally saw that he had carved the image of a dragon into the small piece of wood. The flames eagerly licked at the carving, and it was quickly covered in bright fire. I looked back at Simon, and I knew this was his way of declaring war against The Mistress. He gave me an ominous nod and then walked towards the barracks.

"Commanda! Ol' Ferrin has somfing ta say, he does," Ferrin roared over the fired-up Hunters.

Flayed

Bridain motioned for everyone to quiet down. "What is it, Ferrin?"

"I fink I'd like to stay here a bit. Some ol' ghost has got to haunt these ruins, he does." Ferrin motioned to the large collection of gravestones.

Bridain nodded. "Of course. Your place has always been here, Ferrin. As a guardian of the Silver Lady, you have a duty to watch over her holy places, but you shouldn't have to be here alone…" Bridain started to motion towards Avar, but Ferrin growled.

"Da boy has other places ta be, Commanda. Besides, ol' Ferrin is neva alone. He has the ghosts of all his brothas with him here, he does. Dun worry about ol' Ferrin. He'll be fine."

Bridain just nodded, and Ferrin stalked away from the crowd, giving Avar a wink as he did so. Avar looked like he didn't quite know what to think about that, then Bridain turned towards Brin, Avar, and me.

Before he could speak, Brin said firmly, "I have to track down the wizard known as Grumth. He is connected to the murder of my father. There won't be any journey to Winterland for me."

"I am going with Brin," I said, only to shed any doubt. There was a look of relief on the faces of some of the Hunters.

Bridain looked confused. "Wrack, we may need whatever power you used against her before. You should reconsider."

Shaking my head, I replied, "I have made an oath to Brin that I will help her avenge her father's death. I can only follow one path at a time. With luck, our trip to Flay will be short, and we can come find all of you in Winterland."

"I wouldn't hold my uzkin' breath," Brin blurted out.

Anger lived in the eyes of some of the Hunters. Oddly, many of the same ones who seemed relieved that I would not be coming along were now upset for a different reason. Maybe they

Chapter 1

did want me to come with them, after all. Paying more attention forced me to put that aside. They just didn't like Brin's attitude. The love and hate that lived simultaneously between her and the Hunters I found curiously confusing.

A voice from the Hunters called out, "I am going with Brin." Gordo stepped forward out of the crowd.

Both Brin and Bridain looked at Gordo with disapproving eyes.

"What?" said Bridain.

"Thanks, but I have all the Hunters I need." Brin patted Avar on his armored shoulder.

Without skipping a beat, Gordo turned to Brin. "Unless you want to take on The King's entire army, you will need help to sneak past the thorn walls that surround the city. I have a way in that doesn't involve all-out war at the front gate."

"We are going to need the help in Flay, Brin," Avar said confidently.

"I'm going with Brin too," Tarissa's shy voice called out while Brin fumed.

"Fine!" Brin's temper got the best of her. "Anyone else who wants to uzkin' come along?"

Verif walked over and put her hand on my arm. "I want to come too," she said, looking directly into my eyes. Her lustful smile pushed Brin over the edge.

"For uzk sake. Skulking around the city, looking for Grumth, is going to be hard if we have a parade of Hunters and sorcerers," she said with contempt.

"And Ukumog won't stick out?" I said, trying to bring levity to the tense air.

Flayed

Brin just glared at me and, after a moment, walked away. As I watched her go, Verif put her hand in mine. I just let it happen and stayed listening to the Hunters discuss their arrangements. My mind could not get away from my own journey, and the clinging grasp of Verif did nothing to comfort my worries about Brin and the Hunters clashing.

Buried in my own thoughts, I found a way to escape the crowd alone. Mindlessly, I wandered to the graveyard and found myself near Marec's stone. I sat there with it, watching the moon travel through the sky, and found comfort in its silvery glow. I felt calm and knew that we were doing the right thing. Quietly, I thanked the patron of the Shadow Hunters, The Silver Lady, for that inspiration. Somehow, I felt as if she heard my whispered thanks.

Morning came and found three groups all ready to go separate directions. Our small band said their farewells to Bridain and the rest of the Hunters, then to Ferrin. Avar seemed to take the goodbyes the hardest, especially from Ferrin. The old man gave him a longer farewell than any of the others, and when he came to leave with us, Tarissa gave him a warm hug. Then we were off.

"So, what exactly is your plan, Gordo?" asked Brin.

Gordo smiled. "I have a friend who has a way with doors and gates. She will help us out, but first we will need to find her uncle, Jared. He should be up near Regret."

Brin sighed in frustration. "Regret is northwest. Flay is northeast. That is weeks in the wrong direction."

"Yeah, well…" Gordo paused, like he didn't want to say something else.

As typical, Brin could not let that go. "'Yeah, well' what?"

Gordo rolled his eyes. "Yeah, well… We might have to go all the way to Frostbite."

Chapter 1

"Sundered uzkin' gate! Frostbite is even farther to the northwest! You are joking, right? Tell me that you are joking."

Gordo didn't reply. He just kept walking west.

Behind me, I could just make out the whispering between Tarissa and Avar. Something about their tone made me decide not to listen in, no matter how much my curious nature compelled me to. With Gordo and Brin in front, and Tarissa and Avar bringing up the rear, Verif walked alongside me. It was a little awkward at first; I wasn't sure how to address her clear sign of affection from the night before. Each time I looked over at her, she smiled. They reminded me of the secret smiles that Brin sometimes gave me, but there was something distinctly selfish about them, like Verif was trying to persuade me to trust her through a fake sweet demeanor. Most of the time, I would just try to lull my mind to sleep by watching the dark curls of Brin's hair bounce as she walked through hills and forest.

A few days passed this way. Gordo and Brin kept arguing. Her temper would always get away with her, and Gordo would never raise his voice. He had the quiet sort of anger. Whenever she made him mad, he would just grow quiet for an hour or two. Avar and Tarissa kept whispering, and one night they even curled up together when it was time to camp.

"Those two have a bit of a history," Verif answered my curious stare after everyone else was asleep.

"Hrm? What do you mean?"

She smiled, happy to tell me something I didn't know. "Before Avar went off with Brin, everyone in Sanctuary thought they were going to get married. I am sure that even Garrett was convinced."

This was yet another side of Avar that I had somehow missed. When I first met him, he seemed so simple. Perhaps I let those early moments of his drunken lessons about The Doomed

Flayed

flavor my understanding of who he was. Suddenly, I felt a little guilty for thinking of him the way that Brin always had, like a walking library, a simple answer to all my questions about this world. Now it seemed, though, that I had a new person eager to tell me all the things she knew.

Verif offered to share some slices of an apple with me. At least, I think it was an apple. The flesh of it was rather dark and looked older than one might want to eat. I waved off her offering.

"Oh, I forgot. You don't really need to eat, do you?"

"Not really," I said with hesitation. With Verif, it was sometimes hard for me to tell where the conversation was going.

She sat there, quietly eating her apple, smiling at me every time I looked over in her direction. Eventually I couldn't take it anymore.

"Ok." My tone clearly conveyed my annoyance with the situation. "I know you aren't this nice. What is it that you want?"

She gave me a forced, fake look of shock and said, "Hey! I can be nice."

I raised an eyebrow and only thought about how she had been eager to tie me up with the rope that nearly killed Murks.

Her exaggerated pout faded and the real Verif appeared. "Ok fine. I am not filled with sunshine."

With my head shaking I muttered, "I knew it," and crossed my arms.

"You just aren't very forthcoming." She tried to sting me with blame or guilt.

Confused, I could not help but reply, "What?"

The camp was quiet, and Verif felt the need to check if anyone else was listening to our conversation before she replied. Turning her head to look around, and taking a bite of the dead-

Chapter 1

looking apple, she let the conversation drop just long enough that I thought she wouldn't reply. Then, just as I was about to let my mind wander elsewhere: "Magic," she blurted out.

My eyes narrowed. "What about it?"

She scoffed, "You know things I want to know. How much more complicated does this have to be?"

I glared at her.

"Did you think I was in love with you or something? I was just trying to be friends." She munched more ferociously on her death apple.

Sighing, I replied, "You could have just said something. Besides, I don't know what you probably want to know."

She chuckled a bit. "Playing hard to get. I have known your kind of wizard before."

I rolled my eyes and realized that she did not understand. There was power that was part of who or what I was, but I had no idea how to tap into it. There was no wizard who taught me how to use my power, no scroll that explained what the rules were, and if I was wrong, I certainly did not remember anything about them. Exasperated by her expectations, I could only reply, "I can't give you what you want. I don't have any answers. I am plodding along, just like you are."

She stared at me in disbelief. "But that can't be true. I have seen the things you do."

"Yeah, and all of them just happened," I tried to appeal to her. "It is like a reflex. I don't have any control over it."

A grave concern crossed her face. "That is... frightening, but amazing."

I glanced over at Brin, who had just woken up, probably due to our conversation. Her eyes met mine, and her sleepy smile changed for a brief moment to that secret warmth that she had for

Flayed

me. All my self-doubt from this agonizing conversation with Verif fell away, but only for the briefest of moments, then Verif's last comment sank in, and I felt that dark hunger well up in my chest, that desire that hid inside me. I clenched my fists and used the pain of my fingers digging into my palms to keep it at bay, but I knew that wouldn't work forever.

"People are trying to sleep here," Brin reminded us before slipping back into her slumber.

"You don't have to tell me," I said quietly to Verif, trying to end the awkward silence.

Verif smiled proudly. "Well, I suppose we will have to solve this thing together, then."

I glanced over at Brin, who seemed almost to glow there in the cold twilight of the evening. "Yeah," I said rather mindlessly. "Yeah, we will."

Chapter 2

For days after Verif and I had our little heart-to-heart, the awkward silence continued between us. I felt that I had already said too much, and every time I looked at her, she gave me that fake smile. I didn't really have much to say to her. The two people I wanted to spend more time with were always busy with their prospective partners in our jolly little band of miscreants. Tarissa and Avar drew closer to each other and further away from the rest of us. They thought that I hadn't noticed them holding hands while we were walking, or the quiet giggling that followed whispers. What ever was going on there, I just hoped it wouldn't make either of them sloppy. I remember how Avar was after Matthew was killed; he was a wreck. He became so withdrawn that he never even told Brin or I that Matthew was his brother. It was hard for me to forget little omissions like that.

Gordo and Brin were busy fighting over who was really in charge. He knew where we needed to go, but Brin had issues letting anyone else take the lead. More than once there were hushed arguments filled with whispered fury. Her rage could not overcome her need to remain hidden from the patrols that we believed were wandering the woods around us.

Flayed

Our paranoia was confirmed one evening when we were looking for a good place to camp. Gordo took us to an old overgrown road that used to connect the southern reaches of Marrowdale to some other town that no longer existed.

That night, I was sent out to gather wood for a fire while Brin and Avar went to hunt for food. The sun was setting by the time we had found a good spot, something hidden from the road. The day leading up to this was filled with cold drizzling rain. Everything was wet. I kept foraging for something that might have been kept dry, but was having trouble. It got darker, then I saw a spot of light through the trees.

For a moment I thought I got turned around and that my companions must have found some dry wood, but then I realized that it was actually on the other side of the old road. I immediately changed my movements to try and conceal my presence. Someone had heard me. I knew it.

Moments later, a pair of soldiers, clad from neck to toe in black leather armor emblazoned with the red skull of The Baron, came looking for me. Recalling a trick I had seen Brin do when hunting, I found some wet leaves to lie in, camouflaging my form, then I tossed a rock away from where I was. The two men heard the noise and headed off in that direction.

I knew I needed to warn my friends at the camp, but now I was curious. *Who were these men? Why were they out here? And how many of them were there?* I had to know. So, I started stalking them.

Slowly, I started following them at a cautious distance. Each time they turned in my direction while looking around, I was already prepared to elude their vision. "Use the terrain to break your form," I remember Brin telling me once on our escape from

Chapter 2

Yellow Liver. "The eye looks for the shape of a person or beast. If you are just a rock, a tree, or the wind - they won't ever uzkin' find you."

"Where did you learn all this?" I asked her.

Her face became grave, the way it always did when she thought of her father. "Doesn't matter where I learned it. It works. And if you are going to survive out here - you need to pay more attention."

The nostalgia for our simple trip to the Forest of Shadows suddenly overwhelmed me. The broken form of the world seemed normal back then. But now, things were all sideways. Perhaps they always were — I just didn't know better.

Shaking my mind free of the fog of memory, I continued to follow the two men.

"Oi! I don't fink it is anyfing. Les go back to da uzkin fire, right?"

The second one nodded in agreement. "Too right, my lad. It is too cold up in dis forest for these old bones, it is. Back to the fire, and the sergeant's mead."

Sergeant? I could not help but wonder if they were members of Sergeant Valance's Jawbone Company. Now I was really too curious for my own good.

I made my way across the road after the two men. Their desire for mead had quickened their pace, and it made my stalking more difficult. I looked up just in time to notice that there were also some fortifications in the trees with men watching the road. It was a wonder that no one had seen me cross.

Safely in the dark embrace of the woods on the other side of the road, I continued to follow the two men. Occasionally I could hear them muttering things to one another, but I could make no sense of their conversation. Almost out of nowhere, a fortress

Flayed

suddenly loomed before me. It was heavily camouflaged, as if it had grown there in the woods. Only the movement of men on the walls of the fort gave it away. I pressed myself behind a thick tree to hide from the watchers there upon the walls. The two men I had been following approached a curtain of vines, which parted and let them in. Through this opening, I could see a fire inside some iron box with a door that stood open, where wood could be deposited. While I watched, the tenders of the fire closed the door, presumably to hide the light of the fire.

This brief window of light must have been what I saw, for the fort was not far from the road. Without my two wandering distractions, I felt trapped. Between me and the road were the lookout nests, and I was sure that the eyes of the watchers on the walls of the fort were now paying attention to the segment of the forest where I found myself. I had no choice but to wait for the right time to move.

"Fifteen days it is," a voice from the wall called out.

A scoffing sound came from elsewhere on the wall. "You on about that again? We is here because The Baron says we be here. We be here as long as hims fink us do."

The first watcher grumbled, "It ain't dis fort which be driving me crazy—"

"You was crazy to begin wit."

The first one laughed, "Oi, ye be right about that. Course we all havta be crazy to be out here."

"Dem deadies cannae be as bad as dey say," the second one said.

I tried to get a better look up at the wall. My eyes focused on finding the source of the two voices. If they were distracting each other, perhaps I could make my escape.

Chapter 2

"You wrong 'bout dat, boy," the first one's tone became serious. "I'z seen dem in action. You cannae kill 'em. They jus get back up ifin them fall down. Not like a man. More like the..." His voice trailed off.

My thoughts finished the sentence for him. *More like The Doomed.* Unkillable. An army of deathless things would be impossible to defeat. Even with Ukumog on our side, the blade that already had felled two of the immortal dark masters of this diseased world, it would be impossible to face that many of them at once. And the two we did defeat... Well, one was made weak by hunger and fear, and the other had been trapped for thousands of years. Suddenly I grew afraid of a conflict with one of The Doomed that was really in charge. The Baron or The King came immediately to mind. Then the fight between Valance's men and The Vampire overtook my thoughts. I didn't stick around to see the end of that, but it wasn't going well for the humans that stood against him. An arrow of despair pierced my heart. For one unexplainable moment - I was overwhelmed at the enormity of my position. It seemed that I was at odds with the same powers which had ground the world to the vile stagnation that was all around me. *Even with Brin, Avar, Ukumog, and the hunters beside me how could we hope to overcome The Doomed?*

My chest pulsed with a cold, wracking pain. Flashes of the dream where I had been pierced by those black iron rods and buried by The Baron coursed through my mind. My eyelids fluttered and my breath became labored as I fought the whirlpool of visions that sought to steal me away. I slid silently down the tree I was behind, and pulled my robe tightly around me, grasping for any comfort I could find.

Flayed

"Bah!" the second one called out. "You sound like you a Flayer! Uzk Da King and him's knights. Da Baron am da one who ain't killable! Hims power is so much greater!"

The first one laughed. "Yeah? Den whys we been fightin' dis war for so long, eh? Whys him not just wave dat scepter of hims and win?"

Sounds of stomping feet echoed down from the wall, followed by a shout from the second voice, "I'z gunna gut you, King lova. Da Baron gunna reward us for dis."

"Fink you can take me, son? Uzk you!"

I peered up at the wall from behind my tree. The two men were actually trying to kill each other; one had a knife, and other had a wooden club. The one with the blade made a few aggressive movements before the other one swung his much larger weapon. Being more agile than his opponent, the one with the knife bent out of the way of the club, then immediately lunged in and plunged his knife into the flesh of his assailant.

Shocked by this sudden turn of events, I sat there a little dazed for a few moments. The dance of combat up on the wall rolled down into the fort, and I heard the sound of shouts come from inside. *If I don't move now, there will soon be a number of soldiers out here.*

Quietly and with caution, I slinked away from my spot behind the tree. My robe gathered up with one hand as to not drag on the black, wet leaves that covered the ground, I made my way towards the road and my friends. One last obstacle was in my way – the treetop watch posts.

My pace slowed as I drew near to the place where I saw them before. I lingered until I was sure that I knew where all the watch posts were, then I went south from them and crossed the road in the cover of darkness.

Chapter 2

The dark had changed the forest a bit, and my little adventure had not helped with my orientation. I looked for trees that were familiar and found none. I was lost.

My senses all kicked into overdrive there in the dark, wet forest. The gloom of the rain had put a blanket of clouds between the earth and the sky, trapping the light of the stars and moon on the other side. With my inhuman sight, I could make out the piles of dead leaves that littered the ground. Trees with rough black bark sliced up the terrain. Roots and rocks clashed in a slow and silent war beneath the ocean of decaying leaves, making every direction deceptively treacherous.

The smell of the decaying flora made me think of the Forest of Shadows, but the exact memories evaded every attempt of recovery. I was left with one solid impression: the world had not always been this tainted.

I suppose this wasn't a new realization. My visions hinted at a world filled with vivid colors and wondrous smells, but that place just seemed like a dream. The harsh reality of the contrasting world hit me solidly in that moment.

With every breath, I tried to tear back the stark shadow that was cast over this place. I wanted to see the life that was here before. Like a child learning the limitations of their imagination over reality, I was sorely disappointed. No matter what I focused on, the vivid world filled with life was simply gone. It would have been easier to bring Brin's father back to life, or perhaps even the old man from my visions. That smiling bearded wizard who I called grandfather more than once. Those people were gone. Yet, they haunted me - much like the memory the ancient days of glorious life that once filled this terrible place.

Flayed

"Master should not dwell on these things." Murks had been so silent that I nearly forgot that I always carried him with me. "Dwelling on the past will only lead to sorrow. Master must focus on the future."

With a deep sigh, I purged my sentimental struggle over things I could not change. "Who told you that, Murks?"

"You did, Master."

Now he had my full attention. "I have no memory of that. When did I say that to you?"

Murks hesitated. I could feel his mind fill with worry over how much he should say.

"It's ok, Murks. I am not mad, I am just at a loss here. A little direction would be a good thing."

Sitting on a rock, I reached into my robe and brought out the dark red hemodan from inside. The simply-molded features of his face reflected the worry I felt in his mind.

"When Master was buried by the nasty ol' Baron. Before the Rods of Nekarsli put Master to sleep. Master whispered to Murks' mind."

Now I was rightfully confused. "You mean the rods that The Baron used on me?"

"Yes, Master. The rods were old magic, meant to trap servants of the old gods. The Doomed used them on you to try and make you stay dead."

"It didn't work so well." I smiled.

"Oh, the rods worked perfect, Master. Somehow they got taken away, though. Maybe someone saw them sticking out of the ground and took them."

Chapter 2

"Wait. What?" I had an uncountable number of questions floating around my head, but before I could follow any of their threads, I heard the unmistakable rumble of boots. Hundreds of marching boots.

Murks leapt back into my robe, and I stood up. The sound was coming from the road. Quickly, but quietly, I made my way to the trees that bordered the road so that I could get a better look. Even before I reached those trees, I could see the lights of distant torches. The shrill sounds of birds echoed from the woods on the other side of the road.

From my safe hiding place, I saw the soldiers on the road suddenly burst into action. Marching steps became a hurried charge. The air suddenly glinted with the passing of silent arrows carrying with them death for the watchers in the tree nests. These men of war, all girded in armor and the green diagonal stripe on an off-white field of The King. Without giving it much thought, my eyes searched the soldiers for something. Using my dark sight, I finally saw them. The revenants.

When I say I saw them, I not only mean that I gazed upon them with my eyes. I mean I saw them. There was a hole where they stood, as if they should not be standing there at all. My thirst for life became starkly obvious to me in that moment, for I saw that hunger reflected back at me through the void of their presence.

There were three of them standing just off the road. All of them were wearing ancient-looking armor. Each exposed plate looked like it had seen a thousand wars. They all had the cold strange embrace of a few thick chains riding on top of their armor and livery. All the chains were locked into place with the type of heavy locks you would use to seal a chest. Each of the locks was different, as was the pattern of chains. It was almost as if the chains were part of their uniform.

Flayed

The three of them stood together, working as a unit. One of them was shouting commands that I could almost make out from my distant position. A second was watching edge of the forest, presumably for any of The Baron's men that might try and escape to the road. The third scanned the other side of the road, pausing just as he looked in my direction.

The hair on my neck stood up as he looked at me, and I could not help but look back. I saw now why everyone thought I was one of these revenants. They had the same touch of death upon their form. The same pale skin and sunken eyes. The same black death that floated around their mouth. They were just like me.

"Do you think he sees us, Murks?" I used my mental connection with my hemodan companion as to not make a sound.

He stirred in my pocket. "Murks not know, Master. The Knights are extensions of The King. Hard to even think of what powers they have."

The one who was scanning my part of the woods eventually continued past without saying anything to the other soldiers, and I breathed a little easier. By then, the woods on the other side of the road were roaring with the sounds of combat. I could not help but wonder which side was winning.

"Psst!" A whisper came from behind me, "Wrack?"

I turned to see all of my companions from the camp. Quickly, I held my finger up to my lips, then beckoned them over towards me. Brin was the only one who accepted my invitation.

"What the uzk is going on?" she whispered.

"It seems that The Baron's men and the The King's army have come to blows," I responded calmly.

Brin sighed, "I was uzkin' worried when you didn't come back with the wood."

Chapter 2

"Right." I smiled. "I bet you were actually cursing that there wasn't a fire when you came back from hunting." I motioned to the skinny rabbit that she was still dangling from her clenched left hand.

She scoffed, quietly. "Yeah, well… I don't know if you have noticed, but I am not the most patient person."

I chuckled, then we sat there and watched the chaos on up the road, hough I could not be sure how much of it that Brin could actually see. "There are knights in that group of King's men."

"What? Gaak. We should get the uzk out of here then." She started to creep back to the rest of the group, then turned and looked to see if I was following her. Discovering that I wasn't, she gave me her typical encouragement. "Wrack! C'mon!"

Just before I turned to follow, that one revenant who had looked in my direction before again looked over at me. I almost believed that he saw me. As luck would have it, a soldier from The Baron's men burst from the tree line onto the road. The staring knight moved with such deadly and swift precision as to send chills down my spine. The death of the fleeing soldier was nothing more than swatting an annoying insect. The distraction is exactly what I needed to slip away from the edge of the trees.

When I joined my friends, they were already discussing what to do next.

"No, he said that there is more than one with them," Brin whispered.

Gordo scratched his chin for a moment. "We need to leave immediately. The knights do not uzk around. They will search both sides of the woods, and we can't be here when they do that."

"Then they will set up ambushes and patrols around the whole area, hoping to catch more strays," Tarissa chimed in.

Brin nodded. "I didn't want to sleep tonight anyway."

Flayed

We all started carefully retreating from the woods, putting distance between ourselves and the war that echoed through the forest.

"Where are we going?" I asked after some time had past.

Gordo looked back at me for a moment, then faced the dark path ahead. "The only place they won't go. The temple that overlooks Marrowdale."

For another two days we quietly tromped through the dark wooded hills in search for safe passage. Each time we turned our direction towards Marrowdale, something in our path would make us go the long way around. At one point I felt like we were walking in circles and I wanted to speak up, but I didn't know these woods like my companions, so I tried to make the best of it by looking at the blackened and leafless trees that broke up my view in every direction. They all looked so thin and as if they had been burned.

When I was left alone in my nightly vigil, I decided to get a more detailed look at one of the trees. Their bark was thin and slightly oily. Within the black bark there were grey lines that looked like tiny veins, barely visible to even my vision. I imagined that if these trees were animals, they would be so old and infirm as to barely be able to breath - but yet they still clung desperately to their dwindling spark of life with a ferocity as to turn them mean.

Again, I wanted to see this forest as it once was. Leaves of green and gold, their barks white with black spots, roots deep and strong. Strong enough to carry me into their tallest branches where I could pretend I was flying in that constant gentle wind that would playfully churn the tops of the trees. I would stare the clouds and shout at the sun with challenges as I pretended to be the greatest wizard the world had ever known.

Chapter 2

That forest is gone, and the boy in the tree, was he me? Or is this fantasy just a reflection of what truth I want to believe? Did it really matter?

Lost in these spiraling thoughts, I found myself back at the fireless camp, watching over the shadows of my sleeping friends. Things were soon about to change.

The next day we reached the edge of the wood. There on the hillside overlooking the flattened space where Marrowdale once stood was a ruin of a temple. All the stonework, though weathered, was expertly done. All edges were carved in curves, buttresses that looked like draped curtains staked to the ground around the building. The center was a circle base with a dome on the top. The weathered stones were your average light grey, with tiny flecks that glittered in the mid-morning light, and swirling trails of white streaming throughout.

As I walked around to the front, I could see that the arched tunnel that once stood facing Marrowdale now was mostly collapsed, and to get in that way would require climbing over the moss-covered rubble. Before I could explore further, Gordo and Avar began climbing in through the collapsed entrance. Tarissa and Verif immediately followed, but Brin backed away.

"Go on in if you want," Brin said. Her arms were crossed, and the toe of her boot kicked at a tiny stone sticking out of the ground.

I was surprised at her apparent dislike of this place. In the time we traveled together, I had never known her to shy away from anything. "Are you not going in?"

She kicked the stone again. "Nope. I don't like holy places. They uzkin' make my skin crawl."

Flayed

I was struck by a sudden confusion. All I could say was, "Ok." What I really wanted to ask was why this place was different than the underground temple in Sanctuary, but I held my curiosity in check.

The two of us stood there in silence. Brin had the rock she continued to strike with the toe of her boot, and I had the amazing view of the valley of Marrowdale before me.

I could see the dark shapes that marked the old foundations of buildings. The air was crisp and refreshing here, more so than any breath I had encountered since my awakening, now nearly three years past, or near as I could tell. The passage of time was hard to keep when there is no clock pushing you to old age. My thoughts wandered to the last time we had come to this place, and my eyes and mind fell upon the gateway at the same time.

There it stood, a menacing doorway, standing in the middle of a town that no longer existed. I could almost feel the dread call of the barbed hook upon it. My desire to try and open the door which led to the unknown beyond almost put my feet in motion, but after a few shuffling steps, I held my ground.

"I think I can open that gate."

Brin kept kicking the stone. "Hrm?"

"The doorway down there in Marrowdale. I think I can open it."

She stopped playing with the rock. "That isn't a place we need to go, Wrack. Who knows what sorts of horrors The Baron has locked away down there."

"If he locked them away, wouldn't they be horrible to him? Maybe we could find something in there to use against him." My curiosity was masquerading as hope. I didn't really care what we found inside. I just wanted to go in.

Chapter 2

She shook her head. "No. Not only no, but uzk no. Whatever is inside that place can uzkin' rot."

I could not take my eyes off the silent doorway. It taunted me. Somehow I knew something important was on the other side. Just about the time I had decided to run down the hill and try to open it, Brin grabbed my arm and urged me to the ground.

From our now crouching position, Brin pointed off to the distance. "Men in armor. Probably a patrol from The King's lands."

At first I cursed my luck that that they would appear now, but then I realized that it would have been worse if I had been down there opening the door when they came by. Then the wind shifted.

Black locks of Brin's hair flew into my face and with them came the warm scent of amber and sweat, steel and blood in that specific combination that I only knew as her. Immediately, my stomach filled with tingling, and I could not help but breathe deeply of her scent. It brought me peace. The treacherous demons who ruled my curiosity were instantly held at bay.

I moved closer to Brin and put my arm around her as to stabilize my uncomfortable crouch. She looked over at me, and pushed the curls between us behind her ear. There it was again, that smile. Those eyes, so big and green, but not filled with the cynical bitterness everyone else knew her for.

In the distance, the soldiers continued their patrol. Brin and I relaxed to a sitting position on the ground. Our bodies were close enough that I could feel her warmth. We sat there together and watched the patrol pass into the distance.

"Hey," she said playfully.

"Yeah?" I tried to say, but as soon as my mouth opened, she tossed a handful of moss and pebbles at my face.

She giggled as I wiped the dirt off my face. When my eyes turned to slits and I glared at her, she pointed and laughed.

Flayed

"Oh, that is it." I lunged at her, wrapping my arms around her body and pushed her over.

With the skills that one can only learn from countless fights, Brin quickly turned the tables on me, and soon I was laying on my back with my arms pinned under her knees, and her hand pressing on my chest. She smiled, and I smiled back.

"You two enjoying yourselves out here?" Verif made her presence known.

Embarrassment briefly flashed over Brin's face, which was corrected with a simple, "Wrack was getting uppity. I had to put him in his place." She stood, and then offered a hand to lift me off the ground.

"Yeah. I was embarrassingly out of hand. Good thing Brin was here to save everyone. It would have been messy."

Verif rolled her eyes and crawled back into the temple.

As soon as she was gone, Brin and I had a quiet chuckle.

"You know why I hate this place?" she offered.

I shook my head. "Enlighten me."

"The first time I came here was something like eight or ten years ago. Garrett took me here soon after I found my way to Sanctuary. He said he needed to show me something." She shifted uncomfortably. "It was a particularly snowy winter then, and snow had blown all over the building. It even had dusted the inside with a thin layer of wintery powder. I remember, because it looked so pretty once we got inside. Light was bouncing off the various cracks in the building and filled the whole place with a surreal glow." Realizing she had gotten caught up in the moment, she brushed her hair back over her ears, and focused on the story. "Anyway, once we were inside, Garrett goes through some secret door inside, leaving me alone in the main oval chamber. It was quite like the space under

Chapter 2

Sanctuary, ya know. Altar, pillars, dais, the whole uzkin' deal. The funny thing is that I didn't feel alone in there. I felt like there was someone there with me. It was really strange."

"Yeah?" I tried to encourage more of the story from her, as I could sense that her will to tell it was fading.

She took a deep breath. "Yeah. So... there I was, alone in there, right? And out of the corner of my eye, I thought I saw my father. No... I did see him. Still young, still dressed like the last time I remember being with him... or at least what I think he looked like. It has been so long..."

I knew I needed to step in here, before she shut down the memory. That is, if I wanted to hear more. And I did. "Was it him? Was he there?"

"No." A tear glistened in her left eye. Casually, she wiped it away before she had to acknowledge that it had ever appeared. "When I turned to look, whatever had been there was gone." She pulled her knees up to her chest and wrapped her arms around her legs. "Left me feeling awful."

I hesitated, to see if she was going to continue. When the silence grew too awkward to bear, "I can only imagine."

"I stormed out of there and promised myself I would never go back in. I don't give a uzk if The King was out here. Whatever is in there—" Her voice trailed off.

Unsure of what to say, I blurted out, "I thought I saw an old dead friend in the graveyard back in Sanctuary."

Eager to use any excuse to escape her current train of thought, Brin wiped away the sorrow the memories of her father were summoning. "Oh really? Who was it?"

"Marec. I think he was one of the founders of the Shadow Hunters." My confusion was echoed in the temper of my voice.

Flayed

"I've heard that name before. From what I remember, he is older than the Shadow Hunters, but you should ask Avar. He knows far more about this gaak than me." Her eyes drifted towards the horizon. "Maybe we should just camp up here until spring. Uzk, I hate the cold."

With that, we sat in silence, watching the expanse below.

After a few hours of quiet, I heard Gordo call out from the temple, "Could you give us a hand here?"

I got up to help, leaving Brin to her thoughts. Gordo was pulling supplies through the opening. Once I was there, he and I received the items while Avar and Tarissa pushed things up to us. Food, a tent or two, some other goods for making camp. Once all the supplies were out, those who were inside crawled through the hole, and we were once again ready to travel.

"Where is Verif?" Avar asked.

I looked around. "I thought she was inside with you."

"She was, but then she left," Gordo said.

Tarissa looked around and said quietly, "I will find her."

Avar, Gordo, and I shrugged at each other and started to break down the supplies, making it easier for each of us to carry a small amount. It was getting dark by the time Tarissa returned from around the other side of the temple, Verif along with her.

"It is getting dark. We should just camp inside the temple," Gordo suggested.

Avar stepped in. "No. We should keep moving. We need to find this Jared fellow soon"

Brin nodded in agreement. We passed out every person's burden and headed out. The six of us looked a little odd, carrying tents and such, but I was sure we would be happy to have them the next time it rained.

Chapter 2

Down the hillside we went, towards Marrowdale. Towards that lonely gateway of the prison. Again, the visions of The Baron opening the doorway flashed through my mind. My very blood was drawn towards the doorway. It took all my will to look away.

Breathe in. Breathe out. One foot in front of the other. I could feel Murks squirming in my pocket; apparently I wasn't the only one who heard the silent siren song calling for me to come and open the prison. My thoughts kept trying to force me to turn back, but I clenched my jaw hard enough that I felt as if my teeth would explode. Breathe in. Breathe out. One foot in front of the other.

We passed by the faded memory of the town, and with each step away from the doorway, I felt its call weaken. Before it was completely out of view, I turned back and looked. I thought I could see tendrils of light coming from the door. They were reaching towards me, writhing slowly like smoke in the air. I blinked, and they were gone. In my heart, I knew that someday I would have to deal with that place - but it wasn't that time yet.

Our little band marched on, away from that place and out into the wilderness.

It wasn't long after I shook off the chill of Marrowdale that Brin and Gordo took us off the roads. They had seen fresh signs of large numbers of booted soldiers on the beaten path. No matter who the army called their sovereign, they were not our friend. Soon after, we could see the twinkling glow of campfires in the distance. They were both to the west and the east, with some even in the south. Gordo kept taking us northwest, away from all these unknown armies.

"Where exactly are we?" I asked Verif.

She looked around a bit and pointed southwest. "The space that splits those fires? That leads to Yellow Liver."

Flayed

I took a deep breath. We were near the place where we fled the attack of The Vampire on Sergeant Valance's men, or at least that is where I thought we were. I tried to remember all the faces of the refugees who likely died there. Crushed between the two forces, like so much upturned topsoil. Then my mind drifted to David. *Where had he gone off to? What was so important that he left Sanctuary? Did I make a mistake in healing him with my blood?* These were all questions I could not answer. Best to keep my mind on the travel ahead. Not following the roads always meant danger and struggle. It was a good thing that I still had an eternal well of endurance and strength. My human companions were not so lucky.

About dawn we had to make camp. By then there were no campfires to be seen; we were truly deep within the wilderness.

As tents went up and food was prepared, I noticed that the rabbits Avar was cooking were much more plump than our normal daily catch. Indeed, as the sun started to cast its light around us, the plants and earth seemed much more alive than the grey and black ones I had seen since my awakening. They were not quite filled with the vivid life I had seen in my visions, but still - they were noticeably different.

The air was crisp and stung the inside of my nose as I took a deep breath. I could feel so much life here, almost as if the twisted hands of The Doomed had not reached out to taint this land. As my companions slept, I drank in the life of the place. Energy filled my limbs, and I felt a strength growing inside me. Closing my eyes, I saw light beneath my eyelids, and my lips curled up into a smile.

I do not know how much time passed, but when I opened my eyes, the color that had once been in the trees, moss, and grass around us had dimmed. *Had I imagined their luster? Or had I truly consumed their life? Murks once told me that I fed on life, is this what had happened to the rest of the world?* Perhaps this is what is

Chapter 2

meant by The Cursing that people kept speaking of. The moment in time when The Doomed were created and the world itself began to die. I was appalled by even the idea of it, and horrified by any connection I might have to this slow death of the world.

Many hours later, my companions stirred. I waited for them to comment on the change in our environment, but none of them seemed to notice. Perhaps it was simply my strange senses playing tricks on me, so I said nothing.

We travelled onward through the wilderness. Beyond the camp, I again saw dim life in the plants around us. Breathe in. Breathe out. One step at a time. I did everything I could to keep my hunger in check.

Flayed

Chapter 3

"I am telling you, I know where we can find him." Gordo's tone was not convincing.

Brin didn't even respond, he had been saying the same thing over and over for what seemed like weeks now. I could tell she liked Gordo because she would have murdered anyone else that continued to yammer at her whenever there was a pause in the conversation. This one time he pushed it too far though.

"You don't believe me do you?"

The runes on Ukumog flared, and Brin tried to control her temper. "Just shut up, Gordon. I know, you have the thing for this Elaina girl, and you think she is a member of one of the forgotten bloodlines, blessed by the ancient power of the old gods. I get it. You have been talking about it since we left Sanctuary. But please, just shut the uzk up."

Gordo was visibly hurt by Brin's biting words. Under his breath he muttered, "I don't have a thing for Elaina..."

"Yes you do, Gordo," Brin's voice echoed her frustration. "Just shut up about her and get us to Regret. This Jared fellow better know where she is."

"Fine," Gordo said just to get the final word in.

Flayed

This pattern of conversion repeated itself almost word for word every few hours for the next two days. Between these, he did occasionally make her laugh with a silly joke, or doing something stupid and laughing at himself. Once he told us that the ice on a little brook was strong enough to hold us, and when he jumped up and down on it to demonstrate his point, the ice cracked and he fell into freezing water up to his knees. All of us got a good laugh at that. I became extremely fond of Gordo's silly sense of humor while we travelled. The smell of his drying boots, I was not fond of, however.

As we travelled, I continued to keep my hunger in check. Some nights were easier than others, but I did not pull on the glorious strands of life that were all around me. "This path could only lead to darkness," I thought.

Shortly after we had entered the less tainted part of the wood, I had the feeling that we were being stalked. It was really just a minor nagging, like having a tiny rock in your shoe that every three steps disappears for several miles, only to return for another three steps later on. I kept hoping that I was imagining the feeling and that it would eventually go away, but it never did. I still had a sense that somewhere in the frost-tinted woods around us there was something stalking us. The farther north we went my vigilance over our camp at night required much more focus due to the troubling sense of lurking danger that pulled at my thoughts. The last thing I wanted was that barbed beast to throw its hooks into Brin or Avar and drag them off into the night like they had done to that poor girl Sally. I was happy that I at least still remembered her name. There were still so many names and faces of the Yellow Liver refugees that I couldn't quite remember. The fog of visions still lingered at the edges of my mind, and what they hid frightened me.

Chapter 3

A rustling sound broke my introspection, and I focused again on scanning the area around us. I tried to reach out with my mind, my eyes, even my heart to expand my ability to detect whatever might be stalking us, but with no results. There was just so much life around us, it masked whatever was stalking us out there.

Another day passed, and worry filled my mind. I couldn't stop thinking of Sally's face as she was violently pulled away from our camp months or years ago. To me, it seemed like it had only happened a week ago or so. I could not just silently worry, but I did not want to infect my companions with the paranoia that I was experiencing. That night, I decided to take action.

"Hey, Brin? Can I talk to you for a second?" I tried to act casual when I asked her. I am uncertain I succeeded.

Brin's brow furrowed. "Sure, Wrack. Everything ok?"

"Yeah," I lied. "Everything is fine. Come over here for a second."

We walked far enough away from everyone else that I was sure they would not hear my whispers. I started to speak, but when my eyes caught her silhouette, I was entranced. Stray threads of hair floated about her head, forming lush, black, wavy waterfalls that crashed against her shoulders and curled their way into pools that hung upon the very air at their ends. She stood with such confidence, with one hand on her hip and the other rested on the boney pommel of Ukumog which itself dangled from one of her two sword belts. A fire came to life in the clearing behind her, and my eyes could not escape the beauty of her. I stammered over my words for a moment. Smiling, she stepped towards me, close enough that I could feel the warmth radiating from the scales of her armor.

Flayed

"Did you have something you wanted to tell me?" she whispered.

My tongue was suddenly thick enough to fill my entire mouth, and I tried to remember why I had pulled her aside. In that moment I wanted to tell her how the light made her luminous. No, I wanted to tell her how the warmth of her body was like breathing summer air just after a refreshing rain. No, how her life was the most delicious thing I had ever encountered, and how I ached to drink away her warmth... My own fear of this dark turn in my thoughts made me step away from the beckoning warmth of her presence. "Uh... Yes... I, um... I think something is following us again."

"What?" Both of her hands found purchase on Ukumog's handle as she scanned the trees around us.

"I haven't gotten a good look at anything, and I don't think it is the thing from the Bladed Labyrinth," I tried to calm her.

"Yeah, I shoulda killed that uzkin' thing when we were there."

Marveling at the ease with which she talked about destroying a monster that had made six of us run for our lives, I remained silent for a moment. "I am sure that was not the last time we will see that thing."

Brin scoffed, "Avar thinks that thing is a servant of another of The Doomed."

"What?" I was shocked.

She resumed a casual stance and turned back to me. "Well, if there is something out there, I can't see it. Maybe I will sleep next to you tonight, so you can wake me up if there is any trouble." Her smile was charmingly wicked.

Chapter 3

I returned her smile, sheepishly, but when we turned to rejoin dinner at the camp, I could not help but worry about the hunger which lay in wait beneath my skin.

Even with Brin sleeping inches away from me, I was able to keep my hunger at bay, and for two more days we traveled through the woods. With each passing mile, the trees seemed to become greener and more stout. They were covered in needles instead of leaves, and their branches were long and flexible. The air was more humid and had a sharp smell that was not unpleasant. Again, old memories of an ancient green world filled my mind. *What made this place more like the ancient world from my memory? How is it that this forest had escaped the corrupting touch of The Cursing?* I could not help but wonder if the people here lived in the same squalor as their southern neighbors.

On the third day, the trees thinned, and breathtaking snowy peaks of a mountain range sat just beyond green rolling hills. In the light of dusk, a plume of smoke caught the sunlight and stood boldly against the purple sky. The trail of smoke led to a small cluster of buildings built between two ice covered lakes. Reflexively we all took a deep breath of the chilly air and savored this peaceful moment. For my part, I wondered why more people chose to live in filthy cities over this wondrous expanse of living green. I could have lived in that moment forever, but my friends had other plans. Too soon, Gordo called for us to move towards the plume of smoke, and we complied.

Before the light left the sky, I could more clearly see the town we approached. I counted about fifteen buildings in the center of the town, with outlying buildings scattered around the radius, including some shacks that were built upon the icy surface of the lakes. All the permanent buildings were white or grey with dark

Flayed

structural beams showing through the walls of the structure. Again, there was something familiar about this style. I sifted through the scattered memories that floated in the disrupted pool of my mind, searching for where I had seen buildings like this before. My search was disrupted by a shout aimed at our group of travelers.

"Hey! Hello! Who approaches the village of Regret?" the voice asked.

Gordo shouted back, "A group of travelers from Sanctuary. We are looking for Jared Raast."

The bundled figure that was the source of the voice hesitated long enough for me to adjust my vision. He was covered in many layers of cloth and leather clothing, all hidden under a large fur cloak. He shifted where he stood, and I saw the pommel of a sword hanging from his belt. He rubbed his scruffy chin with a hand that was covered by gloves that left the fingertips exposed. "What do the Hunters want with Jared Raast?"

"We have a private matter to discuss with him," Gordo responded. There was something familiar in his tone, as if he knew this man.

There came an absence of sound from behind us, as if there were suddenly a hole in the wind. I turned to see a massive wolf watching us from just up the hill behind us. Its white fur was shocking against the snow-dusted green terrain around us, and it moved with impossible silence. I could see each of its breaths as well, as if the air were making frost with each exhale. Behind me, Gordo and the man continued to shout at one another.

"Unless the Hunters have pressing business, we suggest you find your way somewhere else."

Gordo grunted, "Sanctuary has fallen. We are on a mission to enter a place that is unfriendly to the Shadow Hunters, or the Brotherhood of Ravens. For this, we need Jared."

Chapter 3

I nudged Tarissa with my elbow, and motioned towards the wolf with my chin. She quickly turned all the way around to face the possible threat on our party's rear flank.

"Where did that come from?" she asked.

"I don't know. It snuck up on us," I said. I thought, but did not say, "Perhaps this is what has been following us for the past several days."

"Master, that is a wolf of Winterland. It should not be here," Murks said in my mind.

"Even so, unless you have business for the Hunters – you can be on your way, Gordon Haas," the man said.

Gordo had finally had enough. He threw his gloves to the ground. "Really, Jared? Why are we playing these games? I never did anything to you or Regret."

"Yes, but she doesn't want to see you, Gordo. You know that," Jared scolded.

A frustrated sigh left Gordo's chest. "Do we have to talk about this out in the open here, Jared? And why is Frost stalking us like we are a threat?" Gordo motioned towards the wolf behind us.

"I know you aren't a threat, Gordo, but that revenant that travels with you is not welcome here," Jared said.

At a loss for words, Gordo just looked at the rest of us and shook his head. "I swear, I will be so happy if I never have to talk to another Raast again," Gordo whispered. "He is with us, Jared. He isn't one of The King's servants."

Jared laughed. "Revenants are bound to The King's will, Gordo. You have been a Hunter long enough to know that. He isn't welcome."

"Listen, Gordo. I can just stay outside town while you do what you need to do," I offered.

Flayed

"No. We trust you, so Jared should, too. I am not leaving you out here on this hill with Frost. Who knows what will happen?" Gordo's frustration was obvious, and it wasn't just about Jared stopping me from coming any closer to Regret.

A pregnant silence gripped us all for a long time. The wolf was standing so still that a few times I almost forgot he was actually standing there; his stillness was tricking my mind into thinking that the stark white form was just snow upon the hill. It was incredibly eerie. With every moment, I felt that it could just leap towards us and start to tear us limb from limb. The tension continued to build, and suddenly the massive wolf took a step towards us. I steadied myself, and pushed all ideas that it would attack from my mind. I didn't have a weapon, but I could distract it long enough for Tarissa to stab it a few times, perhaps even give Brin time to loose Ukumog. Once that blade's edges were given permission to slice open the flesh of this wolf, I felt confident that we would win.

"Fine, Gordon. Bring your friends along. If that undead friend of yours causes any trouble, Frost will tear him apart."

"Deal," Gordo responded.

Six people and two monsters walked down the hill towards the little village together. Like me, there was something unnatural about the wolf. Jared made me walk in the back with Frost, and being that close to him allowed me to appreciate the obvious and subtle things. For starters, he was extremely large. His shoulders came up to the middle of my torso, and his paws were larger than my face. His eyes showed an intelligence that I had not seen in an animal before. He was watching my every move, and quietly growled at me when I adjusted my robe to make sure that I was presentable as we approached the town.

Chapter 3

"Calm down, Frost. I am not here to hurt anyone," I said to it, and he immediately stopped growling, but his vigilance did not end. Much like me, there was much more to this giant wolf than I could see on the surface.

As we walked within range of the town, I could see the concern and fear in the resident's faces. There was but a handful of people there, and all of them seemed to avoid our path. Window shutters were closed. I saw one or two people touch a necklace as if to silently ask for some powerful force to protect them. This was all because of me. It was me they stared at, not the giant wolf at my side, nor the beautiful woman with a monstrous blade at her hip. They were all frightened of me. Where I saw contempt in the faces of the Hunters when I first met them, this was pure abject fear. They saw the monster that lived on the surface, but I knew that they did not see the human that stared back at them from inside my skin. As I had been so many times, I was conflicted by my own fears and thoughts. *Am I a monster or not? Will that simple question ever be answered for me?* I didn't know.

Jared led us to a large house on the other side of the town. We had passed the hub at the center and through the gateway of two lakes to the land on the other side. While we weren't much closer, the immense majesty of the snow-covered mountains to the north of us filled my soul. They seemed as unmovable as the heavens, as peaceful as a lazy summer day, and at the same time they almost judged us like we were an unfortunate anthill about to be trampled. With the cold air in my lungs and this sight before me, I was so struck that I stopped in my tracks and just stared at these giants that stretched as far as I could see to the east and the west. This place belonged to them.

Avar laughed. "See? If his soul was truly as dark and terrible as you feared, would he be overwhelmed like this?"

Flayed

While I heard his remarks and the quiet chuckles of my collected companions – I simply could not look away from the mountains. As I watched, some of the clouds parted and rays of sunshine gracefully touched the white caps of a few of these dark titans before me. My breath was stolen away, and I was transfixed.

"Hrm. Well, we better get him inside, before my neighbors come down here with pitchforks," Jared grumbled.

Brin put her arm around me and walked with me through the open front door of the house. Just before I crossed the threshold, I saw Jared nod to Frost, who then slowly loped away from the house. Jared checked the street one more time and then closed the door.

Inside it was remarkably cozy. A fire was within the fireplace, and the same structural beam design was present on the inside of the house as it was without. The house had meager furnishings, all well worn wood and leather. The various tools of a hunter were neatly arranged in the main room, a bow was by the fireplace, and another was by the door. A belt with pouches and a knife was hanging off the back of one of the many chairs in the room. All the seats were set in a circle, with the fireplace as the foundation of the circle's arch. It was much warmer inside than it was in the wintry air outside. That struck me with the fleeting thought that it had seemed to be winter for a great long time. I thought on this as Brin ushered me to one of the seats at the fire, though not exactly close to it, as Verif and Tarissa had already claimed the seats flanking it.

Had it been winter when we left Sanctuary? That was at least two months past. How was it still winter? My vague memory of times past made me think that perhaps the winter should have passed, but yet it lingered. Perhaps it was our traveling North. *Was this their frozen springtime?* My mind drew ever inward,

Chapter 3

ignoring the people that surrounded me. I was fixated on this fault of perception. *How is it that I should be oddly powerful in areas I could not control and, at the same time, so dim-witted about the passage of time and the basic knowledge of the world around us?*

So utterly befuddled was I at this train of thought that I had not noticed the conversation around me, nor had I even felt the tiny hemodan struggling to move within my robes. Absentmindedly, I must have reached into my robes and started to pull Murks out, for I was shocked to my senses by him shouting in my mind.

My eyes focused on the people around me, who had all grown silent and were staring. "Wrack? Are you well?" Brin asked.

I could feel the surprised expression on my face. "Uh, yeah. I'm ok. Sorry, I was miles away. What are we talking about?"

Jared's face became dark with worry, but Brin didn't even pause. "We were discussing why we are trying to get to Flay."

"Right, the wizard Grumth," I replied.

"You met Brin's father, right Jared?" Gordo interjected.

The worry in Jared's face lessened, but suspicion remained in the glare he continued to give me. "Have you ever hunted a wizard before, Brin?" Jared ignored Gordo's question.

"Actually, I have been hunting this same wizard for what feels like forever. We actually caught up with the uzker a few years ago. That is how I was able to reclaim my father's sword."

Jared rubbed his scruffy chin. "And this sword you claim is the legendary blade of The Betrayer?"

Brin sighed, "Yes. I keep telling you that."

"Forgive me if I am skeptical," Jared said as he put another log on the fire. "You wouldn't believe the number of people who have come here over the years, claiming to be the next mouthpiece of the Silver Lady, or to know how to resolve the power that the dark ones have over this world."

Flayed

"Jared. Come on. You aren't being fair here," Gordo complained. "You know well enough who she is, and what that sword is."

Jared scoffed. "I take it you have told Brin everything then?"

Gordo froze. His silence made Brin angry.

"Told me what?" When no one responded, she demanded, "Told me what!"

Gordo shifted uncomfortably. "My friends and I had an encounter with your sword, a few years before I ever met you. It is a long story, but the short of it is – we found Ukumog in a cave of ice up in the Frozen Waste. We were kinda sent to find it by the Silver Lady."

Brin was so shocked by this admission that she was silent.

When no outburst came, Gordo continued, "It was taken from us, by a group of wizards that called themselves The Eternal Well. Their leader had helped us in the past, but I think they might have just been following us in case we found the sword. Elaina, the woman we need, is actually the one who pulled it out of the ice."

Brin stood up, looked like she was about to say something, then sat down again. She rubbed the palms of her hands on her knees in frustration, then stood up again. "You tell me this now?" She glanced around, looking for something small to throw at Gordo.

"Does it change your plans any?" Gordo obviously hoped that this question would turn her rage in a different direction. "Look, I know this hunt is about finding out what happened to your father. I want answers there, too. These wizards in The Eternal Well, they know things. Things that people have either forgotten, or never knew."

Chapter 3

"Actually, it was The Eternal Well that told the Hunters about Gordo and his friends. That is why we came to Marrowdale to recruit you," Tarissa whispered.

This piece of information was even new to Gordo. "I don't even know what to think about that."

"Certainly does seem to be a lot more going on here than what lies upon the surface," Jared muttered. "Fine. Elaina is in Yellow Liver. She went there to see if she could help any of the people after everything fell apart." Jared paused. "We still don't know what riled up The King, and why the war between His Majesty and The Baron has started up again. It has been more than a lifetime since they were fighting each other openly. Something has changed, and I need to make sure that their attention does not become fixed on us here. Our deal with the gnomes of the frozen waste for protection does not include armies that will come to our aid."

"Gnomes?" I could not help but ask.

Jared looked at me like I had two heads. "Yes. Gnomes. Greedy little buggers that enslave other races and who are always consumed with a hunger for wealth and power. Lucky for us, there is an ancient compact with them so they don't come down here and try and take us over the mountains. They like having friends over here. It helps keep the dark ones at bay."

"The dark ones?" I asked. "You're talking about The Doomed, right?"

Jared winced at the mention of their collective name. "Yes. The gnomes fear them more than they fear anything else. They don't want to upset the balance. I would not see that balance disturbed, nor the balance we have with the earth up here. This place has so far been able to survive the blight that The Cursing brought with it. I would sooner die than have that taken from us as well."

Flayed

I hadn't imagined it. This place did have less of the touch of decay upon it. Then I realized, I had been feeding on the life that was out there, in the wilderness. Suddenly, I was filled with the urge to leave, to go far away. I did not want to rob this place of the precious life that yet lingered in its branches and waters. "Well, we know what we need to. When are we off to Yellow Liver?"

Jared sighed as he stoked the fire. "I hate that name."

I was confused, but Avar spoke before I could say anything.

"I don't see the big deal. Yellow Liver isn't much different than some other names. Skullspill, Marrowdale, Spleen Tear, Flay…"

"Another great thing about The Cursing, my young friend. These towns didn't always have such interesting names." Jared said, growing more agitated by the conversation.

Avar paused, but could not help but continue. "What do you mean?"

Jared's sigh said that he didn't really want to talk about this, but he continued anyway. "Take Yellow Liver for example. Before The Cursing, it was called Little River, because of a beautiful river that ran right next to it. The stories about that place that we still have say that after The Cursing and that ruthless murderer, Palig, was put in charge of the town by The Baron, the land seemed to react to his presence. The bed of the river turned yellow, and soon the river itself was transformed into a sickening sludge. The people started calling the town Yellow River, because of the change. Years passed and the river mostly dried up or changed course, and River became Liver because people in the town were so unhappy that they were drinking themselves into oblivion."

A hush fell over the room when Jared stopped speaking. The crackle of the fire as it popped and sizzled through some moisture in the logs was the only sound inside. Avar shifted

Chapter 3

uncomfortably in his chair; like me his desire to ask more questions was burning him, but he stayed silent. My curiosity was held at bay by a lack of desire to further aggravate our host, and so I let myself be hypnotized by the fire. The warmth of its glow and the comfort that the heat brought me was peaceful. My mind fell into a flickering dream.

"You know Marec, this kid of yours has some real fire in him," Lucien said with a smile.

Marec laughed. "Yeah, but I think he comes by it honestly."

The two men were sitting under the awning of a stable on bales of hay. Lucien was cutting a crisp and juicy apple with a knife. Both the fruit and the implement looked so tiny in his giant hands. Marec drank from a waterskin and wiped sweat from his brow as they both watched me sweep up the final parts of our work cleaning the stables.

"You old men can help me finish, ya know." My voice was filled with youth and mockery. I felt like I could have taken on the world.

They both laughed. "A little bit of extra work is good for you," Marec said with a smile.

Lucien agreed. "Builds character."

"I have enough character."

When I was done sweeping, we left the stable and had a proper lunch. The fruit was ripe and delicious, and the salted meat and cheese were so good I ate more than both of them combined. I was eating it fast enough that Marec had to warn me to slow down. While the young me didn't see it, I could see the pride they both had for me. We were like brothers.

Flayed

After the food, Lucien and Marec took me into the fortress courtyard, to the training area. We all took turns sparring with each other, only when they would spar with me it was more instructional. While the two of them clashed swords, I could feel the competition. Lucien would always start off gentle, but the longer the fight went on, the more his immense strength would come to bear against Marec. The smaller Marec made up for his lack of comparable strength with speed and agility. Overall, they were well matched opponents. As always happened, the longer they practiced against one another, the more a crowd would grow to watch.

Whispers filled the crowd as people came to see if Marec would topple the giant or get crushed like a bug. As I looked around, I could even see some whispered wagers on who would win this particular battle.

The summer had been a mild one, and the banners that hung from the towers of the fortress flapped lazily in the breeze. Their emblem of a black tree with ravens roosted in its branches on a stark white field only showing occasionally.

A few of the children came to watch the fight and brought with them more of the salted meat that I loved so dearly.

"Hello, Alexander," a whisper came from behind me.

I twisted around to see a teen aged girl, only slightly younger than me. Instantly I recalled her name, Lilly. Her hair was dark and silky, and she always made me nervous. "Oh, hi Lilly."

She climbed up onto the low wooden fence that I was sitting on to join me. I could feel her warmth as she sat there next to me. "Did you fight already?"

"Yeah. I almost beat Marec in a game of five touches, but then he got two quick hits on me before I could score that last point."

Lilly frowned. "Aw. I missed it."

Chapter 3

I smiled, but didn't know what to say. Looking back, I know I could have said anything, but teenaged me was brimming with awkward emotions that I could not reconcile. Silently, we watched Lucien and Marec until they finished their match. Marec had won, as he usually did. As the two friends embraced each other and gave thanks for the match, coins changed hands within the crowd, and suddenly there were trumpets from the wall.

The quick blares from the lookouts said that someone was coming to the fortress of Sanctuary, but they were not sure if they were friend or foe. In these conflicting times, it was hard to tell who was whom. Men and women scurried to prepare both for battle and for guests. Luckily for the Brotherhood of Ravens, that meant the same thing – armor and weapons.

The rest of the children were hurried to safety, but I was always treated differently. There was expectation of me.

Marec and I donned our armor and prepared our arms, him in his minimal amount of well-covering plates with shield bearing the mark of The Great Tower, and me in my padded gambeson. As I got ready, I said a secret wish that I could have amazing armor like Marec's one day. That I too could be a guardian of The Tower, but I knew that it was the dream of a fool. The Tower had been destroyed years ago.

The trumpets called again, and this time they spoke of a small party from the kingdom of Ravenshroud. There was a following call that I had not heard before, and Marec reacted with surprise.

He turned to me quickly. "Alex, into one of the barrels out by the stable. The one we emptied earlier. Climb in, and do not get out."

Flayed

Shocked by Marec's panic, I nodded. I felt the fear shoot through my body, hairs standing on end, and tears trying to burst from my eyes.

"Everything will be ok, Alex. Just do as I say. Don't let them see you," he said as he shed the armor that he was almost finished putting on.

I ran from the armory and found Lucien in the courtyard. He was barking orders to various people in armor when he turned and saw me. Similar panic washed across his face, and he quickly came towards me. I pointed at the empty barrel by the stable, and he nodded before turning back to his duties as captain of the Brotherhood of Ravens.

Scraping my leg as I climbed into the empty water barrel, I hunkered down inside and then realized that I did not have the lid. Trumpets blared again, signaling that the gates were opening, and I shot up from my hiding spot. Lucien caught sight of me, and I pointed at the lid. He ran over and picked up the lid for me.

"Stay quiet," he whispered to me as he put the top on the barrel.

I was alone in the dark.

My mind struggled against the rest of this vision. It was as if I had buried the remainder of this day deep within myself, and I both wanted and did not want to remember it. The more I searched for the rest, the faster it seemed to elude me. Frustration turned into anger, anger turned into rage, rage into madness, and madness into hunger. A raw terrifying hunger.

When I grabbed hold of my senses, I was sitting in a chair. It was once a plush armchair covered in expensive leather, but age and use had worn it down in spots. My breathing was labored, and my fingertips were pressed together in front of me, the pair of my forefingers touching my lips. The jagged nails of my fingers dug

Chapter 3

into my soft flesh just enough for me to sense their disrepair. I was no longer the young Alexander, nor did I seem to be the deathly form that was now called Wrack. I was someone else.

My thoughts spiraled in circles as I stared off in space. The twilight of the day was barely illuminating the room, but I could make out a wooden room which reminded me greatly of the inn I had once visited in Yellow Liver, The Headless Mermaid.

I turned to the window and watched the darkness of the night come. All the while, I was lost in thought.

A loud knock at the door to my room startled me, but I did not move or speak.

"M'lord? M'lord, are you well?"

My hesitation was not to cause alarm, far from it. My senses were heightened, yet my reaction had been slowed. I was drunk with something other than alcohol, and I did not want the euphoria to end. Deep inside me, I knew that to open my mouth would somehow let the feeling escape. My beautiful peace would yet again be disturbed. The hunger would return.

"M'lord? M'lord Palig, do you require assistance?" the voice came again, this time more persistent. If I did not respond, they would come in here, and I didn't know what would happen then.

My mouth opened with a terrible slimy feeling, as if I were painlessly tearing open a healing wound. "I am well, thank you for your concern," I gurgled.

I could feel them hesitating at the door, I did not want them to press the issue further. Silently, I prayed to whatever gods there were to let them walk away.

"Yes, m'lord. Should you need anything…"

"Have no doubt, I will send for you. Thank you again."

Flayed

Footfalls faded away from my door, and I knew they no longer hovered outside. It mattered little, though. The hunger was already slowly returning. It was only a matter of time before it overwhelmed me. My face twitched with helpless frustration, and I put my hands to my face. They were still sticky with the blood that covered them. Though I should not have been surprised by this, I recoiled from my own touch and stared at my hands. Caked in gore, with nails thick and dark, like some terrible fungus had taken them. Shaking, I curled my wretched fingers into fists and nearly wept.

Almost as quickly as the despair had come, it fled, and my attention turned to the wreckage of a corpse that lay at my feet. Every part of him was left torn, chewed, or missing. So voracious had been my hunger that I had not even removed his clothes; doubtless shreds of fabric had found their way into my unnatural gullet. This was quickly growing out of control. This corpse had once been Hran, son of the innkeeper. He had only come to ask how he could serve The Baron in his war against The King, and I lost myself.

My mind raced as I tried to ferret the best way to hide this massacre from my most gracious host. Doubtless there was too much mess to hide this shameful mockery. *What would I do?*

As I struggled, the hunger grew and grew, until I could not hold it at bay any longer. I was no longer a man. I had become something accursed.

I awoke feeling the terror of Palig's transformation. It was as real and present as anything else in my life. I was reliving his memories, one piece at a time. The room was colder; the fire had died hours ago. My friends lay sleeping around my chair on

Chapter 3

the floor. For a brief moment, I thought they might all be dead. As the fog of the memories faded, I sat alone in the silent room. The sounds of my sleeping friends reminded me that I was not the monster that had eaten the innkeeper's son. That I was nothing like that particular monster. The first light of morning found me trying desperately to remember more about that day in the fortress with Lucien and Marec. It was like trying to catch smoke with my bare hands.

"Morning, Wrack." Brin smiled.

"Morning. What happened last night?"

She rubbed her face, yawned, and replied, "You fell asleep in your chair. First time I think I have ever caught you sleeping in the years we have known each other."

"...And you are sure I was sleeping?"

"Yeah. Even mumbled a bit in your sleep. You muttered something about someone named Lilly. All seemed pleasant enough. Avar wanted to wake you," she said as she kicked him gently. "Huh, didn't you?"

Avar grumbled and tried to roll away from Brin's bootless foot, and instead rolled over into Tarissa, waking her up.

"Hey! Avar! I'm trying to sleep here," she whined. It was the loudest I had ever heard her speak.

A chuckle came from Verif and she rolled over to face us all. "Morning, everyone." She flashed me an attempt at a sweet smile. It still seemed fake.

Jared came in from the other room, fully dressed and ready for the day. He passed out some smoked meat to everyone, even offering one to me. Brin started to speak, but before she did, I took the meat from Jared's hand. "Thank you, Jared."

"Wasn't sure if you would eat it, but you are welcome to it."

Flayed

I stared at the meat in my pale hand. It reminded me of the meat from the dream. I could almost hear the breeze on that summer day again. When Jared looked away, I stowed the meat away for later.

Living on the road helps train you to be ready to move quickly. Within moments of Jared coming into the room, we were all ready to travel. Frost met us at the door—he had been sleeping on the porch from the look of things—and our two hosts led us back through the town.

At this time of day, most of the townsfolk were either still sleeping or already out hunting. Our walk back through the town did not inspire nearly as many glares as the first time. Perhaps they all assumed that if Frost hadn't torn us all to shreds, we must be alright. Standing on the bridge of land between the two frozen lakes, Jared bid us farewell. "I wish you the best of luck finding my niece, and I hope you find what you are looking for. Gordon, you treat Elaina well, do you hear me?"

"I hear you, Jared. Until we meet again…" Gordo embraced Jared, and we departed back into the evergreen hills of the north.

Chapter 4

A road wandered from Regret through Skullspill, The Baron's capital city, and then continued south to Yellow Liver. Brin and Gordo were wary of the roads, however, and they had no desire to even entertain the idea of going to Skullspill. This meant at least a few weeks of travel through the wilderness, avoiding The Baron's patrols, and watching as the winter turned into spring. While we trekked, I was focused on the life in the wilds around us. The farther away from Regret we got, the harder the wildlife seemed to struggle against some unseen corruption. Plants were darker, animals were thinner and more sickly. As the first days of spring greeted us, the expected sense of rebirth that the season felt like it should bring with it was not present. The air was warmer, and the ground wetter, but that was about the only change. Life was at a standstill the closer we got to the city of Skullspill.

As a group we avoided a few small towns that we passed along the way. Tarissa did go into the towns to trade for some supplies when we needed them. She traded the furs of the rabbits we would sometimes catch for trail food – more salted meats, nuts, bread, and the like. The two towns had relatively innocuous names. One was called Peak, and the other Corner. Avar said that these names had to do with the way they looked on a map, but he had no map with which to explain his point, so I just took him at his word.

Flayed

I quickly lost track of the days we spent traveling, and it seemed like we were going south the entire time. It wasn't until we were almost to Yellow Liver that anything looked familiar to me. We stood on the top of that rocky hill that we had once stood upon while on our way out of Yellow Liver after the fall of The Ghoul. Again, Castle Skullspill could be seen on the horizon. That was the night that Tarissa went into the town called Corner. My thoughts were mostly on David, for the last time we were there, I was carrying him so he had a chance to survive. His sudden departure from Sanctuary still had me puzzled, and as I stared at the city of The Baron on that hill, I wondered where David was.

Just like the last time, it was several more days before we saw Yellow Liver. This time there was no attack by the bloated beast that killed Sally and wounded David. We approached Yellow Liver from the northeastern hillside during the daytime. Even from a distance, Yellow Liver looked different. It was bustling with activity, and the north gate into the city was extremely busy. The wall around the city had been repaired in the time since the attack from The Rotting One and the army from Flay. The new stones within the wall stood out as we got closer.

Unlike my last visit, there were no guards posted outside the gate. People were coming and going freely, and with no one to extract a toll, the ramshackle huts that were built along the wall were abandoned or dismantled. The city looked, smelled, and felt different.

"Just act normal," Brin reminded us as we approached the gates. I had nearly forgotten that we could be high on the list of criminals that The Baron was hunting for the death of his servant, The Ghoul.

Chapter 4

As we passed the stone walls, my thoughts turned to those turned into ghoulish monsters by the old master of this town. *Did they still exist? Did they die with their master, or do they linger in the shadows even still?* I assumed that they might want revenge for what we did to their master. I hoped that we would not have time to find out.

Shivers ran up and down my spine as we crossed the threshold into the town, and they continued to haunt me as we made our way deeper still. They were subtle enough that the looseness of my robe hid them from my companions, and I thought it best to not worry them. As my companions figured out how we would hunt down this woman that Gordo seemed obsessed with, I continued my study of the town.

Where darkness and hopelessness seemed to be the order of the day during my last visit, there seemed to be an undertone of hope in this still-filthy town. The people seemed brighter. There were more smiles as we walked by, and even more shutters were open, catching the spring air.

We travelled deeper into the city, past roads I remember wandering during the siege of The King's army. We even passed the road that led to the strangely familiar part of the town where the guardsman Michael, Avar's brother, was killed by ghouls in the chaos. The events of that time were as unreal and faded as the memories that haunted me.

Brin and Gordo kept taking us farther south through the town's districts and I noticed a slight shift as the day progressed. As the day drew on, and we found ourselves closer to the southern part of the town—the southern gate is where I had first unknowingly watched Brin pummel a city guard—the streets grew sparse, and that old sense of fear and dread returned. Shutters were closed, and before the sun set, we were the only people out on the street.

Flayed

"Uh, Brin? Gordon? Perhaps we should get off the streets," Avar suggested.

Gordo looked at him like he was mad, but then he too realized that we were the only ones out there.

"Come on, the Headless Mermaid is this way," Brin quickly offered, and then started a quick pace down the lane.

We dodged through tight alleyways and narrow streets, all empty. Most of the buildings even seemed abandoned. Something was definitely wrong. So often had I been blessed with the sense of something following our little group that I had grown accustomed to it. This time I was wrong to ignore it.

By the time we were within sight of The Headless Mermaid, the sun had gone down and the streets were lit by only whispers of the flickering stars above us. To our dismay, there was no light from this, our inn of choice, nor was there any sound of movement or drunken revelry that we could hear from down the vacant street. The silence was ominous.

"Head back to the north part of town?" Tarissa suggested.

We all grunted in agreement, and as a group we started sprinting through the streets. Within a blink of an eye, a blur passed in front of me, and as it passed, Verif vanished from view. I stopped dead in my tracks and immediately braced for combat. Instinct took over, and I looked to my left to see a man in filthy tattered clothes perched atop Verif, who was flailing wildly.

"Brin!" I shouted.

"Uzk," I heard her mutter and, rapidly, the familiar *clink!* of Ukumog's leash being removed.

Before anyone could do anything, more loping shapes came from the darkness around us. Ghouls came pouring in from every street and building that we could see, all of them with a ravenous hunger glowing in their eyes. The battle was on.

Chapter 4

Gordon lifted his shield and intercepted as many attacks from the ghouls that he could, while Brin let loose the combined fury of her dark will and Ukumog's unnatural thirst for blood. Avar and Tarissa fought together like a practiced fighting team, both using Avar's shield to block incoming swings, and as distraction for Tarissa's knives to strike lethal blows. I ran to see if I could help Verif, but before I could reach her, smoke started rising from the ghoul, and it leaped away holding its face. I reached a hand to lift Verif off the ground, and she took it with an indignant look.

"Thanks."

I smiled and drew my knives.

Our group was surrounded and outnumbered. Ghoul after ghoul met a bloody end, and each time, their bodies would be quickly snatched away from us, and some of the horde facing us would feast upon the dying flesh of their own kind.

"Have they ever eaten their own kind before?" I shouted to the group.

Avar quickly responded, "That's new."

"Charming." Verif's sarcasm echoed what we were all thinking.

The smell of sweat from my human companions filled the air, and while it did not bother me, our attackers seemed even more driven to obtain the sweet meat that lived just underneath our clothes. I could not help but pity these people. They were once human, after all, and after having the experience of one night of Palig's decent into this terrifying state, my imagination went wild with who these people were before The Curse took them.

Our enemy learned from out attacks, and they shifted their tactics. Instead of going for our torso in an effort to wound and therefore incapacitate us, they started working in teams to distract us up top, while another ghoul went for our legs. Tarissa was the

Flayed

first they tried this on, which was a mistake on their part. The attacker ended up with a dagger slashed across their face. I was the next, and I was not as prepared or nimble, and I fell.

Almost instantly, I was dragged into the frantic mob of frothing monsters that stood awaiting fresh meat. They tore at me, and I felt Murks fall loose from a rip in my robes. The little hemodan started screaming, "Korata arcanas reca sol!" Dark energy pulsed in both his and my hands, and I feared I would lose control. I felt the claws and teeth of ravenous ghouls dig into my side and forearm, and I was suddenly overwhelmed with my own hunger. Not for flesh or for things material, but for the very energy of life itself. Murks' voice called out again, "Korata arcanas reca sol!" Cold shot down my arms, and my spine was on fire. My hands burned with the dark power that I tried so terribly hard to hold at bay, and I cried out.

It was not agony of the flesh, but a suffering of the soul that pressed on me. Even surrounded by all that terror, my thoughts went to Michael's death at the hands of the ghouls, then flashed to the face of the brave little boy lying on the floor of The Ghoul's feeding chamber. I then watched in my mind's eye as Brin was overwhelmed by a sea of this unending hunger. Her flesh was torn from her bones in seconds, and then they did the same to Verif, Avar, Tarissa, Gordo, then finally Lucien, Marec, and Lilly. I couldn't hold onto the rage, the hunger, or the fear any longer.

"NO!" The sound exploded from me, and I heard the combat instantly stop.

The ghouls who had hold of me immediately backed away, groveling to the ground, and as I stood, they all fell to the ground before me. Their posture spoke of misbehaving dogs when their master was angrily displeased. And standing in the middle of them, dark power swirling around my like a black and purple cloud of smoke, I felt them worship me.

Chapter 4

"Master, no!" said a voice nearby.

I turned to Murks, who I assumed was the source of the voice, but instead it was one ghoul who had lifted his torso off his knees, but still held his arms in front of his face as if to both shield him from harm and also to prevent himself from looking directly at me. Murks, on the other hand, was mimicking my every moment, with his own cloud of black smoke churning through the air around his tiny body.

"Master, please! Don't destroys us. We'z is lost wiffowt you, master. Abandoned we was, hungrier than before, but scared is all," the ghoul spoke again.

My human companions stood ready for combat. Brin stayed focused on the horde kneeling at her feet, Gordo looked at me with a horror that reflected my own inner thoughts, but Verif smiled. It was a smile filled with awe and pride, and in her eyes I saw the lust which always lay beneath the surface of her fake smiles.

"We are not food for you," I said to the ghoul, who nodded in reply. "You will go now, back to your hiding places. You will not eat the flesh of the humans in this city. DO YOU UNDERSTAND?" My words rattled the abandoned shutters that lined the street.

The subjugated mass of monsters before me all grumbled in agreement, and I could feel the hunger within them twisting their will against my words. I hoped that it would last, but I could not be sure.

"There must be some leadership among you. Send those who would talk to me to this tavern tomorrow night," I commanded them.

From the edges of the horde, I saw figures scamper off into the darkness. Gurgling cries filled the air as they fled with the burning pit in their gut screaming to be sated. The ghoul who had spoken was the last to leave, and before he did so, he crawled to my robes and wept into the hem. "Please forgives us, master. Please makes us whole again. We'z not deserves dis. Dis hunger is…" His sobs overtook his words, and facing the ground, he loped off into the darkness.

"That's new," Avar said, and Tarissa elbowed him in the ribs. "What?" he complained. "I didn't know Wrack had a hemodan!"

"Yeah, that is what you were talking about," Verif scoffed.

Brin leashed Ukumog with the familiar *clink!* "We should get out of here, before they change their minds."

The dark power faded quickly from me, and I felt exhausted. "Yeah," was all I could summon as a reply.

Our journey back to the northern part of the city was quiet and uneventful. The entire way, I could feel the eyes of unseen ghouls watching us as we passed. So strong was our desire to make quick exit from this cursed part of town, we did so silently. There was no barrage of questions from either Avar, nor whispered compliments about my power from Verif. Silently, we made our way through the dark winding streets towards the sounds of life.

Ahead in the dark streets we could see the lights of torches. Makeshift barricades blocked our path, and on the other side, there were sounds of watchers.

"Hail!" Gordo shouted to alert the watchers as we approached.

A single head popped up off to the side of the barricade. "Oi! What you want?"

Without missing a beat, Brin shouted, "We want out of this uzkin' part of town!"

Chapter 4

"Howz'd we know you izn't ghouls then?" the watcher asked.

I chuckled a bit, and all my companions glared at me.

"Do we look like uzkin' ghouls to you?" Brin said sternly.

The watcher paused, then threw a torch over the wall to illuminate us. Brin leaned over and picked up the torch.

"We aren't ghouls." Exhaustion highlighted Avar's tone. "We just want to find somewhere safe to sleep."

A pregnant pause filled the air as we waited for some response.

"Who is out there?" a new voice came from behind the wall.

We all looked at each other. This new voice did not have the same accent as the residents of Yellow Liver, and it made us wary. Brin kicked her toe into the dirt a few times before her impatience got the best of her. "I am Brin, daughter of Teague, and her companions. Please, these are my uzkin' friends. Please, for the love of my father – let us through."

Again, there was a pause, and some whispering on the other side of the wall. I could hear hushed angry tones, and I started to brace for some sort of attack. Out of nowhere there was a cracking sound, like someone had just been punched in the jaw. Then another and another. Then silence again.

"Oi, Brin. Youz still there?" the first watcher's voice came over the wall.

"Yeah. We are still here."

The barricade came to life with noise. Rapidly, a hole appeared in the wall, large enough for one person to fit through. Brin breached the wall first, followed by Gordo, Avar, and Tarissa. Realizing that they might not let me pass, I pulled the hood of my robe over my head and made sure that Murks was hidden within

Flayed

the folds of my tattered robe. The tears in my garment would sometimes flash sections of my pale flesh but it would have to do. Verif gave me a slight smile as she walked through the opening, then it was my turn.

The barricade was made of scraps of wood and metal. There were pieces of furniture, bands of metal from the outside of barrels, broken wagon wheels, and the glint of a host of nails. My robes got caught as I tried to shuffle through the opening. Tugging on them, I tried to free myself, but heard the fabric tear.

"Havin' a bit of a problem?" the watcher asked.

"My robe is caught, but I think I have it," I replied

Everyone stood there, waiting for me to push through.

"Movement on the other side of the wall!" a shout came from nearby.

The watcher was agitated. "Youz gotta move. Wez gotta fill this hole, we do."

Giving up on trying to free the fabric from the nails, I just moved forward, tearing open the side of my robe. I quickly grasped the fabric around the hole, and lifted them towards my body, trying to hide the opening. As I stepped away from the barricade, the watchers all reassembled the interlocking pieces of the wall. Within moments, their work was done, and they went back to watching the streets and rooftops on the other side of the wall.

The streets weren't busy, but they also were not barren. The light of flickering torches illuminated the lane in every direction. Watchers and others to support them wandered scheduled paths and stood in watchtowers built on the roofs of nearby buildings.

"This is new too." Avar was half kidding, but we all nodded in agreement. "The people of Yellow Liver all organized against their enemy. Never thought I would see that."

Chapter 4

Off to the side, there was one man who was obviously knocked unconscious and tossed to the side. Small bits of leather armor peeked out from under his black tabard, which was adorned with the red skull of The Baron.

"Perhaps organized against more than one enemy," I muttered.

"Oi, you're Brin?" An older man with an eyepatch approached our group and spoke in Tarissa's direction.

Tarissa blushed and pointed at the dark haired woman next to her.

"Who wants to know?" Brin said, her hands on her hips.

The old man gave a toothless grin. "Follow me, m'lady." He beckoned us with his fingers and just started walking away.

With a shrug Brin started to follow, and Gordo grabbed her arm. "It could be a trap," he whispered at her, loud enough for me to hear.

Brin pulled her arm away from Gordo, shooting him a look that scolded him for touching her. "Trap or not, this might lead us to your precious Elaina. You have a uzkin' better idea?"

The old man stopped in his tracks and looked at us with his one good eye. "You'z comin'?"

"Yeah, old man. We're coming." Brin shot a glare at Gordo.

We didn't have to follow the old man far before we reached an old shop that was being used as a command center of sorts. The old man stood to one side of the open doorway and motioned for us to go in. "Ere we are, m'lady. The Cap will wants to talk wif ye."

Brin gave him a bit of an odd look, but did as he asked.

The main room of this one time shop was mostly dominated with a table, and on that table was a map of Yellow Liver. Pins and wood carvings covered the map. Even to my untrained eye, I could see that this was a general's strategy map. The wall of barricades

Flayed

were plainly denoted by carved wooden walls. Figures represented every watchman and every tower along the wall. Pins with large red heads were pressed into several places on the ghoul side of the wall, and grotesque carvings showed where the ghouls were sighted.

A stream of runners constantly came and went from the room to the street outside. Two of them pressed their way through us, dropped a note, and then quickly pushed their way back out to the street. The notes were snatched up instantly by one of two men that stood at the table, and they responded by moving, removing, replacing, or adding more figures to the map. On the far side of the room, a well armored man wearing the black tabard of The Baron whispered to a rather plump woman who was dressed like a baker, complete with apron and a dusting of flour. It was then that I realized that this shop was actually a bakery, with the tables for customers all piled to the sides, and the serving counter was the large table the map was stretched over.

"Captain..." Brin started to say, obviously expecting the man in armor to respond.

The man in armor finished speaking with the baker and then pushed passed all of us to the door. Brin's eyes followed him until he walked passed her, and then she turned back to the baker.

"How can I'z help ya, miss?" the baker Captain said.

From behind me, I heard a gruff voice hum a few bars of a slow, sad tune. This particular tune I had heard a few times before, and when it came to the right moment, I whispered to myself, "We know their names..." When I looked behind me, the old man with the eyepatch was standing in the doorway, leaning against the doorframe. He winked at me with his good eye, and I turned back to the baker.

Chapter 4

"Lady Brin! I'z didn't expected a visit from ya or your friends, course it isn't as if you'z would even know ta contact me." The woman was a bit frenetic in her communication, as if someone extremely important had unexpectedly entered her presence. She came from around the table and walked towards Brin. "I'z Melanie Amarand. Baker by day, watch captain by night." She smiled, and before Brin knew what was happening, Melanie embraced her in a warm, gentle hug. Brin went stiff. It was like she didn't know what to do, but the hug lasted long enough that she brought one of her arms up and awkwardly patted Melanie on the back.

Melanie released Brin and gave us all a warm smile. "Welcome back ta Yellow Liver," she said as she returned to the far side of the map. "Whot can we'z do to help ya?"

Brin dusted flour off the scales of her armor. "Actually, we are looking for someone here."

"A woman named Elaina Raast," Gordo said before Brin could continue. "Short, brown hair, a little clumsy, but with a warm heart."

"And who is you, sir? I see dat you travel wit Brin," the Captain asked.

Gordo paused for a moment, weighing his words. "My name is Gordon Haas. I'm just a friend and companion of Lady Brin."

Melanie smiled. "I'z know Elaina, actually. She'z been helpin' us keep da men along the wall fed durin' dese long nights. Especially when it's deadly cold owt there. A bit of warm bread and a bowl of hot soup can go a long way in da dead of night."

Gordo nodded.

"I'z also know her liddle girl, Gordon."

Flayed

Though I could not see his face, Gordo immediately stiffened at the mention of Elaina's daughter. There was more here than he had been letting on.

The captain continued, "Elaina talks about the man who abandoned her and their child to go run off and fight some foolish crusade against The Masters. Before I would subject my friend to any discomfort, I would know your intent."

Uncomfortable silence lingered in the room before Gordo responded sharply, "With respect, Captain. That is a matter between me and Elaina."

The Captain was displeased with this answer.

"Look, Captain, we are in a bit of a hurry," Brin butted in. "We came through town just to find this girl and have a bit of a chat. We didn't expect to find the city in the middle of an uzkin' war."

Now the Captain was annoyed. "Oh? Youz didn't expect dat owr little town would continue to try'z and clean up the mess whot YOU left behind?"

"Cap," the old man behind us said. His hand was raised in the air.

Melanie took a breath and calmed herself. "Yes, Harold?"

"Wut happin'd tween Elaina and dis Gordo fella ain't none of owr bizness. Lady Brin needs owr help," the old man said.

The captain let loose a sigh. "You're right, as usual, Pop." She grabbed for a cloak and as she latched it around her neck she said, "Follow me."

The streets of Yellow Liver were still lit with torches come dawn. As the sun first scorched the sky with a warm light, we walked up on the backside of a run-down public house. This pub had the welcoming smells of stew and bread wafting down the breeze-swept streets. People all around the building hungrily

Chapter 4

slurped down the warm meat and potatoes in their bowls, each so happy with their meal that they barely noticed our company moving towards the building.

Through the back door, we entered the kitchen, which was a complete mess. There were two fireplaces with massive pots sitting over the fires, and built into the chimney of each was a stone oven where fresh bread was being pulled out. Unwashed pots, still partially filled with stew, were pushed over to the side of the room. Crusts and crumbs covered nearly every surface in the large room. Trays for the huge loaves of bread were stacked haphazardly on the center table, most of them empty of the golden delight that I could still smell in the air. People absolutely whirred about the room, cleaning, cooking, preparing dough, chopping both meat and vegetables, and delivering food to the people collected both inside and out.

Melanie weaved through the machine of the kitchen and went right to one of the women chopping vegetables. The woman stopped chopping, but did not release her grip on the blade before coming over to talk with us.

"Elaina," Gordo said as she came walking up.

"I wondered when you might crawl back here, Gordon. What do you need this time?" Elaina said, wiping the blade in her hand with her apron.

We were all shocked into silence, especially Gordo. I certainly did not know what to say, and for my part, I was still glad that no one had made note of the fact that our company had one undead thing in their midst. I half expected someone to accuse me of being a spy for The King, making this entire situation explode.

When Elaina got no response, she continued to rant, "Nothing? Nothing to say for yourself? Four years, Gordon. She is four years old, and she doesn't even know her father."

Flayed

"Oh, this is *that* Gordon?" a man working in the kitchen shouted out as he continued to work.

Gordo sheepishly muttered, "Sorry."

"Sorry? Sorry is all you have to say?" Elaina was now gesturing with both hands, including the one with the knife.

Gordo just hung his head and kept his mouth shut.

"It is almost dawn, and I will have to go take care of OUR daughter." Elaina scowled at him for a moment, then turned to the rest of us. Her face lit up and a smile appeared instantly. "Hello, everyone. I don't mean to be rude. This isn't even my tavern, I just help out at night for Mel."

"And you'z are amazin', Elaina," the Captain offered.

Elaina smiled again. It was a warm and happy smile. She was brilliant at hiding the anger and bitterness that came flowing out at Gordo, as if it were held in reserve for him. "As you probably know, I'm Elaina Raast. Who are all of you?" She held her hand out in friendship.

Brin quickly took her hand, seeming almost impressed at the speed that Elaina had dressed down Gordo. "I'm Brin-"

Elaina gasped. Her face went from joy to one of shock, almost as if she had seen a ghost. "As in the daughter of Teague, Brin?"

Brin nodded, her black curls bouncing.

"So, Avar is with you, then?" Elaina said.

Avar was surprised to hear his name, but stepped forward. "I'm Avar," he said as he shook her hand.

"I have heard about a lot about you." Elaina smiled, confusing all of us even more. "Oh, and Brin has Ukumog! That would explain a lot." She punched Gordo in the arm. "Why didn't you say who you were here with?"

"You didn't give me a chance," he muttered.

Chapter 4

Elaina paid no attention. "And who are the rest of your companions?"

"I'm Verif," our cat-eyed sorceress commented from the back. "We've met before."

"Oh, yes!" Elaina remembered, then pointed at Tarissa. "And you are, Larissa?"

Tarissa whispered a correction, "Tarissa."

"Right! How are Bridain and Ferrin? Wow, I haven't seen all of you since before we went up to the Frozen Waste," Elaina said.

At the mention of the waste, Melanie perked up. "You'z been to da Northern Wastez?"

"Long story, Mel, and I really should get going." Elaina smiled. Turning to the rest of us she said, "Come on, you lot. Hopefully my flat is big enough to fit us all. Might be a bit cozy."

Back into the morning streets of Yellow Liver. The sun was glinting off the damp rooftops of the town sprawling out before us. Smoke and steam could be seen, fleeing their earthly bonds to try and reach the open sky above. Elaina said farewell to Melanie and Harold, and we wandered a few blocks to a tenement building that looked like it was once the manor home of someone important, but then a city grew up around it. Like an open wound on pristine flesh, it stood out among its neighbors. The construction was more elegant and aged, but it was aging better than all the buildings around it. As we walked through the main doorway, I saw the keystone was labeled with 'TB' engraved into its surface. It looked like the mark of either the maker or the original owner of the home, but even under the protective awning of the porch, it appeared ancient and worn.

Flayed

The stairs in the main entry room were oddly short, but they did the job easy enough. Their awkward height made the two tall men in our party, Gordo and Avar, take more than one step at a time. On the second floor, we went down a hallway and found the room that Elaina then unlocked, and we all went in.

The room was furnished comfortably, if shabbily. Still, it was more lush and homey than any place I had ever seen in Yellow Liver. A small child sat on the floor with an older woman, and they were playing some game involving colored stones.

"Sorry I am late," Elaina said to the woman.

"You say dat like it doesn't happn' every night, lass. It is perfectly alrite. If I wuz a bit younger myself I would be out dere wit ya." The old woman smiled and struggled to get up off the floor.

Gordo and Elaina both rushed to help her get up.

"Thank ya, dears," the old woman said. "Oh! Ain't dis a handsum man, Elaina. You should…"

"Tried that once already, Daisy." Elaina looked over at the small girl on the ground.

The old woman immediately got angry and gave Gordo a light slap on the arm. "Dis girl is a gem, I'z tell ya. A gem. Ya ain't worthy of her." She turned back to Elaina. "Ya be needin' me to stay?"

A funny smile crossed Elaina's face. "No, Nana. I think I will be alright. He won't try anything with his friends here."

Nana glared at Gordo. "Don't ya be makin' her sad, ya hear me? Else ya havta answer ta me!"

"That's not my intent, Nana. Never was," Gordo admitted.

The old woman continued to glare at Gordo, waved goodbye to Elaina and the little girl, and then made her way out the door. She never really even acknowledged the rest of us.

"Well," said Gordo, "she is a character."

Chapter 4

Elaina laughed, "You don't know the half of it."

In that tiny exchange, I saw it. I saw the love that still existed between these two estranged friends. I didn't know what caused this rift between the two of them, but I knew that if Gordo let himself choose, he would be right here with Elaina. For her part, Elaina wanted to be with Gordo, but she was done with adventure. She was settled into her tiny little home, with her tiny little girl.

Gordo crouched down to look at his daughter. "Hi," he said in that soft, playful voice that adults sometimes use with children.

"Don't confuse her, Gordon. Life is hard enough here as it is, and I don't suppose you are staying." Elaina's voice was calmer now, but still scolding.

"You know I can't stay. Sanctuary has been destroyed, and with everything that is happening…"

Elaina turned away, and I saw her wipe away forming tears, but she pretended to be picking up after the child. "I know, Gordon. I know."

Silence filled the room, until the little girl stood up and gave Gordo a surprise hug around the neck. Gordo laughed. "Hi!" he said again. This time it was he who quietly wiped away the tears.

"What is her name?" asked Verif.

"Gwendolyne." Elaina smiled. "But I call her Gwen."

We all just stood there and watched a father play with his daughter for the first time. Brin turned and looked at me. Her green eyes were filled with tears. I caught one of them as they fell from her face, and then felt one drop from my own lashes. This moment showed us what it was we were fighting for, and I think that even Brin realized there were greater things in this world than revenge.

Tarissa moved forward and kneeled down next to Gwen. "Hi Gwen. I'm Tarissa."

"Hi," Gwen said shyly.

Flayed

"And I'm Avar," he said as he sat down next to Tarissa.

Gwen just smiled, her eyes filled with shy curiosity.

Verif seemed afraid to approach. She took a step forward and gave an awkward wave. "I'm Verif."

Gwen looked up and stared at Verif. She was fixated by Verif's strange and brilliant cat-like eyes.

Brin took my hand and whispered, "This is beautiful."

My mind drifted for a moment to the vision of Brin playing with her father. Those few happy moments when she wasn't much older than Gwen, but then something out of the corner of my eye pulled me away from the memory. The white runes on Ukumog were gleaming, its radiant light pulsing gently. Even it had been made calm by this happy meeting, but like all things, it would not last forever.

"So... Why did you really come, Gordon?" Elaina asked.

Gordo ignored her question and continued playing with Gwen. The happy laughter of the tiny girl echoed through all of us. None of us wanted the moment to end.

Elaina walked over and picked up Gwen. Holding her in her arms, Elaina asked Gordo again, "Why did you really come here? I assume it wasn't to see her. Some quest you are on?"

The happiness was broken. "Something like that, Elaina. We need some of your blood."

"What? No! You are going to do something foolish with it." Elaina was angry at the mere suggestion.

Tarissa turned to Avar. "Why do we need some of her blood?"

Avar shrugged and asked Gordo the same question.

Gordo sighed. "Elaina is from the bloodline of openers. Her blood can be used to open doors, gateways, portals—"

Chapter 4

"Walls made of thorns," Verif interjected.

"Exactly." Gordo nodded.

Elaina walked away from Gordo and the rest of us. "You are going back to Flay? We only used my blood to get out of there once, and we had Grimoire's help."

"Well, he isn't around. I don't know where he is," Gordo said. "I should have known this wouldn't work," he grumbled.

"Elaina." Brin was forceful yet calm. "We need to get into Flay so that we can find a wizard who is hiding there. He knows something about my father's murder, and maybe it can lead us to The Doomed that killed him. I want revenge." With those last few words, the runes on Ukumog flared white hot.

Stunned for a moment, Elaina considered her options. "And if I say no? Are you going to hurt anyone?"

"Mommy!" Little Gwen yelled.

"Calm down, baby. No one is going to hurt you," Gordo said and shot a glare over at Brin.

I stepped forward, not knowing exactly what to say. "Listen, this is one step forward on a much longer journey. If you lend us the power of your blood, it will make things easier for all of us, including Gordon. We will find a different way if you deny us, but those ways will be far less safe."

Elaina looked at me as if it was the first time. I realized that she skipped over me in the introductions at the public house, and she never even seemed to realize I was there. "What was your name again?" Her eyes were wide with anticipation.

I paused. It felt a little like her curiosity was a weapon, and she was aiming for my head. "Wrack. Pleasure to meet you, Elaina and Gwen." I gave a slight bow.

Flayed

When I looked up, her eyes were filled with tears. "Are you the one who killed The Ghoul? I hear your name in whispers around here. There was even a soldier from The King's army who defected and now helps in our kitchen. He said that you faced off against The Rotting One when they attacked the city the night The Ghoul died."

Something warm flushed my soul. This recognition from a stranger for doing good things was ever so different from the scorn I usually received. A smile curved my dead lips upwards, and I said, "I am he."

"Oh, Elaina. Why do you keep ending up in these situations? First the doorway in Papa's inn, then Ukumog, now this? Why can't you stay out of trouble?" she asked herself. "Fine Gordo, I will give you the blood you want, but on one condition. When this whole thing is over, you come back here, back to us! Not to some silver monastery in the clouds or wherever you Hunters go. We need you. I need you."

Gordo nodded. "When this is done, I will go back to being a smith." He produced three small vials and a sewing needle.

For the next little while, they carefully collected Elaina's blood, then sealed each of the vials with wax, so that no moisture could escape. While they did that, I thought about one thing she had said. The doorway in Papa's inn. Elaina was the girl I had seen in that vision. The one of the children from Marrowdale opening that doorway that still stood in the ruin of the town – only it wasn't a ruin when they opened it. It was the same vision that had shown me Gordo's face. They were both much younger in the images I saw, but it was them, nonetheless. *How was this all connected?* The doorway, Ukumog, the Frozen Waste, the bloodline of openers, and me. These kids knew more about what was happening that they were letting on. *Did Brin catch all of this?*

Chapter 4

"Master thinks about things that don't matter too much," the mental connection to my hemodan came to life.

I chuckled to myself. "Yes, Murks. I know. Maybe one day I will have all the answers."

Suddenly, I could feel his terror, and it made me frightened, too.

"Right, all done," Gordo said as the last bottle was sealed and cooled.

Tarissa sighed, "Wonderful. Back to hiking through the woods. How far away is Flay?"

"Much farther than Sanctuary," said Avar. "Will take us months to get there, I would wager."

Verif growled at the thought.

"We can't leave yet. We have to meet our new friends tonight," I reminded everyone.

Brin ground her teeth. "UZK! Really? I thought that was a ploy to get away. How do we know your little tricks will work again?"

"Let's not trouble Elaina anymore with our silly quests," I said, reminding her that there were happy children present.

"Right. Thanks for the hospitality, Elaina. Bye bye, little one." Brin tried to sound cheerful, but it came out a bit grumpy.

We all said our goodbyes, and Gordo wanted a moment alone with Elaina. We stood out in the hallway while he whispered his farewells, and kissed his two girls goodbye. I wondered if Gwen even realized that Gordo was her father, or if she would remember him after we left. I found myself wishing that she would.

Flayed

Chapter 5

We went to try and see Melanie, but her bakery was open for the day and she was nowhere to be found. While my companions focused on what to do for the day, I found myself lost in worry. It felt like I was walking in shadows, and at any moment the light would shift and suddenly all the people of Yellow Liver would realize a monster was in their midst. My torn robes added to this feeling; I was a ruined thing, and I needed time to repair myself.

"I am going to the Headless Mermaid," I blurted out while they were talking about something else. "If you want to come with me, that's fine. If not — I will meet you at dawn at Melanie's bakery."

"Right," said Gordo. "I am going to find someplace to sleep for a bit."

"Me too," followed Tarissa.

Avar looked torn for a moment, but then said, "I guess I will go with them. You don't really need me, anyway."

"I want to come," Verif said, taking a step towards me.

"Bad uzkin' idea," Brin suggested. "I know you want to see what kinda spell Wrack has over the ghouls, but you look like a tasty treat, and most of those ghouls looked like they hadn't eaten in a while. Wrack will be fine."

Flayed

Verif scowled at Brin and crossed her arms. "I can hold my own against some ghouls."

"Uzk, Verif. I never said you couldn't. This just seems to be one of those things that Wrack needs to take care of alone, without us uzkin' things up." There was apology and fear in the look Brin gave me. Immediately, I got the impression she still felt as if she had done something wrong when she used Ukumog to separate me from The Mistress.

"Perhaps Brin has a point, Verif. Either both of you should come, or maybe I should go alone."

Brin chuckled a bit and took Verif by the arm. "Come on, Verif. Let's get some rest. We will be traveling for a while in the morning."

Verif groaned at the thought of it, but complied with Brin's pull. The two women waved and followed the rest of my friends into the city. I was alone.

Slipping past the guards into the southern part of town was easy. During the daylight hours the barricades were left open, and small groups of people, mostly adventurous types or looters, were traveling into the ruins of their former neighbors. No one even looked at me twice as I passed.

For the next several hours, I walked the streets between all those abandoned buildings. Mindlessly, I wandered and quickly found the spot where Murks saved be from an onslaught of ghouls. I touched the cobblestone alleyway, and the wall that I had punched in my frustration.

"Everyone needs saving sometimes, Master," Murks said as he crawled out of tattered folds of my robe.

I sighed. "I feel like we are right back where we started."

Chapter 5

He considered the comment and let me dwell on it for a moment before gesturing at the town around us. "Are we, Master? When last we was here, the city was about to consume itself—"

"Not funny, Murks."

He sighed. "Murks not trying to make jokes, Master. Murks mean it. City was about to fall apart. We stopped that."

I leaned against the wall and slid to the ground. "A lot of people died that day, and probably the days following."

"But how many didn't die because of us? We stood up and protected them, Master. That is how it works…"

The little hemodan had a point. "Ah, Murks," I said smiling, "always so wise."

"Murks had a good teacher, Master." The impressions on his clay-like face morphed into a smile, and he sat next to me.

We watched the shadows crawl across the walls for a while and listened to the scrambling of people in the abandoned buildings around us. Anyone who saw us there probably thought we were either a dumped corpse or just a pile of tattered black cloth. Well, until someone didn't and came to search me.

As he moved quietly towards me, I could hear him muttering. "It's just a body, someone just left himz here. No ghoul owt in da sunlight. Thems don't need der stuff anymore…"

It was Murks who moved first and stopped the man in his tracks. "You should go. Master doesn't want to be disturbed," he said to the man.

"What are you, liddel fing?" said the man as he produced a knife.

"You should heed the hemodan's words, friend." My tone was intentionally ominous. It was my attempt to ward off the desperate man before he resorted to violence. He was slack-jawed as I stood up and pulled my hood back.

Flayed

"Wha—what are you den?" He threatened with his knife as he backed away. "Some kinda ghoul fing?"

"I assure you that I am no ghoul, sir. Please, just leave us be." My pale palms were open towards the sky to display that I had no weapon at the ready.

The man paused. I could see him playing through several scenarios in his head. Each time he looked down at Murks, he shifted backwards.

"Go home," I continued. "Surely there is a better life for you than looting the abandoned memories of your unfortunate neighbors."

His face lit up with anger. "Look, if dey no need these fings no more, den why is it a problem if I'z takin' them, then? Eh?"

"And what happens when there isn't anything left to take?" I asked. "Who will you take from then?"

Waves of anger crushed his face into a scowl, and for a moment I thought he might lunge at me, but with each cycle of his eyes and thoughts, he would take tiny steps away.

"Begone," I waved at him, and started walking away. When I heard his feet shuffle against the stone, I looked back and saw him running down the empty street, towards the barricades.

Murks and I wandered a bit more, and try as I might, we could not find that strange part of the city again. The one with the elegant and ancient buildings, and where Matthew died. All roads seemed to lead back to the street where the Headless Mermaid was. Taking this as a bit of a sign, we went inside.

The place was a wreck. Everything had been turned over or shattered. The rank smell of old, spoiled drinks stained the very air. Upstairs was no different. Every mattress had been sliced open

Chapter 5

and searched, every pillow mutilated, every cupboard tossed upon the floor. The storm of greed and desperation had come through some time ago, though, for there was a layer of dust over everything.

I sat on the floor in the room where Brin, Avar, and I had first stayed in Yellow Liver, and I looked up through the cloudy window at the fading sunlight. "It is good that the innkeeper had at least repaired the window," I said. "The last time I saw this particular window, I had just fallen through it." I rubbed the back of my head to soothe away the phantom pains of memory. "I was so helpless then. Seems like a lifetime ago."

"It was..." Murks paused, his head suddenly turning towards the door. He had heard something from the common room below.

Footsteps.

"It isn't dark yet. I would be surprised if it is our hungry friends," I thought at Murks.

"Murks hopes it isn't a gang of robbers come to take whatever they think Master might have."

The panic I felt was quite curious. I wondered if Grumth had felt this way when he knew that we had found his hemodan in the woods the day we reclaimed Ukumog. I felt the tiny mask that I collected from Jugless poke me in the side. I had forgotten I still had it.

"Hello?" A familiar voice called out from below, "Wrack?"

"Verif?" I shouted back as I walked out into the hall.

As I approached the top of the stairs, I saw her standing in the middle of the common room. The moment our eyes met, she smiled at me.

"What are you doing here?"

Flayed

Her grin was dangerous. "I wanted to see you work your magic over the ghouls. I told you before, I want to learn from you." The lust in her eyes was almost intoxicating now. I had trouble thinking clearly.

Murks saved me from saying something stupid by suggesting to Verif, "If you wants to watch, you will have to be out of sight. The ghouls cannot know you are here."

I nodded in agreement. "There is no telling how many of them will come."

"But you won't let them hurt me, will you?" She drew closer, and with each step I felt a hunger grow within me.

Holding out my hand to keep her at bay, "Uzk, Verif. Just do as I ask. Stay upstairs, but out of sight. You should be able to see and hear most of what is going on, but even if they attack me — stay hidden. Ok?"

She pouted. "Fine." As she went upstairs I looked over at Murks who just offered a frustrated shrug. Then she shouted, "Can I at least have your little hemodan as company?"

With a defeated sigh I responded, "Sure."

Graciously, Murks followed without a gripe and went to climb up the short flight of stairs that lead to the rooms. Knowing that it would take him time to climb each step, I picked him up and put him down at the top.

"Thanks, Master," he whispered.

"Thank you, Murks. Don't let her get into trouble." I smiled at him.

The next few hours passed quietly. There was no way to know exactly when our company would arrive, and I dared not leave the common room of the inn lest they stalk quietly in and find me spending time with Verif. From my connection through Murks, it seemed that the two were getting along and that Verif wasn't being

Chapter 5

overly pushy. Unless specifically directed into communication, we shared our emotional state, and his never went away from his general hopeful state.

Shortly after the light of the sun completely faded from the sky, I could hear movement outside the inn. Shadows moved across the hazy windows, and I could hear murmuring come from outside, yet nothing came within. Rummaging about, I looked for a source of light to let them know I was within. My search was met with success, as I found a box of old candles and some wooden matches. I lit some candles and put them upon the bar, then took one more and placed it upon the one table I had set upright in the room, and sat behind it.

The murmuring quieted, and the movement outside was impossible to see. Having more light on my side of the clouded windows gave whatever was lingering outside the advantage. So, I waited. These dark denizens of Yellow Liver needed to come to me on their own. I knew that if I tried to control them it would start our relationship on a different level than I wanted, but I wasn't entirely sure what I did want.

"Having an army of ghouls at your command would be a useful thing," I thought. "Bolstering the people of Yellow Liver against The Doomed by ridding their friends of their curse would also be useful. Can I even do such a thing? Is that within my power?"

Before I could continue this line of thought, the front door of the inn creaked open. Many pairs of eyes flickered in the candlelight. They waited on the other side of the doorway, as if for an invitation. Unnerved by the awkward situation, I stood and came partway around the table.

"Come in, come in," I beckoned them.

Flayed

Cautiously, a few pairs of eyes breached the darkened doorway's threshold. They were wretched things, these ghouls, some of them looking a bit like the humans that they once were, but with grey skin, thin patchy hair, and mouths that looked more like the maw of a flesh eating fish than any human I had seen. Their dark eyes remained fixed on me, and I could sense their awkward hesitation. For my part, I wasn't sure what I was doing there either. My mind filled with discordant thoughts. Some part of me wanted to run, another to slay all these terrible things, but in the back of my thoughts I could almost hear the whispers of Palig screaming for lordship over these monsters of his making.

The more of them that came within, the more that wanted to, and what was at first just a small handful of ghouls sharing my light quickly became a chorus of hungry souls. Just being there, I too felt a hunger. Hearing their whining stomachs, I could feel the empty part of my soul, the dark hole in me that hungered for the light of the living. I was grateful that Brin had decided not to come, for against the grey host of living things within this world, she was the brightest. It was her sweet delicious sunshine that I wanted to devour more than anything in that moment. My eyesight shifted, and I felt my eyes twist. I blew out the candle nearest to me to cease the light searing my vision.

Clenching my jaw, I tried to swallow back the hunger. This darkness did not suit my purpose, and I needed to hold it at bay. I remembered the lush green of the world my memories had revealed to me and, painful as it was, I let the sunlight burn away my hunger. It would not last, but it had to last for long enough.

"Welcome, my friends. Doubtless you should know that I am aware of your struggles." There it was. The word that Palig had said over and over again. Doubtless. *Was this me speaking, or some ghost of him using my lips as a vessel of dark design?*

Chapter 5

Before I continued, they all collapsed to the ground, even the larger host of twisted souls that could not fit within, and so lingered in the street outside. On their knees, they faced the ground, their arms outstretched, as if reaching to touch the hem of my robe. My mind reeled with the power that flowed through it.

A rush of burning cold surged through me, and a twisted smile appeared on my face. I was like a god to them. I was their savior, their lord, their master. They would do anything I asked. Of course, that is how they got here, by embracing my dark gifts. Sacrificing their mortality for a greater power and understanding. These would be lords of this world bowed to me.

"I am not him." Words came from my lips without my invitation. "I am someone different."

A few of their heads slowly lifted to meet my gaze. Worry and doubt blew through the room like a foul wind.

"Your master, The Ghoul, who gave you these gifts and the hunger that is your burden, is dead, his life consumed by the dark blade Ukumog," I said without thinking. The horror of my words frightened me. My soul cringed at the thought of my own death, and it was then I realized the struggle that went on inside my soul. Palig was here with me.

"Doubtless, you will all still follow me. I am your master! Doubtless, I am your GOD!" I screamed.

The host of ghouls around me shifted and tried to inch away, all trying to maintain their submissive position.

My minds eye saw The Ghoul standing there among his subjects. His hunger undeniable, his power was absolute. There was nothing he could not do. For a moment, I reached for one of the knives that should have been hanging from the harness across

Flayed

my torso. Finding only a tattered robe, I grew confused, and this confusion gave me the moment of doubt I needed to wrestle back control from my unseen enemy.

I called upon my own dark hunger and summoned it forth. Like a tidal wave of anguish, it came rushing forth and filled every part of my soul. From somewhere nearby, I felt a wall of fire pressed around me, keeping my hunger from overflowing into the world around me. Churning in the black waves of this dark magic, I clung to the shores of my mortal self. Like a predator living inside the ocean of my consciousness, the hunger sought out the silver of Palig's thoughts and bit down. Hard.

An unearthly wail burst forth from the deepest part of me and rippled out into the world around me. The wall of fire pressed down on my struggle and forced the darkness back. As it passed over me, I could hear the giggle of a child and the raspy chuckle of an old man. "Alright now, Alex. Vanquish it," the old man said.

"I will." Reaching out my will like a massive iron hand, I clutched the fire and that which it contained and crushed them both into oblivion.

The ghouls stared at me with frightened silence as I gasped for breath. "Master, you ok?" a ghoul asked.

"I am fine," I lied. "Just had to deal with an unexpected unseen force… Where was I?"

"Youz am owr god, master," the helpful ghoul volunteered.

Collecting my composure, I said, "Right. Well, that is what I would expect your old master to claim, am I wrong?"

There was a murmuring collection of nodding heads in response.

"I am not your old master. My name is Wrack, and I am he who killed Palig The Doomed. He is no more."

Chapter 5

From outside came pained wails of sorrow. The host of ghouls before me shifted uneasily.

"But I wield his power, his might, and I can command you. I have taken his place as your new master." This seemed to soothe their already troubled souls.

"How we knowz you are owr master?" A dissenting voice came from the crowd. "How wez know you got hims powa?"

Gazing over the crowd, I tried to find the source of the concern, but only found questioning eyes. "Fine," I sighed. "You want an example of my power?"

The response first came in a hesitant whisper and ended in shouts in agreement. They wanted me to prove myself.

Holding my hands up to silence the noise, I considered what I should do. My magic was far too unreliable for me to summon at will, but my voice was under my own control. They had heeded my commands to stop the fight before; perhaps giving them another to force their wills would be enough of a show. Forcing their wills. I sounded like one of The Doomed, clutching my immortal fist over the will of the people. Still, I wanted to end this fight between the ghouls and the people of Yellow Liver. How else could I do that?

"Heed my words, minions. I am your master now, and you will obey my commands. From this day forth, you will not prey upon the humans. You will not attack them and feed upon their flesh. You will not dig up their newly dead. You will find other food to sustain your hunger — and you will do so without threatening the people here. This is our city, and the humans here are ours to protect as well. Not because they are cattle for the slaughter, but because they are our friends, our family, our neighbors." A hushed gasp rippled through the sea of undeath around me. Before they could ask me any questions, I continued. "Any ghoul who breaks this rule will be punished most severely."

Flayed

Silence and hesitation filled the room.

"Do you understand me?"

None of them moved.

"I SAID, DO YOU UNDERSTAND ME?"

They nodded in agreement, some of them scowling at me as they did so.

"Good. Now that we understand each other, there is one more thing. I will not be staying here in Yellow Liver, so I will appoint some of you to take charge while I am away."

Greedy grins flushed many faces with the grimy glint of savage teeth. Immediately I knew this would be a difficult task. Scanning the crowd, I looked for any glimmer of humanity left in the crowd. I walked out the front door of the inn and into the streets. As I emerged, the host of ghouls that I had not yet seen immediately groveled in my presence, save four that sat upon a distant rooftop. They were different than the other ghouls, larger in some strange way, and their silhouettes made them seem less human. I could see the dark embers of their eyes, even at this great distance, and I had no doubt that they heard me.

"Those four will be trouble," I made note to myself and Murks.

Every few feet, I would stop and look at the faces of the ghouls around me. I wasn't entirely sure what I was looking for, but I kept searching. Deep inside, I was horrified by the twisted faces that surrounded me. The ones that still looked mostly human were the worst of all. It was harder to think that they were always these grey-skinned vessels for an undying hunger.

Pausing for a moment before continuing my search, I took a much better look around me and marveled at the sheer number of these poor souls. They kneeled in the streets, perched on rooftops, hid in alleyways, lingered in doorways, and seemed endless. Each

Chapter 5

time I thought I had seen all of them, there were more that I hadn't noticed. I wanted to weep at how far this corruption had spread, but the pride I had in my newly-found army kept my compassion at bay. More than ever, I understood who Palig was, and yet — for all his hunger and lust for power, he did nothing with this army of undead that was at his command. *Was his fear this crippling? Had The Baron beaten down his will so far that he could not act on his desire for power and control? Or was there something I was yet missing in this great puzzle?* I decided it must be the latter, but only The Baron had the real power to answer my questions.

The clouds shifted above, and I saw a silver beam of moonlight from the sky touch the faces of five of the ghouls. They were spread through the crowd, and at first it seemed odd that these five would catch the light as they did. I beckoned them over, I felt a strange relief wash over me, as if a warm blanket had been wrapped around my resolve, giving me great comfort. For a fleeting moment, I felt the warm embrace of love, but then it was gone.

When the five ghouls had come to me, I looked them over. Two of them looked mostly human, one of them having not yet given in to the grey skin that came as part of the curse. The other three were older ghouls, their flesh scarred by the eternal hunt for food, but in their eyes I still saw the glimmer of humanity. A slight chuckle left my nostrils as I realized — I hadn't made this decision alone. Someone or something was aiding me in this choice. I only hoped that they had the best interests of the town in their hearts as they did so.

"You five. What are your names?" I commanded, loud enough for all to hear me.

"I'mz Chargil, sir," one of the human-like ones answered. Her features were unmistakably female.

Flayed

The next one grunted before speaking. "Wez Dargan, masta," it gurgled.

Another human-looking one spoke up, out of turn, "I'm Shawn, master. Dese otha two are Ulaar and Lerg. Demz don't speak much."

I nodded at Shawn, and the other two ghouls bowed their heads in recognition.

"Very well. You five shall be my champions here in Yellow Liver. While I am away, you will keep your brothers from stepping across the line, and it falls upon you to help the lost ones find their way. Can I trust you to perform this?"

All of them except for Shawn nodded quickly in response, and I saw Shawn's eyes dart over to the four lurkers that I had noticed earlier.

"All of you, be warned," I shouted. "The world you know is changing. Be prepared to change with it. Now, go!"

The dark souls who lingered on the fringes or hid in darkened doorways were the first to flee at this dismissal, then the rest of the twisted host followed, save for the five I had named my servants, and the four that lurked upon a distant roof.

My hand found purchase on Shawn's filthy shoulder. "Who are they?" I asked the five.

Lerg gurgled something and coughed up a handful of slime trying to talk.

Shawn winced at the future that might someday be his, then looked at me with worried eyes, "Dey are da elda ones. Dos four are da only onez dat remain frum the first group dat The Ghoul gave himz blessin' to." He looked up at them with fear and reverence. "Dem not like what youz doin', masta."

Chapter 5

I stood tall in the moonlight. From this distance is was hard to feel any fear of the large lurking shadows with embers for eyes. "They will fall in line, or they will be destroyed, just like the one who cursed them."

"Curse? Youz fink dis is a curse?" Hope rang like a bell in Shawn's voice.

I smiled at him, and found the same hope in all five pairs of eyes that looked up at me. "Yes I do, Shawn. A curse that I hope to break."

Five menacing maws curled up into terrifyingly hopeful grins. Dargan drooled black ichor out of one side of her mouth, and Ulaar wiped it away with his claw, then scraped it off onto the stones at our feet.

"Do what you can. The humans are no longer food. Kill any that will not obey. Leave those four to me."

A mixture of gurgling acceptance was uttered by my new friends, then they all loped off in different directions in the empty part of the city. Yet the four lurkers still sat upon the distant roof, like unhappy gargoyles. I paid them no more mind and went back inside the inn.

I found Verif and Murks both sitting in the main room. Verif was bursting with excitement.

"Wrack!" Verif quietly screamed. "That was amazing! I thought they were going to kill you when you told them that they couldn't eat humans anymore."

"Yeah, I thought they might, too."

She leapt forward and hugged me. "Wow! I have never seen anything like that."

Her warmth was nearly intoxicating. The hunger of the ghouls felt contagious, and I had not yet acclimated. I wanted to hold her closely and have her form melt away into mine. Before

Flayed

I could give into this dark desire, I gently broke the embrace and urged her to arm's distance. As soon as she was gone, the cold air stole away her delicious heat. "I wasn't exactly sure what to expect myself."

"So, how long have you had this power over the ghouls?"

I laughed. "Now it is question and answer time?" Walking over to the window, I checked to see if the inn was still being watched by any of the lurkers. Finding them missing, I said, "Perhaps we should get back to town."

"Aww. So soon? I kinda like having you all to myself." Her eyes were filled with lust again, and I did not trust that my hunger for her life would stay under my control.

"I need to be around living people right now, Verif. Not just you and me. It is hard to explain."

She pouted a bit. "Fine. Let's go find everyone else." I could tell she wasn't happy.

Even with my current edict, I could not be sure that we would not fall under attack, so we took great caution returning to the barricades. Once we found the one closest to the bakery, I waved at the watchmen and said, "Oi! Can we be let through please? We are friends of Brin. Ask the Captain if you need to."

A head popped up over the barricade and a familiar voice called out, "Wrack is it, then?"

"Yeah, Harold."

"Right boyz, let 'em in."

Many hands on the other side worked to disassemble the puzzle of a barricade to allow us through. Once inside the living part of the city, Harold escorted us back to the Bakery, where we waited until morning. Verif curled up in a corner and slept, but I sat and watched the messages coming and going. Before long, the map on the captain's table was empty of ghoul markers.

Chapter 5

"It dunna make any uzkin' sense!" Melanie exclaimed. "Why wuld all dem ghouls jus vanish? Dem usually at least one tryin' to get over da wall, or watchin' us."

Had it worked? Did the ghouls retreat from this nightly siege? "Perhaps they have decided to look for food elsewhere," I offered. "Even still, I wouldn't let your guard down."

The captain laughed, "Tonight has been diffrent, dats fur sure." She paused to adjust some of the markers on the map. I could see her scanning for a hole in their patrol or something else they had missed. "But only time will tell us, eh?" She gave me a worried smile.

Sitting back in the corner near Verif, I thought about telling the captain everything. That I had been the one to kill the ghoul, and that somehow Ukumog had given me some of his power, some of his personal memories — but that also sounded like a bad idea. There was also no real assurance that the ghouls would continue to follow my command, especially after we headed to Flay. "Better to let them continue to be paranoid, might save some lives," I thought to myself and my hidden hemodan.

He agreed.

Early morning rays of sunshine started creeping into the bakeshop, and that cued the captain and her night watch to start preparations for the daytime. I let Verif sleep a little while longer, hoping that Brin would come looking for us in the bakeshop. Just after the doorway gleamed with the sunlight from the stone street, Harold slowly walked through the threshold. His steps carried with them the weariness of old bones held up by a powerful heart. As if it were his own shop, he pulled off one of the stacked chairs and rested his tired bones.

Flayed

"Strange night, dis one," he said. "Never seen dem ghouls act like dis."

"Yeah? Have you been watching them long?" I complied with his desire to start a conversation.

Melanie called out from the back of the building. "Pop! Youz not helpin' us git ready?"

Harold made a face and motioned towards me. "I'm entertainin' youz guests, Cap!"

She smiled at him wryly. "Sure Pop. Thats wot you is doin'."

He nervously rubbed his palms on his knees, trying to summon up the correct words. "Yeah. Iz been watchin' em a while now. Even befur all dis mess startid." Sudden shame assaulted his words, and his face showed the signs of the struggle to fight it back. His abrupt silence gave way to a tiny laugh. "Watched fur long'r den wez shuld hav, I reckon."

My mind turned to the first time I was in Yellow Liver, the morning where I was attacked on the street by the ghoul who stabbed me with the black talon. I remembered the frightened faces of the people on the street, and how the shutters of the nearby buildings were shut as my attacker and his minions came walking down the street.

"Yellow Liva wuz a city ruled by a monsta. Wez wuz all scared before." His words echoed my thoughts. "Somethin' happened dat night, da night when dat army attacked. It wuz like we all just woke up. Da enemy wuz always in da room wif us, but somfing made it ok for us to see dem." There was a passionate relief in his words. Simply said, but they spoke volumes.

I nodded quietly in return, but could not help but wonder when they would wake to see me as the monster in the room with them. I hoped it wouldn't come to that.

Chapter 5

"Maybe it is true, wot dems say, da master ghoul is dead. Good riddens, Iz say. Time for a change, Iz say." The embers of revolution burned in his hushed tones. Though, with The Ghoul dead, I wasn't sure who he was hoping to overthrow.

"Pop," Melanie called from the back of the shop, "youz remember dat Sargent Valence is comin' inta town dis mornin', yeah?"

My face reacted with surprise, and I saw that Harold noticed.

"Iz rememburr, Cap," he responded loudly, eyes still fixed on me. His gaze shifted to suspicion as he rubbed his chin, then he whispered, "Youz know da Sargent?"

With a sigh, I considered lying to the old man, but for some reason I decided to tell him the truth. "I've had a run in with him. He arrested Brin and I, along with a handful of refugees from the attack here, out on the road near Marrowdale."

"Marrowdale?" His voice was filled with surprise and wonder. "Dats far away, lad. Wot wuz all of you doin' up dere?"

"Fleeing, mostly." I paused, uncertain what I should or should not say. "Brin believes that there is someone in Flay who knows more about her father's death."

Harold nodded, solemnly. "Eyes like fire, dat one haz. Gunna get all you lot in trouble one day, iffin she hazint already."

I chuckled. "You don't know the half of it."

He smiled. "So, wot happind wiff da Sargent?"

"Well. He tried to take us all back to Skullspill, but we were attacked by some of The King's men, and we fled in the chaos."

Leaning back in his chair, he stroked his chin. "Was dis when dat Vampire Prince attacked?"

Without thinking, I nodded.

Flayed

"I heard himz talkin' about dat night. Barely escaped with himz life, he did. If dem werewolvz dinnae show up, himz said he wuld be dead fur sure! Sounds like a right nasty fight ta me."

"I wouldn't call it one of my favorite experiences." Instantly, my head was filled with echoes of that night. I could almost feel the raw power of The Vampire all over again, but then my thoughts turned to my strange meeting with The Rotting One in the woods. It still confused me why The Rotting One turned against his own army in order to help me escape. Some of his words rang through my thoughts: "Remember yourself, Wrack. Only after that will you be able to help her…"

"Wrack? Youz still with ol' Harold?"

Shaking away the memories I said, "Yeah, Harold. Sorry. I get caught up in my own thoughts sometimes."

"Itz ok, boy. It happen to uz ol' geezers." A rumbling dry chuckle rolled out of Harold's chest and quickly turned into a cough.

"Pop! Are you still out there?" Melanie shouted again from the back of the shop.

Struggling to stand up, Harold called out. "Yeah, Cap. Keep your britches on, Iz comin'. Youz don't need to keep shoutin."

As he shuffled towards the back, I said, "Good to meet you Harold. I think we will be heading out today."

"So soon?" He sounded disappointed.

"Yeah. Brin really wants to get to Flay."

He smiled. "Well, youz be careful, dems Flayers cannae be trusted."

Brin stormed in through the door. "See, Avar! I told you that they would be here."

Coming in after her, Avar sighed.

"Glad to see that you two aren't uzkin' dead."

Chapter 5

Woken my Brin's exclamations, Verif quickly got to her feet. I followed.

"Mornin' lady Brin," Harold said cheerfully. "You lot want some biscuits before youz head out? Ol' Harold can git ya some. Iz know da owna."

Brin nodded, her mood shifting instantly to match Harold. "That would be amazing, Harold, thank you."

"Me too, please," Verif added.

Soon, all six of us wayfarers watched the Yellow Liver come to life while we filled our bellies for the road ahead. None of my companions asked about the night before while we ate, and as soon as we were done, we said farewell to the sleepless Captain and her exhausted father and headed out the north gate of the city.

The stone walls of the city were still in view when we saw the small company of men wearing the red and black livery of The Baron marching down the road. They had a pike with a horse's jawbone tied to the end of it, and at their head marched Sergeant Valence. Quickly, we skirted to the side of the road and let them pass. For a moment I thought I saw him give me a subtle nod as they passed, but I just thought I was seeing things.

Flayed

CHAPTER 6

The journey to Flay took more than a month, perhaps even two. I watched the world wake from the wet warmth of spring into the dead heat of summer. With every league we travelled the life around us shifted. The struggle for everything to survive was less and less harsh. In the west, near Yellow Liver, the plants were grey and stunted, and the water was filled with a poisonous sulfur that had to be boiled away to make it drinkable. These maladies of the world changed with every step. Before long, my companions could fill their waterskins directly from a stream, and the plants changed from grey to green. Jared's words about The Cursing poisoning the world were driven home for me. Both in the frozen land of Regret and here in the East, things were different.

Brin kept us away from the roads, but we were never far away from them. The noises of skirmishes between small groups of armored warriors were frequent when we left Yellow Liver, but they became less so the farther we travelled.

Conversation was light during our journey, and even the events of the travel were nothing to speak of. As we passed Marrowdale, Avar insisted that we go back to the ruin on the hill so he could collect supplies. When I asked how he knew that there

Flayed

would always be supplies there, he just shrugged and said that someone always made sure that the secret stash of Shadow Hunter supplies was always filled. I did not press him anymore about it.

Up to the north and east of Marrowdale we travelled, and that is when the marvel of the world's fresh bounty really pressed home. At first I dismissed the change of the air to the change of the seasons, but the further East we got, the trees stood taller and the other plants did not seem to be struggling just to survive. My hunger for the energy of life that surrounded me was a beast I fought the entire way. The nights were long and lonely, as I spent every hour keeping my own monster caged within my heart. I was determined to leave this place as unspoiled as I could. As hard as I tried, I was not always perfect. Occasionally, I would watch the color of a branch leached from it as I brushed by, the dark green corrupted into a dark grey. Contact between my hungry soul and this thriving wilderness was dangerous. It made me hesitate to touch anything living, even my companions.

One hot morning, we crested a wooded hill, and through the trees I saw what looked at first like a huge bird's nest on the horizon. It took a moment for me to realize that the gleaming shapes inside the nest were actually buildings, and once I realized that, the size of this nest shocked me. We were still a great distance from the gleaming city on the horizon, but the scale of it surprised me.

"There it is," Brin said as we crested another hill. "Flay. Capital city of the Kingdom of Ravenshroud and seat of power to the most powerful of all The Doomed, The King." She pointed at the nest I had seen hours before.

From this new vantage point, we could see more details of the city. That dark twist of vegetation surrounding the pointed roofs was the thick wall of thorny brambles. It had given me the impression at first that instead of a city, it was a giant nest. So tall and

Chapter 6

thick it was that the city did not need stone walls to keep its enemies at bay. Nature itself was guardian to this place, and it boggled my mind. Archways of stone were set into the dark brambles, housing large metal-bound gates. Towers jutted out of the thicket like spears pointed at the heavens, and I could see the movement of watchmen within their tips. The land surrounding the city was mostly flat, and was partitioned into more farms than I cared to count. The smell of manure grew stronger as we approached the farms; no doubt they used it to fertilize the rich dark earth for their crops. The contrast of this place and the dour cities and towns of the west was shocking to me, but I had no answer for this difference, so I tried to push the thoughts from my mind.

As the day pushed on, we travelled carefully, as to not be seen by any of the various patrols or the farmers. We darted between clusters of trees and hid behind barns until there was no choice but to stop until nightfall. We found safe haven in a group of trees between two farms, and settled in until nightfall.

Gordo reached into his pouch and pulled out two vials of Elaina's blood. "One vial to get us in, one vial to get us out." He held them up for all of us to see. "Just a drop on each thing you want to open for you, and then a simple thought or word to will it open. That is all you need."

Tarissa held out her hand, and Gordo handed her one of the vials. The wax-sealed cork had kept the blood safe and wet during the entire journey. My thoughts went to Elaina and her small child. I imagined her keeping busy helping others in Yellow Liver, but hidden behind her smile was the worry that she would never see any of us again, Gordo most of all.

Suddenly, this whole mission seemed selfish and pointless. I could not imagine what the next step might be. *If the wizard Grumth implicated one of The Doomed, what then? What if it were*

Flayed

The King himself? Would we charge the mighty palace inside this massive city? These questions simply could not be asked, however. I swallowed my doubts and shook off my fear. A promise was made to this woman whom I cared for, and that promise I would keep. She was the first person to show me any kindness, and that gift had carried me all the way to this point. It was silly to even consider trying to sway her from this troubled path. Her personal darkness was just too strong. The only way I could bring light to her was to help her.

I looked through the trees at the wall of thorns before us. No longer were the gleaming spires of the city in view; we were too close to the towering wall of brambles. Along the barrier to the North stood one of the large stone archways, flanked on either side by a handful of soldiers wearing the green and white of The King's men. Banners bearing the same stripe of green on a field of white danced lazily in the breeze ushered in by the setting sun.

After the light left the sky, fires were lit at the gates, and more light could be seen from the towers, which stabbed the sky from behind the wall. Soldiers with torches began patrolling the wall. Brin and Gordo started watching them, waiting for the correct moment to lunge forward to the wall. They had already picked a spot to pierce the defense of the city. It was far enough away from both the gate and the towers above that they thought it the best place to enter. They just hoped it also had the required buildings on the other side to protect them from the watchful eyes of the nearest towers. To find ourselves out in the open would be a potentially fatal mistake.

Hours passed by like years, but in the darkest part of the night, Gordo finally spoke. "Ok. It is now or never."

"Then it is now," Brin said defiantly.

The rest of us nodded.

Chapter 6

After the next guard passed by, we slinked out of the tiny cluster of lush, tall trees and crawled towards the wall. We slithered on our bellies shoulder to shoulder, so that we would all hit the wall at once, rather than doing so in a single line. We wanted to limit the window where the watch towers might spot our arrival. Once we were at the wall, none of us took a breath. We waited to make sure that we hadn't been seen or heard. When no guard called out or alarm bell rang, we found comfort in that brief moment of triumph, but there was still work ahead.

Gordo kept pushing forward through the hedge with enough speed that the closing branches behind us never became an issue, but I will admit that I was worried for a moment when I realized that they were continuing to close. For a brief moment, I imagined the six of us impaled and trapped halfway through the wall of brambles. That momentary panic, however, was completely unwarranted.

Gordo produced his vial of Elaina's blood and broke the seal. Carefully, he placed tiny drops of the red vitae on branches of thorns. All of us held our breaths as we watched branches. Doubt creeped into my mind when nothing happened. Gordo's explanation of how this magic worked was vague at best, and it did not take long for me to lose faith that it would work at all. Pressed together as we were, I could feel Brin's temperature rise as her silent anger started to grow.

"It will work," Gordo whispered.

Tarissa leaned back and looked down the wall in both directions and shook her head at Brin, who then sighed with relief.

All of our attention was on those glistening drops of blood that sat upon the branches of thorns. It was as if the extension our will was slowing down time itself. Or perhaps that is a grand joke that gods play on mortals: the more you focus on something involving

Flayed

time, the longer it will seem to take. Brin was growing even more impatient than usual. She kept shifting within her crouched stance, and I could hear the metal hook on Ukumog asking to be freed from its captive ring on her belt.

Again, Tarissa checked the wall for incoming danger. This time her response was to point a finger along the north side of the wall.

"Gordo," Brin whispered with dire urgency, "we are running short on time. Make this magic uzkin' work already."

"Have faith in the magic, Brin. It will work." Gordo was so calm about this. I couldn't help but believe that it would work.

Verif sighed. "Is there some incantation or word you have to say to make it work?"

"Uh." Gordo's calm demeanor fell apart, and my faith was shattered instantly. "Elaina never had to say anything to make it work."

"Uzk!" Brin hissed. "Do you even know how to use this without her?"

"Guys?" Tarissa asked sweetly, but was ignored.

Avar chimed in, "All the magic I have read about requires will in order to make it work. If it is connected to Elaina when she uses it…"

"…maybe she doesn't require words," Verif finished Avar's thought with hushed excitement.

"Guys, the guard is coming!" Tarissa whispered and hunched in closer to the wall.

"Ask it to open, Gordo," I suggested calmly, but a storm of worry was brewing in my heart.

"Please open?" Gordo's hushed voice nearly cracked.

Nothing happened.

Chapter 6

Verif sighed, disgusted with Gordo's pathetic attempt. "You have to command the magic, Gordo. Tell it to open. Don't be so weak!"

Tarissa put her hand on Verif's shoulder to quiet her escalating volume. "He is two hundred paces away and approaching slowly."

"By all means, Gordo," Brin said, "Take your uzkin' time."

A quieted *clink!* filled the air, as Ukumog was unleashed from Brin's belt. The terrifying blade's freedom suddenly put us all on edge, and I could feel the hunger of its edge bleed into the air around us. A fight was coming.

"Gordo. Gordo, listen to me," I said aggressively. "Just tell the blood what you want it to do."

He looked at me with worried and confused eyes. I could feel Verif nodding behind me. With the two of us encouraging him, he turned back to the emotionless crimson drops. I could smell the iron in the blood as he whispered to the branches, "Open."

The branches came to life with the natural creaking and rustling of a sudden wind. Brin's fist was tightly gripped around the leather-wrapped bone handle of Ukumog. As the layers of thorny branches moved aside to allow us entry, Brin wasn't moving with the rest of us.

"Brin," I called to her.

Without looking at me, she replied, "Just a moment. This guard is going to see us."

"Brin, you don't have to kill him. Stop listening to the sword, and listen to me." It was just me and her; the rest of our companions were already crawling through the treacherous tunnel through the hedge. After she didn't respond, I said again, "Brin."

Flayed

She looked back at me with anger in her eyes. When our gaze met, something shifted in her, and I saw her grip on the blade loosen.

"C'mon, Brin. Hurry," I whispered.

She turned her body towards me, and with a flip of her wrist, Ukumog clinked with protest as it was leashed to her belt. I let her pass me before I crawled into the tunnel, and as I passed the threshold of the hedge, I whispered, "Close."

Behind me, the thorny branches rustled back into place. I could hear the armor of the patrolling guard chiming with each of his footsteps. The wall of the hedge sealed behind me before I could see them. We had made it just in time.

At the head of our group, Gordo was placing drops of Elaina's blood on branches and commanding them to open. I could hear him whispering to each of them in turn, his voice growing more and more sure of itself with every word. The ground beneath us was damp and rough. The soil was soft enough, but the hardened roots of this massive wall made the ground painful to crawl over. From my connection to Murks, I could feel him wince each time my robe got snagged on a thorn. Each time this happened, I just kept moving, which more often than not ended with the fabric of my robes tearing.

There was a moment, while crawling inside that thorny tunnel, where the air suddenly shifted from musty earth and sweat to smoked meats and fresh air. Light from torches in the city poured in through the hole that Gordo had opened at the far end. My nerves were steeled as I pushed through the last length of my crawl. I was prepared for a fight once we set foot on the streets of Flay. To my surprise, none came.

Chapter 6

As Brin pushed forward to make the crawl up the slight hill and into the city, the heel of her boot made an unexpected quick movement back and up, colliding with my face. I was both surprised and enraged for a brief moment, and even with the grunt I know I made, Brin did not even acknowledge the violence she had committed against me. I could taste blood in the back of my throat, and I saw a drop of dark fluid drip from my nose into the musty earth below. Something wise and old inside my soul pushed away any concern I had for my wound, and whispered worry to me. My blood still had power I did not understand, and the thought of leaving it here in this thorny tomb I found deeply troubling. I dabbed at the earth with my robes a few times before trying to scoop up as much of my blood as I could from the moist earth.

A hand came through the threshold of the thorns and helped to pull me up and out. Instinctively, I started brushing the dirt from my tattered robes. At our feet was the evidence of our trespass, as the rest of the street we had entered was completely devoid of dirt or debris. From where we stood, I could not even see a plant growing out of place. Even in the dark cover of night, I could see enough of the city to be overwhelmed with memories. I knew this place, and apart from the stains of weather and time, it was exactly the same. The stones in the street were flat and precise. The buildings were blocky and efficient, yet carved with detailed beauty. Compared to all the filth and misery I had seen since crawling from my mossy grave, this place was clean and ordered. Where Yellow Liver had a stench of filth that loomed over everything, here the wonderful smell of smoked food and spices filled the air.

My companions all whispered to each other as I breathed in my surroundings and got lost in the beauty of them. Somewhere in my trance, I somehow discarded the clod of dirt I had been

Flayed

clutching. Panic set in for a moment as I looked at all the dirt around us and realized that it was gone. Hope tried to flush my worry away, but with only a promise of success.

"We should get moving," Brin said. "When the guards find all this dirt, they will know that someone snuck through."

She was right. The wet earth was smeared along the sharp edge of the road, and the distinct texture of footprints could be seen against the surface of the stone.

"Where are we going?" Avar asked.

Brin looked around for a moment. "This way." She pointed down the length of the wall, away from our place of entrance.

Without another word, my companions and I started skulking through the streets of Flay. Before we got out of sight, I glanced back over my shoulder at the spot where we had entered. The hole that had allowed us entry was completely gone, and for a moment I thought I saw a flower growing on the thorny vines.

"How odd." I said to no one.

We skulked in the shadowy backstreets for hours, dodging armored soldiers on patrol. Each of them wore the colors of The King's men, the off-white with a green stripe, but few of them wore the tabards that I had seen before. These soldiers often wore ribbons wrapped around their belts the trailed off alongside their swords. Their armor also rarely looked dented or worn. It made me question if any of these particular soldiers had seen any of the war that existed outside the walls of this city.

I was impressed by the design of the city. The streets marched in perfectly straight lines, save for where they met the stones that patrolled the round wall. The buildings all stood straight and had fresh stoney faces. Poles with burning lamps lined the streets at nearly perfect intervals, easily lighting the interior streets of this grid of homes efficiently. When we got to the main

Chapter 6

thoroughfare, I stood for a moment in awe of the marvel of it. With a bow strong enough, I could have shot an arrow straight through the center of the city, passing over the massive statue at the center of the city center to finally find rest in the first gate that led up the hill to the seat of The King himself.

The statue was equally as stunning. The base was a large basin of water, and in the center of this living water was a fountain that gently cast the water up into the air and back into the basin. Above the fountain stood a regal man wearing armor and casting his stern gaze to the southwest. His cloak almost seemed to wave with the motion of the water as it dripped off his shoulders and pooled into the water below. The hands of the statue were wrapped around the handle of a mighty sword, the point of which was planted solemnly between the man's feet. Upon the man's shoulder was a raven delicately holding a crown in its beak. The statue was so lifelike, that for a brief moment I thought I would see the raven place the crown on the head of the regal man, and I was almost disappointed when it did not.

"That's him, isn't it?" I muttered to Avar.

He squinted through the darkness at the statue and nodded. "I can't really see it, but if you are talking about the statue in the town center, yeah. That is The King. Or at least who he was."

"Who he was?"

Avar sighed. "The King was once King Darion Kalindir, King of Ravenshroud. He who would be Emperor. The Cursing changed him. It changed all of them." His face filled with sadness before he turned away and continued to follow Brin back into the side streets.

"What happened to him?" I couldn't contain my curiosity.

"He was consumed by his own greed and arrogance," Tarissa answered.

Flayed

Avar sighed. "He is nothing but a shadow, a ghost. Or at least that is the rumor."

"The rumor?" I asked.

"Yeah," Tarissa replied. "All the people of Flay pretend that they can see him when it is announced that he is walking among them, but it is just that – pretend."

"The revenants that serve The King directly run the city, and they can be strict with people who do not play along with what they say about His Majesty." There was a hint of nostalgia in Avar's voice.

"If he isn't real, doesn't that mean that there is one less of The Doomed in the world?"

"It isn't that simple," Avar said. "Fighting him is like fighting a belief. It doesn't matter if he is real or not, the people believe, and many of them worship him as a god. That is the one faith that hasn't been made illegal here in his kingdom. It is hard to save a people from a monster that lives inside their hearts and minds."

"Even if he were real, and someone was able to kill him, how would anyone ever know it happened? Would anyone believe it?" Tarissa chuckled. "If they did believe it, you would have thousands of his subjects willing to die to avenge the death of their god. It would be a nightmare."

I nodded. "Sounds like a complex problem."

"Yeah, but things are even more complex now. About five or six years ago now we got word that The King's son had returned the Flay. Prince Rimmul was gone for thousands of years, and then all of a sudden he was back." Tarissa spoke like she was giving me some kind of spy report. "His presence has done work to destabilize the city a bit. There are factions of people who are now secretly worshiping him instead of King Darion."

Chapter 6

"I hadn't heard the details about that," Avar said. "What is happening with the eight great houses of Flay?"

My curious ears just listened.

Tarissa took a deep breath. "Too much to talk about right now. I would need some time to lay it out for you, and my information is about two years out of date."

"Ah," Avar said. "The Mistress attacking Sanctuary would do that."

Silence fell between them, but my desire to know more burned too brightly. Tarissa had always been an enigma to me. She didn't wear the same armor as the other Shadow Hunters, nor did she have the soldier demeanor of Bridain. Where Avar was liberal with the information he shared, she would often refrain from commenting on anything people said, but it was clear to me now – she was extremely familiar with the politics around us. Verif had told me once that those who were wizards were often scarred by the supernatural. I had seen no evidence that Tarissa bore such magical corruption. My instincts told me that Tarissa could just vanish into the crowd here in Flay, or blend in with the people of Yellow Liver with just as much ease. "What is it that you do for the Shadow Hunters, Tarissa?"

Surprised by the question, she looked back at me. With a sweet smile, she deflected the question, but I could see her expert eyes searching my face for some reason to say more. Without saying a word, she turned back to the journey ahead of us.

"She collects information for the Hunters," Avar responded.

Tarissa's blond ponytail shook back and forth in front of me. "What have I told you about that, Avar?"

Avar was briefly silent, and then spoke, "Right..."

Flayed

While I wanted to ask more, the sudden silence was filled with such awkwardness that I could not find a good way to break it. Swimming in this silence, we continued skulking the streets until the sky started to lighten up.

"Where exactly are we heading?" asked an out of breath Gordo as we weaved up the hill towards the castle gate.

Brin just continued to march forward.

After a moment or two Gordo asked, "Avar? Do you have any idea where she is taking us?"

"Not a clue."

"Great," Gordo said sarcastically.

The light grew in the sky and the city came to life. Grey stone shone brightly in the morning sun, and the first of the citizens came trickling out of their homes. Many of the houses had a shop of some sort on their street level. It was there that people did their work. Doors to the front gardens of these houses opened to reveal bakeries, butchers, wainwrights, coopers, cobblers, blacksmiths, and every other sort of craftsman. Within the short span of an hour, the streets were teeming with the organized flow of life.

In Yellow Liver, the foul smells and horrible buzz of life were an assault on the senses of anyone unprepared. Here in Flay, the people were polite, generous, and washed. I could smell the smoke from craftsmen's shops, but along with it was the burning of soothing incense. In every section of the city there were large community bathhouses where the smell of scented oils and fresh water would wash the very air around them. Even to my supernatural senses, things seemed to balance out. Knowing this was the domain of at least two, if not three, of The Doomed, I kept waiting to see the horror that lay lurking under the surface.

"Let's find a way to get our clothes clean," Tarissa suggested. "In the day, we are going to stick out."

Chapter 6

Brin nodded.

"There is a catch." Tarissa continued, "Anyone who washes our clothes might report all the dirt to the guard. Word in Flay about strange events travels fast. Best not to give the people in the bath house any information."

Everyone muttered in agreement. Brin started to walk towards the bath house, but Tarissa grabbed her arm.

"You should leave Ukumog out here," Tarissa started.

"Uzk that," Brin spat.

Tarissa nodded, but continued, "Wrack cannot go in there anyway. A revenant going into the bath house looking like he does would be severe cause for alarm. We give him all our distinctive items," she pointed at Gordo and Avar's silver shoulder guards, "and he protects them from somewhere safe."

"What do we do about Wrack?" Avar asked for me.

Tarissa looked at me with compassion. "We will just have to figure that out later."

My companions reluctantly piled up their prized possessions, including Ukumog, and headed to the baths. At the last moment, Verif changed her mind and stayed with me. "My eyes will stand out too much," she offered as an excuse.

The two of us sat there in silence until she fell asleep with her head on my lap. I pulled a blanket out of her pack to cover her. Something pulled at my mind until I found myself staring at the glowing runes on Ukumog's surface. The saber shape of the blade was mysteriously gone, and it had returned to the long rectangle that I had originally known it as. Likewise the runes now glowed with their original blue, instead of the white it had been since Brin attacked that thing the Shadow had called a seed.

Flayed

With each of the slow pulses of Ukumog's runes, I felt fear and anger growing in my heart. Images of The Ghoul's death flooded my mind. The darkness that I had felt in my soul at that moment was the only thing that pushed the fear away, but the anger was trying even harder to get in. I closed my eyes and tried to think of something, anything, else.

With Ukumog in my hand, I walked the stone road up towards the castle in Flay. Behind me the city was on fire, the grand statue in the center had been cracked, the raven cut in half, and the head of the regal man lay in the leaking basin below. In my other hand I held the large bronze crown from the statue. Blood ran from my hand down the crown and dripped onto the hot stones of the street, where it sizzled and smoked. There were no cries of panic, no one running for safety. All the people of Flay were either gone or dead, and I didn't care to know which. Purple flames rose from Ukumog as I ascended through the first gate and into the high city of Flay.

I saw the banners of all eight of the great houses of Flay, and I knew their names. First came the house called Horn, with the banner of two pairs of antlers. These antlers were stacked, one set on top of the other, and the top ones were much larger than the bottom pair. Next came a banner with three inkwells and one quill. Each of these items was in a separate quarter of the space, with the quill being in the upper left quarter. This was the banner of house Juindar. Next was the banner of house Xyan; it was a simple banner with nothing but a triangle in the center. The banner that followed was of a hammer and shield, and belonged to house Numerum. House Aeochael stood out against the rest, as their banner had

Chapter 6

wavy lines coming together in the center forming a stylized cat's eye. The banner of three mountains belonged to house Ruthrom. House Chundai's banner was of a stalk of wheat and an ear of corn crossed in front of a green and growing tree. The gruesome banner of house Grunnax was that of a hand with palm facing outward, but with a large slice missing between the thumb and forefinger. The white raven on house Ellarin's banner had rubies for eyes and was carrying a simple ring in its beak.

I passed each of these houses with their banners flying in the wind, and as they fell behind me, flames consumed first the banners and then the buildings themselves. As I reached the great gate leading into the castle itself, I saw the banner of House Kalindir itself: A mighty sword pointed downwards, with raven's wings on either side of the sword, as if the sword were the body for these wings. Hovering over the pommel of the sword was the regal image of a crown.

Without saying a word, I walked directly up to the gate and, casting the bloody crown to the ground, I grasped Ukumog with both hands and lifted it over my head. I screamed in anger, frustration, and pain so loudly that the castle trembled before me. The banner of The King's house burst into purple flames over my head and I brought Ukumog crashing down into the massive gate of the castle. The gate's doors and portcullis reacted as if a mountain had come crashing into them. Wood splintered, metal twisted, and stone exploded.

Before me, I saw two figures wrapped in smoke and dust, each wearing a crown. Rage built in my chest, and I wanted to raise Ukumog again and charge into them, but suddenly there were more figures with them. These were like the shadows I had seen before in my visions. Before I could do anything, I saw them erupt into action, and to my surprise it was not me they engaged in combat,

Flayed

but each other. As I watched these men, women, and monsters dance with violent intent, I heard a soft and subtle chuckle from somewhere behind me.

The ground erupted, and some giant unseen thing from under us sent the burning ruins of Flay into the air like a handful of dirt.

These images were so powerful and their sudden end jarred me, and my fear, out of the dream and back into the world.

My transition away from the dream was not a pleasant one. Restless and afraid, I prepared to defend myself from some unseen enemy. Before I had come to my senses, I was standing in the street. My first thought was that of Verif, who had been resting her head in my lap when I went to sleep. Dazed, I nearly lost my balance as I moved around to look for the cat-eyed woman, and I was even more confused when I did not find her.

The mist of my vision started to lift, and I realized that the light in the sky was much different than when I had fallen asleep. The dream had overtaken me in the morning, as the day had just begun, but now it was clearly the afternoon. There was some small panic in my heart as I went to our small pile of equipment, but I was relieved to see the angry runes of Ukumog glare back at me when I removed the packs that it hid behind.

"Where is everyone?" I asked the air.

Murks responded, startling me, "Master, Verif went into the bathhouse after…"

The unmistakeable sounds of combat rolled up the street from the bathhouse. If Murks continued to talk to me, I didn't listen. This all seemed unreal, like something from one of my visions. It

Chapter 6

wasn't until people spilled out from the many archways that led from the dark interior of the baths to the streets that I realized this was actually happening. Scattered through the crowd of about twenty people were my friends, and following the crowd was a set of soldiers wearing the green and white livery of The King's men. At least two of these warriors wore the touch of undeath on their exposed flesh. Revenants.

Tarissa ran up the street towards me, shouting something and motioning with her hands. Just behind her was Avar, holding most of his clothes in his arms and using a short pole to deflect the attacks of the soldier assaulting him. Off in the crowd to the right, I saw Brin whirling around a shovel, parrying and striking soldiers with great skill. I could not find Gordo or Verif as I scanned the fleeing faces.

"We have to get out of here," Tarissa said with calm urgency as she ran up to the pile of gear. "They know we are here now."

Gordo emerged from the crowd, wielding a wooden pole in both hands, and attacked the soldiers that were attacking Avar. This gave Avar a chance to escape up the street to where Tarissa was pulling her equipment from the pile. With deft grace, the blond woman pulled her knives and swords out of the pile and then quickly rejoined the fight. Avar struggled to speedily put his pants on before reaching for his silver shoulder guards and then his weapons. Brin slowly started making her way through the combat and the panic towards us as more soldiers started to pour in from the streets beyond the bathhouse.

Flashes of the dark power from my dream pulsed through my mind with each heartbeat. Fear and indecision held my feet to the ground and paralyzed my brain. I had seen our small band overcome terrible enemies, but something about this place terrified

Flayed

me. We were the chaos come to the doorstep of order, and while we thought we were a storm, we were nothing but a breeze upon the stone wall of The King's mighty city.

"Wrack!" Brin shouted. "Wrack! Bring me my sword!"

My blank mind had finally been given a purpose, an order. Without thinking twice, I reached behind our pile of gear. My fingers wrapped around the red leather of Ukumog's handle, and I was struck by lightning.

The calming sound of my breath filled my ears as the lids of my eyes lifted, and there was a quiet moment of piece as I realized that I was now standing in the middle of the fray. The blood of The King's soldiers dripped from Ukumog. Men clad in green and white continued to press on my position. As if I had done it a thousand times before, I raised Ukumog to defend me against a storm of swords. Brin found her way to my side, and in the first pause she placed her hand on my wrist.

"Thanks, Wrack," she said.

Lost in the warmth of her touch, my hand loosed and she easily stole Ukumog from my grip. I stepped back and, exhausted from my short time holding the haunting blade, I was again unsure what to do. I took a deep breath, and finally saw Verif near the bathhouse on the other side of the forces arrayed against us. Even in the light of the afternoon sun, I could see her eyes glowing with a bronze-colored light. Her lips were moving as she stared at the backs of the armored men between us. At first I thought she was trying to communicate with me, but I was wrong.

Without any warning, there was a flash and a boom so bright and loud that I was rendered both blind and deaf. I stumbled backwards trying to get away from the smell of burnt hair, hot metal, and acid, but I tripped and fell to the ground. Slowly, the ringing in my ears and the light that had overwhelmed my eyes

Chapter 6

faded. The clashing of steel and the pounding of boots filled the air. Brin was still fighting soldiers, yet dozens of others lay smoking between her and the bathhouse. Nearby me, Tarissa was shouting at Avar as the two of them gathered all of our gear. Gordo was nowhere to be seen, and I looked down the road just in time to see the pommel of a sword come down on the back of Verif's head. She felt instantly to the ground, and her assailant stood over her body staring down at her. The tabard that rode over his body had seen many battles, and his decaying armor betrayed its ancient age. His shield had likewise weathered uncounted battles. With his well-used sword, he motioned for the humans around him to take Verif away, then he looked up at Brin with a cold intensity.

"Brin!" I shouted. "Brin, we have to leave!"

Behind the bathhouse, I could see more soldiers running towards our position. We were soon to be swarmed by The King's men.

Brin looked at me with a nearly feral face, but then I saw the reality of the situation sink in. "UZK!" she screamed as Verif was lifted off the ground and carried away.

Avar and Tarissa had picked up all of our things, handing me Verif's pack as they yelled, "Let's go!" and started running up the street away from the oncoming horde of swords and shields.

"Brin!" I shouted, just as Gordo sat up from a pile of smoking bodies. His hair was burnt and sticking up in strange ways. A stunned look was on his face, and he obviously did not know where he was. Brin had been pushed back from where Gordo was and the only weapon I had was Verif's pack. "Brin! Get Gordo!"

Something shifted in Brin's stance. To my untrained eye, it looked like she changed her focus from defense to lethal offense. In a blur of black and white, Ukumog split a soldier like a log for the fire. With amazing speed, Brin removed the soldier's

Flayed

sword from his dead hand before his body could even fall to the ground. Instantly, Brin became a whirlwind of spectacular death. She sliced, kicked, bashed, and hacked her way through multiple soldiers trying to move towards Gordo. "HEY! GORDON, GET THE UZK UP!"

With one hand on the side of his head, Gordo tried to stand. He was so unsteady that he appeared almost drunk.

A roar came from the street on the other side of Brin followed by the bang of a shield colliding with something. Brin went flying backwards and the ancient revenant moved forward to close the gap. The clattering of his armor sounded like chains hanging in the wind.

"Be it known," he declared, "that I, Ser Marius Juindar, place ye under arrest in the name of His Majesty!" He shouted so loudly that everyone in the street could hear him.

Brin leapt to her feet in one motion, still holding Ukumog in one hand and the claimed sword in the other. Ukumog's runes were glowing, but not nearly as brightly as I would have expected. Something about this fight was different. Suddenly I could sense that Brin's rage was not fueled by the sword, but instead this was all her. *Could she defeat this ancient warrior without the help of the accursed blade?*

Marius marched towards Brin, who did not shrink away from him. She brought her off hand sword across his path to try and create an opening where she could strike with Ukumog. He parried it easily with his sword and just kept walking towards her.

"In the name of The King! I command thee to lay down thy weapons and surrender, woman!"

The small army in the street behind the revenant moved forward to take the stunned Gordo into their custody and tend to their wounded. They rest just seemed to stand back and watch Brin

Chapter 6

and Marius clash. Again and again, Brin brought her swords to bear against Marius' body, and each time he easily turned the attacks aside.

"Surrender! Thy! Arms!" he shouted at her with an unyielding ferocity.

Looking over my shoulder, I could see the forms of Avar and Tarissa much farther up the street. Avar, who was lagging behind, turned to look back at me and waved his arms telling me to follow. Marius continued to walk towards Brin, forcing her to continually back away. As she started backing up towards the wall, I called out to her so that she would reposition herself towards me and the direction that Avar had fled. Her swings started to lose their ferocity and speed, and I could hear her breathing become more labored. I could hear the boots of soldiers echoing through the side streets as they started to surround us.

Desperately, I searched for something I could use as a weapon. The daggers I had carried at one point were lost, probably somewhere with Avar and Tarissa. All I had was the pack in my hands. My hand dove in through the opening under the top flap and started recklessly rummaging through the contents. My hand then emerged holding a bottle of ink. Without thinking I tossed the bottle at Marius and he blocked it with his shield, shattering the vial and splattering ink all over the street. His cold gaze shifted, looking me directly in the eye. Even from this distance, I saw a slight confusion appear in his steeled face. This gave Brin just the opening she needed, and Ukumog would not miss its chance to shed blood.

There was a blur of black and white as Ukumog flew upwards between Marius' sword and shield. With terrible speed, the blade sliced upwards through the knight's neck and face, shattering bone, and spraying ancient black blood into the air. Marius was

Flayed

lifted up off his feet and fell backwards onto the stone street where he lay, unmoving. I did not pause to watch the blood streaming from the two halves of his face. Instead I said, "Brin" with enough urgency to pull her from her battle frenzy.

The two of us streaked up the street towards the fleeing forms of Avar and Tarissa. The dread of leaving Gordo and Verif behind wounded me deeply. The panic rooted itself deep in my heart, and I could not even stop to think how we could save them.

"Run! It matters not! His Majesty shall find thee!" Marius' voice echoed in the street.

I turned to see him standing on his feet, with no wound in his face, but the evidence of his wound staining his tabard and the street beneath him. In my heart, I knew this would happen. It seems that the revenants and I had a lot in common. Perhaps Avar was right. Perhaps I was once a servant of The King. In that moment, however, I was not about to stop and ask questions.

Brin's breathing became even more labored as we barreled up the street. I looked over to see if she was ok, as her pace also began to slow, and when I looked back Tarissa and Avar were gone.

"Where did they go?" I asked.

"I… I think they turned left up there." Brin waved her hand in front of her, not really pointing at any specific street.

Not wanting to make her clarify, I asked a different question. "What happened back there?"

"Yeah. Verif said she woke up and you were asleep. Ya know, for a guy who never sleeps, you have been doing a lot more of that recently." Brin chuckled.

I grunted with resentful agreement.

Chapter 6

"So," Brin took some deep breaths. "So, we are in the baths, right? Well, some of us had finished and were waiting on the others. Tarissa and Avar were taking their sweet time. Can't say I blame 'em. Circumstances being reversed, I prolly woulda taken advantage of a little alone time myself…"

"Ah," was all I needed to say.

"Are they chasing us? Uzk. All this running…" Brin started to look over her shoulder and almost lost her balance, so she stopped trying to look back and just kept running forward. "Uzk," she muttered.

Looking back, I saw no one following us, nor did I hear boots beating against the stone streets behind us. This worried me more than if they had been following us. "Doesn't seem that they are pursuing us. But let's not slow down to find out."

Brin slowed her pace a bit. "Yeah."

"So, what happened in the bathhouse, exactly?"

"Oh yeah. So we are in there, relaxing, and suddenly there is commotion all over the place. I heard raised voices, and I knew something was uzk'd. We all hid wherever we could, slinking away from the people who were searching the place. We didn't have any weapons or anything, so we just found anything we could."

"Yeah, I saw that."

"Anyway, then I heard Verif come in, and she was distracting the guards or something, getting flirty with them. Then BAM, gaak was on fire and exploding, soldiers rushed to fight her, and she held them at bay with uzkin' bronze colored lightning and gaak. She gave us time to collect our clothes, some of which had been gathered by the guards, and get out into the street. You saw the rest." Brin paused, solemnly. "I hope she doesn't pay a hefty price for helping us get out of there. Things would have been very uzkin' different if she hadn't come in there."

Flayed

"Sorry I wasn't there." Guilt weighed down on me. "I don't know what is happening with me. These visions are different. They feel a lot more like dreams than memories."

Brin gave a wheezing laugh. "Maybe being out of the uzkin' ground is filling you with more life!"

I was horrified to think that I was feeding on the life around me, and Brin's comment made that even more real for me. I worried about the future of my hunger and where it might lead me, but I didn't have a lot of time to wallow in that future sorrow.

"Turn here!" Brin said.

We turned the corner to find yet another street, straight as an arrow and filled with people. Sprinkled into the crowd was the glint of armor and the colors of The King.

"Uzk!" Brin pulled me back behind the building. "The streets are crawling with those uzkin' guards."

"What do we do?" I asked while trying to form a plan myself.

Murks crawled out from my robes and up to my shoulder. The three of us were looking around and listening for the sound of armor and boots.

"Where the uzk did those blond uzkers go?" Brin asked the air.

"Up," Murks responded.

Brin and I looked up and saw Tarissa waving at us from one building over on the second floor. Once all of us were looking at her, she pointed towards the door facing the street. With some hesitation, the three of us started walking towards the door. I heard the familiar clink! as Ukumog was attached to Brin's belt.

The door to the building opened, and out on the steps walked someone I didn't expect. It wasn't the tall but strong man with blond hair and a boyish face that I expected. It was instead a

Chapter 6

short, funny-looking man with a skull cap and a black robe. With his left hand, he held the door open, and his right arm clutched a large and ancient tome. Then it hit me, I had seen this man before. He was the one who appeared in the Headless Mermaid and called me Wrack, then vanished. While I hadn't thought about that moment in years, I suddenly knew that his appearance was not a coincidence.

Brin's pace slowed, but I continued to stride forward. Sensing my confidence, she continued forward, but put her hand on the red leather wrapped handle of Ukumog.

The old man nodded as we approached. "Hello there, Wrack," he grumbled, then turned to Brin. "Pleasure to meet you, Brianndwyn."

Brin stopped walking forward at the strange name that this odd man called her. "How do you know... Where did you hear... Who are you?"

The old man nodded. "There will be time for questions later, daughter of Teague. Please, come inside quickly."

What could we do, but follow his invitation and our own curiosity into that strange house? Perhaps inside we would finally get more answers.

Flayed

Chapter 7

We were barely inside the door before the strange little man started speaking to us.

"I am sure you both have enumerable questions, but there is a task which requires immediate attention."

I was still stunned by this encounter. This little man had shown up twice before. The first time he said something to me that made me pick my current name, and the second was to wake me after Brin and Avar had been taken by the guards of Yellow Liver. It seemed extremely curious that he would show up now.

Inside the tiny house, I could hear the creaking footsteps of people in the side rooms and on the floor above us. They were all coming to the room where we found ourselves. Most of the figures that entered were robed in black cloth, not unlike my own robes. The only faces I recognized were Avar and Tarissa, however, as they pushed through the crowd to get to us. Tarissa came right to Brin and gave her a hug. Brin didn't fight away the blond woman, but her eyes told me that she knew this was mostly for Tarissa's comfort.

"I'm ok," Brin said.

"For a moment there, I wasn't sure we would see you two again," Avar said lightheartedly.

Flayed

I sighed. "When the revenant showed up, I wasn't sure we would see you either."

The mirth drained out of his face. "What?"

"Yeah. Said his name was Marius something," Brin said, gently pushing Tarissa away.

"Marius Juindar being your enemy is nothing to take lightly," the old man cautioned.

Brin raised an eyebrow. "And just who are you?"

The old man chuckled. "We get that question from both beggars and kings, but the answer is always the same. We are The Eternal Well."

"Oh uzk," Avar muttered.

"Relax, young Hunter. Not all the stories about us are true."

"Wait! The wizard Grumth is in your stupid cult!" Brin shouted.

The old man held up his free hand. "Calm yourself Brin. We are not your enemy. The sword was in our possession after it was taken from its icy tomb. We merely held it so that The Doomed would not claim it for their own."

His words had not soothed the storm in Brin's heart. "Look, I don't care WHY you kept the sword. I just want information about who killed my father!"

The old man sighed. "I understand your pain, Brin. Revenge is a parasite that lives inside the soul of many, and some use the rage it grants as part of its curse to do great things. One must be careful not to let the monster devour one's sight, however. Else it will no longer be you wielding the sword…"

Chapter 7

Everyone was silent. I waited for the explosion of expletives and rage to burst from Brin's face. I could see the fire burning in her soul. She took a step towards the little old man and instead of a torrent of rage, a single tear escaped her eye, and she turned away from him.

Cutting the silence, I asked, "Didn't you say there was something immediate that we need to do?"

"Yes." The old man's face lit up as he remembered. "I understand that Gordon Haas was your guide into the city. It is important that we free him before The King discovers exactly who he is."

"Why would The King care about Gordo?" Avar asked.

The old man stared at Avar for a moment, then looked over at Tarissa before finally looking me in the eye. "Gordon is one of the last of the bloodline of makers."

I was confused. "What is that?"

"There are many magical bloodlines in this world, Wrack. No doubt you know about the Wayfarers..." The confusion in my face made him continue, "They can use their blood to open any lock or doorway. They create a path where there was none before."

Avar nodded. "Ah, like Elaina."

"Yes. Gordon's family has the power to make powerful items, should they mix their blood into their craft."

Tarissa shook her head. "That sounds like evil magic."

"It isn't. The bloodlines are some of the oldest magic there is," the old man said. "Gordon's blood in the hands of The King would change the great stalemate immensely. We must free him from his prison."

A new figure entered from a room connected to ours. This new person leaned over and whispered to the old man, and then retreated back the way it had come in.

Flayed

"Excellent," the old man nodded to himself. "Well, we know where Gordon is being held."

"What is the bad news?" asked Tarissa.

"They have decreed that both Gordon and Verif will be executed at dawn. I have no doubt it is a trap."

"Why would they care to set a trap for us?" Brin was growing impatient with everything.

"Marius Juindar has seen that sword before, Brin. Undoubtedly, he has already told his master that it is in the city, and The King will stop at nothing to claim it."

Brin groaned.

"Outside the walls of this once great city you can be as reckless as you like, Brin. In Flay, there are ancient monsters more cunning and more skilled than you can imagine. Regardless of how you feel about me, we must free your friends. We have only until dawn."

"Ok..." Tarissa searched for a name. Apparently he hadn't given it to her, either.

"Grimoire," he said. "Yes, like an ancient tome. I am the keeper of the Eternal Well."

"Ok, Grimoire," Tarissa said. "Do you already have a plan?"

"There is only one vulnerability to the place where Gordon is being kept. We will have to go in through the sewers."

Avar sighed. "Great. Uzkin' sewers again."

"Flay keeps their sewers uncommonly clean. However, they have other precautions in place down there." There was a dark tone in Grimoire's voice.

"Like what kind of precautions?" I asked without thinking.

Chapter 7

"The sewers can be flooded as a security measure. As if that weren't bad enough, there are gates throughout the entire network of tunnels that can be used to control both the flow of water and access to the different sections."

Again, I could not help but ask, "Where does the overflow go?"

"The north side of the city sits on a cliff, much like the castle in Skullspill. The overflow tunnels cast the water down into the chasm below."

Tarissa furrowed her brow. "That seems like a huge vulnerability. Hasn't an army ever climbed the cliff and gained access to the city through these tunnels?"

Grimoire chuckled. "There was a group of three soldiers who did actually make that climb, but they were lucky and well prepared. A larger force would be seen before they reached the summit. At one time, the beasts of the chasm grew fat on the flesh of soldiers that came to kill The King, but that was long ago."

Tarissa nodded.

"Well, doesn't seem like we have much choice, does it?" Brin did nothing to hide her disappointment.

"There is more," Grimoire said. "The Well cannot be seen to help in this endeavor. We have our current access because we appear neutral—"

"Oh! Here it comes!" Brin threw her hands in the air.

Grimoire was visibly annoyed by her outburst. "We can aid you in making sure that the gates are open before you make your way. We can even help to make a distraction, but we cannot go into the tunnels with you."

"How do we know YOU aren't the trap?" I asked.

Flayed

Grimoire face reacted like I had just said the most insulting thing he had ever heard. "We would never betray those who bring hope to this world, Wrack. Teague's daughter, however brash, is still the most powerful weapon against this darkness." There were tears in his eyes as he spoke.

Brin's eyes welled up with tears, but was otherwise speechless. She and Grimoire locked eyes, and he nodded at her. Trying to hide her emotions, she turned away and looked out the dirty window.

Breaking the awkward silence, I said, "What else do we need to know?"

Grimoire shook away the emotions that had boiled up inside him. "Ah. Yes. Um. Near where you will enter the sewers, there is a T intersection. Etched upon the wall is a map of the tunnels. It is scrawled in a magical ink that will only appear in the light of the moon."

Annoyed, I asked, "How will we get moonlight down there?"

"I can take care of that," Avar spoke up.

Before I could ask him how he was going to manage that, Grimoire spoke again.

"You will need to find the entrance to the market barracks. The sewer drain you are looking for is in the middle of the holding cells beneath the barracks. Caution must be used, for the barracks have controls for both gates to block off the sewer, and flood controls within. If the guard even smells a prison break, they will not hesitate to block off the prisoner's escape, and perhaps even flood the tunnels. Trapped within the gates under the barracks, one would have little choice but to either return to their cell or drown."

"Let's hope it doesn't come to that."

Grimoire nodded gravely.

Chapter 7

We had to wait until darkness fell before we moved to the sewers. During the day that passed, most of our little company slept and ate the food that the robed members of the Eternal Well brought for them. Each time, I was also offered food, but I refused. Each time, the robed person reacted with quiet surprise and a nod. After the early twilight of the spring evening, we moved.

Grimoire had members of the Eternal Well already in place, and created reasons for the people in charge of the gates in the sewers to have opened each gate to allow for our journey, supposedly. I was still wary of these strangers who wore my same robes. I could not deny the unusual feeling that I knew more about these men and women, but it was like a family I hadn't seen in a lifetime or more. Their mannerisms were strange and yet familiar. Only Grimoire really spoke to us, but I could hear them whispering to each other when needed. Never did they say anyone's name, just called each other brother or sister, and spoke more with a look and a pointed finger than with actual words. I could not help but feel that this was because we – or more specifically, I – were around. They treated all of us with a reverence and suspicion that was alien, and I say this after dealing with the love/hate that the Shadow Hunters showed to Brin and me.

They had given each of us black robes, like the ones they wore, to get us through the streets. "Won't this give away your involvement?" Brin asked.

"Most ignore men and women in robes," Grimoire said. "It is one of the reasons we wear them."

I quieted my suspicions as we headed for the entry to the sewers. It did not take us long to get there through the busy streets. The day was winding down and the orderly citizens of Flay were returning to their homes to celebrate one more day survived in the

Flayed

dark shadow of The King. Our destination was a small building that looked more like a grand shed than anything else. The four of us, along with Grimoire, slipped into the shed while the other robed figures stood outside the building, and as soon as we were safely inside, they moved on.

In the center of the shed, a hole with a grate that had already been lifted away to allow access to the stone lined tunnel into the ground. Another black-robed figure stood off to one side, holding a grubby-looking man by the throat. As we entered, Grimoire nodded to this new person. In turn, they tightened their grip on the grubby man, producing a shiny bauble and lifting it to point it at the grubby man's face. The unnamed robed figure said with a man's voice, "The Eternal Well is the giver and receiver of all memory. Be at peace."

A dim light suddenly came from the shiny thing he held, and the grubby man's face went from fear to complacency in the blink of an eye. As quickly as it happened, the light faded and the robed figure put the shiny object away in a hidden pocket within his robes. He nodded at Grimoire and left the shed with the grubby man in tow. I could feel the tension in the room as we all wanted to ask what had just transpired, but no one asked.

Tarissa ignored the tension, and was focused on the task at hand. "Once we are down there, which direction do we go?"

"At the bottom of the ladder, head northeast, which will be to the left." Grimoire gestured to help orient us to which direction he meant. "I will be here, waiting for your return. There are more robes stashed in here for when we escape with two more friends."

"It really seems like you are taking a risk here," Avar said.

Chapter 7

"Some things are worth the risk, young Avar," Grimoire scolded. "Should this be the time when the forces here within the city actually turn against us, then so be it. I am prepared. Are you? Are all of you?"

His question elicited no outward response from anyone. Instead, my companions stripped off their robes, we all checked our gear, and made ready to descend into the sewers. For Avar, Brin, and me the anticipation could not have been more terrible. I hoped with all my heart that these sewers would indeed be nothing like the horrors that lay below Yellow Liver. Only making our way down into the darkness would tell.

"Uzk," Brin muttered. "Let's get this over with." Then she promptly climbed into the hole.

One after the other, we descended the metal rods built into the side of the stone wall beneath the hole. We passed about ten feet of solid earth and stone with room for only one person in the tunnel, but then it opened up into the tunnels below. The tunnels themselves were not tall or wide. The well-crafted stonework that surrounded us was only a foot or two above our heads, and we could uncomfortably stand two people across, but the gutter of stinking sewage that ran through the center of the tunnel floor caused us to move through single file.

Brin was in the lead, followed by Tarissa, who whispered directions to her. Next was Avar, who had not brought his shield with us on this trip, but unlike the trip into the sewers of Yellow Liver, he did have a lit torch, which was our only light source. I was in the rear, and I could not help but have flashing memories of the ghouls who attacked from the darkness behind me the last time I was in a sewer.

"I've heard about pockets of gas that can build up in places like this," Avar whispered to me. "Gotta be careful with the torch."

Flayed

I shrugged, but Avar didn't see, and he offered no follow up. *What was one more thing to worry about?*

The echo of trickling water was ever present all around us. I found it impossible to tell if the noise was coming from the gutter of sludge beside us, or was the sound of the hundreds of holes throughout the city that fed these disgusting waterways. The people in front of us stopped suddenly, and I saw Brin put her hand on Ukumog's handle, but the group sighed with relief when a few rats scratched their way by on the other side of the gutter. Soon after our expedition began, we arrived at the intersection spoken of by Grimoire.

"Ok, Avar. This must be it. Do your thing," Brin commanded.

Avar gave me a smile. "Hold this for a second." He handed me the torch.

Both Brin and Tarissa stepped away from the facing wall of the intersection to give Avar space. He stepped forward, facing the wall, and began whispering into his cupped-together hands. After a moment, he folded his hands together, like he was holding a baby bird, then opened the side that faced the wall. A silvery light illuminated the wall from Avar's palms, and a great diagram rapidly faded into view upon the previously blank wall. He kept his palms facing the wall so that we could take in the enormous detail that appeared before us.

Blocks and lines made up most of the maze that appeared before me. Each section was labeled after what I presumed to be sections of the city. Looming over the entire map were the words 'City of Flay' with a large space between the two last words. The very stone between them even look scored, as if someone had scratched away whatever writing had been there before.

Chapter 7

"Previous name of the city, no doubt," I shared my thoughts with Murks. He agreed.

Tarissa and Brin began inspecting the routes between where we were and the marketplace garrison while my eyes drifted to the edges of the map itself. While the main city shared the same sewer, the map showed that the high part of the city was on its own system of tunnels, and there was a smaller set of tunnels that were off to the side, near the castle.

"Different systems to protect against siege, I suppose," I thought. Murks again agreed.

A tiny mark revealed where all the tunnels led out of the cliffs into the gorge to the north of the city. Following the lines, I could see that four trails actually led out. The unexpected fourth line led back to a space near the castle, but just ended in a strange circle that was not labeled.

"Ok. Got it," Brin said.

Tarissa nodded and moved her head to indicate I should follow them. Avar dropped his shimmering hands, and within a heartbeat we were off down one of the tunnels.

It took us the better part of an hour to navigate the tunnels to our destination, but we were also trying to be quiet. Even in that short space of time, I was able to disregard most of the horrid stench that lived down there, but each time I had nearly gotten used to the smell, something else foul reached my senses. We traversed the dark tunnels, occasionally encountering arched gateways set into the sides and ceiling of the tunnel. As I passed through one of these things, I saw the glint of looming steel inside the gap that hid inside the arch.

"These must be the gates Grimoire mentioned," I offered to anyone who was listening.

Avar was the only one to respond. "Hrm? Oh. Yeah."

Flayed

Closer to the market, the smell of rotted flesh danced with the rank smell of sewage, creating a sickening stench. I could taste it in the air, which made things far worse. When we actually reached the market, we could hear whispered echoes of the bustle taking place above our heads. Bones and the half-eaten flesh of things unrecognizable littered the tunnels there, and the rats became much more frequent. Most of these tiny nuisances scuttled away at the mere appearance of Avar's torch, but braver ones waited to see the four of us tromping through their putrid feasting grounds before running away.

Finally, we reached another set of metal rungs leading up into a hole. We were all more than eager to escape the squalid fright that was our current situation. Brin started to move to the ladder first, but Tarissa placed a hand upon Brin's shoulder. "Let me."

Brin paused for a moment, but then nodded and stepped to the side.

Tarissa slithered up the ladder so silently that I near forgot she was there. Once she disappeared into the hole above those metal rungs, I heard not a sound, save for a quiet clunk as she loosed the grate at the top of the tunnel. I held my breath, awaiting noise of complaining guards from the surface, but none came.

"Your girl is uzkin' amazing, Avar." Brin smiled.

He beamed with pride. "You should tell her that, after we get out of here."

Brin chuckled. "I will."

Avar went up the ladder after we heard a quiet "psst" from above us. As soon as he was up the tunnel and out of view, Brin placed her hands on the metal rungs and looked up through the hole. Turning back to me, she smiled. "Can't wait to be out of this uzkin' stinkhole."

Chapter 7

"I dunno. Kinda grows on you, being down here. I mean, look at all the food." I motioned towards the rotting fragments of picked-over carcasses. "I could live like a king down here."

She laughed. "Yeah, but you don't even eat. Really, it is the uzkin' smell. Why would anyone choose to use a sewer as their base of operations? I will just never understand that monster we—you—killed."

"Yeah. I suppose you could get used to the smell, but then you would probably stink. Hard to feel good about being near people when you smell like death and gaak."

A shiver ran through her. "I can't imagine anyone wanting to get close to that inhuman monster."

Her words were flaming arrows striking my heart. "Palig," I muttered.

"What?" Her brow furrowed, unsure about what I was saying.

"His name was Palig. Before."

"Ah." She nodded, brushing off my foolish and subtle attempt to show that even The Ghoul was once human. That *I* was once human.

She started her ascent of the ladder without another word, but as she passed through the hole in the ceiling she called back, "You coming?"

Her call to action pushed away the sadness in my heart for a moment. "Yeah."

"Love is good, Master." Murks' tiny voice entered my mind. "Master mustn't forget love."

"Is that what this is, Murks?" My thoughts sought answers.

"Murks doesn't know, Master. Murks knows you care for Brin, but Murks doesn't know what love means."

Flayed

"Why would you tell me that then, if you don't know what it means?" A moment later when my comment burnt the fog of rage from my thoughts, "Oh. Let me guess. One more thing I told you to remember."

"No, Master. Master's friend Teague told me. He said that I should always remind you that love is important, that love matters. He said that it was love that allowed the Silver Lady's light to still shine into the world and give people hope."

My hands froze at the mention of Brin's father. After Murks stopped speaking to me, my mind spiraled into every memory or vision I had of the bard. The cacophony of noise that came back from the void of my shattered mind was overwhelming. Grey tears leaked from my eyes, and my head hurt. One deep breath followed another until I came back to the present, and I had gained no insight.

Torchlight flickered from above, and the tunnel was empty. One hand over the other. One foot then the other. Slowly, I crawled to the top of the ladder.

The drain that was also this access tunnel was in the floor of a small prison. Two rows of cells lined opposing walls, while the drain was in the middle of the walkway between them. The floor sloped slightly, so that all fluids would find their way into this middle drain.

"Lovely," I commented to no one.

Of the eight cells, four to each wall, only two were occupied. The others had evidence of recent use, but nothing but a stray shoe or remnants of a hay bed remained within them. The two that currently held our friends, Verif and Gordo, were the farthest away from the entry door to the chamber. Avar, Brin, and Tarissa were gathered over by Gordo's cell, whispering through the bars. A metal-bound wooden entry door had a tiny sliding window at about face height, which seemed to have no mechanism for being

Chapter 7

opened on this side. Light flickered under the door from unseen torches beyond the prison. I could not help but wonder how often they checked these cells.

Tarissa was working to pick the lock on Gordo's cell while he whispered to Brin and Avar. My attention was drawn to the cell across from Gordo's. Inside, Verif lay motionless on the floor. Heavy manacles were locked around her ankles and wrists that were so bulky she would need help moving. While unusual, it was not these restraints that got my attention. Stretched over her face was a mesh of woven silver. The top and bottom of this mesh had straps made of leather running through the weave that were used to hold the silver mask over her entire face. From ear to ear and the edge of her scalp to under her chin, the mesh was pulled tight. The tails of the leather bands were covered with barbs and spikes which dug into the flesh of her face as they made their way to the tangled mess of her normally silky, smooth hair to come together in the back. This mask looked of elegant design, save for the sadistic barbs, but the joy with which it caused suffering could only be a reflection of the craftsman who made it.

"Oh, Verif. What have they done to you?" I asked, hoping she could hear me, but she just lay there, unmoving.

Avar placed his arm around my shoulders and whispered into my ear, "That is a ssligari mask. A miserable contraption." He shook his head. "They were used by The King ages ago when his men were hunting down all the sorcerers in these lands. The masks render their wearers unable to use magic."

"Ssligari? Isn't the Silver Lady named Ssli'garion?" I asked.

Avar's jaw flexed. "Yeah. The sick bastards named their instrument after the goddess of hope and inspiration. Don't even get me started on how uzked up that is."

Flayed

"How do we get her out of that thing?"

Avar sighed. "Very carefully. If we are too rough, the barbs will tear apart her scalp and might even tear open parts of her throat. The people who use these things don't intend to pull them off a living person."

In the dark of the prison, I could see the movement of Verif's eyes under the mesh. This my the only signal that she was still alive. "We have to get her out of there." Even I could hear the fear in my voice.

"I can only pick one lock at a time, Wrack," Tarissa said calmly.

I sat on the floor just outside Verif's cell. My hands wrapped around the cold steel bars that separated us. Guilt over feeling annoyed at Verif's flirtation and desire for my magic stung me. I felt helpless, a feeling I was growing weary of. My mind toyed with thoughts of waking the dark strength inside me and tearing the bars off her cell, then I heard noises coming from the other side of the door.

"Shh!" I stood up, and everyone went silent.

Footsteps scraped their way down the hallway towards us, and while I could not be sure they were coming to check on the prisoners, we had to be ready. "Someone is coming."

The four of us erupted into action. Brin and I pressed ourselves to either side of the wooden door while Avar made his way back into the tunnel. There was a quiet click, and Tarissa gave a sigh of relief before following him and pulling the thin metal grate over the hole. I reached into my robes to discover that I still hadn't recovered my knives. I silently cursed myself for being here and being unarmed.

Chapter 7

"*Clink!*" Ukumog said, as it announced its release from its prison upon the oxblood belt wrapped around Brin's waist. The sword again looked long and thin, with a curve that was more pronounced at the top. The runes glowed only dimly with a pale white light. I found it difficult to look at the sword, for its shifting form confused me. In my mind the sword should have been a long rectangle of black metal with a tip that was flat, yet edged, and runes that glowed with a cold blue fire. *Why was it suddenly different in Brin's hands? And why did it keep changing back and forth from my understanding to this saber-like version of itself?* Disoriented by this maze of thoughts, I lost track of the task at hand for a moment, but when the window in the door slid open, I came back to my senses quickly.

"Hello, my lovelies," the voice on the other side of the door called out in a tone that made my skin crawl. "Are we both still alive? Ready for the big day tomorrow?"

"Begone, you filth," Gordo responded.

"Aww. Still got some fight in ya, do we? Well, we will see how much fight ya have left in the morning."

"Why don't you come in here and say that?"

Brin's eyes lit up, and she nodded at me. She—and Ukumog—were ready to shed blood. The door of the jail opened out, most likely to prevent any prisoners who escaped their cells from pulling out the hinges in the doors and disappearing into the barracks. Apparently the builders of this place had great confidence in the security measures within the sewer.

"You really are an angry one, aren't ya? Well, Sir Marius will be here soon enough. He will burn that anger right out of ya. I only hope he lets me watch."

Flayed

"You would like that, wouldn't you? You sick uzker. Does it give you thrills to torture that helpless girl?" I could see the inferno of murderous rage building up inside Gordo's eyes. I began to worry that he might open his recently unlocked cage just to get closer to the twisted man on the other side of the door.

"She is a pretty one, that is for sure." The sound of metal keys chimed in through the window. "Perhaps I will come in and take one more look at her before Sir Marius ruins her for good." Sounds of a large key entering the iron lock on the door were followed quickly by the clunk of bolt being turned back.

I pressed myself against the wall and made ready for the fight that was on its way.

The door opened, and a fat man wearing leather armor and the colors of The King's guard came shuffling in. He didn't bother to close the door behind him, and kept the ring of large keys in his hand, rather than return it to the clasp on his belt. As he crossed the prison towards Verif's cell, he scratched his head through the leather cap, and I saw tuffs of stark white hair peeking out from its edges. When the irritation on his scalp was dealt with, he began searching through the ring for the key to Verif's cell. I mimed to Brin that she should wait until after the cell door was open before setting Ukumog loose upon this despicable man. I could see the fire of murderous desire in her eyes as she nodded at me.

"I'd say, without a doubt, that you might be the loveliest little thing that these cells have ever seen," the man said in Verif's direction as he slid the key into its lock, but he never got a chance to turn it.

"Hey, uzkstick," Brin said as she walked towards him.

Shocked, the man left the keyring dangling from the lock of Verif's cell and started reaching for the sword on his hip. I leapt to action and closed the chamber door as quietly as I could.

Chapter 7

There was a blur of glowing steel as Ukumog lunged for the man's exposed throat, and a spray of dark red as it bit deep. Instinct took over as the man tried, in vain, to keep his precious life from leaking out through the chasm between his head and his body. Moments later, he lay face down on the floor, with his blood racing towards our method of escape.

I flew from the door to Verif's cell, turning the key that still was stuck in the lock to no avail.

"What's wrong?" Gordo asked.

"Idiot had the wrong key." I pulled the key out of the lock and started fumbling through the ring trying each of the keys that looked like the one the dead guard had tried.

Tarissa suddenly was at my side, giving encouraging words to Verif as she lay there, the shoulders of her weakened body shaking with grief and fear. Finally, there was a clunk as the lock of the cell opened. With urgent speed, Tarissa began trying to pick the locks on Verif's shackles while I fiddled with the ring of keys, trying to find the correct ones to set Verif free. Time pressed down on me as my mind spiraled into thoughts of what would happen if the guards above discovered us before we were away. Trying to push these thoughts away, I breathed deeply and focused on the task at hand.

Tarissa was able to unlock one of Verif's ankles before I found the key that would open up the iron around her wrists. Heartbeats after that, Verif was free of all but the mask.

"We don't have time to deal with the mask," Avar said as Verif sat up.

I could hear her quietly whimpering. Her hair was matted with blood, which trickled down her body from various punctures caused by the terrible mask. She tried to reach up and pull the mask off, but I stopped her hands.

Flayed

"Not here. We have to get you safe first," I said.

Avar was already in the tunnel by the time Verif was on her feet. Gordo took the sword from the guardsman and followed, making an audible grunt when his nose met the stink of the sewers. Tarissa followed, and Verif went directly after, with me helping her find her way into the tunnel due to the mask's limited view.

Brin stood there, defiantly motioning for me to go first. Her posture made me think that she actually wanted more men to come bursting through the door so she could shed more blood.

"You go first, and I will close the grate behind us," I said.

She nodded and complied. Still, I worried that one day the sword's lust for mayhem would remove all her reason. I had no idea how I would deal with her, should that ever happen.

As I pulled the grate back into place, I heard footsteps outside the prison door. Quietly, I made my way to the bottom of the ladder, where Gordo was holding Verif up. She reached out a hand and placed it on my arm.

"Thank you, Wrack," she said weakly, then she nearly collapsed.

Gordo handed me the sword in his hand and scooped Verif in his arms. "Everyone else is slightly down the tunnel already. We should get moving." With that, he turned and started following the light of Avar's torch.

Before I could take more than a few steps, I heard a voice from the room above, "—dead!? Go fetch Sir Marius!"

I sprinted up to Gordo. "We haven't got much time. They already found the body."

"Uzk," Gordo said, picking up his pace.

Chapter 7

We were about halfway to the ladder that would lead us up to Grimoire shack when I heard them behind us. Boots pounded the stone and splashed in the filth. I heard some of the echoes get farther from us, and others draw closer.

"They are splitting up," I told Gordo and Verif, then cries came from behind us.

"The portcullis is up! Return to the surface and make the others aware! I will handle things down here!" The voice belonged to the revenant who fought us in the street, Marius Juindar.

Our pace quickened, but in moments my dark eyes saw his shadow running through the tunnels towards us. "We have company back here!" I shouted, hoping that Brin would hear me. Neither Gordo nor I stopped running.

A grinding noise came from ahead of us, and I realized we were just about to reach the final gate between us and the exit. If it fell before we were on the other side, we would be trapped in here with Marius.

From behind there came the sound of an object in flight, and suddenly a knife appeared in the back of Gordo's thigh. The large man stumbled and fell to the ground, screaming with shock and pain. Verif tumbled forward and rolled through the muck. She immediately started scrambling towards one of the walls so that she could use it to prop herself up.

"Ye cannot flee from me, fools!" Marius taunted us, and his pace slowed.

I ran to Verif and helped her stand up. Blood poured out of a massive gash in her throat from where the mask had done its terrible work. She was losing blood rapidly. "Verif! Verif stay with me!" The warmth of her life was fading before my eyes; her form grew weaker by the second. I had to do something.

Flayed

All the guilt over what happened in Sanctuary with David and John when I gave them my blood faded in that moment. I had a way to save Verif, I thought, and I had to use it. I took the sword and sliced open my hand. Casting the sword aside, I covered Verif's gushing wound with my own, and when our blood met, I could feel my dark power mending the wounds. The cold I knew would come pulsed down my arm and into Verif. Dark thoughts filled my mind. I wasn't entirely sure what I was doing, where this power came from, or what would happen to her. I just knew that I could not let her die.

Holding Verif in my arms, I looked back to Gordo standing with the sword I had discarded in his hand, and facing Marius, who was striding down the tunnel at him.

"Gordon!" I shouted. "Let's go!" I stood, holding Verif in my arms, just as a massive noise rumbled through the stone over our heads. I stood there helplessly as the interlocking steel of the portcullis crashed down into place, with Gordo and Marius on the other side.

Dumbfounded, I stood there trying to think about what I could do, but Gordo flashed me a resigned look before he moved forward to clash swords with Marius.

"I told you that you could not flee, fool," Marius said, his sword flashing towards Gordo in the dim light. Slash after slash met awkward resistance, and with each blow that landed on Gordo's flesh, a tear left my eyes.

"Gordo." My words were impotent things. Hollow husks of effort and desire. I could do nothing to change what was about to happen, and both Gordo and I knew that.

Brin's hand landed on my shoulder. I heard her heavy breathing from running back to help us. Ukumog was loosed, but as impotent as my desire to help. Avar and Tarissa came shortly

Chapter 7

thereafter, Avar's torch shedding enough light to allow Gordo to lash out at Marius with a few swings, but what little strength he had was already fading.

"C'mon, Wrack. We can't help him. We have to go." Brin's voice carried a bitter disappointment, and it burned.

Verif's strength was growing, and she moved to stand on her own. I directed her to Tarissa and Avar, who happily lent their support.

With a steely tone I said, "You go, Brin. See them to safety. I won't abandon Gordo. Even if I cannot save him, I will be here so he doesn't have to die in this filthy pit alone."

Brin was stunned at my stern reply, and said nothing. Avar and Tarissa helped Verif walk back towards the exit, taking the light with them. Upon the light's exit, Gordo again cried out in pain as Marius sword became a blur in the darkness and sliced through another part of him.

Marius shouted down the hall, "FLOOD THE TUNNELS!" Then with words made of barbed malice, "Thy friends won't get far, fool. If they don't drown in this dank dungeon, we will find them."

A loud grinding noise filled the tunnels, making me jump. From far away, I could hear the roar of water, and instantly there was growing eddy of fresh water flowing through the gutter at our feet.

"Go, Brin. I can't have you drowning down here."

The hand on my shoulder squeezed, and she nodded. "If you don't come back, I will find you."

I didn't react.

"Do you hear me? I will turn over this whole uzkin' city to find you again," and she kissed me.

Flayed

So stunned was I at this turn of events that I am not sure my lips even moved, but I remember the soft warmth of her lips upon mine, and for a moment I did not smell the filth that surrounded us. All my senses were dedicated to her, the warmth of her flesh, the brush of her hair against my face, and the wave of amber scent that followed. For the briefest of moments I forgot where we were, and I remembered what it was like to feel the sun from that long forgotten green world on my living flesh. I was home.

When she broke contact, the rank air stole away her warmth and her scent, replacing it with the foul stench of the sewer. Without another word, she ran down the tunnel towards the exit.

"One day," Gordo's tired voice roared over the sound of rushing water, "your master will fall and this curse will be lifted from the land, Marius!"

Marius stood there staring at Gordo's crippled form, and with flat emotion he said, "If that day indeed comes, thou will not be here to see it, Shadow Hunter." He chuckled, and then walked back the way he came and against the current of the quickly rising water.

I rushed over to the gate and tried to pull it open as Gordo crawled towards it. He hadn't made it far before the power of the rising water pushed him forward, crashing him into the gate. Another weak cry of pain came from him. The fetid water rushed past his body, pinning him to the gate. "Wrack?" he cried out, and when I didn't respond immediately a second cry came, "Wrack!"

My hand found his white knuckles gripped around the gate. "I'm here."

He looked at me through the grid of iron that separated us. Sadness filled his eyes, and his chin quivered. "Wrack, you have to finish this. Finish what you started."

Chapter 7

I had expected some message to be given to Elaina. Some dying message of love or hope, but not this. Not some demand for continued war against the dark forces of the world. "What about Elaina?" I asked, Brin still dancing through my thoughts.

He hung his head as the water rose past our waists. Pulling himself up the gate so that he was pressed flat against it, he said, "Tell her the truth. Tell her I died down here, fighting against The King. Tell her my death was not in vain!"

I nodded, tears falling from my face and into the stream of disease that swirled around us. "I will."

"I believe in you, Wrack. You and Brin. You will find some way—" The water surged, covering his face for a moment. It had quickly risen over his shoulders.

Even on my side of the gate, the current had knocked me back. My head submerged, and I struggled to get back above the water. "Gordo!" My hands searched the dark water for his.

I saw his face pressed against the gate. "PROMISE ME!" he gurgled.

"I promise, Gordo!"

With one final wave, the water filled the tunnel. My fingers clung to the gate while the current tried to steal me away, but I was stronger. Opening my eyes in the disgusting flood, I could see the shadow of Gordo on the other side of the gate. He was still screaming something, but the rush of water through the gate masked all of his words. He slammed his fists into the gate, causing loud banging to echo through the water. His thrashing and gurgling slowed, and far before I was ready, it stopped. I stayed there with him, helplessly holding onto the gate, while I watched him drown in the filth of a city that hated him. Alone, I sobbed in the darkness. The foul-tasting water burned my lungs, but I didn't care. I was overwhelmed with the loss of this gentle friend.

Flayed

It was he that accepted me in Sanctuary. Thoughts of how he cared for the wounded filled my thoughts. I remembered his laugh, his smile, and the way he looked at his daughter when they met for the first time. It was only here, in this dank hole that he ever lost hope, and even when his mettle was tested – he never truly lost. His last wish was for me to bring that hope to all the people of this accursed land. Oh, how I wished I could be the man he thought I was. I did not have his strength, his joy, his sense of purpose.

My rage bubbled forth from my lungs, and the sound of it echoed through those halls of refuse. I decided then and there that I must find the strength, the will, and the path to make this world whole. I would not cast my promise aside.

Murks approved. His loyalty and commitment to me, even while bound through magic and blood, was absolute. Even if no one else would help me, we would have each other on this doomed quest, through success or failure.

I remained there, submerged in the dark water for what seemed like eternity. Thinking about what Grimoire had said about Gordo, I did not want his blood falling into the hands of our enemies. I broke bones in my hand, forcing it through the gate, and with my nails, I tore open Gordo's lifeless neck. My hope was that the movement of the water would pull the blood out of his body, rendering his gift useless to the enemy. I did not stop until I saw trails of dark fluid flowing from him into the current surrounding us.

I searched his belt for the empty vial that once held Elaina's blood and opened it next to the wound in Gordo's neck, gathering his essence from the wound in his throat. I tried to prevent the disgusting water from mixing with his blood in the vial, but I knew I could not entirely prevent it. Once corked with the stump of wax that had been its seal, I tucked it away in my robes.

Chapter 7

"I promise, Gordo," I gurgled through the water in my lungs, coughing as I delivered my final goodbye to this loyal friend. I pulled my hand back through the gate, and after the bones in my hand knitted themselves back together, I swam away into the darkness. Gordon's last plea haunted my thoughts as I navigated the vile maze back to the metal rungs which led away from this place to where Brin was waiting for me.

Flayed

Chapter 8

Immediately upon my hand breaking the surface of the stinking water, I felt a hand catch mine. Friend or foe, it did not matter; I needed to escape this watery tomb. The first face I saw was Brin's. Her eyes were filled with worry, but her lips came to life with that secret smile I knew so well. The mask that had been on Verif's face lay harmlessly upon the floor of the shed, and I watched helplessly as Avar, Tarissa, and Verif cried in silence. It seemed that they had been in the throes of grief for a long time. Brin was keeping her composure, though I could tell that eventually that dam would need to break.

"I do believe that robe has seen its final days," Grimoire said. "Since it seems we now have an extra robe, perhaps you should take it, Wrack."

With my current frame of my mind, I thought for a moment that he was mocking the loss of Gordon, and a quiet anger illuminated my soul, then I saw that he too had been fighting back tears, and so I nodded and took the robe from him. Murks crawled out of my secret pocket, and everyone in the shed turned away while I stripped off all the clothes I could, including my filth-soaked boots. From the hidden pocket, I took the tiny mask from Jugless the hemodan and the vial of Gordo's blood. Murks took his sewing needle, knowing that he would indeed have to repair the

Flayed

new robe someday. That mysterious key that still hung around my neck I kept, and the leather ties around my wrists I still could not remove, but everything else from my old cloth skin I discarded.

"Are you sure you don't want this?" Grimoire offered the braided red and black belt with silver skulls.

I shook my head. "No, I think I am ready for a fresh start."

"Well, if you are prepared then." Grimoire picked up my discarded clothing and boots. "We should be off before the guard starts searching the area."

Without any more talk, the others donned their robes, and we headed out into the street. Waiting outside was a small handful of other black-robed figures, one of whom Grimoire handed my old things as we passed. I caught a glimpse of the face under the robe, and it looked familiar, but my grief held my curiosity at bay, Gordon's final plea still planted firmly in the front of my thoughts.

"With the result of this journey, I will have to take you someplace other than where we were. Some place far safer." There was something ominous in Grimoire's tone. "The Well does have a powerful ally here in Flay. We have already arranged to settle you in his household for the time being."

There was no idle chit chat on our way through the streets of the city. The dark streets were dead quiet, and we took a route off the main thoroughfare to reach our destination. Still, through the open windows, we could hear the citizens of the city talking excitedly about the executions that were to happen in the morning. My willpower was tested on that night. I wanted to challenge the ignorance of these fools who would look forward to good people being murdered by an unholy tyrant, but debris from the street cut into my bare feet as we walked. Odd as it may sound, this damage

Chapter 8

to my feet helped keep me centered and focused on the moment. Should I have kept my ruined boots to protect me, I do not know if I would have been able to keep my grief under control.

We passed through the open gates to the upper district of the city, where the rich and powerful families of Flay called home. Immediately upon our passage through, we returned to the alleys and back paths that ran between the estates. Very near the gate, we came to an old and run-down property. The wood and stone that were the bones and flesh of the main building looked rotten and dead. A certain doom lingered over this place, yet this is where we were headed.

Grimoire took us to the back door, while the other members of the Well split up and went different directions through the streets. They were quite clever. Easy to discount the travels of black-robed figures if the robes were everywhere. No way to tell one group from another, impossible for witnesses to direct authorities to one group over another.

We walked up to door near the back of the large manor house. This entrance was clearly meant for servants or secret guests, of which I assumed we were the latter.

"Here we are. Now, I warn you – this man is your ally, like it or not. Any hostility towards our host will result in an end to our dealings." Grimoire looked at each of us to confirm acknowledgment, then knocked upon the door.

I looked up at the faded banners which flew over this estate in the night air. In dim moonlight I could see it: the sigil of three mountains, the sign of house Ruthrom. My eyes grew wide. Mindlessly, I whispered, "This is the house of—"

The door creaked open and strong perfume mixed with the stench of rotting flesh rolled over us like a wave, and a figure with wild wispy hair stood backlit in the doorway.

Flayed

"Mavren, I apologize for our arrival at this late hour." Grimoire gave a shallow bow. "I trust you received my message about unexpected guests?"

"Indeed, Grimoire, I did." Mavren's voice had an unnatural reverberation that sent shivers down my spine. "Are these faceless robes before me the aforementioned travelers? Pleasure to meet all of you. I am Mavren Ruthrom, grand steward of Flay, but you, my friends, may know me by another name."

"The Rotting One," I muttered.

Mavren stepped forward into the dim moonlight. Half his face was covered in the ancient silk mask that he always wore. From neck to toe, he was clad in regal, yet threadbare, clothing. "Indeed. A horrible name, but one well deserved as I, and my family, are cursed. But I do not tell you anything you do not already know."

I could not fathom why Grimoire would bring us here, to this house. The Rotting One was a member of the same tyrants who ruled this city and brought The Cursing down upon the entire world. Their action and their will brought ruin to the green places of my memory. How could he be trusted? Why wasn't Brin unleashing Ukumog upon this foul creature? I felt as if my entire world had been turned upside down.

"Please, weary travellers, enjoy my hospitality. I am sure you have many questions. The time for answers is at hand, my friends. Tomorrow this city will find a new dawn, and in the wake of the ripples you have already caused – nothing here will ever be the same again."

Grimoire walked past Mavren and into the estate without hesitation. The rest of us did not move.

"I see." Mavren nodded solemnly. "Understand this, friends. I want the same thing you want, yet I am not ready to pull my mask down and expose my heart to the tyrant. If you wish to

Chapter 8

take your chances upon the streets, I implore you to do so, but know this: Curses can be broken, torments undone. And in their joyous passing, unsung tunes will be sung. Throw off your chains..."

"We know their names," Brin quietly sang.

The Rotting One smiled at Brin and nodded his head. Without another word, Brin walked past and into the estate, and everyone except me followed. I heard a sigh of relief come from our Doomed host, and his eyes then met mine. I stood there, defiant.

"It has been a long time, old friend," Mavren whispered. "No harm will come to her here, but you must all stay hidden. They know of your presence here, within our sacred walls. However, none would dare conceive that you are here within my home. Please, old friend. Help us."

His plea felt genuine, and his one dead eye reminded me of the friend I had just watched drown under the streets of this city. My heart melted, and against my better judgement, I met my friends on the other side of the estate's accursed threshold.

"Welcome to my home, friends. Please, make yourself comfortable." The Rotting One brought us deeper into his decaying lair. The place was clean, yet it was a reflection of its master, a crumbling husk. Ancient marks marred the walls. Paintings lay where they had crashed to the floor some unknown time in the past, the wall above their resting place discolored to tell the story of where they once hung. "Let me show you to your rooms."

We passed by many rooms, all filled with disintegrating furniture. Carpets were tattered and frayed down to the wood floors beneath them. The ceiling bore marks of water damage, and some walls leaned awkwardly. It was rather amazing that the building was still standing at all. The smell was not much better. The stagnant

Flayed

air that hung in these hallways was infused with the unmistakable aroma of rotting flesh. Several times, I saw my companions wince or gag at the offensive odors that lived here.

"We do not have guests here often, I'm afraid. Indeed, I will have to sort out how we will get you the provisions you need, as I do not keep food within the estate." The Rotting One seemingly amused himself with these thoughts. It was apparent that he had not thought about the mortality of others in quite some time. "We did keep servants for some time, but we haven't had need of them in so long," he droned on as we climbed a flight of stairs to the second level of the house. "Ah. Precious May." He sighed. "She was the last of our servants. I'm afraid it has been long enough that I do not remember exactly how long ago it was. She was a kind and gentle soul. Unfortunate, how the gentle ones and dedicated are always the ones..." There was little doubt that he could have gone on longer, but his words trickled and slowed as the conversation took place inside his own head.

A few simple turns in the upstairs hallways and we stopped. "Here we are. You may select your own rooms. I did a small amount of preparation before you arrived. Please let me know if you need anything."

We all nodded and mumbled our thanks for safe haven in this hostile city.

"One note, however," he said, gravely. "At the other end of this hall is a room that you must not enter. Indeed, you may hear noises from behind the closed door, but they are simply the sounds of my beloved wife. Or rather, what she has become. It is our preference that she remain undisturbed by your visitation here, and we also do not wish for her escape." His face became tight with concern and grief.

Chapter 8

"Indeed, old friend," Grimoire said. "We should get some rest. I will consult with our friends here on the arrangements of their stay here."

Mavren nodded his rotting head. "Good night to you all," he said, then made his way towards the very room he had just warned us against.

With my magical senses I could hear slight noises from that room, as if a sleepwalking person shuffled around behind the closed door. As Mavren grew closer, the unseen person within began a low moaning and gurgling that was quiet enough. I was sure none of my companions could hear it.

"Hush dear, tis only I," Mavren whispered before he disappeared behind the door.

In short order, we picked out our rooms. Mine contained a bed that had long since fallen apart and would have required hours of work to return to working condition. "I don't really sleep," I reminded my friends so they would not need feel guilty about my choice of accommodations.

Days passed in that rotting prison. Human servants came and delivered food, even preparing it for later consumption, then left again. Often, our host would leave the estate to take care of his duty to the city and his liege. It did not take long for me to feel the crushing force of the walls that kept us within. The weight of my promise to Gordo was a burden I was not really prepared to carry, and I dared not share that with anyone else.

The first week went by smoothly. My friends were sullen at first, and there were conversations about Gordo and his memory. I would always escape the conversations before it was my turn to share anything. This drove a wedge between me and my friends, and they started to give me a wide berth in the house. It wasn't long

Flayed

before I was spending most of my time alone in forgotten parts of the estate. Lost in my own thoughts, I forgot about the passage of time.

One cool summer morning, Brin found me in the abandoned barn on the property. I found the open space and dashes of morning light in the decrepit building to be soothing, and I often watched the rays of the sun travel across the dark wood that held the building together.

Standing in the open doorway she asked, "Are you ok?"

Only her shadow was cast across the cool dirt floor where I sat. She did not even have Ukumog with her. I wasn't sure how to answer her, so I didn't.

Closing the door, she stepped forward with a few hesitant paces. "We are worried about you."

"Yeah?" I whispered.

She drew closer and sat on the floor near me. "Wrack."

Our eyes met. Her dark hair glowed with a beam of morning sunlight, and she smiled.

"I'm worried about me too," was all I could offer before my eyes went back to the dirt.

Murks, who had been sitting beside me in the dirt, climbed up into my lap and sat on my thigh. It was hard to be sullen with Murks as my hemodan. Most days, his brimming optimism kept me from spending the entire day wallowing in self pity, but sometimes even his encouraging words could not punch through the darkness of my thoughts. This had been one of those mornings.

We sat in silence for a while, watching the light move across the walls of the barn. It was comforting, having her there with me. After a while, Murks climbed out of my lap and started playing in the dirt, like a child. He was happy not to be trapped within my robes. His silly antics even made me smile a time or two.

Chapter 8

"Mavren has plans, Wrack," she said after I giggled at Murks.

"Yeah? I am sure he does." My words were acid. "They all have plans."

Brin sighed. "He wants to bring down The King. We had an extremely frank discussion the other evening."

"And what happens after The King is gone?" Anger lifted the volume of my voice just enough to make my point. "One of the others will just step in to rule in his stead. Just getting rid of The King is not enough." My fingertips felt the tickle of cold power slowly collecting in them. My fists hidden in my lap, I tried hard to push the power away.

"Actually, he doesn't want that either." She paused to frame her words properly. "He said something about wanting to lift The Curse. The whole uzkin' thing."

"Won't that kill him?" I asked, refusing to believe that this could be a genuine motive for one of The Doomed.

"That is a risk he seems willing to take."

Shaking my head, I said, "If he and Grimoire want to end The Curse, what do they need us for?"

Her head tilted to the side, telling me that I should already know the answer to that question. "They believe, just like everyone else, that the end to The Curse has something to do with the line of bards. The storytellers who speak the words of Ssli'Garion, The Silver Lady."

"And they think you are the next one in that line." It wasn't a question, just a verbal acknowledgement of where her words were leading.

She nodded. "Yeah, they do. Having Ukumog doesn't hurt either, I suppose."

Flayed

"What is stopping them from just taking the sword and doing the dirty work themselves?"

"Grimoire said something about how The Betrayer made the sword. How its existence is anathema to The Doomed."

"Hrm. I saw what happened when The Vampire tried to pick it up."

"Yeah," she said. "Uzker got the gaak zapped out of him."

We shared a chuckle.

"I dunno, Brin. There is still something about all this business that I cannot wrap my head around. Mavren was there in Yellow Liver when The King's army showed up. He was there in the woods when The Vampire attacked our forced march to Skullspill. He has his fingers in many pies. I am not sure his agenda is as cleancut as you make it out to be."

"We all have secrets, Wrack. You of all people should know that."

There was nothing I could say to that; instead, I just nodded.

"Mavren has been working to gain support from the other households in Flay. He wants me to meet some of the ones he has already formed a secret alliance with." Her tone did not have any excitement.

"You sound upset about it. Do you not want to do it?"

She sighed. "No – I mean, yeah. I dunno. Really, the whole thing makes me feel awkward. He is talking about me like I am some kind of legendary icon. I don't like the thought of anyone's hope relying on my success. I mean, look at how well I have found my father's murderer." She gave half-hearted laugh that turned into a frown. "Gods, I need to stay away from you when you are like this. You are making ME sad."

We laughed together.

Chapter 8

"Sorry I am ruining mood, your majesty." I laughed. "Wait, what do you call legendary saviors?"

"Martyrs," she replied with amazing speed followed by a laughing smile.

"Well, I hope it doesn't come to that."

"Yeah, me either." Her tone became more somber. "I rather like being alive."

All our laughs evaporated, and she stood up.

"You really should spend more time in the house," she said, dusting herself off. "At the very least, you should talk with Mavren so you can judge his intentions yourself."

I found comfort watching Murks play in the dirt while Brin made her way to the door. I heard the door creak open, and then, "You coming?"

Looking over towards her, I saw that playful, warm smile that always lifted my spirits. With haste, I lifted myself off the ground and dusted the dirt from my robes. "Yeah, I'm coming. C'mon, Murks."

Murks sprinted over and leapt onto the hem of my robes. The brightness of the outside overwhelmed my eyes as Murks deftly climbed up my robe and into his secret pocket. In these new robes, he had made the pocket a different shape and size, claiming that he needed more space to make it comfortable.

The sounds of Flay washed over the walls around the estate, but we were alone on the grounds. This place was like a forbidden park inside the bustling city. I could not help but imagine what it looked like before the rot took Mavren's family... or at least that is what I assumed happened to them. Try as I might to dig up memories of Mavren, nothing came to the surface of my thoughts. Perhaps I did not have as much knowledge of The Doomed as I thought.

Flayed

That day I spent puttering around the house, passing time. It wasn't until Mavren came home that things changed.

Late in the afternoon, Mavren came back to the estate, and with an excited grin he said, "Well, it is all arranged, my dear. Tonight, we will have guests." When he saw me sitting in the room with Brin, his eyebrows went up. "Oh my, I didn't realize that you were in here, old friend. Might I have a word with you privately?" He motioned for me to leave the room with him.

"Alright," I said, shooting Brin a confused look. She gave a shrug in response.

Once we were out in the hallway, he closed the door to the study where Brin and the rest of my friends were. "My dear boy, you simply cannot attend the feast tonight. Furthermore, my guests cannot even know that you are here. We are so close to forming our treasonous alliance, and I do not want anything to poison the well."

"You think my presence will interfere?"

He gave a tight frown. "Indeed. An unexplained revenant being present in my home might push some of these fine folk away from the negotiation tables. I would rather not have to explain to them who you are."

Folding my arms, I asked indignantly, "And who is that, exactly?"

Mavren paused, his mouth quivering a bit. "My boy, you are the unexplained revenant. All our guests this evening know that the revenants serve His Majesty The King, and it will give them a fright to know that one of them is here. I doubt they will believe me if I were to tell them that you were able to wrest control of your own facilities and strike out on your own accord. Nor do I want any of them to even whisper about your presence to anyone. There is no telling what Marius and Tiberion would do should they discover even a rumor of an unknown revenant being under my roof."

Chapter 8

"If you worry about whispers about your guests, shouldn't you be concerned about people talking about Brin being here?" His shutting me out of this gathering after Brin had convinced me to come back to the house was making me angry.

Mavren gave a wheezy chuckle. "My boy, I am counting on them whispering about it. This is how we will bring more into our fold. Those who are with us will whisper that their savior has arrived, those who are against us will be too afraid to say anything. Besides, these humans don't really know about the sword, but they do know about Teague and his songs. Some of their ancestors were worshipers of the old gods, and many of the houses hold onto traditions, even in secret. This is how we have them, you see? Playing upon the sentiment for ancient history, and a promise of freedom from the thumb of a ghastly tyrant will help us win the hearts and minds of our new friends."

Scanning his face for deceit, I found none. There was even a glimmer of hope in his white, glassy eye. The desire to press him for his plans almost came tumbling out of my mouth, but just after my lips parted, my thoughts were flooded with images of Gordo.

"Fine," I said abruptly. "If you think it will help for me to be out of sight, I will be."

Mavren's putrid face lit up. "Wonderful! If it will help, I can show you a passage on the second floor where time and neglect have allowed for the sounds of the feast hall to drift in. It will at least allow you to hear what is going on. The trick is that you will needs be as still as death up there, else we will all hear something banging around on the floor above. Will this be acceptable?"

"Sure." I resented the comment about death, but I wasn't about to say anything.

"Good, I am glad we understand each other." He turned to open the door.

Flayed

"One more thing," I said, stopping him. "I need to know, Mavren. What do you get out of all this?"

All the joy drained from his rotten face. His white eye darted side to side as he searched my eyes. I could feel the biting cold power fill my spine and rush to my fingertips. Again, I made fists to keep the power from flowing forth into the room.

"I get what I have always wanted, Alexander. I get to go home." A foul tear formed in his cloudy eye, but he wiped it away before it could manifest. A deep, sharp breath was forced from his lungs as he shook away the sorrow and let the joy lift his face once again. With his mask back in place, he walked into the room with Brin and my friends.

Not sure what to think, I stood in the hallway even after he closed the door. Alone, once again.

A few hours later, I was hidden up in a broken space between the walls of the upper floor. It might have once been a narrow secret passage, but the floor had rotted away to almost nothing. I lay across two beams that once held up the missing floor. It wasn't comfortable, but I found a way to make it work. From my hidden place, I could hear the dinner feast as the tables were set by hired servants. Aromas of the charred meat, spices, roasted vegetables, and savory sauces also slithered through the gaps in the walls to my perch.

As the noises from dinner began, the murmur of polite conversation drifted easily to my eager ears. There were gasps the first time that Brin said uzk loudly at the table, and she didn't even think to apologize. Tarissa talked with Mavren's guests about the weather and traveling outside of the city. Avar tried to bring up the plight of the people in Yellow Liver, but the subject was quickly changed by Mavren. Verif was unusually quiet for the whole meal, making me think that there was something going on that I could

Chapter 8

not see. I tried to push my senses to get more of a picture of what was happening in the room, but to no avail. Bored as I was with the drivel that was being discussed, I wished that I could move. I wanted to get out of the tight, decaying tunnel and see the stars. I wanted to feel the night air on my face and escape the rot which oozed from every surface of this ancient estate.

"Now friends," Mavren's voice boomed through the hall. "I do hope that the food was to your liking, but we have matters of import to discuss this eve, and I believe the time for such discussions has come. Verif, Avar, Tarissa, thank you for your company this evening."

There was a pause before Avar said with confusing in his voice, "Oh, ok. It was a pleasure to meet all of you." The sounds of three chairs shifting around on the threadbare carpet preceded the audible exit of my three friends.

Briefly, I considered what I would do if Brin suddenly was in danger. The plaster and wood in the wall between me and the dining hall looked weak enough. Perhaps I could burst through and enter in time to stop any harm from coming to her, or at least I could make enough noise that Verif, Avar, and Tarissa would return.

Mavren cleared his pus filled throat. "Well, gentlemen, lady, I give unto you that which was promised. As I am sure you all suspected, this is Brianndwyn, daughter of the Bard."

Heavy silence filled the room. I could almost see the disbelief in the faces of Mavren's hidden guests. At least one of them sipped their wine, waiting for someone else to ask a stupid question. They didn't have to wait long.

A old voice wheezed out pleasantries. "Pleasure to meet you, Brianndwyn."

"Just Brin, sir. No one has called me Brianndwyn since my father's murder," Brin interrupted.

Flayed

"Very well, Brin," the old voice responded. "I only met your father once. He was here in Flay, singing his forbidden songs. Whispers came to me through friends of friends on where he was. It was in an old basement, if I remember correctly. He was singing his heart out while some local boy played a fiddle that his family had hidden away. When his throat was dry, I offered him a drink." The old voice stopped for a moment, savoring the memory for a moment before continuing. "He was the warmest soul I had ever met, your father. I'm told that was his last performance here in Flay, perhaps ever. I was devastated to hear of his loss, even if His Majesty considered him an enemy."

"He was an enemy, Gregor," a woman's voice pushed its way into the conversation with a polite intensity.

"It was a different time then," Gregor wheezed.

"I'm sorry." Brin sounded a little frustrated. "You all know who I am, and who my father was, but I know almost nothing about you or your houses."

"My apologies, Lady Brin," Gregor offered, nearly gasping for air. "I am Gregor Chundai. Our family has been in charge of feeding this bustling city since the time of The Cursing itself. My companions, if they will let me speak for them." He paused long enough for a nod from each of them. "To my right is Warden Julia Grunnax. Her family leads the armored might of His Majesty. While Julia is not head of her house, she speaks for Hara Grunnax, the general and head of the household."

Brin interrupted, "I thought I was meeting with the heads of the households."

Chapter 8

"It is complicated, as Hara is one of the revenants that serves His Majesty," Julia offered. "Her oaths bind her in such a way that this meeting would be impossible without her giving you up to the agents of the crown. Rest assured, I speak for all living members of the household."

"Is she the only revenant in your house?" Brin asked.

Julia answered, "Aye, m'lady. She has been at His Majesty's side ever since house Andoleth betrayed the crown."

"Why do I know that name?" Brin asked.

"Um," Mavren muttered. "You would know him as The Baron..."

"Uzk – I mean... Uh. Sorry... Please continue, Master Chundai." Brin held onto her polite veneer.

"To my left is Titus Xyan. The Xyans were once the wizards of His Majesty's court. However, their power has waned—"

A calculating voice butted in, "What the good master is trying to say is that our power has been subverted by the selfish interests of house Kalindir."

"Which is the royal house?" Brin sounded unsure.

"Mavren, I think she is starting to get it." Gregor laughed, which quickly became a wet cough.

"Sorry for the mold, old friend," Mavren replied. "I'm afraid that I just can't keep up with this old house alone."

Gregor coughed again. "It is nothing, Master Ruthrom. This meeting is worth every moment."

"So what happens now?" Brin's voice betrayed her growing impatience.

"I need to know if you actually have a way of defeating the tyrant, or if this is all just empty hope and vanity." Julia cut right to the point.

Flayed

Brin chuckled. "I think that is the first time anyone has ever called me vain." She laughed again, then her tone changed, "If we were in a pub, I would uzkin' punch you."

"I was hoping you might say something like that. Mavren, where can I test this little girl's mettle?" Julia barked.

"Ladies," Gregor whispered, "there is no need for such violence."

"Actually, old friend," Mavren said with delight, "I think there might be. Come ladies, we can handle your base needs for inflicting harm on one another out in the garden, by the barn."

Helplessly, I lay there between the walls, unmoving, while the entire dinner party headed out of the house. Once I heard the door at the rear of the house close and the shouting began outside, I quickly crawled across the dusty beams and out into the main body of the house. Moving swiftly, I went from room to room upon the second floor, trying to get a view of what was happening out by the barn. I made it through three rooms and knew the next one would give me the view I wanted, before I started hearing her.

"RrrRrrrrrrrrrrugghhh..." The inhuman moaning came from Mavren's forbidden room where what remained of his wife was trapped. She scratched and shuffled around in the room, banging against the door.

Curiosity overcame my sensibilities, as it had many times before, and I crept up to the forbidden door. With each step, I could hear her agitation grow. Her moans became more desperate, and when I was nearly within reach – threatening. Standing just on the other side of the door, I could hear her shuffling, but along with it, the chiming of a chain. Murks silently screamed in my head words of desperate warning, but I ignored them. I could not help but wonder if she had been leashed within the room, so I opened the door.

Chapter 8

The smell of death washed out of the room as I opened the door. The walls were moldy and rotten, the beams that held the room in place could only remained there by some magical force, as they were falling apart. The carpet was worn through to the floorboards, and those boards were warped and decaying. The piles of debris in the room may have once been furniture, but now they were nothing but heaps of dusty trash. The wrecked piles of wood and paper were probably once great bookshelves. The only thing untouched by The Rotting One's corruption was a painting on the far wall. The couple in the painting were old, yet not festering with rot. The burgundy half mask and white hair let me know that the man was most certainly our host, Mavren Ruthrom. The woman I surmised was his wife, yet there was nothing the painting had in common with the shuffling corpse that stood before me. She stared at me with empty eye sockets. For a moment, I thought she did not realize that I was even there.

Much of her flesh had fallen away ages ago, and what remained was covered in fungus and ichor. What muscles that endured upon her body twitched just before she lunged at me, roaring with unearthly hunger. She moved with inhuman speed, but was hindered by the rusty chain that tethered her ankle to the far wall. I, too, could move quickly, and used my speed to close the door before I tested the theory about the limits of said chain. I stepped away from the door, the handle rattling erratically.

There was no time to catch my breath as Mavren's voice started shouting up through the house, "I am coming my love! All will be well!"

"I could run," I thought to myself.

Murks disagreed. "Even if Master ran, The Rotting One would know what has happened."

Flayed

"So I stand here and face punishment for breaking his hospitality?"

"He will hide you from his guests, Master. Remember, he does not want them to know you are here." Murks was brilliant.

As Mavren topped the stairs with a speed that no human could ever possess, I waiting silently in the hallway. When his gaze met mine, I could swear I saw green flames awaken behind his milky eye. "What have you done?" His whisper was filled with a dark and ancient rage.

"I am sorry, Mavren. I thought I heard someone else in there," I lied.

From the first level of the house, I heard excited chatter that could only be Brin swearing. Mavren was torn between his guests and his rage. He took a deep breath, ooze leaking from the pustules on his neck. "Hide, foolish boy. I will deal with you later."

Before he could utter another word, I slid into one of the side bedrooms to avoid our honored guests. I could immediately smell the sandalwood of Verif's perfume. This was her room.

Outside the door, I could hear Mavren calming his ravenous monster of a wife, pain and frustration pouring forth from each of his calming words. The dark part of my soul was amused by his suffering. After all, didn't he deserve The Curse? His wife, on the other hand, was probably a poor soul who married the wrong man. How horrifying it must have been to watch everything she cared about rotting away before her eyes, yet continuing to live. Curses were terrible things, and this one was the emperor of all curses. A curse that poisoned an entire world was something impressive indeed.

Without wasting a moment I started trying to piece together everything I knew about The Cursing. Isn't that what I had promised? To remove The Curse from the world? Surely something

Chapter 8

this penetrating would not dissipate when all The Doomed were gone. There must be something, someone, that was tying it together, fueling it.

Avar had said something about The Doomed all coming together and sealing themselves together with magic, and it becoming that which was known as The Cursing. Was that the original intent? There was something I was missing, and it was just out of my grasp.

The door opened, and Verif walked in, raising her eyebrows when she saw me sitting upon her floor, but she casually closed the door anyway. She joined me on the floor, and we sat there together in silence until the noise upstairs had returned to the main floor of the house.

"What did you do?" she whispered.

I took a deep sigh and said nothing, yet Murks climbed out of my robes and said, "Master went where he should not have and riled up The Rotting One's wife. He is very sorry."

Verif smiled and give a tiny laugh. "You are terrible, Wrack. Always doing things people say you shouldn't."

"Yeah," I chuckled. "I didn't mean to upset her. I just heard her moving around in there. It is terrible the way he keeps her alive like that."

"Was she all rotten?"

"Yeah. Worse than I could have imagined. I am not sure there is anything left of the woman she was before."

"Mistress Ruthrom was a kindhearted woman. She does not deserve this," Murks muttered.

Verif's eyebrows furrowed. "Murks, did you know her?"

Murks looked at Verif blankly, then over to me.

"Don't look at me. I didn't know her." I shrugged. "At least, I don't remember knowing her."

Flayed

Verif's face was overcome with confusion. "That makes no sense. How could you not know her, but your hemodan does?"

"I have no idea. Magic is a strange thing." I was similarly confused.

Verif scoffed, "Yeah. You are right there."

"When I made Murks, I had no idea what I was doing. I was just idly playing with some dirt."

She was stunned and retreated into her own thoughts. Noise from the main part of the house settled, and many boots were making their way up to the second floor.

"And you are sure he is YOUR hemodan? I mean, you can feel his emotions and things?"

"Yeah. Why?" I had no idea where she was going with this question.

She shrugged. "Just an old tale about a hemodan who killed its master, long ago. Something about the spell being corrupted by a shadow, and the hemodan having a will of its own. That story is one of the reasons not many sorcerers have them anymore. Well, the few sorcerers that are around, anyway."

"Really? How did the shadow corrupt it?"

Before she could answer, there was a knock at the door, and without waiting for a reply, Brin walked into the room. Her face was cut and bruised, and she was brimming with joy. "Wrack! There you are! We have allies. Uzkin' allies!" She stepped around Verif to nearly crash into me, giving me a extremely enthusiastic hug.

Verif pulled away a bit, and sighed. "That's great, Brin."

"Uzk yes, it is!" She released me from the hug, and I immediately wished that she hadn't. Her warmth was calming, and the smell of amber was almost intoxicating. "These are real allies.

Chapter 8

Leaders in Flay. We are going to start having more meetings, some of them off the Ruthrom estate. We cannot let the other families get too curious about them coming here all the time."

"Do you really think that is wise?" I asked.

Brin scoffed, "What choice do we have? It isn't like we can really leave the city safely. Besides, this may actually lead to a real end to the tyranny of The King and his son."

"Since when are you a crusader against The Doomed?" I asked, testing the waters.

Brin shrugged. "It isn't like I am getting any closer to finding my father's murderer. Besides, I want to kill Marius Juindar."

"Ah. So we *are* still in the revenge business."

Brin thought about it for a second, "Yeah. I suppose we are."

Silence filled the room. I retreated to thoughts of Gordo, my promises to him, the vial of his blood that I still carried, and the pointless struggle of his final moments.

"I should let you both get some sleep," I said, standing up. "You will need your rest for all the politicking you will be doing."

Brin groaned, "I hate politics."

We left Verif in her room and made our separate ways to our rooms. Mavren was waiting for me in mine.

"Do you have any idea what you have done, boy?" His tone was stern and angry.

I said nothing.

"It has taken me a great deal of work to awaken the person that still lives inside the corpse of my wife. Most times it isn't there at all. Your disturbance has ruined that for me."

Without thinking, I responded, "Perhaps you should let her go."

Flayed

Green smoke streamed out of Mavren's eye sockets, and I again saw the tiny flames behind his milky eye. "Do you really want to tell me what I should do with my wife, boy? What do you know of love? What do you know of anything?"

Cold shot down my spine, and my hands came to life with the bite of dark power. Wisps of purple and black smoke slowly danced around the openings of my sleeves. I ground my teeth, but held back my anger. He was right. I knew nothing about love. I knew nothing about Mavren, his wife, or The Curse that tore apart his family. "I'm sorry, Mavren."

"From this day forward, you are confined to the house, do you understand? We cannot risk any of your reckless antics while Brin is working towards forming these alliances." His tone made me feel like a child.

"I understand."

Still fuming, he walked passed me and out the door. The creaking of the house and rotting walls immediately pressed on me. I was tired of being helpless, of being useless. I wanted to help Brin, and fulfill my promise to Gordo. Every time I did anything on my own, I ended up as a prisoner. I was tired of this, but I would play along. I took my frustration by using the dark smoke to tear the broken bed apart, splinter by splinter, thread by thread, until nothing but a pile of dust remained. It took days.

The next two months were riddled with secret meetings and plans that I was not really a part of. When it was just us at the house, they invited me into their collaborations, but almost instantly I was beyond my depth. Names from all the different houses of Flay became like a language that I did not share with my companions. When I expressed my frustration at being excluded, it always came back to the same thing. I was a revenant, and not under The King's

Chapter 8

control. When I tried to explain that this would be a good thing, they always countered that there was no way to actually prove I was not just a spy for His Majesty.

I could see my frustration echoed in Brin's eyes, yet I also saw how much hope this whole mess was giving her. It seemed like the goal that had been driving her for more than twenty years had finally faded to the background. She even said to me one night when we were alone, "What better way to avenge him than to destroy the beings he believed were killing the entire world. For once, I feel like I am on the right path."

I could not do anything to damage her upturn in attitude. Perhaps I had been wrong all this time. Perhaps Ukumog's dark will was not poisoning her mind. Nothing seemed certain anymore, save for the tomb of The Rotting One's estate. The walls still held me tight, like a cell that was shrinking, one inch at a time.

Each time I brought up going outside to our host, he likewise talked about how important it was for their combined mission. While his words were filled with genuine concern, his tone hid notes of anger. He still hadn't forgiven me for my encounter with his tormented corpse of a wife. The more upset I got, the more he seemed to enjoy it. Yet, I was conflicted about what I had done to him, and I could not focus on plans where I was not valuable, so I found other ways to keep myself occupied.

While they worked their plans I roamed the house alone, being careful to avoid the forbidden bedroom of Mavren's wife. Exploring the halls, I did occasionally hear her scratching at the walls of her room and moaning that unearthly moan. My running thoughts always seemed to turn back to Gordo, however. I was fixated on his loss, and I could not bring myself to really care about Mavren's mission for Brin. The dark thoughts I had dancing in my

Flayed

mind about Gordo's death paled in comparison to what Mavren must have suffered all these years. Yet something kept drawing me back to the door behind which held the corpse of his wife trapped.

More than once, I found myself sitting in the hallway, just down from her room, listening to her. I imagined how helpless Mavren must have felt as he watched his beloved wife transform over weeks and months into a twisted shadow made flesh. I sometimes wondered if I wouldn't be doing him a favor if I ended her life, freeing both him and her from this mockery of a family that haunted the halls of his home. One day I found myself standing on the other side of her door with my hand outstretched to turn the handle, and I knew I needed to escape this house, even if just for a little while.

All my time alone in the halls had given me a great understanding of every entrance and exit. Some ways around the house seemed so dusty and in ill repair that I doubted even Mavren knew about them. It was the cellar that allowed me my egress, however. One window, just large enough for me to escape, and with just a simple latch on the inside. One of the panes of the stained glass was missing, and it was large enough for Murks to fit through it. I squeezed through the opening, then Murks climbed back through and locked the latch, just in case.

I was careful while wandering the streets alone. Leaving the shelter of the house was one thing, but to put my friends at risk was another. I kept to the back streets while I wandered around. Each time I ran into a sewer grate along the street, I thought about Gordo drowning right before my eyes. His desperate gestures while he tried to talk through the water in his lungs would not leave me be. *What was he trying to tell me?* His last request was an impossible one, perhaps his dying gulps were about more of the same. *What can I do against these titans of darkness that loom over us all?* His

Chapter 8

request, and my promise, seemed impossible. Yet, Brin and Mavren seemed so certain that they could topple an empire eons old. I just didn't see the way through.

Whispering from up the street broke me from my trance. It sounded like someone was trying to get my attention. My curiosity took hold, as it often did, and forced my feet to move towards that sound. The streets in the high city were mostly empty at night, and hiding from the guards was easy enough that I had no trouble following the whispers.

"Master, where are we going?" Murks asked me telepathically.

I responded in kind, "I don't know, Murks. I keep thinking I hear my name."

"Master shouldn't go this way. This road leads to a forgotten place that should stay that way."

"Why?" His warning only helped to fuel my curiosity.

"Some things should stay forgotten. Master once told me that."

"One day I would really like to meet this wise old master you once had." I was caught in the grip of my own desire, his enigmatic warning only succeeding in making me angry.

He went silent.

The whispering sounds led me up to the north end of the city, towards the castle. I started to believe that it was indeed drawing me right into the arms of The King or his blood-drinking son, but instead I found a street that ran along the east side of the wall that separated the castle from the high city. I crested the hill and saw the street rapidly decline and twist around to the west, still following the wall of the castle. All of my senses were now screaming that Murks was right. Whatever was down this street should just be left to lie there, forgotten. That same dark thing that

Flayed

caused me to enjoy the fear that Palig suffered before I ended his life awoke within me. It was unafraid, and it wanted to venture down this street to who-knows-where. I became a mere passenger and had no choice but to follow.

Carefully, I walked down the steep street. Many of the stones had become loose, and the road was treacherous. Focusing on the road in front of me allowed more reason to enter my desire to move forward, and I decided I should turn around and go back.

Then I saw it.

At the bottom of the street's decline, an opening caught my eye. It was wide with a narrow arch at the top. The doorway was laid into the same wall that surrounded the castle, but I was so far beneath the spires that this entrance would have to lead into the dungeons, or perhaps to something below the castle itself. Opposite this simple, yet ominous, entrance was a wall, the same one I had been following this whole time, a exterior perimeter that lay between me and the cliff on which the castle and the city were built. This was not like the thorn wall that surrounded the lower city, but was instead an extension of the stone wall that protected the high city. However, there was something uncomfortably familiar about this spot.

I froze there, staring at the entrance below the castle and the dark space beyond the city wall. I knew that out beyond the curtain of darkness, there rose majestic mountains covered in snow. That the ravine that lay just on the other side of this exterior wall was deep and dangerous. Somehow I also knew that it could be climbed, both up and down, and that if I followed the ravine east, I would find my way beyond Flay and into the tundra of Winterland.

"How do I know this place, Murks?"

Chapter 8

Murks hesitated. "Master has been here before. This is where Master Marec and Master Lucien came to collect Master from Flay, so long ago."

Suddenly it came flooding back. The smell of that incense, the days in the dark temple below the castle, lessons in cosmology from Se'Naat. The hairs on my neck stood up, and a shiver went up my spine.

"I shouldn't be here," I said out loud to no one.

Murks agreed, but before I could move, I saw robed figures emerge from the dark portal underneath the castle. Swiftly, I stepped into the shadow of the outer wall, pressing myself silently against the stone.

The forms pulled the great oak doors of the temple shut with a grinding sound as the hinges protested. There was a deep rumble as the doors closed, and the figures seem to put a bar on the outside of the door.

"They are keeping something in there?" I thought to Murks, who had nothing to say in response.

After the figures spoke to each other for a moment, they then followed the curving street to the west, which seemed a mirror of the street I was on. I had no doubt it curved around the castle and would lead them to the other side of it.

For the briefest of moments, I was tempted to remove the bar and enter the ancient temple, but I was able to overcome that desire and quietly fled up the street and into the high city. That night, I did not stop for anything else. I just headed straight for Mavren's accursed estate and crept my way though its tattered halls to my shredded pile of a bed. In the quiet of the night, I promised myself that I would not go back to that dark temple.

Murks agreed.

Flayed

The next morning we were all paid a visit by the Eternal Well. There were eight of them in total, and most of them stayed out in the yard and waited on Grimoire and two others.

"What brings you by this day, old friend?" Mavren welcomed them at the back door.

"It seems that duty calls us away from Flay for a time, Mavren. I came along to say my farewells," Grimoire said, his two attendants remaining silent, as was their way.

Mavren seemed sad. "'Tis a shame to see you go, old friend. When shall you be returning?"

"I doubt we will return before your business has progressed." Grimoire seemed disappointed.

"I can't believe you are leaving," Brin said. "There is so much left to do. How are we going to handle the Juindar situation? Or progress the deal with House Xyan without you?"

Grimoire sighed. "I am sure you will figure things out, my dear. Really, it has been your charm and strength that has gotten us all this far."

I stood in the back as they continued to chatter about houses and deals that I knew nothing about. Grimoire gave Brin some papers from the book he always clutched. Verif gave Grimoire a hug and whispered in his ear. Avar and Tarissa likewise said their farewells.

"Wrack, can I talk to you outside a moment?" Grimoire caught me by surprise.

Mavren looked at me and motioned his head towards the door.

"Sure," I stammered.

Outside, it was just me and the members of The Eternal Well. Their black robes were all the same as mine, but I could see the mortal faces that lay within the depths of their hoods.

Chapter 8

"I wanted to give you this, before I go. It is my hope that you won't need it, and that you will keep it safe." Grimoire held his hand out, and sitting in his palm was a little jeweled scarab.

I raised an eyebrow and did not move to take it.

"This bauble contains memories, memories that The Eternal Well has sworn to protect. There are members of our order who have died keeping this from the hands of corrupt forces. It is no small thing I give to you, though it may look it."

My brow furrowed, and while I reached out to take the tiny bejeweled thing, I said, "Why give this to me?"

"Because these memories are yours."

My hand stopped just before touching the scarab. "Mine?"

"It was no accident that I met you in Yellow Liver, years ago. I know you suspected that, but it is true. I was there, in that city, because of you."

The other robed figures shifted uncomfortably.

I searched Grimoire's wrinkled face for an answer, something he wasn't saying. In those wrinkles I saw an ancient and undying wisdom. Something great and powerful was there, looking back at me, and I could not explain it.

"Son, take the scarab, and protect it. I would warn you that you should never use it, but should you need to, place its belly against your forehead. It will do the rest. Then make sure you break it afterwards, I would not want it to fall into corrupted hands."

I was completely confused and overwhelmed. Something was happening there, in that moment, that I did not entirely understand. "How did you end up with my memories? Why would I give them to you? Who are you?"

"All excellent questions, my dear boy. If only I had the time to answer them all. Yet, here I offer you this gift. A gift that you entrusted to me, and now it is time I should return it."

Flayed

Bewildered, I followed his urgings and gently removed the scarab from his palm. It was silver and bronze, with purple gemstones for eyes and cut opals covering its shell.

"As I said, you should not use this thing. Not yet." He had the tone of a teacher when he scolded me, "Most warnings I know you will not heed, for that is not your way but this one, you should weigh gravely. Do you hear me, Alexander?"

Suddenly, I realized I was breathing heavily. This whole moment was overwhelming. "Yes. Yes, I hear you."

"Good. Oh, and do not let Mavren, or anyone else for that matter, know that you have it." He paused and seemed about to bid me farewell, but then he took a deep breath and said, "Also, I thought you should know. After your mission to save Gordon Haas, Tiberion Juindar had his body strung up on display in the marketplace."

His words felt like a punch in the gut.

"I am very sorry," he continued. "I know you were close with him. Well, I must be on my way. We will meet again, Wrack." With that, Grimoire turned, and the other members of The Eternal Well followed.

Before they were out of sight, the figure in the back turned to look at me, and I saw his face. It was Grumth, the exact wizard that we had originally travelled all this way to Flay to find.

"He had been right here with us, the whole time?" I whispered.

"Who, Master?" Murks asked.

"No one," I responded, placing the scarab into the pocket with Murks as I walked back towards the house. "It doesn't matter anymore."

Chapter 9

Months went by, and I watched the seasons change from inside that rotten prison. Each day I would follow a similar routine. As my friends stirred and made their plans, I would listen with no interest and no context, then I would wander the halls aimlessly, repeatedly finding my way back to a place where I could hear Mavren's wife moving around in her room. My mind would drift from this place into dreamlike thoughts, and I would almost always find myself playing with the jeweled scarab. Murks would always mention that I should keep the scarab secret, and I would comply. At night, my companions would come home and share info about their day. It was always some version of how House Chundai and House Grunnax were trying to get House Horn and House Numerum into their conspiracy; the level of success or failure is what set the tone of these conversations. Having no context, and being sullen about my lot in this whole business, I didn't much care for their plans or conversations. On rare occasion, I would share my viewpoint on a question asked, but I would shortly forget even what they asked me. I wanted to care, I just didn't.

The heat of summer blew away with the leaves on the estate's diseased trees, and for a brief moment most of the days were filled with rain. I stirred one morning to hear the silence of

Flayed

winter upon us. Snow had fallen in Flay, and it dulled the sounds of the city I could not see. All this time had passed, and I had done nothing to keep my promise to Gordo.

One evening, Brin and the others came back to the estate and found me by the fire in the great hall. It was a particularly cold evening, and I found watching the flames dance the wood into ashes to be soothing. Brin had a sense of purpose in the way she sat next to me, and she looked me in the eyes before she said anything.

"Wrack, I have something important to talk with you about," she said with a slightly condescending tone.

A sigh escaped me. "Yeah? What is it? More talk about how House Xyan might betray you and how you need to know more about magic? I told you, I don't know how it works. You should talk to Verif, at least her magic makes sense."

Brin shook her head. "No, that is not it." She took a moment to consider what she was about to say.

It was then that I cast aside my childish defiance. Something about this moment seemed actually important.

"Tomorrow night we will have a unique guest in the house. Someone very powerful and extremely dangerous."

I expected Mavren to enter the conversation and give me a lecture about following the rules. "Ok…"

"I need you to be ready to fight, in case he starts one."

"Who? You haven't told me who the guest is."

She sighed. It was a sigh that told me that this wasn't just some head of a mortal house. It was something far different than that.

Chapter 9

My mouth hung open as I contemplated the idea of The Vampire or either of the Juindar brothers attending our dying hidden palace. "It is one of the Princes of Broken, a city from across the sea. Prince Gelraan Darkweaver." She paused, searching my face for a reaction.

At first I had no idea what she was talking about, then something twitched in the back of my mind. Memories locked away came trickling out, and before I knew what I was doing, I said, "He is one of The Doomed."

"I know," she said somberly. "We are trying to get them to turn against each other."

"You can't trust him," I said, my voice stern with cold anger.

"It is too late. House Grunnax already made the arrangements. Mavren isn't happy about this visit either. He yelled at me just before I came here to tell you, saying that he did not want to open his home to that monster."

The idea of The Rotting One calling anyone else a monster I found a little funny, so I chuckled.

"This is serious, Wrack. I really need your help here."

"Sorry, just… Nothing. What do you need me to do?"

"I need to you to hide and listen in on our conversation. Like you did before."

"Right, I get it. Stay out of sight so that he won't think something strange is afoot." I was fed up. Now I felt like I was not only being excluded, I was being treated like a child.

Brin paused, she seemed surprised by my negative outburst. "Are you upset about something?"

I looked over at Avar, Tarissa, and Verif, who were listening quietly nearby. "We should talk about this alone."

Flayed

"Alright." Brin's tone changed to one of grave concern. "Could all of you give us a moment, please?"

"Sure," Tarissa said, taking Avar's hand, leading him out of the room.

Verif rolled her eyes. "I guess I can find somewhere else to keep warm," she said, before leaving in a bit of a huff.

Once we were alone, I spoke before Brin could. "I feel left out, Brin. Ever since we have gotten to this godsforsaken place, I have been excluded from your plans."

"I am not trying to exclude you—"

"But you are," I interrupted her. "I am trapped in this house, and I am going a bit mad. My mind seems focused on Gordo and a promise I made to his as he drowned almost literally in my arms."

Brin's back straightened. "What promise?"

I sighed and looked at my boots. "He made me promise that I would keep fighting against The Doomed. That I would find some way to release this world from their corrupted grip."

Brin turned and stared at the fire, her face devoid of emotion.

"His last words weren't about Elaina or Gwen, Brin. They were about us, you and me. He said he believed in the two of us, and that we could find a way to make this all happen."

"You shouldn't have made that promise, Wrack. Uzk."

The energy in the room changed, and now I was the confused one. I was uncertain why Brin was taking this promise so seriously, but I couldn't stop myself. I had to keep pouring out all this that I had been bottling up. "Grimoire told me, you know. That Gordo's body was on display in the market. They strung him up with a sign that called him a traitor. I can't just let this go, Brin."

Chapter 9

"Uzk, Wrack! We are trying to cause an uprising. We are trying to make a change here. Why can't you see that?"

She was right. I had been blinded by being told that I could not do and had lost an opportunity to help from a distance.

"Why didn't you uzkin' tell me about this promise, Wrack?" Brin strained to keep her voice down, but her frustration and anger were clear.

"I'm sorry, Brin. Everything just happened so fast, and then I felt like I was being excluded."

She sat back on the threadbare furniture and crossed her arms. "Is there anything else you need to tell me?"

Sighing, I relented. "I often think about going upstairs and killing Mavren's wife."

Brin shifted in her seat. "I do too, actually. I want to put her out of her misery."

"Seems like he is keeping her safe more for his own peace of mind than for her," I said.

"Yeah." Brin gave a tiny chuckle. "See? Sharing isn't so bad. If we are going to be a team here, Wrack, I need to know I can trust you. There have been men in my life before, and most of them could not be trusted. Some of them even tried to kill me." Her smile said that she was joking, her eyes said the exact opposite.

"I would never harm you, Brin. Not on purpose, anyway."

She nodded. "That is what makes you different. Different from most people who are alive, different from me. I have hurt people before, just because I could. Maybe I have finally bought into the whole ideal of the Shadow Hunters, that we can make a difference and push back the evil. I dunno, mostly you make me want to care. I see the way you look at people, even people you don't

Flayed

know. You care about them, about their lives. I think a lot about that uzk'd up night in Yellow Liver where we were trapped in that burning building. Do you remember that?"

"I remember."

She sighed. "There was so much fire, and the people in there, they were like animals. As soon as there was a tiny hole, they put their body between Ukumog and the wall that I was carving. That one man... I still see his face sometimes when I sleep. Before you came into my life, I wouldn't have had any remorse for killing some pathetic idiot who got in my way... Now I am just rambling." She wiped away tears that I could not yet see.

I moved closer to her, and took one of her hands in my cold, yet gentle, fingers. "Maybe Gordo was right," I said.

"First time for everything." Brin laughed away her tears.

"Hey now, he isn't here to defend himself."

"Way to ruin the uzkin' joke, Wrack." She slapped my knee, playfully.

I smiled at her. This small confrontation lifted my spirits, and for that moment I forgot that I was a prisoner in this decaying cage of a house. "What do you need me to do?"

"Hrm?"

"At the meeting with Darkweaver..." I reminded her.

"Oh right! Uzk. My mind was far away. Um. I can't bring you into the meeting, nor can I carry Ukumog in there. Just seems bad form to have the supposed sword of The Betrayer on my hip when I meet with one of The Doomed."

I nodded.

"So, I was hoping you could hide nearby where you can hear the meeting, and if he starts anything, you could bring Ukumog with you."

Chapter 9

My mind flashed back to the visions I had about me carrying Ukumog through the streets of the high city of Flay, with all the banners of the houses burning. "Ok. Maybe there is more I should tell you."

Brin tilted her head to the side, obviously put off my by sudden need to confess more secrets.

"Ukumog scares the gaak out of me. When all of you went into the bathhouse after we arrived here, I had a vision where I carried it through the streets of Flay, and the entire city ended up destroyed. Whatever happened when I wielded it against The Ghoul, that wasn't me. It was something Ukumog awoke within me."

Brin's brow furrowed and her gaze turned to the dancing flames in the fireplace.

The silence became too much rather quickly, and I continued, "I worry that if I use the sword, the same dark thing will awake, and I won't be able to control it."

"Yeah," she said flatly, her eyes still focused on the fire. "I know what you mean. Sometimes I am not completely in control of it either. It is almost like I am just watching myself wield it, ya know?"

"I do."

She smiled at me with a warmth I had never seen before. I felt as if a giant weight had been lifted and a barrier between the two of us had been breached.

"I am so very glad to have found you, Wrack. Something about you makes me feel not so uzkin' alone. Ya know?" Tears appeared in her eyes again, and they obviously made her extremely uncomfortable.

Flayed

The surface of my face did not betray the depth of my feelings; I remained rather stone faced. Inside my heart, however, there was a storm brewing. I could feel the dark power coursing through my spine, and I was choking back the hunger for Brin's life. To see this woman, whom I regarded as a invulnerable titan, so overwhelmed with emotion; it was doing something great and terrible inside me. Words boiled to the surface and I said, "But you wield the blade, just as your father before you. Does this trouble you?" These words I spoke, but I was not convinced that they were actually mine.

Brin thought for a moment before responding. She wiped a tear away before it fell from her dark lashes onto her face. "No. No, it doesn't trouble me. Just like with you, though, I wish the sword was more my partner. We would be much more effective if I could actually work *with* it. Does that make sense?"

Again, I was flattered and confused. This woman was always so confident, and this moment she seemed exactly the opposite, like the mask she wore to hold the world at bay was finally off. I didn't dare respond in kind. Was Wrack the mask? I shook away the cobwebs of this age-old question. This was no time to get lost in my own self pity.

"If you need me to hold onto Ukumog while you talk to Darkweaver, I will do so. If something happens, however, the handle of that blade will find its way to you. I would rather not tempt fate again. Who knows what the sword might drive me to do."

"Fair enough," she said. "I will feel better just knowing you are there, lurking in the shadows ready to lend aid." She smirked.

"Don't squires hold onto the swords of knights until they need them?" I said with a wide smile.

Chapter 9

Brin didn't miss a beat. "You forgot, 'Dame' Brin. Really, Wrack, if you are going to be my squire, you will have to do better than that. Uzkin' etiquette, man."

"Yes, my lady," I mocked.

Quiet fell over the room, and we stared at the fire. Somehow her head found its way to my shoulder, and we sat there on the ancient furniture sharing her body heat until she fell asleep.

The pain of my unholy hunger was like having a knife buried in my gut that I didn't want anyone to know about. I focused on the dancing flames and the amber smell of Brin's hair. Eventually, I too nodded off.

The next day was filled with preparations for our special guest. Great care was taken to prepare the house, which included bringing in people to clean and repair portions of the estate. For most of the day, I spent time confined to the barn, watching the rays of the sun move across the walls and ground. Luckily, I wasn't alone all day. During various points, Verif, Avar, Tarissa, and Brin all were banished to the barn while the cleaners cleaned, the builders built, and the cooks cooked. After sunset, it got very cold very fast in the snow-covered barn, and promptly we were all allowed to return to the main house.

"I don't know how you stay sane being trapped on the estate, Wrack," Verif joked.

I shrugged. "If I was ever sane, that was gone a long time ago."

She chuckled and gave me a playful shove.

"Ok. Everyone knows the plan, yeah?" Brin changed the mood instantly.

"Yeah, we all hide while you talk with Prince Darkweaver. Seems simple enough," Avar said.

Flayed

Brin nodded. "Yeah, but if something happens and you hear the screams, shouting, or clashing steel you need to come running and ready for battle."

"But Brin," Verif said with a smirk, "you are always yelling."

"Yeah, yeah. Very uzkin' funny," Brin said, obviously annoyed. "You know what I mean."

"And Wrack will have Ukumog in his hidey-hole?" Tarissa was not distracted by Verif's shenanigans.

"Yeah," I said. "But I won't be wielding it."

Verif, Tarissa, and Avar all gave me looks that told me that my protest over holding the blade was perhaps a little stronger than I would have liked.

Brin ignored the awkward stares I was getting and proceeded with the plan. "Wrack will be the only one of you that will be able to actually hear the conversation. It will be only Darkweaver, Mavren, and myself in the room." Brin shivered a bit. "Just the thought of being in a room alone with two of The Doomed is giving me chills."

"As it should," Avar said, with arched eyebrows that conveyed the fact that he thought this meeting was a bad idea.

Brin nodded. "Well, it is too late to change our minds now."

We all groaned in agreement.

A short while later, I was again in the dusty, crumbling crawlspace between walls. The velvet curtains that had been hung in the feast hall to cover the decay muffled the sounds from the room a bit, but not enough to cause me trouble. I lay across the same support beams, hoping that they would not chose tonight to be the night to finally collapse. Laying down the length of my body was

Chapter 9

Ukumog, wrapped in a blanket. Even in the dark space between walls, I could see the bone pommel of the sword in the middle of its wrapping.

Last time I was in this particular crawlspace, I found myself staring at the plaster wall that was the barrier between the dining hall and me. Not this time, however. This time I could not take my eyes off the pommel of that accursed sword. Even without being able to see the glowing runes on the black metal surface of the blade, I was uneasy. I wasn't entirely sure if it was the sword I did not trust, or if it was that I did not trust myself. A fear lingered in the back of my mind. It was as if I had Jared's winter wolf lying in that crawlspace with me; the sword was just as dangerous and unpredictable, even if we had made friends with it somehow.

I lingered in a long period of quiet while I waited for our guest to show up. The Doomed arrived when they damn well felt like it, and we needed everyone to be in place well ahead of time. After a time, it was almost as if I had fallen into a trance. A thousand years could have passed outside, and I would have been just fine. I fell into a strange place wherein I could not move, fear and worry gripping my heart, but the emotional wound was so deep that I had become at one with it. I welcomed the peace that might be on the other side of the death that was coming for me.

A knock at the main door of the estate shocked me out of my trance. Suddenly, I could hear blood rushing through my own veins, my heart was pounding. Living with one of The Doomed over these many months was enough, but now I would be within feet of two of them. Nothing about this plan was good. I began to doubt everything we had discussed, and I was wracked with worry for Brin. *Those monsters could do anything to her. What if this had been their plan all along?*

Flayed

"Calm yourself, Master. Murks believes in you. If something happens, we will save Brin. Murks knows we will." Murks' thoughts were calming.

The pressure in my blood eased. My heart slowed. Closing my eyes, I reached out with my senses to try and listen for our guest and the impending discussion.

"My, my, Ms Brin. You are far more beautiful than Mavren told me you would be." A deep and charming voice slithered through the walls to my ears. His accent was unlike one I had ever heard before. The vowels all seemed rounder somehow, and his voice seemed anything but harsh.

The mere sound of him, though, sent my skin crawling. I felt the bite of my dark power run through my spine, and my hands burned with cold. My jaw clenched, and I choked back this sudden rage that boiled my dead blood.

"Pleasure to meet you, Your Highness," Brin was perfectly polite.

"No need for formalities tonight, Ms Brin. In this private company, you may call me Gelraan. I trust you remember Julia Grunnax," the charming voice said. "I couldn't very well meet with you without her present. After all, it is she who brought us together."

Murks got nervous. "She wasn't part of the plan."

"I know, Murks. We will just have to hope for the best," I responded telepathically.

"Always a pleasure to see you, Julia," Mavren's voice oozed. "Shall we have a seat? Dinner is already prepared."

"Ah, yes! Your gatherings never disappoint, Mavren," Gelraan said. "I look forward to the food, but I am mostly here for the company and conversation…"

"Well, I hope that you won't be disappointed," Brin said coyly.

Chapter 9

"I am sure I won't, dear. How could anyone be disappointed in you? You are a rare gem in this dying world. If you are not careful, I might have to steal you away to Onisvaal myself!" Gelraan gave a deep belly laugh, which everyone else politely mimicked. I hated him already.

"I would love to see Onisvaal someday, but if I do, it will be under my own terms, Gelraan," Brin said firmly, but politely.

"My, Mavren. Your girl does have a bite, does she not?" Gelraan responded, his tone unable to hide from me the fact that he was upset. "Shall we have dinner?"

"Indeed on both counts, Your Highness," Mavren sniveled.

The group of them moved into the feast hall and shut the doors so that the servants Mavren hired would know it was not proper for them to just hang about in the room. Most of dinner was polite conversation, talking about how cold it was here in Flay versus the beautiful weather and ocean breezes in Broken. Gelraan would take any opportunity to talk about the beauty of his city, and would almost always include some subtle proposal that Brin should come visit. He was persistent, I will give him that. Brin, however, always avoided his invitations, politely changing the subject to ones about adventure or the political climate in the world. The war between Skullspill and Flay was a convenient talking point that her dinner companions were always quick to abandon.

After all the food was finished, and the guests had moved on to drinks, the serving staff was dismissed for the night. It wasn't until all the other persons in the estate were gone that Mavren returned to the feast hall and said, "Friends, we are finally alone."

"I have come to understand that you want my help in overthrowing the royal family of Flay. Is that right, Brin?" Gelraan moved directly to the point. His tone even changed from charming guest to verbal combatant.

Flayed

My heart fluttered, as I hoped that Brin was up to the task of taking Darkweaver head-on.

"Indeed, there seems to be a sentiment within the city that a change of regime would be favorable." Brin was calm and collected.

"That is our girl." I shared my joy with Murks over our telepathic connection.

There was a pause in the conversation. I heard someone, whom I assumed was Gelraan, sip from his glass and let loose a gasp as his thirst was quenched delightfully, then he said, "What do the Princes of Onisvaal have to gain from such a change? We have excellent relations with the royal family and, indeed, almost all of the houses of Flay. Why would we throw in our lot with an upstart, who cannot actually even change things? Hrm?" He paused, but before Brin could get a word in, he started again, "Frankly, I am surprised that you would even be a part of this, Mavren, after everything that has happened, the sacrifices you have personally made to assure peace in the realms. This will just throw us back into a never-ending state of war."

"But we *are* in a never-ending state of war, old friend," Mavren stated calmly. "After thousands of years, Andoleth and His Majesty are still trying to best one another. I hear tell that there is still strife between Onisvaal and the lost kingdom of Dias. The lords who were supposed to protect the realm have corrupted it, Gelraan. You know this. Why pretend everything is just as we planned? Indeed, old friend, we are far from that idyllic moment. Age has given me the wisdom to see through it, and the death of Palig has given me hope that perhaps our grave mistake can, at last, be undone." His words held as much passion and conviction as when he scolded me for my visit to his wife.

Chapter 9

In the silence afterwards, my heart stirred with emotion. If one of The Doomed had hope that their horrors could be undone, perhaps we did have a chance to succeed.

"It is true then? Andoleth's assassin is dead?" Gelraan asked.

"Yes," Brin responded coldly. "I killed him, with my father's blade."

"Ah! You neglected to mention that part." Gelraan had hesitation in his voice. "Julia, why did you not tell me that they had the sword of The Betrayer?"

"I— I didn't know they had it, my lord." Fear lived in Julia's voice.

Gelraan laughed. "Would you even know Ukumog if you saw it, dear girl?"

Julia did not respond.

"That is what I thought." Gelraan sounded disappointed. "You Flayers see only what your king and his son want you to see." He sighed. "So, if I were to engage with your secret group of conspirators, what then? Do you have a plan to make this all happen?"

"Yes, actually," Brin responded immediately. "Once we have most of the houses on our side, we can start to slow the production of food. We will divert the flow of cash to the royal family and remove some of the luxury that the high citizens now enjoy. With the city starved for all things normal, we will flood the city with whispers that it is The Curse that has caused this, and begin a movement to have the people rebel against their king. Eventually, The King or his son will have to move against the people. We then simply stab whichever of them is on the field in the

Flayed

back with the sword of The Betrayer. The other will probably try to get revenge or flee. Either way, we will meet their challenge and destroy them in similar fashion."

"Is that all?" Gelraan sounded sarcastic. "You will just stab whichever Kalindir is on the field and that will end it? Don't make me laugh."

"You have a better plan?" Mavren now sounded annoyed, but he was trying to contain it.

Gelraan sighed. "The first part of your plan might work. You can drive the city to revolt, but to count on the proper moment to prevent itself so that you can just stab them is childish. You do know that Darion spends a vast majority of his time in an incorporeal state, do you not? How can you make him take form once a revolution has begun? What is to stop him from just staying ghostly until you and everyone you know is dead from old age, then returning to claim his rightful throne?"

"There is nothing rightful about the empire he built," Mavren commented.

"Rightful or no, this is where we are," Gelraan said. "Darion was the strongest of us before he was killed, and he remains as such even without a body. If you want my help, you are going to have to come up with a better plan than this."

Pregnant silence filled the room. The fact that Darkweaver had not just left the room in disgust, I found to be a good thing. In truth, I didn't know what would happen if he refused Brin and Mavren. They couldn't really let him leave, as he might tell the Kalindirs our plan, which would certainly spell all of our deaths, perhaps even Mavren's.

"So help us then," Brin said simply.

"What?" Gelraan responded.

Chapter 9

Brin repeated herself. "Help us. We want this change, and we could benefit from your wisdom here. Teach us what we need to know in order to make this all happen. We don't just want you to be an ally on paper. If this plan is to work, everyone must get their hands dirty, and I would rather work with a team than have an army of mindless undead who just do what they are told. If you have better ideas, I want to hear them."

After a bit of silence, Gelraan let loose a booming laugh. "Girl, you are really something special, you know that?"

"That is what my father used to tell me, yeah."

He laughed again. "Fine. You want my help, we can arrange that. But make no mistake, if this goes sideways, I will save my own skin here. I have a whole nation of people to consider."

"A partial commitment is better than a flat no," Brin said.

"Ah, now just wait a moment. If you want my complete loyalty, you will have to buy it. I want something in return that will also show me how committed you are to this cause."

"What is that?" Mavren asked.

"First I want to know what you get out of this, Mavren. Tired of living in the shadow of a king you once thought dead? Or just want revenge for Darion crushing your ancient kingdom?"

Silence again. This time it was wrought with tension that even I felt. After several moments and a deep sigh, Mavren responded, "I get to go home, Gelraan. When all this is said and done, I can go back to the lands that were Stonefall and carve out a new life, away from curses and kingdoms. I will finally be free."

"I knew a king once," Gelraan waxed poetic. "A king who cared more for his people than he did for himself. He was a strong man, with a loving wife and two strong sons. It wounded my heart to see him fall to his knees. If this plan lets that king be free of his conqueror, so be it."

Flayed

Again there was silence, mixed with a few whispers that I could not quite make out.

"So we have a deal then?" Brin broke the silence.

"Not yet, pretty lady," Gelraan flirted. "I want something from you as well."

"Oh? And what might that be?" Brin sounded skeptical.

Gelraan took a deep breath. "I want to help you convince the remaining houses to join our cause." His emphasis on the word convince was rather harsh.

"We have been working on that for months," Julia said.

"I am thinking that we offer them more of an ultimatum. Either they join us, or they will face the consequences. Regardless of their decision, it will speed up your timeline a bit. If you wait until spring and the city is in revolt, then Andoleth will undoubtedly send an army here. He does so want this city as his own. Fighting both armies would be rather exhausting and might cause some of the weaker house to reaffirm their alliances with Darion out of fear of our skeletal friend."

"Fine. How would you want to do this?" Brin asked.

"Bring them all to the estate, and we will have a talk with them. This would be a different kind of meeting, though. We need to show strength. So, bring Ukumog instead of that corset, as lovely as it is." Gelraan's tone made my skin crawl.

"Fine, Mavren will work the details out with you," Brin responded. She sounded done with the entire evening.

"Excellent." Gelraan sounded extremely happy. It struck me as odd, considering his position on the entire idea of the rebellion just moments prior. Something was off, but I wasn't sure what.

Julia and Gelraan said their goodbyes and made their way out of the estate before I was able to climb out of the space between walls. I was grateful to have Ukumog off of my chest, and I realized

Chapter 9

afterward that the entire time Gelraan was there, I was staring at the pommel of the blade. Part of me wished he had started a fight, so that I could have burst through the wall swinging the blade. I tried to brush those thoughts aside.

"So?" Brin asked me in front of everyone. "How do you think things went?"

Shrugging, I said, "Seemed to go well enough, I suppose. He certainly seems at least interested in what you are up to."

Brin nodded. "Yeah. It was a bit odd how quickly we changed his mind, though."

"Perhaps he was already on the fence," Mavren said. "I do know that he has had a intimate relationship with the Grunnax house for quite some time now. Julia is exceptionally persuasive when she sets her mind to it."

"What does that mean?" Tarissa asked, quietly.

Mavren seemed unsure how to answer that. "It means that she gets things done when she wants them done. Indeed, it was she who approached me some time ago about something akin to our little plot. We have been keeping each other's secrets for some time now."

The silence in the room told me that no one wanted to press Mavren about these secrets that he had been sharing with Julia. The looks on their faces, however, told me that they all thought that something was not quite right about this whole situation.

We helped Mavren clear the dining hall and clean the kitchen. When I had him alone while washing up the dishes, I asked him, "What secrets were you talking about earlier? Does this conspiracy against The King go deeper than we know?"

He gave me an odd look and then gave a quiet, yet unearthly, chuckle. "No, Wrack. The conspiracy does not go further than you know. We are all in this ship together, my friend."

Flayed

Try as I might, I could not conceive of a follow up question to ask in that moment, so it passed, and after a short few days, we were prepping for yet another meeting.

Gelraan had picked this guest list himself, even though it had been Mavren who invited these people of station in Flay to his home. As usual, the plan included me being stuck in that dusty space between walls. However, this time Brin would have Ukumog on her hip. For this, I was grateful, even if I was tired of being in that space. Tarissa, Avar, and Verif would be again out of hearing range, so it did rely on me to alert them to any trouble.

"It is important that you all know who will be here tonight," Mavren told us in afternoon, prior to the meeting

"You may have to give me a rundown on what the various families do, as well," I said. "It isn't like I have been out there talking to these people."

Brin shrugged. "I somehow doubt I have talked to all these people, either. These are the ones who have not yet joined our cause."

"Which is actually most of the houses…" Verif snidely remarked.

"Oh hush," Mavren scolded. "Shall I begin?" After the briefest of hesitations, he started going down the list in his hand. "We expect that Houses Ellarin, Xyan, Horn, Numerum, and Aeochel may be in attendance." He paused and glared at the paper in his hand. "Is that right? Aeochel? I cannot imagine Patrox being engaged in scandalous talk such as this. Highly unusual, indeed. Oh, it does say that these people are invited, not that this is the confirmed list. I see," he said, mostly to himself.

"Who are all these people?" I asked, bluntly.

Chapter 9

"Ah, indeed. Well, we assume that the invitation were to the heads of these households." He scanned the page in his hand, "Ah! Yes! The actual people who were invited are listed at the bottom of this letter: Derek Ellarin, Titus Xyan, Nicholas Horn, Katarina Numerum, and Patrox Aeochel. Indeed, it also says that Patrox declined our invitation."

"You don't even know who was invited?" Verif rolled her eyes.

"Indeed, perhaps I should not have let Gelraan use my name to invite people. I should have insisted on writing these letters myself. This whole business has made me, perhaps, a touch too trusting. Hopefully he does not betray that trust." Mavren gave me a funny stare before continuing, "You had asked what these houses do, yes?"

I nodded.

Mavren began, "Well, Derek Ellarin is currently His Majesty's chancellor. He often steps in for The King in matters of foreign relations. One cannot imagine how hard it is to negotiate with someone that you cannot see."

"The King is invisible?" Avar perked up.

"Indeed," Mavren said. "Darion cannot normally manifest during the day, and even at night he requires the blood of the living to become visible to your average human. His revenants and son, however, can always see and hear him. Indeed, he could be in this room and we would not know, save perhaps for a slight chill in the air."

The simple thought that The King, chief among The Doomed, could secretly be inside the house on Mavren's estate sent a chill through my bones.

"Shall I continue?" Mavren asked.

"Yeah. Please do," I said.

Flayed

Mavren resumed his teacher-like pace of speech, "Titus Xyan has been here once before. The Xyans are an ancient house of wizards, originally hailing from the lands known as Dias. Their magical power has faded over time, however, and now the Xyan household are but a parasite upon the Kingdom of Ravenshroud."

Ravenshroud? That name was both familiar and terrifying. Before I could say anything, Avar spoke up.

"Ravenshroud? Isn't that the old name of the kingdom?" Avar already had his trusted notebook open and was taking notes.

"Indeed, Goodman Avar. Ravenshroud is an ancient kingdom which once tried its hand at being an empire. Darion Kalindir has been its liege for thousands of years. It was the betrayal of Andoleth, whom you know as The Baron, that destroyed the kingdom and put us all in this terrible state."

Mavren's words were soaked in the smooth butter of propaganda. With everything that was going on, I found it hard to trust that Mavren actually believed the drivel that he was spouting about The Baron being the cause of the horrors that now besieged the world. I searched my shattered memory for some moment where I know The Baron and The King were actually working together, but I was cut short by Mavren clearing his throat.

"Shall we continue?" Mavren asked. "Perhaps this time with fewer interruptions?" He glared at Avar, who just looked down at his notebook. "Where was I? Oh yes, next would be House Horn. They are tax collectors. Fat from the riches that His Majesty grants them, they are comfortable in their current state. Then there is House Numerum. They assist the kingdom in the regulation of usurers and the royal treasury. As such, they work closely with House Horn. There was a time when one house watched over all of these things for His Majesty. Things did not go so well over time."

"What about House Aeochel? What do they do?" I asked.

Chapter 9

"Ah, yes. House Aeochel holds a position that my house once did. They are in charge of the spiritual well-being of the people. These days, it is a church devoted to the divine right of His Majesty that they force the common people to believe in." There was acid in Mavren's voice. "Patrox is a lovely man, as well. His Majesty gave him the gift of undeath only a few hundred years ago, I think it is now."

"From your tone, it does not sound like you are unhappy that Patrox will not be here." Verif's smug smile was somewhat playful.

Mavren chuckled. "Indeed. I dare say that my estate is not up to snuff as far as High Priest Patrox Aeochel is concerned. That, and I haven't been to his religious services in ages."

The Rotting One's sarcasm gave us all a bit of a laugh.

"Honestly, it wounds me what they have done. Our world does have divine patrons. I have never understood why men need to elevate themselves to that position. It is a thankless job, and we are ill suited to meet its rough conditions. Even as immortal and powerful as some of us have become." Mavren trailed off into his own sullen thoughts.

None of us wanted to pick up this line of the conversation, so we all went on our separate ways to prepare for the dinner the following night.

When night fell, it found me in my usual spot between the walls. The house was creaking in such a way that I thought that this would be the night that the support beams would give out. I prayed to whatever divine patrons Mavren spoke of that afternoon that my fears would be unfounded.

The house was busier than it had been since the Eternal Well left. First it was Gelraan and his many servants that flooded the house, then the various honored guests with their retinues. I

Flayed

finally understood why I was deeply hidden in the house. If one of the servants found any of my friends, it would have been less surprising to find some unknown human than to uncover an unchained revenant lingering in the hallways of this run-down house.

Once dinner began, the noises from all over the house quieted to a hush. Even the conversation in the dining hall, I could barely hear over the sounds of the meal itself. There were occasional pleasantries or group laughter, but nothing worth paying attention to. Around an hour or so into the gathering, another party showed up to join the meal. Since I did not have a list of actual attendees, I was concerned that perhaps Patrox of house Aeochel had actually decided to show up and surprise everyone.

"Titus! I was worried you would not be able to join us! Please, sit! Eat!" Gelraan's booming voice put my worries at ease.

"My apologies for being late, I had a conflict that turned into a meal, so I won't be eating." Titus' voice was short, as if he were upset at something. "Thank you again for your hospitality, Mavren."

"Always, my friend. The house of Ruthrom is always open to you." Mavren's glass clinked as he raised it in salute.

Many other glasses made noises as they were risen in the air. "To unity of purpose," Gelraan said.

"Indeed? To what purpose would you call us together here?" a woman's calculating voice responded.

"In the guise of a simple party, no doubt. It must be exceptionally scandalous," a man responded.

"Katarina, Derek, I think you know why you are here." Gelraan's chair creaked. "Tonight we discuss a change of guardianship here in Flay."

Chapter 9

A few gasps came from the collected people, followed by a pregnant silence. I did not even hear the sound of a fork or knife tearing at the flesh of whatever roast beast they were devouring. The sound of their shock was upsetting. I took that moment to examine the wall between me and the dining hall, concerned that I might need to actually bust through it.

The man who spoke before, Derek, broke the silence, "Just what, exactly, are we talking about here?"

"I think I have heard enough, and I suggest that any of you who do not wish to be traitors follow me out the door now." Katarina's chair growled as she pushed it back.

"Do you know what that is?" Gelraan said calmly. No sound of footsteps or further protests answered his question, so he continued. "Lady Brin, would you show them?"

"A sword with a bone handle?" a man's voice I had to assume was Nicholas Horn answered.

Derek scoffed. "A grotesque and unwieldy sword. Look at it. It is huge!"

"By the sundered gate... That's— That's—" Titus fumbled.

"At least one of you humans is aware," Gelraan mocked the collected guests. "This, my dear humans, is the sword of The Betrayer, Ukumog. Do you see how the runes glow with an angry light? Do you feel that chill in the air? That, my friends, is because this sword reviles we who are blessed. We precious few who have been granted powers beyond your mortal ken, some call us The Doomed. This sword was crafted by one of us. Its purpose is simple – murder, destruction, mayhem. It wishes to undo the blessings placed upon us."

"Kill her!" Katarina yelled.

Ukumog responded, "*Clink!*"

Flayed

In my head I imagined the next few moments being streaks of blazing blue light as Brin allowed Ukumog's savage edge to do what it needed to do, but in my imagination, she turned the blade on Gelraan, and then she hesitated for a moment before turning the blade on Mavren. Explosions of accursed blood painted the walls of the dining hall and everyone in the room. When the guests fled, Brin did not bother to stop them; she let them run back to their master so that they could warn him that she was coming for him and his son. Sadly, this is not what happened next.

Gelraan laughed. "Kill her? Who are you talking to, Katarina? Me? Mavren? The sword wants to kill *us*, Katarina, and yet the sword's owner is here as our guest." His laughter became more insulting. "Did you really think that shouting a command at me would cause me to do your bidding, human? Have you learned nothing from Darion and Rimmul?" There was just enough pause in his speech for a shrug. "Perhaps you have not. A shame really. We could have used your talents. Do you wish to leave?"

"Prince Darkweaver, I cannot bring myself to plot against His Majesty," Katarina said defiantly.

Derek's chair was pushed back so quickly it crashed into the wall between him and me. "Nor can I. You call yourselves blessed and claim to share the same power as His Majesty, but I say unto you: blasphemy! You are unworthy to be in the same space with his divine power, you filth."

"Really?" Gelraan responded with amused calm. "Is that your official opinion as lord chancellor? Indeed, I could cease all trade agreements that I have with the Empire. I am sure you do not have need of our craftsmen, our gold, or, indeed, our food." He paused to let his words drive home. "I was looking forward to sharing this wine that I brought from Onisvaal with all of you, but I

Chapter 9

suppose I should just—" A loud crash coming from the dining hall made me jump. I moved into an upright position and prepared to leap through the wall, but a voice from the other side stopped me.

"Oops..." Gelraan said mockingly. "You didn't want to actually drink that, did you? Filthy traitor wine, after all."

"Now, Your Highness, I do not think—" Mavren interjected.

Gelraan hushed him, like a parent might shush a child. "Mavren, that is the problem, you don't think."

An uneasy silence flushed through the room. All my senses screamed that something terrible was about to happen, that Gelraan's pretense for bringing all these people to Mavren's home was nothing but a part of some twisted game he was playing. "Brin is in trouble, I must do something," burned through my mind. Cold power shot down my spine, and my hands were ignited in dark flames.

Before I could act further I heard Gelraan say, "For all of your parts, I hope that you serve your master better in death."

Without thinking any further I shielded my head with my arms and leapt into the plaster wall. As I hoped, it exploded in a cloud of splinters and dust, throwing me onto the floor of the dining hall. I heard the sound of several sharp objects fly through the air like arrows seeking the heartsblood of a distant foe. When I stood, my robes and skin covered in grey dust, I saw what was happening. Several fragments of glass from a shattered bottle that lay upon the table had been cast through the air with blinding speed. Gelraan must have used magic to propel them, as he was standing too far away from the debris to have thrown them, and the accuracy at which they drove through the air at the necks of their targets was uncanny. Katarina and Nicholas were already fountains of mortal

Flayed

blood, their necks perforated by the broken glass, which continued to travel with such force as to imbed itself in the plaster behind them.

Titus muttered an unheard word, and the glassy projectile just scratched his neck, leaving a rather nasty flesh wound. I looked over at Brin, and immediately reached out with my dark power and pulled the glass out of the air before it made its way towards her. Sadly, this distraction proved fatal for Derek Ellarin, as the glass headed for him found its mark, cutting a second mouth into his throat. Blood spurted from all three of the mortally wounded guests and showered the remainder of the food upon the feast table, the walls, and the floor.

Mavren moved forward with unnatural speed and punched Gelraan in the face with such force it would have killed a normal man. He screamed, "How DARE you?" with a voice that made the building tremble.

Gelraan responded with only laughter as he reached forward his hand and, with an unseen force, threw Mavren through the closed door into the kitchen. The wood exploded into millions of wooden splinters, and Mavren disappeared into the other room. "Remember your place, Ruthrom," Gelraan shouted.

Brin looked completely taken off guard. All of this action had happened in a blink of an eye, and she seemed unaware that Gelraan had even attacked her in the first place. Taking a defensive stance, she gripped Ukumog with both hands, and just as her second hand wrapped itself around the handle the runes on Ukumog burned brightly with blue fire. "What the uzk?!"

"Oh come now, girl. You did not see this coming? While I agree with your goals, I have my own agenda to pursue. Now, who is this new guest? Hrm?" Galreen looked over at me, his face filled with smug victory.

Chapter 9

His skin was the darkest I had ever seen, approaching the color of my robes, he was dressed in yellow silks with fine embroidery, and across his body was a deep blue sash that also seemed to have great detail. A pearl earring encased in gold dangled from his right earlobe. His face was handsome, save for the scar that cut a diagonal line from the middle of his forehead down to that expensive earring.

With a flick of his wrist, the candelabra from the middle of the feast table was in his right hand, and as our eyes met all the laughter instantly drained away. "I knew this was too good to be true," he said to himself. "Fight me or save your friends, the choice is yours," he said directly to me.

In one smooth motion he threw the lit candles into the hole that I had come through, and then he transformed into a bat and flew out through the open kitchen doorway. Behind me, the hungry flames on the candles found the dry and rotten support beams in the belly of the house and immediately spread from floor to floor. Within seconds the fire spread through the house like kindling bursting into flame.

Before any of us could take any action, Titus Xyan jumped to his feet and bolted for the door. He was gone before we could even call out his name.

"We have to get out of here," I said to Brin.

"What about uzkin' Darkweaver?" she said.

I looked down at the three corpses at my feet, their hearts still pumping fresh blood out through the gushing wounds in their throats. "Another time," I said moving across the room and holding out my hand.

The door to the main part of the house opened. Smoke was already filling the air out there. "What the uzk happened?" Avar said.

Flayed

"We have to get out of the house. In moments it will be a raging inferno," I said.

Verif asked, a hint of panic in her voice, "Where is Mavren?"

"I will get him," I said. "Get out into the garden, and keep a lookout for bats."

"Bats?" Tarissa said, as they all ran towards the back door.

Alone, I ran into the kitchen. Mavren, with his head down, leaned against one of the preparation tables which was still covered in food. His stance was that of a man defeated. The room was already filling with smoke, and the ancient plaster was cracking from the heat. "Worry not, old friend. I am alright."

"Mavren, we have to get out of this house. Gelraan set it on fire," I said, trying to contain my sense of urgency. While I hadn't yet experienced the bite of flames on my flesh, I did not relish the idea of testing my body's ability to regenerate.

"Plaster does not burn, friend. We shall be fine," he said.

"While that may be true, the wooden supports that hold all the plaster in place is what is actually on fire. He threw the flames into the space between the walls."

Mavren looked at me with a shocked eye. "That would, indeed, be terrible. We should flee."

The two of us bolted out the door into the garden where the rest of us were waiting. The flames had already reached the roof, and embers from the burning wood flew into the air like a malevolent pestilence, and shortly the entire estate was ignited.

"SELENA!" Mavren shouted at the house and then sprinted towards the door.

Tarissa muttered, "Oh uzk, his wife…"

Chapter 9

Before Mavren's supernatural speed could carry him into the house, the side where his wife's bedroom was collapsed, showering the area with dust, splinters, and flames.

"SELENA! NO!" Mavren screamed at the ruined estate. He stood there. Even with all his power, he was helpless to save his dead wife from the crushing flames that now sat upon her ravaged corpse.

"We have to get out of here, Mavren," I said to him. "The guard will be here soon, and they won't like what they find. Assuming that Gelraan didn't already have a plan in place for this. If he did, well, then we need to leave right now."

A viscous green tear oozed down Mavren's rotten cheek. For the blink of an eye, he looked like the regal man with the mane of salt and pepper hair from my memories. The rot was gone, his clothes were restored to how I remembered him, and the shadow of The Curse had been lifted, but then the moment was gone and he was again the disgusting dead thing known as The Rotting One.

"Come with me." He quickly strode towards the back exit from the estate. "I know a place no one would dare look."

"Where?" Verif asked.

Mavren looked over his shoulder with a look that said that he wished she hadn't asked that question, then, looking directly at me, he said, "An ancient and forgotten temple."

Murks was immediately filled with dread. Over our telepathic link, I heard him say, "Oh, uzk."

Flayed

Chapter 10

Billowing smoke floated over the whole of the high city of Flay. Glowing embers danced in the windless night air. Even at this late hour, the city was alive and focused. The fire had called up workers from the low city to help extinguish the flames of Mavren's old life. A primal fear clung to those who watched the smoke and flames with blank faces. It was as if they were waiting to see if their lives would be so swiftly destroyed by uncontrollable elemental hunger. Rich or poor, well fed or starving, dirty or clean, it did not matter. They all feared the flames that they felt were waiting at the edges of their life to devour their very souls. *Did they know that hungry flames such as these had been given life and walked among them?* One such primal terror was their beloved king, another was his hungry son, and yet another pushed his way through the awestruck crowd. Mavren, his oozing rot leaving traces of pus behind on humans he brushed past, was one such flame. Yet this elemental terror now seemed to long for an end to all of his mockery of life.

Not only had he conspired with humans, one of which held the key to his own destruction, but he let in the worst thing possible: hope. It was this hope that had allowed Gelraan Darkweaver to turn the tide against him. This trust got his shadow of a life reduced to a burning pile of forsaken rubble. Even as we moved through the

Flayed

crowd, there was a change in Mavren. His polite demeanor had been replaced with a dark focus which was currently aimed at getting us away from the burning remains of his human life. The look in his eye made me worry that this sequence of events had unleashed the monster that always had been hidden deep inside his dead flesh.

Murks refused to say anything, even over our telepathic bond, while we darted from shadow to shadow, leaving the gathered crowd behind us. Much like my worry for Mavren's emotional shift, I worried about the change in my hemodan. Indeed, much of the things that happened since we arrived in Flay gave me much to worry about.

Having broken through the other side of the collected audience of Mavren's ruination, we found the rest of Flay's high city streets to be completely empty. Our pace eased once we were far enough away from the crowd that we could no longer hear individual shouts. Glancing over my shoulder, I the ominous glow of the inferno through the haze of smoke that loomed over the city. Mavren had truly lost all his earthly things. I could not help but wonder how he felt. Apart from the obvious grief of his wife's loss, I hoped that there had also been a weight lifted from his heart, yet I worried that having nothing to ground him might turn him in the dark direction of Palig's fall. Only time could answer that question.

Much as I had suspected, we weaved our way through the quiet streets towards the road that ran down and behind the castle to the same exact doors that had spooked me the one time I went wandering without my companion's knowledge. The closer we got to those dark forgotten doors, the faster my heart pounded.

"You ok, Wrack?" Brin asked. Her face was smudged with black soot, but I could still smell the amber she wore through the scent of burnt wood.

Chapter 10

Taking a deep breath, I responded, "I think so. Just shaken from how quickly things escalated back at the estate. I mean, I feel like I should have seen it coming."

"I think we all thought Gelraan was up to something. I, for one, was caught completely off guard," she said, trying to dilute my self blame.

"So I saw."

She smiled, her eyes filled with a warmth that was beyond the simple smiles she had given me a thousand times. "Thanks, by the way. If you hadn't burst through the wall back there, I would probably be dead."

"You have done the same for me, countless times, Brin." I returned her smile, which made her face light up. My heart fluttered, and I lost track of what I was saying for a moment. "Next time you can save me."

"Deal," she said, reaching out and taking hold of my cold hands. "Aah! Your hands are extremely cold!"

"My hands are always cold. I'm not exactly alive," I said with a hint of sarcasm.

"Not this cold." Her tone had a touch of curiosity.

I lifted my hands into view, and saw that they had writhing dark power dancing around my fingers and palms. Without saying a word, I flexed and relaxed my fingers a few times, trying to focus on making the power retreat. The moment my mind directed the power, it vanished. "Huh," I said aloud. I felt as if I had finally connected to this power that haunted me. The next time I had cause to use it, I intended to exert my will more directly over it, though I silently, and foolishly, hoped that moment would never actually arrive.

Upon seeing the darkness fade, Brin reached out and wrapped her hand around mine, giving me a huge smile.

Flayed

From behind me, I heard Tarissa comment, "Well, there you have it."

"You didn't see this coming?" Avar laughed.

Behind them, Verif made a huffing noise.

"We are nearly there, old friends. Once inside, we shall be safe from those without, but there are secrets kept in this place like a vault. We must be wary while we seek refuge here. In a few days' time, after our wounds have scabbed, we will forge our plan anew and leave this ancient place of worship," Mavren said, keeping his eyes on the road ahead as we descended behind the castle.

At we approached the large carved doors, a shiver ran through me. Brin squeezed my hand, and while I enjoyed feeling her silent reassurance, the monster in me was screaming for her warmth. Using the excuse that we were about to be in possible danger, I found a way to separate my hand from Brin's. Instantly the winter air stole the heat of her hand from mine, and I wished I hadn't ever let go.

Mavren walked directly up to the bar that held the door shut, and removed it with a sharp tug. He set it aside and answered the question I was about to ask, "Don't worry, I can replace the bar and meet you inside."

"How will you do that?" Tarissa asked.

"You forget, my dear, I am one of the accursed Doomed. There are certain magical perks." He smiled.

Tarissa nodded.

Once the doors creaked open enough for us to fit inside, we went in one at a time. Brin insisted on going first, followed by Avar, Tarissa, and then Verif. I waited a moment, shooting Mavren a raised eyebrow.

"Go inside, Wrack. Once I secure the door, I will transform and follow you through the opening under the door," he assured me.

Chapter 10

I remembered that he had transformed into a green smoke before. I did have a momentary twinge of worry that he might just lock us inside the temple and leave, but looking at the wooden bar, I was pretty sure we could break it from the inside if we needed to.

Once inside, Mavren closed the doors and barred them. Green smoke drifted through the crack under the door, but in the darkness, I was the only one who could see it. Moments later, Mavren reformed out of the cloud, almost like he had been in it the whole time and suddenly just walked forward out of it, leaving tendrils of the twisting green to dissipate into the air. I was impressed at the subtlety and elegance of the transformation, especially in contrast to the jarring power of Darkweaver's transformation into a bat.

"Can all The Doomed transform?" I asked before a torch could bring light to my human friends.

Mavren looked at me through the darkness and responded, with a thoughtful look, "I believe so, yes. Though the transformations tend to be always the same." He walked over to a torch hanging on the wall, and it ignited slowly without him doing much anything else. "Darkweaver can transform into a bat, obviously. I believe that Rimmul can change into a wolf. His majesty once could take on the form of a gold eagle. I am unfamiliar with Andoleth's transformative state, nor can I recall Palig's transformation. As for the others who bear this curse, I do not recall their powers. Most of them have been locked into a terrifying form for at least a thousand years now, many of them worse than my ruined shell. I shudder to think how The Maiden looks now, wretched creature she was in her life."

All of us followed Mavren, and his torch, deeper into the temple. Beyond the small foyer we found another door, which was left partially open. The hinges of that door groaned as we pushed them open to gain access to the main worship hall. It was a large

Flayed

room, supported by large pillars which were placed around the room so that the view of the far end of the hall would not be blocked from the many pews that rested in half-ruined rows between us and the dais at the other end.

Walking on the crumbling carpet that lined the main aisle proved awkward and destructive, as the carpet nearly disintegrated at our passing. Overhead, in the vaulted ceilings, loomed balconies that I thought must contain more pews for worshipers to sit and watch the proceedings at the dais. The sides of this hall were covered in the flecking remains of elaborate murals, painted with pigments made of precious metals and inlaid with gemstones. Most of the gems had been pried from their embedded nests, and the paintings were so ruined that I could only make out designs and not details of the story they undoubtedly once told. The air in the belly of the temple was stale and smelled of decay, and the light from the torch showed us the wispy clouds of dust that our presence was kicking up. Beyond the dust, and at the far ends of the hall, I could see doors in the far wall, and the side walls that led off into dark forgotten hallways. Lying in front of these doors were piles of rotting dark fabric which once were undoubtedly curtains that obscured the doorways from ancient eyes.

On the raised floor of the dais sat the remains of an altar. Long ago this sacred remnant of ancient worship had been defiled. It was smashed and ruined. The surface of the metal looked melted and burned by some long forgotten fire. Elaborate candlesticks lay broken and covered in dust around the altar, and the ancient tang of death hung in the air over the ruin of this place of worship and sacrifice. As we got closer, I could see the dusty bones of animals long slaughtered over this ruined heap of metal and wood. I could feel the hatred that still lingered over the dais itself, as if the defiling of the altar was such an act of burning hatred that the scent of it

Chapter 10

could stain the mere presence of the thing. It made my stomach turn. The runes upon Ukumog, however, seemed to feed on this ancient rage. With each step, the flickering blue of those magical symbols intensified, until we were standing near the dais and they looked as if they were about to burst into flame right there upon the black surface of the blade, their light brighter than Mavren's torch.

"The sword does not approve of what has been done to this place," Mavren noted. "I share its animosity for those who perpetrated this most heinous of crimes. But rest assured, these people have met their end, most of them ages ago, perhaps even before Ukumog was forged. Ah, what madness led us to this point?"

"Greed?" Avar offered, his tone making it more of a comment. Looking at him, I knew he believed the answer to be that simple.

"Aye, Goodman Avar. Greed was indeed a motivation for some. For others, it was a twisted piety, a fanatical devotion to an unspeakable evil that caused us to end up on this road of terror. A road from which there seemed, for a long time, to be no escape." Mavren rested his undead bones in a pew three rows from the front. "And now... Now it seems we have come to escaping this city being our only way forward." His eyes focused on the glimmering light reflecting from the ruined altar. "I, for one, will be glad when that dawn finally comes."

We sat there in silence for some time. Brin's hand again found mine and recoiled from the cold which was wrapped around my limbs. I again willed it to recede, and it obeyed. We held hands, just being there in the quiet place, and remained contemplative for long enough that my human companions began falling asleep. Brin rested her head on my shoulder, and while she slept, I kept my eye on Ukumog. Here in this place, I thought it was perhaps the most dangerous thing within these forgotten halls.

Flayed

After a time, my mind slipped away, ushered by distant whispers, the same sweetly malicious whispers that led me to this temple before. I resisted their call, but their song had lured me to sleep. Like many times before, I found myself lost in the dreams of a past that may have once been.

"Come now, boy," a calculating voice called out to me. "Show me what you are really made of."

The only light in the room was coming from a candle on a table in the center. The room was round and carved out of stone, with only one exit, and the door was shut. The light flickered on the figure of a man that stood between the table and the exit. He was tall and was wrapped in dark robes tied with a simple cord. His face was long, with sharp features. His dark hair was smoothed back over his head, and his expertly trimmed beard brought his face to a point at his chin. His intense gaze was entirely fixed on me, and his fingertips were pressed together, forming an almost sinister yet pious steeple out of his hands. His pose seemed to be one of nearly unearthly repose, but didn't seem awkward or strange for him, more akin to the way that some people talk or think with their hands. This severe man that challenged me was Se'Naat, the high priest of the temple. It was by his word that the divine wishes of all the gods made their way to the masses of the Kingdom of Ravenshroud. His raw cunning was a machine silently running behind those dark eyes, and his presence made me extremely nervous. My thoughts were racing with the desire to leave the room. I was scared, exhausted, and stubborn. I knew what he wanted, but I didn't think I could accomplish it. The more he pressed me, the more I didn't want to do what he was asking anyway.

Chapter 10

"I don't think I can," I said.

Se'Naat stared at me with those piercing eyes. It was obvious that he was not going to budge. His motionless gaze was unnerving. "Fine," he said quietly, startling me. "If you do not think you have what it takes, then you can leave the city. I have no use for a talentless apprentice." He motioned towards the iron bound door.

The fear gripped me more solidly. I didn't want to leave the safe confines of the city, or the temple for that matter. Flashes of horror and violence filled my mind, and I did not want to return to wherever those images came from. "Let me try one more time," I said, like a child who finally realized the consequences of their decisions.

"If that is what you wish, Alexander." Se'Naat smiled. "Show me then. Vanquish the candle's light."

The way he said that reminded me of someone else. Someone far away and long gone. A fool who abandoned me to a harsh and unforgiving fate. Hate burned in my heart, and I let it fester, let it grow. I thought about the old man's beard, his demanding pressure to prove myself to him. Over and over, the memories of test after test with little to no success. A thousand candles stood against me in my mind and taunted me with the mocking laughter of my old bearded tormentor. That man, who called himself my grandfather, that man who abandoned me. Finally, I would prove him wrong. Finally I would let go of the nightmare of his sick games of light and shadow.

My fingers became fists and my palms were bitten by my nails. I could feel trickles of blood squishing between my fingers. The room was so silent that the drops of blood hitting the stone floor echoed through the small room. So focused was I on that mocking candle, that I didn't wince when the pain in my hands came, nor did I react to the thunder of my blood crashing into the floor. Se'Naat

Flayed

and the room vanished from my sight. I was so intent upon finally defeating this candle that it became only me and it locked in a duel to the death.

The flame stood there calmly. it didn't wave, flicker, or bend. It simply was unmoved at my anger or my will. Focusing so intensely on the flame, I took a deep breath, and the sweet incense that was always burning in the temple filled my lungs and went straight to my head. As I used my rage to push away everything else, my mind became a focused weapon of hate.

My lips were pressed so tightly together that I thought they might fuse in place. I focused the wheels of my mind into engines that tore at the curtain between our world and the hidden one that lay just beyond the veil. That hidden world is where the power of the universe could be tapped, where it could be harnessed by mere mortals. Beyond even that was a doorway into the realm of the gods themselves. Past that forbidden gate lay the power of creation itself. While my mind ground away the barrier between me and the unseen world, I pondered the forbidden gate. It was said that only one true wizard would live within our world at a time, one who was given the key to all things forbidden to others who might touch the power of the divine. My previous tormentor was thought to have been the holder of that sacred mantle.

Since the death of that coward, it was Se'Naat who held the office, and while he did not live in the ancient home of the wizard, he held the keys to the divine source in secret away from those who might try and gain access without the will of the gods. If I proved myself worthy, then I would become his apprentice. I would someday own the keys to the deepest of arcane secrets, but I had to defeat this uzkin' candle.

Chapter 10

Then I felt it, it was as if my mind had pushed through the hard barrier that lived between me and the hidden world. The drill of my thoughts sank deeply into that well of secrets, and my thoughts lit up as if they were made of the same fire in the stars. The world suddenly smelled of sunshine and spring mornings, and my heart was flush with love. From nowhere, my thoughts were invaded by something confusing. Thoughts unravelled like old memories suddenly reawakened. Images of a young girl and her sweet smile. Memories of two men dueling in the courtyard of a keep, one man smaller with salt and pepper hair, the other a blond giant. The happiness in my heart grew too sweet and too sorrowful. I felt tears leave my eyes and run down my cheeks.

"Alexander," Se'Naat's voice was calming. "Stay here, in this moment. Do not let your thoughts take control. You must master them. Harness the power and bend it to your will. It is you who is the master, boy, not the fickle whims of the universe."

These thoughts that filled my mind were all lies. Se'Naat had shown me what the old man did to his students. The wizard was always seeking his successor and would take promising students to his tower, far away. I had been taken as a small child and kept prisoner in the wizard's keep. Se'Naat had used his powers to unlock some fragments of my own memories for me, but had also revealed the truth. He removed the lies, and I saw the squalor in which the old man had kept his students, all the while pressing on them the memories of families they never had. Trying to find one of them that would take on the identity of his "grandchild". All these memories, all this joy, it was all lies. My anger over my stolen life coalesced in my thoughts into a dark mass. Into this shapeless thing, I poured all my anger, frustration, and misery. This dark thing hung over the images of sweet spring like a giant storm cloud about to burst. My thoughts soared over the landscape of this imaginary place, and I

Flayed

tore apart the weave of magic which gave it form in my thoughts. Just as Se'Naat had taught me, I took those anchoring threads of magic and sewed them into my formless anger, and created a spell. There it hung in the vastness of my hungry mind, waiting to be given form in the world.

I looked up into the divine heavens of my thoughts, and saw countless stars shimmering and shifting over me, and out of the corner of my mind's eye, I saw something shining brighter than any of these stars. I held onto the spell I had made, but I let my thoughts soar through the sky of the unseen world towards this glowing thing, and as I drew close I saw it for what it was. A gate, made out of light that seemed hidden there in the sky. I was ashamed that I could see the gate, for I did not feel worthy to even know it existed and yet, for a moment, I was tempted to forget about my challenge. My curiosity wanted to get beyond the gate, to see the divine secret that lay just on the other side. In my arrogance, I believed that all I had to do was touch the gate and it would open to me. All of the divine power would wash over my mind, and I would be illuminated.

"Alexander," Se'Naat called me back from my foolish quest in the hidden world. "Remain focused. Vanquish the light."

I opened my eyes, and without saying a word, I called forth the spell that I had crafted.

Power shot through my spine and down to my tight fists. My eyes felt as if they were on fire with raw energy, and the room was ablaze with light that only I could see. There on the table sat my unflinching enemy, that accursed candle. With this power rushing through me, I felt omnipotent. I could have torn apart the table, disintegrated the candle, and blown open the iron bound door. This blatant display of power was not the test, however, and now I understood why. To harness the arcane secrets of the universe

Chapter 10

and to be seduced by their secrets, but then to lose control would be to fail. To summon the power and only use enough to blow out a candle, that would show mastery and control.

My lips curled into a capricious smirk as I silently congratulated myself on solving the riddle that had so long plagued me. With a simple word, I brought my test to an end, "Out."

With the spell finally cast, I felt the power leave me. In the dark room, I could smell only the incense and the smoke from the extinguished candle, and I smiled at my accomplishment. Wielding that power had drained me, however, and I leaned back against the stone wall, breathing heavily.

Clapping echoed in the tiny room. "Well done, my boy," Se'Naat's voice called to me through the darkness. "You have passed the challenge of the candle." Blue light came to life in the room, and I saw Se'Naat pull his fingers away from the now-lit wick of the candle. The unusual light came from the flame that now danced on the wick, moved by some unfelt breeze. "I knew I was right to pick you, my boy."

"What happens now, Your Grace?" I asked, still out of breath.

"Oh, great things, Alexander." His toothy smile gave me chills. "Great things indeed."

From outside the body of my younger self, I watched as he and Se'Naat walked to the door. As it opened, I heard the anguished screams of a tortured soul, followed by the rending of flesh and bone. I followed them out into the hallway, and with each footfall of my younger self, I heard the sound of a hammer pounding an anvil. My mind reeled at the sounds, as they did not belong. Not here, not in this moment. My eyelids pressed together, trying to shove away the screaming and pounding, which grew louder and louder with every step of my younger self. Frustration boiled up through

Flayed

my body, and I screamed, only to open my eyes and see an even younger version of myself, dirty and lost in some dark woods. He looked at me dispassionately and raised a finger to his lips, urging me to be silent.

I screamed again, but there was no noise, and I was left alone in the dark woods. All the trees were barren, and the life of the land was gone. Green lushness had given way to grey cracks, and I felt the death of every living thing.

My body jolted awake with all my limbs coming to life at the same time. I was a bit embarrassed at the uncoordinated movement of my body, so I sheepishly looked around to see if anyone had noticed my sudden waking. Everyone around me was still asleep. Brin had shifted, with her body lying entirely on the pew next to me, but her boots still touching the stone floor. Tarissa and Avar were seated a row or so away, both their heads lying on the other person for support. I did not see Verif at first, but then I noticed her boots resting up on the armrest of one of the pews several rows back. Mavren, however, was nowhere to be seen.

I scanned the dark room around us and saw no changes to our environment. The doors that led to the street were still closed, and I assumed they remained barred. Standing up, I focused my senses to see if I could hear Mavren moving around somewhere beyond the main body of the temple. The whispers again drifted to my ears, and while I could not make out what they were saying, I knew that something foul lay at the other end of them. The shattered memories I had of this place, and of its ancient high priest, made me wary of anything that might remain here. Then I heard a muttering voice from the rooms beyond the altar.

Chapter 10

With hushed speed, I glided over to the doors that led to the hallways beyond and, once there, stopped to listen further. Someone was certainly in the deep recess of the temple's furthest rooms, and they were talking out-loud. The actual words I could not make out, but I could hear them. Looking back at Brin and finding her still asleep, Ukumog glowing fiercely by her side, I decided to see if I could discover the source of the voice. Surely, it had to be Mavren, but who would he be talking to?

Stalking through the hallways, I passed by doorways that led to empty barracks, abandoned kitchens, barren pantries, and a looted armory. The hallway split into two paths, and I listened carefully to see from which direction the sounds were coming and took that path. Emotions pushed through the fog of lost memories, and the hair on my neck began to stand up with every step I took. I was drawing close to the home of the foul priest himself. *With everything that had come to pass, it wasn't possible that he would still be down here, was it?* To push away my growing fear, I tried to think about what happened to Se'Naat. Try as I might, I could not remember what became of him. The cast of characters that played in the fragments of my dreamlike memory – I wasn't even sure what was entirely true either. These thoughts proved an ample distraction, and before long, I found myself at the doorway that led into the high priest's chambers in this dark temple.

Inside there was no light, but I could see through the darkness well enough. As I breached the doorway, I felt a gust of air rush past me, and it made me shiver. The furniture within the room had long since turned to formless debris. My eyes caught the texture of a scrap of elaborate cloth, and the glimmer of gold trim through the dust, but there was nothing of true value down here.

Flayed

In the back of the room, however, I found Mavren kneeling, facing the back wall. The wall itself had seen better days. It was cracked and broken open. Subterranean water trickled through the stones that used to form a wall, and then disappeared into the cracks and holes that replaced it. The wet stone cave was large enough for me to crawl through, but showed no signs of being carved by the hands of men. Mavren kept muttering to himself until I drew close enough to see that he was kneeling in front of a small altar much like the one from the main hall of the temple, thought it looked unspoiled.

"Can a sorrowful man not find a brief moment to pray?" Mavren broke his muttering and said to me without looking over his shoulder.

"I heard noises, and I had no idea where you had gone." I took a step back, not wishing to interrupt. "Sorry to disturb you."

"I grieve for the loss of my wife," his voice broke.

I nodded. "I know, Mavren. I'm sorry."

"No, you are not, Wrack. Did you think I could not perceive the pity in your face when we spoke of her that night? You are like all the others, you simply do not understand. I lost my sons to this curse, and when my wife could not be pried from her mourning and the madness began to take her, I swore that I would not let The Curse ruin her. Yet, for all my power, I was unable to stop it." He silently sobbed, never turning to show me the pain in his rotting face, "I was helpless, just as I have ever been. I failed my kingdom when Darion's army came. I failed again when my king fell to Andoleth's assassin, and again when I led our people into a ceaseless war. Then, to watch my family rot into nothing… I failed again. I cannot bear it!"

Chapter 10

I had no idea how to help him. None of the words that flashed through my mind seemed to be the right thing to say. Most of them seemed like they had a great chance to make things worse, so I just listened.

"Do you hear me, gods? Have you forsaken your most loyal of sons? I hear your whispers, but cannot make sense of the words."

My eyes grew larger at the mention of the whispers. Was he hearing the same thing I was?

"Abandon me not, oh dark lady! Most brilliant of kings, I call unto you. All the children of the heavens and the earth, I need your guidance! What is it that your humble servant should do? Please! Do not forsake me any longer!" His angry prayers were riddled with sobbing.

So passionate was his plea, so desperate his loneliness, that I was greatly moved. I wiped away a flood of grey tears from my own eyes as he begged the motionless altar. For my own part, I wished that they would answer him so that I, too, would know for certain that we had not been forsaken. As he talked, I felt the need in my soul for redemption rising. This darkness that we had all grown to understand as normal was a pestilence that must be lifted so that we could one day feel the warm sun upon our faces and know the sweet smell of life once again.

Yet for all Mavren's pleas and my silent hope, the altar did not move.

Eventually the shattered man who shared the room with me had poured the contents of his soul into the darkness, and receiving no reply, he collapsed into sorrow.

Trying to stem the flow of sympathetic tears from my own eyes, I closed my lids, and clenched my jaw. Silently, I called out for something, anything to give Mavren some hope. In part, my wish

Flayed

was a selfish one, for I feared what Mavren may do if he were lost to the maddening grief that gripped him. Unwilling to leave him alone, I found a space on the floor to sit and just be there with him, waiting until he could find the other side of his grief.

After a great period of silence, I saw the light of a torch coming down the hallway, and I called towards it, "It is alright. Mavren and I are back here. Please, do not come closer."

The torch stopped approaching, and Tarissa responded, quietly, "Very well. Call if you need anything." After that, the torchlight flickered its way away from Mavren and me.

After more time, I could take the silence no longer. I felt I needed to say something. I needed to show him that he was not alone. Without thinking, words just started spilling from my lips. "For what it is worth, Mavren. I do not consider you to be a failure. Through all this misery and torment, you still are fighting. Rather than give into the power that haunts you, your goal is one of redemption, not selfish greed or further power. These things that happened to you are terrible, and a lesser person would have been so wracked by misery that it could have consumed them. You are strong enough to have taken a different path, and through it all, you still hold onto that regal bearing that I know you had before. There is something to be said for that."

About half way through those words, he started to look at me, rather than at the floor or the altar. After taking a moment to think about what I had said, he responded, "Indeed, Wrack, your words are most gracious. While I do not entirely believe everything you have said, I appreciate you showing me another side of my plight. I believe that I have settled on a course of action. Come, let us discuss this with the others."

Chapter 10

We picked ourselves up off the floor and shook the dust from our clothing. Awkward silence travelled with us as we made our way back down the hallways toward our companions. Entering the main hall, we found them all still gathered there, and they spoke first as we approached.

"What the uzk were you doing back there?" Brin demanded.

I smiled. "Sorting out a few things, nothing to worry about."

She did not look satisfied with my answer.

"I scouted around. There are no supplies here," Tarissa said. "We will need to get food and water in short order. Would be helpful to gather information about what is happening on the surface, as well."

I nodded in agreement.

"That doesn't solve the underlying problem," Verif offered. "We need a longer plan than just surviving in this pit. Maybe we can get word to Bridain in Winterland."

"What are the Hunters going to do, Verif? Lay siege to Flay? We need to figure out what to do next, even if we get no further help." Avar sounded upset.

"Uzk, Avar. You don't have to bite her head off," Brin said. "We are just kicking around ideas."

"Sorry," Avar said. "I am tired and hungry. I didn't mean it."

Verif nodded, but she still looked hurt.

"I think that Tarissa's plan has the most merit. We need some uzkin' supplies if we are going to stay down here," Brin said. "What do you think, Wrack and Mavren?"

Flayed

"I know nothing of the Shadow Hunters in Winterland, so I'm afraid that I cannot give meaningful commentary on that specific plan, but I agree that we need to get you supplies. However, my plan is slightly different," Mavren offered.

"I'm listening," Brin crossed her arms and looked skeptical.

Mavren smiled. "I go to the castle that looms over our heads and I speak with my lord and master, Darion, about all of this mess. I twist the truth to make Gelraan the usurping villain and replace myself in His Majesty's good graces."

I thought for a moment and then started shaking my head. "I don't know, Mavren. Without knowing anything about the political climate out there, you could go out and never return. We need more information and we need supplies now." Motioning towards our human companions, "They could starve waiting for you to come back. Seems too risky."

"Excellent points, Wrack, but I still believe it is our best option," Mavren said, shaking his head. "If I know my liege at all, he will understand and believe me, but only if I act swiftly. Too many of Gelraan's whisperers spread rumors through the high city, and there will be no convincing him."

"How about this?" Tarissa interjected. "Wrack and I go out there and gather news and a small amount of food and then come back. Once we have more information, then you can act on this plan of yours. Certainly The King will not harden his heart to you in one day."

"Hrm..." Mavren rubbed his chin. "Your plan has merit, I grant you that, but I still think that a conversation between The King and myself would be the best move here." Without another word, he started moving towards the door.

"Mavren!" I called out. "Where are you going? We haven't made a final decision."

Chapter 10

"Begging your pardon, Wrack, but I do not need your permission to go and attend my king's court..." Mavren replied, a dark impatience brewing in his voice.

Brin shifted, and Ukumog creaked on the ring on her belt. "I say we let Tarissa go out and gather information and supplies. We need to be pragmatic about this, right, Mavren?"

Mavren stopped in his tracks. "My dear, when I suggested that you should practice more restraint when on this path, it was meant for just you. Please do not lecture me about prudence. If anything, I have been the most patient of participants in this scheme. Now it is my turn to take action!" His voice echoed through the temple.

This was unlike the Mavren Ruthrom that I had come to know over the past year. "Mavren, you are not acting like yourself."

"Indeed, Wrack? I am pleased that after ages of this tormented life, I can still surprise those who barely know me!" Mavren was anything but calm. Green embers glowed behind his white eye, and I feared he was about to lash out with power against me.

"Is this what Serena would want?" Verif casually tossed the words at him, but seemed to know that they would plant hooks in his mind. "Turn yourself in blindly if you want, but I do not think that she would see reason in this plan."

The embers burst forth into a green fire burning out of his eye. While his rage was evident, he spoke with an unnerving calm. "Do not ever speak of what my wife would or would not want. You did not know her as I did."

"True." Verif was unaffected by his obvious rage. "I did talk to Grimoire about her a great deal before he left, though. Did he know her? It sure sounded like he did."

Flayed

Instantly, the fire stopped licking the air around Mavren's brow, but the glow still remained. "Fine. Go forth and recover your information and supplies. When you return, however, I will go and see my king."

Without missing a beat Tarissa said, "C'mon Wrack, let's go."

Avar started gathering his things.

"No, Avar. Just Wrack and me," Tarissa said immediately.

"Why him?" Avar pouted.

"Because, with that black robe, he can blend in. He also can see and hear things that you cannot. Sorry, sweetheart, but you would just distract me." She smiled at him in the same way that Brin always looked at me. It was the first time that I had caught this particular look from her.

"Very well," Avar groaned. "You keep her safe, Wrack. Do you hear me?"

"Aye aye, captain." I responded.

Mavren stepped towards the door with us, and his human form disappeared into a that living green mist. He glided under the door and opened the bar for Tarissa to step out into the daylight beyond.

Having grown used to the darkness of the abandoned temple, I shielded my eyes from the rays of the sun. Tarissa pulled her leather hood up over her golden hair, and I followed suit.

Murks let me know that he, too, was ready for this mission, and crawled up into my hood and hid behind my neck to provide a third set of eyes on this dangerous venture.

"You ready?" Tarissa asked, slinging an empty bag over her shoulder.

Chapter 10

I nodded and looked down at the place where my shadow should have been. Against the stark grey of the stone road, it was easier to notice that I cast no shadow. Pointing to hers, I asked, "Do you think that will be a problem?"

She shook her head. "Not at all. Just be my shadow. Let me do all the talking and keep your eyes out. We will be fine. If we do our jobs right, no one will even notice us."

Her confidence was infectious, and for that I was extremely grateful. Taking a deep breath, we started the long climb up one half of the horseshoe road that lead back into the high city.

Flayed

Chapter 11

"Just let me do all the talking," Tarissa ordered me as we walked up the path. "If you just follow me around and watch my back, we will be fine. Actually talking to anyone might cause them to pay more attention to you, and we could end up in trouble that way."

I understood, but I immediately felt incensed that my participation would be nothing but listening all over again. "Why did you bring me with you if you just needed someone to watch your back?"

Tarissa gave a quiet giggle. "I needed someone, and you seemed to need to get out of that place. Seemed like a good match."

I chuckled. "Alright then, let's get this thing done."

"We are going into the low city. I know a pathway there that is never guarded."

"Don't we want information about what happened after the fire?" I asked.

She glanced over at me briefly. "We do, but it is unlikely that we will get real information in the high city. People will just spout what The King wants them to say. No, we need information from the real folks here in Flay. They always know the truth. Even

Flayed

if the masses here eat up the lies that Kalindir serves them, there are some who do not. Thankfully, this is not my first time to Flay, so I know exactly who to ask."

We avoided the guard and most of the people on the roads in the high city. Often, I got the feeling that we were being watched, and glancing over my shoulder I would see nothing but The King's castle looming behind us. A few times, it gave me shivers. When we arrived at the wall that separated the high city and the low city, Tarissa made a line directly for a cellar door that seemed to be built into a building that was right next to the wall. The space between the wall and the building was barely enough for me to stick my hand into and was overgrown with vines.

Once we were safely inside the abandoned cellar, Tarissa said, "There wasn't always a wall between the high and low cities here. This building, I'm told, was a pub once. No one uses it anymore. Well, no one except smugglers, thieves, and spies."

She walked over to a wall and tapped the stones three times. Shortly after, the wall moved inward, and a small door receded into the wall a bit and slid to one side. A bald man wearing ragged clothing peeked out from the hole. "Ah, Tarissa. Good seeing you again. With all the bustle in high city, I didn't know if we would be seeing you again." He looked over at me. "Who is your friend."

Pressing something shiny into his hand she said, "I thought you weren't in the business of asking stupid questions, Tomas." Her wry smile told me that these two knew each other well.

"Yeah, yeah. Sometimes I forget meself, that's all." He checked his palm. "Right, off you go, then." He disappeared through the hole.

Tarissa moved to follow him, and looked back at me. "Tomas is in the business of keeping secrets. Don't worry about him." She smiled, and then also disappeared.

Chapter 11

The other side was much like the room we had come from, except this one looked like the cellar to an actual pub. Kegs lined the wall of the cellar, and the stench of stale beer assaulted my senses. Tarissa motioned for me to keep following her, and I heard the stone door close behind us. We weaved our way through the maze of kegs and storage to a stairway that led up to the main part of the pub. We found ourselves in a hallway that led both to the kitchen and to the main room. Following the latter route, we ended up in a rather busy common room. The service was abuzz with lunch, which also seemed to have no end of demand for the beers and ales that were kept in the cellar below. The noise and commotion made it easy to vanish into the crowd, and so we did.

I followed Tarissa through the crowd to a staircase that led to a second common room. This one was mostly filled with shadowy booths with heavy velvet curtains that could be drawn over the openings out into the center aisle, where servers moved around taking care of their customers. The booths were mostly empty, but the people who were in there gave me the feeling that they were all up to some shady business. I tried not to stare at the people as I scanned the room, but when my eyes did meet any of the guests' within the booths, they invariably returned my glance with a malicious glare.

Tarissa made her way directly to a booth near the back of the room, which we found empty. Once inside, she pulled loose the rope from one of the curtains, and when I tried to loosen the other one, she gave me a light tap and shook her head, then motioned for me to come sit next to her on her side of the booth. I was extremely curious what she was up to, but I followed along. We sat in silence, undisturbed even by the girls taking orders for food or drink, for a great while. Then I heard someone cough from the other side of the

Flayed

closed curtain, and Tarissa responded by putting a coin on the edge of the table that was open to the aisle. Swiftly, a hand scooped up the coin, and then Tarissa closed the other curtain.

"Sorry for all the odd behavior, Wrack," she whispered. "There is just a way of doing things here, and I don't have time to explain it all to you. Just play along and keep your hood up."

I remembered how Avar said that Tarissa used to collect information for the Shadow Hunters, and I could not help but feel like I was now tied into some strange game of intrigue where I did not know all the rules. Still, I complied with her request and checked my hood to make sure that it kept my face in shadow, even from anyone who might sit with us in the booth.

After a short time, the curtain parted, and a man dressed in the well-worn garb of a gentleman sat opposite us and closed the curtain behind us. His oiled hair and trimmed mustache made him look a bit silly to me, but from what I saw in the high city, I was sure he was just being fashionable.

Without wasting a moment he whispered, "Tarissa, darling, it is wonderful to see you again." With speed and grace he, gently took one of Tarissa's hands and kissed her knuckles.

"Oh, Joseph, always the charmer." Tarissa gave a flirty laugh as she retrieved her hand.

He smiled, completely ignoring me. "As much as I would like for you to come here to visit me, I know you are here on business," he whispered playfully. "What is it that I can do for you?"

"I need to know what is going on in the city. I hear rumors about some big shakeup in high city, and I need the truth, not the rumors of peasants." Tarissa was direct, but maintained her flirty tone.

Joseph chuckled, "The truth isn't cheap, little dove."

Chapter 11

Before he could even finish the word, Tarissa placed a small embroidered pouch on the table between them. "White fern seeds, from Skullspill."

Joseph's face lit up. "How did—"

"Mariano sends his regards." Tarissa smiled. "I know you two don't get along anymore, but I was there, and I knew you wanted these for your garden."

He looked conflicted, but he reached towards the pouch.

With graceful speed, Tarissa stabbed her forefinger through the loop of the strings of the pouch, preventing Joseph from scooping it up. "We have a deal?"

He gave an unconvincing smile. "Of course we have a deal, Tarissa dear."

She smiled and was silent while he checked the contents of the pouch. His long nose entered the mouth of the pouch and he inhaled the scent of the contents deeply before sighing with relief.

"If you inhale them all, you won't have any left to make more seeds," Tarissa playfully reminded him.

He gave an uneasy smile. "Of course, dear. You have arrived just in time, too. Planting season for white fern is upon us, and I have space in my garden."

"Don't let those Chundai farmers catch you growing this stuff near their plants. They get rather particular about their soil."

"Please, you talk to me like I have never had to deal with those elite farmers before. I live here in Flay, don't I?"

Tarissa laughed. It seemed genuine, though I didn't find our company to be particularly amusing.

Joseph tucked away the pouch and asked, "Specifically, what is it you want to know?"

Flayed

"Well, I know about the criminal that the guard caught months ago. The one that they were calling a traitor. I think they strung him up in the marketplace, is that right?"

I hadn't told Tarissa about Gordo's body being on display, but she must have heard about it during those months I was locked away inside Mavren's estate. My interest was suddenly piqued, but I made sure not to change my stoic demeanor.

"Forgive me, Tarissa dear, but you don't often visit me and bring a friend."

"Don't mind him, Joseph, he is with me."

"But, my dear—"

"If you don't want my business, I will happily take my gift and go elsewhere." Tarissa's tone suddenly had an edge – nowhere near the harshness of Brin's conversational tone, but for the soft and quiet Tarissa to adopt threats, it seemed a little strange to me.

"Hold on now. There is no need to be drastic." Joseph pulled away from Tarissa, and placed a hand over the pocket where he had shoved the pouch filled with seeds. "I will tell you what you want to know, and then some. I just can't be too careful. Things are going crazy in the city, my dear. I have never seen days like this before."

"What do you mean?" Tarissa asked.

"Well…" Joseph started. "That traitor being strung up in the market was really just the first stone in an avalanche of issues. Supposedly, there were more criminals on the loose in the city that were friends of the one they put on display. Tiberion came here himself to ask about them, but all of this was news to me. I remembered that they had announced the capture and execution of traitors, plural, and it seemed odd to me that there was only one on display, and that he was already dead."

"Did Tiberion believe you?" Tarissa asked.

Chapter 11

Joseph nodded. "I believe so. Though his brother came by a few more times and disrupted my business. Said he was looking for someone carrying a strange looking sword. Again, I had nothing to offer him."

"His brother? You mean Marius?"

Joseph gave her a serious look. "Do you know of another revenant that calls Tiberion his brother?"

"Hrm, I suppose not. What has them all riled?"

His eyebrows went up in exasperation. "That is just it, no one knows. I even did some poking around on my own. It was refreshing to seek out information again. I think having this place has made me soft."

Tarissa laughed. "I can't imagine trying to retire like you did."

"Tarissa dear, who said I ever retired?"

"You did!" She laughed again. "When you bought this place you said that you were stepping out of the game. Too much trouble, you said."

"Yes, well… Old habits, I suppose." He smiled and waved his hand in the air. "Never mind all that, where was I?"

She calmed her sweet laughter. "Um. You were seeking out information."

"Right!" he said, sliding back into the groove of his story. "I asked all my old contacts and some new ones. No one knew what was going on. I heard something about a prison break which led to a sewer flood, but apart from the flood, I couldn't find any sources on that. Then there was this whole thing with Lord Mavren Ruthrom."

Tarissa furrowed her brow. "What happened there? House Ruthrom has been close with the royal family for countless years."

"So everyone thought." Joseph leaned towards Tarissa and whispered, "Word is that Mavren is a traitor."

Flayed

Tarissa's face shifted to one of complete disbelief. I knew it was an act, but she played it well. "What?"

"I know, hard to even imagine. His majesty is putting out the call for Mavren to return to the castle so that they can get to the bottom of a fire that completely leveled the Ruthrom estate. People are saying that multiple bodies were found in the ruins of the place, and a few people even died trying to put out the fire."

Reflexively, Tarissa covered her mouth pretending to be shocked at this news, most of which I knew she already knew. "Is there some conspiracy brewing? It seems unlikely that Lord Ruthrom would plot against The King. They are both ancient and immortal. What would he stand to gain?"

Joseph shrugged. "Got me. My people inside the castle say that His Highness, Prince Rimmul, was the one to break the news to the court. Also, Gelraan Darkweaver is also at the castle. I have it on good authority that Prince Darkweaver rushed into the castle on the night of the fire and only wanted to speak to Rimmul. People in the know are saying that Darkweaver may have been the one to uncover the plot."

"Uzk." Tarissa leaned back, and ran her hands over her face. "What the uzk is happening in the city?"

Joseph nodded. "War is happening, my dear. War. I got a report this morning from a merchant that was outside the gates when they went up at sunrise. He said that The Baron's army was marching en masse towards Flay. I imagine it is only a matter of time before that news starts a flood of panic. My money is on Juindar pressing the court to institute martial law until the threat has passed. If I were you, Tarissa, I would get out of the city while you still can."

Chapter 11

We sat in silence as Tarissa absorbed those last details. I tried to imagine how we would deal with the city if martial law was engaged. It seemed like we only had one option – escape. Either we use Elaina's blood to open the thorny walls of the low city, or we climb over the stone wall behind the castle and into the ravine below. Maybe head for Winterland and let The Baron and The King wage their war on each other. Except I knew what that meant, the innocent people here in Flay would suffer. No matter how deluded they were in believing that these cursed men were their saviors, they did not deserve to be torn apart by this never-ending tug of war over the dying hills between here and Skullspill.

Tarissa broke the silence. "How far out is the army?"

"If that merchant is to be believed? Two or three days."

A sigh escaped Tarissa's lips.

"I don't know how much you know about armies, my dear, but that means that there are probably scouts already outside the city, and perhaps even spies inside these walls. It seems that our years of gluttony and contentment may be at an end, at least for now. There is no conceivable way that The Baron's men will be able to breach the walls of the lower city, and even if they do, I have my escape route already planned out."

"I can't even think about what else I should ask," Tarissa admitted, still overwhelmed by the news.

"That's good, because I don't have much more to offer. Unless you want to know who has been stealing dogs over by Pigeon Street," Joseph chuckled.

"We should get going, we have plans to make." Tarissa shifted in her seat.

Joseph nodded. "For what it is worth, my dear, I have no doubt that you will be fine. You have always struck me as a resourceful survivor."

Flayed

"Until next time, Joseph," Tarissa said.

He nodded. "Until then. Tell Mariano thank you for the seeds." He pushed apart the curtain and left, leaving the curtains closed.

"Well. I didn't expect that," Tarissa whispered.

"Which part?" I asked.

She shrugged. "The part with the army at the gates."

"That's funny," I said. "I always feel like there is an army following us."

After throwing me a glance that told me that she thought I was an idiot, I shrugged. The shrug claimed a tiny chuckle from her.

"Right, well, I suppose we should walk around, get a sense of the air, and then head back to the temple." She pulled the curtain aside, and we disappeared back into the crowd.

Instead of heading down into the cellar and back beyond the stone walls high city, we went out into the streets of the low city. I immediately took note of the looming thorny walls, lined with watchtowers that hugged the small metropolis. It was both comforting and confining to see those walls. As we walked, I remembered how the air felt right before The King's army attacked Yellow Liver. The air here felt calmer. It still had the controlled serenity that I had noticed upon first climbing onto the streets. Everything was so finely crafted and orderly, I could not even imagine what it would be like with an army at the gates. My mind tried to picture machines of war lobbing flaming balls of stone over the high walls, the thorny brambles themselves ablaze, chaos and death charging through the streets and claiming the lives and minds of the citizens of this calm place.

Chapter 11

Everywhere I seemed to go, destruction followed me. First, the devastation to Yellow Liver, and then the ruin of Sanctuary. I did not want to see this beautiful city that was filled with artists and craftsmen laid low by a harrowing battle between bickering immortals. I felt helpless to stop the grinding machine of war. Pushing the dire thoughts from my mind, I tried to focus on following Tarissa through the streets.

We found ourselves in the marketplace of the low city. Smells from the various food, perfume, and incense vendors assaulted my senses. The sheer volume of color, sound, and motion was akin to a battle in and of itself. Merchants barked from the safety of their carts, calling for passersby to purchase or sample their goods. The pathways through this space were overflowing with a river of people. The outer edges slowed or stopped at the carts of vendors, but the closer one became to the center of the street, the faster the flow was moving. At times this movement went in both directions.

I let all the sounds, smells, and sights in and reveled in this beautiful mess that lay in the heart of a city so organized, one would never have expected this haven of orderly insanity. We would stop to see the goods or try a sample of some food along the way, all the while Tarissa's trained ears were absorbing the chatter of the people around us. Her collection of secrets and information grew rapidly from the wildfire of information being casually discarded around us. Eventually we found what she was looking for, the same vendor that had seen the army of The Baron's men.

"I heard something about an army headed this way," Tarissa casually whispered to the merchant.

The man stopped what he was doing, and gave Tarissa a wide-eyed look.

She shrugged. "So that wasn't you that I heard about?"

Flayed

"Who ye been talkin' to?" he asked, wiping the sweat from his face with a rag that came from one of the pockets in his heavy coat.

The merchant's black tangle of hair curled out from under his colorful pie-shaped hat. His coat was made of wool and had alternating dark colors in the many panels with made up its loose folds. His hands seemed clean, save for the dirt which outlined the yellow nails which crusted the ends of his stubby fingers.

"I'm a friend of Joseph Swift," Tarissa responded, her eyes drifting over the knickknacks and strange fruits on the merchant's cart. "Is that a green fruit?" Her hand came up from the cart with a green fruit that looked a lot like an apple.

"Um... Yeah, that is a green fruit from Skullspill's orchards." The merchant seemed taken aback by Tarissa's quick change of subject.

"I love green fruit." Tarissa smiled. "They are just so crunchy and juicy! Yummy!" She took a bite from the fruit. The flesh of it was green, even beyond the peel, not like the apples I remembered from my various glimpses into the past. "That is a really good green fruit."

"That'll be two silver, m'lady," the merchant said and then took Tarissa's money. He helped other customers buying his goods, giving Tarissa and I sideways glances.

When she finished eating her green fruit, Tarissa wiped some of the emerald juices from her chin. With a satisfied smile on her face, she casually said to the merchant, "That was an excellent green fruit. I haven't had one like that since I was sitting in Mariano's office."

The merchant gulped.

"You know Mariano, don't you?" Tarissa asked; her voice was sweet, but had a bite in her inflection.

Chapter 11

The merchant reached up and took the hat from his head, exposing his balding scalp to the sky above. The difference in skin tone showed that his hat did not often leave its proper perch upon his skull. "Yes ma'am. Mariano be me source for the green fruit. You know 'im?"

"Bastard owes me a favor or two." Tarissa smiled and then leaned in to whisper quietly, "So, tell me what you know about the coming army."

The merchant threw a blanket over his wares and then motioned for the two of us to meet him over by the wagon parked behind it. Once the three of us were collected, he started to speak, "Well, miss, we was bringin' our wares here, like we always do this time of the year. We like to spend the winter here in Flay and then head back to Skullspill with the bounty of the spring. House Chundai has been payin' us for years to bring green fruit up this way. We thinks they're tryin' to make it grow up this way. Won't work though. Gotta have some of that slime what bleeds from the falls for the trees to grow properly. Anyways, our cart travels a bit slow, and we made a stop in Corner before makin' the long trek down The King's Road. Well, when we connected back with the road, there was a cloud of dust behind us durin' the daytimes, but I never saw no fires at night. Odd thing, we thought, but we have seen worse…"

"Army probably did not want to light fires so that they could stay hidden. Poor soldiers," Tarissa offered in the merchant's pause.

He nodded. "Makes a fair bit of sense. Anyway, about a day after passing Marrowdale, a handful of men on horses passed us. These weren't no ordinary travellers. They all had armor emblazoned with the red jawless skull of The Baron's men. They even gave us nasty looks as they passed our cart. We were scared,

Flayed

so our pace slowed a bit. After another day or so, the army actually started to catch up to us, because we were slowin' our pace. Scared us, it did. We could see the outlines of big carts, which we think were war machines, and at their front was the banner of the Jawbone. You know who the Jawbone is, yeah?"

Tarissa nodded. "The Baron's personal hit squad. He doesn't commit those men to anything that isn't important."

"Yeah." The merchant wrung his hands nervously. "After we saw the banner, we picked up the pace a bit. After another day or so, they started dropping back, and then we were able to outpace 'em. Never saw that handful of horses again, though. We figure they were scouts or something."

"They probably were." Tarissa produced a few coins from a pouch and handed them to the merchant. "Thanks for the news. Any word from Yellow Liver? Corner is close to it. Did you hear anything while you were there?"

"Not while I was in Corner, no. But when we was in Skullspill there was talk about Yellow Liver. Apparently there is a new mayor there, Melanie something. She has organized a small militia and such to help keep order. The Baron even took his men out of the city some time back. It is like he doesn't care about the place anymore." He rubbed his nose with the handkerchief before continuing, "Can't say we blame him. That place is nasty, and now with them ghouls running rampant – not a safe place for anyone."

"What about the ghouls? Any news about them?" I broke Tarissa's rules, but my curiosity could not be contained.

The merchant looked at me like he never expected me to speak. "Haven't heard much about them. As far as we can tell, the ghouls are keeping to their part of the city. Still too risky for our

Chapter 11

blood. Those flesh-eaters gotta eat eventually. Only a matter of time, we think, before they come rushing over the walls in waves with a dark hunger that won't be denied."

"Thanks," I said.

Tarissa gave me a sour look before speaking to the merchant, "Yes. Thank you for your information. Mind if I take another green fruit for a friend?"

"As long as you're paying, I don't mind one bit." He waved us back to the front of his booth where he sold Tarissa another green fruit, and we were on our way.

Cutting through the crowd was like walking through a constantly shifting maze. More than once I lost Tarissa in the crowd, but I was able to eventually find her again, her blond ponytail standing out against the wash of grey stone and dark colored clothing. Distracted by trying to make sure I kept up with Tarissa, I completely missed our rapid approach of the raised platform in the center of the marketplace. To one side of it was a frame made of mismatched wood tied together with stained and fraying rope. How it was constructed, however, was not what drew our attention.

Tied to the frame, with arms and legs spread into an x, was the ruined corpse of our dead friend Gordo. My eyes fell on this body, and at first, I had no idea who it was, the body was so destroyed, but then a tuft of remaining hair, the general height, and the sign that read "traitor" hanging over his head clued me in. It felt like someone put a rock in my throat and kicked me in the gut. Fear of exposing our connection to him was the only thing that prevented me from falling to my knees. Tarissa stood under the gruesome scene of our dead friend stripped of all his clothes and most of his flesh, for a moment, emotionless. I, too, was in utter shock.

"Let's get the uzk out of here," she said.

Flayed

I nodded and followed her without saying a word. Brin flashed through my mind, and worry grew in my soul like a wildfire unchecked. With every step, my fear grew, and I had a primal need to know that she was safe. Tarissa seemed carried by a similar worry. The two of us left the market with as much speed as we thought we could get away with, and when we were sure no one was watching, we sprinted towards the place where our loved ones were hopefully safely stowed away.

Our journey back to our friends was like trying to outrun a storm. The thoughts of Gordo's corpse filled our hearts with fear. If that wasn't bad enough, it felt like the whispers and worry over the impending attack by The Baron's army was rolling through the city in our wake. Trying to blend in, we had to contain our desire to speed through the streets back to the forbidden temple where we hoped our friends remained undetected. In my heart, I knew that the Juindar brothers had not forgotten about us; Gordo's corpse had told us that. It made me further worry that our friends were not safe.

As we swam through the streets crowded with the evening traffic of Flay, I felt as if eyes were always watching us. It was the same feeling as when we were stalked by the hooked wielding monster that attacked us on the road, and even how I felt went Frost was stalking us near the town of Regret. Each time I looked over my shoulder, I saw nothing overtly stalking us. Still, my senses told me otherwise.

Trying to forget the feeling of being watched, I silently followed Tarissa as she wove our way back to Joseph's pub, the Golden Swan. Inside the tavern, the room was packed and loud. Boisterous folk were screaming and laughing. There was barely enough room to push through the people standing in the aisles between the tables. After what we had seen, just a short time

Chapter 11

earlier, I found their celebrations bordering on offensive. Logically, I knew that they were not celebrating the terrible display of my lovely friend, but my rage was not willing to listen.

"We should check in with Swift before we pass back over," Tarissa said.

"I don't have time to wait for him," I said. "There is a fire in me, and only knowing that Brin, Avar, and Verif are ok will put it out."

Tarissa nodded. "I feel the same. Screw protocol, let's go."

Without another word, we headed for the stairs that led to the cellar. Just before I turned the corner to descend into the belly of the pub, I felt the same sense that someone was following us. Looking over my shoulder, my eyes met with someone who was certainly focused on us. His eyes didn't flee from my gaze. Instead, it felt like a battle of wills. He was standing in the middle of the common room, staring at me through the hallway. Dark was the skin of his face, darker than the fair skin that was prevalent in Flay, but not nearly as dark as Prince Gelraan's. His mustache was thick and brushed away from his mouth, but curled a little at the ends. His manner of dress looked like nothing else I had seen before, here in Flay or elsewhere.

Suddenly, one of the serving girls bumped into this unknown man, breaking his unblinking gaze, and I was freed from the contest. Before turning away from him, I saw a dagger tucked in his belt that looked familiar, but I could not place it.

As I moved swiftly down the stairs to catch Tarissa before she vanished through the secret passage back into the high city, I pored over all my memories and thoughts, and came up with no reason why this man or his dagger should be familiar to me. It was a puzzle that haunted me all the way back to the doors of the hidden temple.

Flayed

Tarissa pulled back the wooden beam that barred the door from opening on the inside, and quickly we had returned to the dark safety of the temple. Before we could even make it through the hallway that led to the chapel where we left our friends, raised voices travelled to our worried ears. It took me no time at all to realize that Brin was upset about something, as it was her voice that was muttering and then mixing in loud exclamations. The voice that grumbled in response was low and reserved. This told me that it was Mavren.

"What is going on here?" Tarissa broke the conversation as we entered the room.

Our collected friends all gave us frustrated looks, but it was Verif who answered, "Mavren is still trying to leave."

"Some of us have the faith in our ancient alliances. His Majesty will not betray our unique bond," Mavren said. He sounded like someone who was trying exceptionally hard to convince himself.

"I am so tired of this uzkin' conversation," Brin muttered under her breath as she walked away from Mavren. "What news from the world outside this dark box?"

I moved over to meet Brin and gave her a hug. She returned it warmly, and I saw the fiery anger in her eyes fade to their usual smolder. As usual, I found the smell of her to be a welcome intoxication, but I dared not linger in that happy place for long. Shifting to take Brin's hand, I took a seat in the pews, but she was not interested in sitting, so she let go of my hand as I moved out of reach. She was focused on Tarissa, who was now resting against the side of one of the pews on the other side of the aisle from us.

Chapter 11

"Well..." Tarissa started. "The word from my savvy contacts is that Mavren is being sought for questioning, and it didn't seem like a polite request." She turned to speak directly to The Rotting One, "It seems that the fire has done more than raised concerns, and Gelraan seems to be in league with Prince Rimmul."

Mavren's shoulders dropped.

"That isn't even the start of the best news..." Tarissa sighed. "It seems that our old friend, The Baron, has his army not far away."

No one was happy to hear this news. Verif sat up with shock. Avar stood with alarm. Mavren hung his head and planted his face in his rotten palms. Brin grabbed Ukumog's handle, and her jaw flexed.

Tarissa continued, "We have a day, maybe two, before they arrive."

"What is the composition of said force?" Mavren asked.

"I couldn't get a troop count, but the merchant who saw the force said that they might have siege weapons. It sounds like a full-on assault," Tarissa said. "Our best course of action is to use some of Elaina's blood to flee through the walls and get out of the city."

Mavren shook his head. "If I flee, then Rimmul will use Andoleth's attack to poison the well of good faith I may still have with his father. No, I cannot run."

"Did you not hear me, Mavren? The Princes are conspiring against you already. The court already believes that you are to blame for the deaths of all the bodies found in ruins of the house, even though we know it was Gelraan who did it." Tarissa showed her frustration. It was the first time I had actually seen her angry. It was a cold whispering anger, the kind you might expect in calculating murderers. The look in her eyes was a bit unsettling.

Flayed

Brin shook her head. "If we wait too long, The Baron's army will circle the walls, and there will be no way out."

"What about Grumth?" Avar asked.

"I don't know if he even matters anymore." Brin gave a frustrated sigh. "But if we leave, then all our work here is for uzkin' nothing."

"I'm pretty sure that the work we have done here is already ruined," Verif seemed to enjoy saying to Brin.

"Uzk!" Brin screamed and began pacing around.

Avar took a step towards Brin. "What is our goal here now? Our contacts and the efforts we were making through Mavren have gone up in smoke..." He suddenly looked embarrassed and turned to Mavren. "Sorry. I didn't mean—"

Mavren waved a hand at Avar with a sullen look on his face. "I understand."

"Without those allies, we are stalled." Avar's selection of words seemed more carefully chosen. "So, what is our next step? We need a goal."

A pregnant silence filled the temple.

Mavren straightened his back. "I dare say, it seems I am the only one here with a plan of action."

"Uzk!" Brin howled with frustration. "We are not letting you go back to your murderous master. There is no telling what he will do to you, or what information he will glean from your mind."

"While I cannot be certain, I doubt that reading minds is in His Majesty's wheelhouse," Mavren said. "We must take some action. Staying here seems like a terrible idea."

Avar lit up. "Did either of you happen to bring back any food or water?"

Tarissa's face fell. "In our rush to return, we forgot."

The humans in the temple groaned.

Chapter 11

"I did bring back a green fruit, but only one. I wanted Avar to try it."

Avar's face lit up. "Oh! You always talked about the green fruit from Skullspill," he said as he moved over to Tarissa.

"How will that feed the rest of us?" Verif scoffed.

"We can share it," Avar offered.

Verif rolled her eyes and sighed in frustration.

"It is better than nothing," he said.

"I cannot take any more of this," Mavren said as he started walking towards the door. "I am going up to the castle to speak with His Majesty."

"The uzk you are." Brin's hand still lay threatenly upon Ukumog's handle. Blue light from the runes upon its surface grew in slight intensity.

Mavren twirled around to face Brin as he strode down the aisle, still continuing to move away from us. "I can appreciate the pressure of this current predicament, Lady Brin, but I am simply not going to remain here while my city is under attack."

The same strange whispers I had heard before started drifting to my ears from deeper inside the temple, and I found myself distracted.

"Mavren... I am warning you." Brin's voice was sharp.

Mavren laughed. "You are warning me, Brin? Perhaps you forget who you are talking to, my dear. I am thousands of years old, not to mention the power my accursed state grants me. Don't flatter yourself."

"*Clink!*" Ukumog replied, its runes blazing with bright blue fire.

Flayed

"Ah, so that is how it will be." Mavren stopped moving towards the door. "You would bring the weapon of The Betrayer against me in order to stop me. Now that does sound interesting. Perhaps we should see what all the fuss is about."

Brin brought the black blade up and held it with both hands, leaving her other sword in its scabbard. "We don't need to fight." Brin's tone said otherwise. "If you would just see sense here..."

Mavren laughed, the green light in his eyes slowly coming to life. "My dear, you are the one who is not seeing sense. There is no other option. Only The King can grant us safe haven here in this city. If we delay, we will be fighting both him and Andoleth's army. Imagine facing both of the Juindar brothers, Prince Rimmul, and a host of other revenants. Is that what you want?"

The whispering slowly grew louder, like an insect daring to get closer and closer to my ears. Looking at my companions, I seemed to be the only one troubled by this particular annoyance.

"Master, you must do something!" Murks screamed in my head, bringing me back to the conflict that was playing out before my eyes.

Verif, Avar, and Tarissa starting moving to flanking positions around Mavren.

"Ah, so now your friends have entered our little game? Eh?" Mavren mocked. "Please, step back. I have no desire to hurt any of you." Mavren's hands started leaking a green mist that drifted slowly to the ground.

As his power awakened, so did mine. Energy shot through my spine, causing dark power to stream upwards from my hands like plumes of black and purple smoke.

Chapter 11

Mavren's eyes caught mine, and he snarled. "So, this is how it is? All of you turn against us? I thought that at least some of you would see sense here. No matter, things have turned how they must."

"What the uzk does that even mean?" Brin shouted.

Mavren smiled and raised his hands, throwing clouds of billowing green mist in Brin's direction.

The circle around Mavren widened as those surrounding him avoided the mist. As it crawled over the pews, I could see decay ravage the remaining life from the wood. The Rotting One smiled at me with a sadistic grin.

"Mavren!" I shouted. "This isn't who you are."

"I'm afraid it is, old friend," and with a quiet roar, he lunged at Brin leaving a streak of green mist which hung like a pestilence in the air.

Brin swung Ukumog in an arc in front of her just in time to deflect Mavren's acidic touch. Mavren howled in pain with an unearthly voice.

"It bites deep, this blade, but not deep enough," Mavren muttered through a feral snarl. With a growl, he leapt at Brin again, bouncing from pew to pew, tossing them, breaking and throwing them as he went by.

Verif muttered something and a streak of silver light flashed through the room striking Mavren before he could pounce on his target. He crashed through more pews and landed a few paces from where I stood.

"We don't have to do this, Mavren!" Brin screamed.

Flayed

"Hush your screeching, child! You know not what forces are arrayed against you!" Mavren's unnatural voice boomed through the temple as he stood up, splinters of shattered pew falling off his rotten body like heavy snowflakes. "You simply cannot win, not even with that foul artifact that you have no right to wield."

Brin's face was flushed with anger. Her fingers tightened around Ukumog's leather wrapped handle. "I have every right, foul thing," she said calmly.

Mavren turned to me, his sadistic smile oozing green ichor. "Behold, Wrack. I shall make your beloved girl suffer."

While he was fixated on me, Brin leapt across the room with inhuman speed and brought the black blade down upon the distracted Mavren Ruthrom. Ukumog burned with terrible glee as it sliced flesh and broke bone. The Rotting One howled like the monstrous thing that lay behind his glowing eyes.

Before Brin could loose the blade from Mavren's shoulder, he turned and threw her across the room. Brin gave a ferocious battle cry as she sailed over pews and crashed into one of the stone pillars some distance away. Without missing a beat, Mavren started moving towards the door that led out into the street. Avar and Tarissa moved to intercept him and ended up standing side by side facing Mavren who was moving with dire purpose.

"Mavren, why are you doing this?" I shouted across the room.

The Rotting One stopped in his tracks, laughed at the two blond humans standing in his way, then turned to face me.

A flash of worry came to me from my connection with Murks, and he popped out from his pocket and slid out my sleeve to the floor. My focus remained on the undead man who I had finally come to think might actually be our ally against the darkness.

Chapter 11

I was sickened by the twisted look on Mavren's rotten face. Without thinking, I said, "Surely this is not what Serena would have wanted."

His face shifted from gleeful malice to burning rage and his eyes flared with green fire. Quietly he said, "Don't you speak of my wife. You do not know her will. I told you before, boy, this is no game. Do not attempt to manipulate me with my memories of love."

"Mavren, you said that you wanted to be free of this curse, that you wanted to go home. Those were your words. Has that changed?" I asked.

The annoying buzz of the circling whispers grew significantly louder, and Mavren suddenly held his head. All of us stood there as he writhed in agony from an unseen assailant. The stalemate between him and the hidden attacker was broken when he loosed a scream into the air above that rumbled the bones of the temple itself. Dust fell from the stones over our heads, and the very earth seemed to shake with the power of Mavren's pain.

"She is still alive, Master," Murks said over our connection. I knew he was talking about Brin, which brought me some relief.

In response to Mavren's howl, another roar rumbled through. The sounds of rage were mixed with the noise of rending fabric. Avar had used my distraction to call out the guardian that lay inside his skin. No longer did the blond, lanky man with the boyish face stand inside his boots. Instead, this beast with wolf-like features and rippling muscles prepared to pounce upon Mavren with claws and fangs ready to cleave flesh.

"You're not leaving here, Mavren," the Avar beast growled.

When Mavren turned to look at Avar, his face was not visible to me, yet his pause gave me the impression he had not expected this change in the dynamic of the fight. The two monsters stood there, staring at each other, when suddenly another battle

Flayed

howl came from Brin as she charged through the wrecked pews and crashed into Mavren with her shoulder, Ukumog still burning in her hands.

Mavren took the full force of her blow, and it knocked him off his feet, but he was able to roll backwards and back onto his feet. He took a moment to look at the five of us scattered around the room, and then laughed. "Truth be told, I have no need to fight you. This little scrap has been fun, I will admit. Time to say farewell."

I knew exactly what his next plan was, and I extended my arms to call forth the power still pouring out of my limbs. Suddenly the whispers grew so intense as to cause me pain. It was as if the great insect that had been whirling around my head had finally found a place to plant its stinger. I tried to shout a warning to my friends, but all I got out was, "Mist! Turn to mist!" My hands found their way to the sides of my head, and I tried to squeeze away the pain that was bouncing around in my skull. The pain made most of the world around me disappear.

Wide arcs of blue and black streaked through the darkness. There was a flash of white light, and a tearing sound. A roar rolled through the stone room, and I felt more dust fall upon my skin. The whispers grew more intense, and I could not hold back the pain any longer. My scream shut out the rest of the world, and I fell into complete darkness.

I refused to submit to this invading force, and I pushed back against whatever was attacking me. Through the pain, I imagined a shield made of brambles, much like the wall around Flay. I watched the vines twist and bend, folding and weaving through each other, then once they had found their place, the thorns came. They burst through the surface of the vines like thousands of tiny daggers being thrust outward through the surface of the flesh of the vines.

Chapter 11

The trick worked. I felt the grip of my unseen assailant release and then retreat. Opening my eyes, I found my senses dimmed, and through the fog I could make out the continued sounds of battle. I had no way to tell how long I had been subdued, but I was determined to come to the aid of my friends.

Standing proved difficult, much like it did when I first woke from my grave all those years ago. Just as I came solidly to my feet, I heard a loud crash and saw a flood of light pour in through the tunnel to the outside. Stumbling on my weak legs and using the shattered pews to help pull me along, I stepped out into the aisle.

Moonlight flooded the entry hall from the outside. Tarissa lay prone at the exit from the temple, her blond hair pooled upon the ground. Avar, still in his guardian form, pounced through the opening and raked his claws through what seemed to be open air, roaring in frustration as he did so. Brin and Verif charged through the opening after him, stepping up on the temple door that now lay flat upon the street, its massive hinges nothing but torn scraps of metal. Both doors were battered and twisted, as if made of clay that had warped during their time in the oven.

I rushed over to Tarissa's prone body and found her still breathing, though her clothes were torn, and some of her flesh looked burned by acid. One of her legs bent unnaturally below her knee, and I could see something hard pressing against the inside of her form-fitting pants. Without thinking, I used one of her blades to slice open my hand and squeeze my dark blood out into her mouth. One drop fell onto the side of her face, and she shook her head, pushing me away.

"What the uzk are you doing?" she screamed.

"Take my blood. It will heal you," I urged.

Flayed

She gave me an angry look. "Do I look like a vampire to you?" Pushing herself away from me, she winced from the pain in her leg and started at me with distrust.

Outside, Avar stopped chasing the unseen enemy, and Brin cursed loudly. I could hear her screams echo off the mountains on the other side of the ravine. The three of them came back into the temple. They looked like they had been fighting for hours. New scars were evident on Brin's armor, Verif looked completely disheveled, and Avar had unusual anger in his bestial face.

"What the uzk happened to you?" Avar growled, his features already returning to their boyish form.

"Something unseen attacked me, but I was finally able to wrestle free of it," I said. "It may have been influencing Mavren too. He certainly wasn't acting like himself."

Brin stared down the moonlit hallway into the temple, her face filled with quiet rage. "We shoulda trusted our instincts to begin with. More than once we could have killed that uzker in his own house. At least then the world would be rid of one more of the uzkin' Doomed." She spat, clearing the cottony guck from her tired throat.

Verif crouched beside Tarissa and wiped the blood from her face. "We have no supplies, what are we going to do about Tarissa."

"Oh, uzk!" Avar said. "Tare, are you ok? What the uzk happened?"

"You kinda happened, Avar." Tarissa said, a dose of bitterness evident in her voice. "When Mavren tried to charge through us, you knocked me into the wall and broke my leg."

Avar hung his head, remorse filling his face. "Sorry, Tare."

Chapter 11

Tarissa let him languish in his regret for a moment before saying, "It's ok, Avar. It was that uzkin' mist that burned me." Her fingers touched the burns on her side.

"I tried to heal her with my blood," my paranoia forced me to admit before it could be turned against me.

"Your blood can do that?" Verif's attention was now completely on me.

"Ferrin said that mine can do that too, Verif." Avar said, pulling back his tattered sleeve. "I haven't tried it yet."

"Not sure what kind of company you are used to traveling with, Avar, but I am not an uzkin' vampire," Tarissa protested.

Brin's gaze was still fixated on the depths of the temple. "We have no other way of speeding your healing, and we have no supplies here, Tarissa."

"I am not drinking anyone's blood," Tarissa replied, wincing with pain.

"We should get out of this doorway at least. Anyone comes down here, it would be better to find the doors torn open with no one inside," Verif suggested.

Brin sighed. "Just means that they will come down here with more people to investigate, but maybe it will give us more time. Let's take her into the back rooms."

Verif quickly made a splint out of some of the shattered pews and set Tarissa's leg, then Avar and I lifted Tarissa carefully off the floor and slowly carried her towards the back of the temple. Brin was quietly griping to herself about the fight with Mavren and never sheathed Ukumog. The runes on the black blade were still extremely bright, so we needed no torch to guide us through the back tunnels.

Flayed

As we reached the hall that led to the room where I found Mavren praying, I began hearing a strange hissing. My pace slowed, and Avar stopped in his tracks.

"What is it, Wrack?" he whispered.

"Do you hear that hissing?" I asked.

Brin quickly shot me a focused glance, then turned her attention to the tunnel ahead. Grasping Ukumog in both hands, she move silently ahead of us and approached the doorway that led to the ancient bedchamber of the high priest.

There was a crashing sound and suddenly something formless flowed into the hallway from the back room. Brin jumped back, and Ukumog's runes shone like a collection of tiny blue suns as it arced through the air at the monster that was now before us.

Time seemed to slow, and the whispers that haunted me before returned in full force, but my mind was still protected by the thorny shield. The hallway seemed to lengthen, and where Brin was only a few steps in front of us, now she seemed much farther away.

"Brin!" I shouted, not knowing what else to do.

The blue light glistened off the undulating skin of the thing in front of her. To me it seemed like the light of Ukumog's runes was being reflected in thousands of eyes, each with no border between it and another. Out of the gelatinous mass, tentacles burst through the surface, and I immediately recognized this type of creature.

"What the uzk is that... thing?" Tarissa asked.

Remembering my encounter beneath the well in Hollow and what the Shadow had told me, I replied, "It's a seed."

"What the uzk is a seed?" Avar asked.

Ukumog arced back and forth in the dark hallway, casting quickly-moving shadows throughout the shifting hallway. Space and time ceased making sense, even for me, and I felt as if the

Chapter 11

darkness which lived between the stars had come to consume us all. From where I stood, it seemed like Brin was scoring hit after hit on the monster which threatened to swallow her, and each time, Ukumog flashed with brilliant light and the beast recoiled. With the speed with which it seemed to be advancing, however, these moments of retreat were only slowing its plan of attack, not preventing it.

"Brin! Get the uzk out of there!" I shouted down the hallway.

Verif moved between us and Brin and held her hands up towards the seed. Her hands glowed with a golden light, and from her fingers, tiny shining darts shaped like finger bones began rushing down the length of the hallway towards the beast. When these golden bones collided with the shifting flesh of the beast, they burst, causing a small explosion of sparks. This magical barrage of streaming finger bones helped to slow the progress of the shapeless form that was starting to ooze over the walls and ceiling of the hallway.

Looking down the disorienting length of the hallway, I shouted, "Brin! Brin we need to get the uzk out of here!"

She shouted something in response that I could not make out over the shower of sparks from Verif's sorcerous assault.

Frustrated, I looked at Tarissa. "I know you don't want to drink either of our blood, but we need to get out of here, and once we are out in the city, we will be vulnerable. I trust you will make a prudent decision." Nodding my head at her to confirm my words, I looked at Avar, and shifted my share of Tarissa's weight towards him.

Avar scooped Tarissa up, and she screamed as her wounded leg twisted. I gave them both one more look before I charged past Verif down the hallway towards Brin.

Flayed

It seemed to take minutes to travel the gap between Avar and Brin. I watched as Ukumog sliced through the seed over and over again, each time the wound healing just quickly as the blade would pass through it. Getting closer to the monster I saw it in greater detail. The dark mass of the seed was like insanity given flesh. The patterns within its rippling surface formed into demented images of humanoid faces or single elements, yet showed no true signs that it was made of anything than a semi-translucent formless mass.

A guttural growl was coming out of Brin as she whipped the dark blade in the air around her, keeping the monster at bay. The whispering was almost deafening as I came up behind her. Straining to be heard over the ambient noise, I screamed, "BRIN!"

Dark power shot through me with an intensity that I had never felt before. Even Ukumog in my hand when I faced against The Ghoul was nothing compared to the cold fire which burned my flesh. Every inch of me sizzled with power brought forth from the unseen world. I felt as if I were being burned alive.

The pain held me in place for a moment, but then a deep and ancient voice filled my soul with comfort. "Vanquish it," the voice said.

Ignoring the pain, I pushed forward and placed my hand on Brin's shoulder and cried out to her. She whirled around with Ukumog raised as if to strike me. Her eyes were solid black, and her face was slack and emotionless. She hesitated, cocking her head to one side, as if she were trying to place the figure that stood before her.

With Brin's whirling blade halted, the seed pressed the attack, attempting to smash us both with one of its tentacles. I stepped between Brin and the seed, lifting my arm to shield us from the attack. A shield of black energy formed out of the smoke rising

Chapter 11

from my hands and deflected the attack. While I had prevented that one strike, I felt as if my magic had somehow fed the beast that stood against us, and in that I was terrified to my core.

If my dark power would feed this thing, and even Ukumog seemed unable to cause a lasting wound, how could we fight this formless horror?

"We have to get out of here, Brin. Do you hear me?" I continued to try and connect with her. She shook her head and turned back to look at me. I saw the darkness fade from her eyes, and it was replaced with fear.

Another tentacle prepared to strike us, and I again raised my arm to defend us. Without saying a word, Brin leaned forward and kissed me on the cheek, filling my dark form with a bit of her warmth. She still smelled of amber and sunshine.

Images of my youth flooded my mind, and I remembered the challenge of the candle. Over and over I tried to extinguish the light, and suddenly I remembered something, some secret hidden within that place of power, and my mind filled with clarity. Purpose filled my soul, and as the tentacle of the beast fell upon us, again the black shield formed. This time, it was I that fed upon the power of the seed, and I felt its emptiness plunge my soul into the darkest of torments. Where my flesh stood was a void in space, a meaningless speck of dust within the ever-burning stars of the heavens. I saw the corruption of all things and the turn of the world towards entropy and ruin.

Time stopped, and my breath was stolen to a forgotten realm, sealed away from the dreams of mortals. I felt myself die.

Suddenly the connection between my soul and the seed was severed by the hungry blade of Ukumog. Brin pulled me away from it with her left hand and threatened the monster with the fiery blade in her right.

Flayed

Ukumog's runes were no longer just aglow with rage. The entire sword was burning with dark blue fire. It was like I had seen in my vision where the entire city of Flay was upturned by an unseen force, and I knew that this seed was that enemy. My mind grasped for an anchor of truth, and I was struck speechless.

Brin and I slowly backed away from the creature. It allowed us to flee, and flee we did. Not just into the temple's heart, but breathlessly we ran all the way out into the moon-soaked streets of Flay.

Chapter 12

We stood there, in the moonlight, outside the doorway to the temple. The doors that once blocked the entrance were now bent and broken, one of them lay on the ground, its hinges torn. The street was silent, but my mind was screaming over the encounter we had just had. My thoughts were still infected with the hollow vision of the seed's empty secrets. Though the fog, I had to keep my focus on things mundane to prevent my consciousness from slipping away to somewhere unknown.

"What the uzk was that... thing?" Tarissa asked again.

Assuming she hadn't heard me the first time, I answered. "I believe that those things are called seeds. Someone told me once that they are monsters from a secret brood of twisted chaos. I don't know much else."

Frustration was evident in Tarissa's pained expression. "That doesn't make any sense."

"I've heard the same thing," Brin said. "And you're right. It doesn't make any uzkin' sense." She took a deep breath, "I will tell you one thing, though. Ukumog certainly hates those things."

Avar gave Brin a confused look. "Have you run into one before?"

Flayed

"Yeah," Brin said. "There was one under Hollow. Ukumog did not want me to stop fighting that one either. It was different this time though. Don't know why."

"Ukumog scares me," I said.

Verif nearly bounced with excitement. "Isn't it glorious?" she asked, staring at the glowing sword in Brin's hand.

Brin furrowed her brow, and then leashed Ukumog to her sword belt. "Well, what the uzk do we do now? I want to get far away from that uzkin' thing." She pointed towards the deep parts of the temple.

"We don't really have a place to go," Avar said.

"Can't we just leave the city before the army gets here?" Verif suggested. "We could head northeast to Winterland and find Bridain."

"I still have the vial of Elaina's blood." Tarissa patted one of her pouches. "But I am not sure we can get out of here before the army gets here."

"Especially with you in this condition," Brin lamented.

"Yeah." Tarissa's voice fell.

Briefly I entertained the idea of us all climbing over the stone wall and into the ravine below. My memories had only given me a brief hint that it was possible, and that I had done it before, but I knew that we were not prepared for that kind of journey, especially with Tarissa's injuries.

Brin looked around. "Let's move away from this spot at least. The last thing we need is the guard coming down here to investigate the noise and finding us all standing here like idiots."

"Fair point," Avar said.

Each of us looked at Brin in silent agreement and followed her when she picked a direction and started moving. Ukumog's runes grew silent as we put distance between ourselves and the

Chapter 12

temple, and so, too, did the whispers vanish from my mind. I breathed easier the farther away from that forsaken temple we put ourselves, but the scars upon my soul I did not think would ever heal. Yet, I pretended that nothing was different.

We kept to the back alleys and roads that went behind the large estates of the high city, just as Tarissa and I had done when we had scouted earlier. The night watch were out in force, and so our journey took much longer than it did before, and it was dawn before we arrived at the abandoned pub. Once inside, Tarissa could not take it anymore, and she uttered in frustration, "Avar. Heal me."

"What?" Avar looked confused.

Tarissa did not have patience. "Use your blood to heal me. I can't go in there like this, and we don't have time."

"Are you sure?" Avar asked.

"Yes, I am sure," she said.

Avar placed her gently on the ground and pulled back his sleeve. Tarissa handed him a blade, and he held it over his arm pausing only to make sure that she wanted him to help her. She nodded at him, and he cut himself deeply. Blood gushed out of the diagonal wound across his forearm and dripped onto the dirt floor. Tarissa's face displayed regret and disgust, but she pressed her lips to Avar's wound and drew the blood into her mouth. Avar's eyes grew wide, and he winced with pain. Tarissa's eyes checked with Avar to make sure she should continue, and Avar nodded.

Verif curiously watched the transaction of blood with a macabre interest shining in her cat-like eyes. Brin stood off to one side with her hands on her hips, waiting impatiently. There was worry in her eyes, however, and she refused to directly look at anyone else in the room. My thoughts drifted to Gordo. How I wished that I could have saved him with some of my own blood. I missed his sense of humor and the way he casually spread his

Flayed

certain kind of optimism. Our little band of rebels did not seem the same since he was gone. Then I realized, no one seemed to talk about Gordo much. Surely that was due to the pain discussions of him might bring up, rather than simply forgetting his importance to us.

I thought of others who had faded away. Garrett, the previous commander of the Shadow Hunters and Avar's late father who died at the hands of Lucien's Doomed armor. Sally, a refugee who had simply vanished into the darkness at the end of a barbed hook. Tikras, companion of those strange barbarians and a wielder of bizarre magics who sacrificed himself to save us all from The Mistress. Lastly, I wondered about David, the man who I had carried nearly the entire way from Yellow Liver to sanctuary, and who was healed by my blood. I could not help but wonder where he had gone, and if he was, indeed, still alive. Those thoughts led me to thoughts about Matthew, Avar's brother, who had been torn apart by the ghouls in Yellow Liver.

Musing on the near ruin of the first city I had encountered after my rebirth from my mossy grave, I remembered how terrible that all was. Then I thought about him. The little brave boy. He was the first human to treat me like I mattered. Even though he barely said any words to me, his face was burned into my memory. However, those moments turned out the same as they always did. From his bravery and kindness my mind shifted to his lifeless eyes. Those eyes lingered in my memory stronger than even his kindness. The rage I felt then, seeing that brave boy's gnawed body lying there in the feeding pit of The Ghoul, I recalled in an instant. The dark part of me wanted to kill Palig all over again, and it scared me.

Tarissa cried out, breaking my drifting thoughts. With blood running down her chin, her hands rushed to her wounded leg. Her cries became almost like a growl for a moment, and I saw

Chapter 12

a silvery light flash through her eyes. Her head flew back, and she gave a roar to the sky, then fell silent. The power had run its course through her, and had exhausted her in the process. Covered in sweat, she motioned for Avar to help her up. With a groan and a little help, she stood on her own.

Brin clapped quietly and said, "Great. Can we get the uzk out of here now?"

"Yeah," Tarissa said, shooting Brin a nasty look.

Limping a bit as she went, Tarissa moved to the secret door and rapped upon it three times. Just as it had the previous time we came through, the door opened. Gasps of surprise came from Avar and Brin, but to Verif this opening seemed unimpressive.

"How did you know that was a door?" Avar whispered to Tarissa.

She chuckled. "It is my job to know secrets, remember?"

Avar smiled sheepishly.

"Secrets," I thought to myself. Somehow that word unlocked something in my memory.

"Lucien!" I heard Grimoire's voice call out. "Lucien, we have to do something else. This plan will not work."

"I am cursed, little brother. We are all cursed. I feel it in my bones," the blond giant said with a relieved smile.

We were in the courtyard of that same keep I had seen in my visions before. Years had passed, however. I could see the time reflected by the creases in Lucien's face as he talked. Marec was there too, his hair more grey than black now. He paced back and forth, each step filled with frustrated worry.

Flayed

"Killing yourself will not break The Curse," Grimoire said. He was a great deal younger than the shriveled man I knew from the Eternal Well, and robes he wore were white, not black. They were trimmed with black and silver, and embroidered into the chest was the tree with ravens nesting atop its branches. His hands moved as he talked, and his voice was filled with anger.

"What is done is done, Grim," Lucien said. "You weren't there. I don't expect you to understand it."

The three of them stewed in silent rage while the people around them continued with their work. Some carried bales of hay, others tended to the horses. I found myself searching the faces of the people, looking for the gentle features that belonged to Lilly. I knew that I had no seen her for years, but I hoped she would remember that silly boy who enjoyed the simplicity of a lazy afternoon, despite the fact that I was no longer that simple boy.

My thoughts filled with a hazy darkness, and I tried to shake it off.

"Alex?" Marec rushed to my side. "Alex, are you alright, boy?"

I waved him off. "I am fine, Marec. My head is just filled with a little mist."

Grimoire raised an eyebrow. "That happened before Alex. Do you remember that?"

"Remember what?" I said.

"Uzk!" Grimoire stood up and paced in a circle. "That bastard did it again, Luc. Can't you see what is happening? He has a plot, and we cannot defeat it with noble gestures of suicide or force of arms alone."

Marec sighed. "Darion will win by any means, but we are just soldiers, Grim."

Chapter 12

Grimoire's face lit up, and he returned to the stump which he had just left. Looking at me intently he said, "We need to preserve your memory, Alex. The power of the old man is still inside you, and we can't let that fade. We need to make sure it never leaves."

His intensity was upsetting, the fire in his eyes threatening to burn me, and I backed away from him.

Lucien rolled his eyes. "How do you plan to do that, Grim? Stick the boy in a box? We tried that once, and Andoleth found him anyway."

Grimoire's shoulders dropped. "I am, as yet, uncertain."

"That is what I thought," Lucien scoffed.

There was a flash, and the dream took me away from the keep.

A small circle of black-robed figures chanted softly, all of them focusing on the middle of their circle. I stood several paces away from them, watching and waiting for them to be done. As the chanting grew more intense, I realized that they were actually singing. The tune became louder and more dynamic, with a mix of voices all woven together in unison. A light appeared from the middle of their number, casting the shadows of those participating away from the circle and across the orderly grey stone street. When the magical singing stopped, a burst of light came from the middle of the circle, and then was extinguished.

"There," Grimoire's voice came from the circle of figures. "The cache is made."

Black robed men and women moved aside, and Grimoire appeared from their number.

"Grim?" I asked him as he approached to confirm the spell's completion.

"Test it if you like, Alex. I do believe that the cache is complete," he said.

Flayed

I was annoyed with that name. It was an old name for a boy who was long gone. "Alexander is dead, Grimoire."

Stone-faced, he said, "Not to me he isn't."

Ignoring his comment, I asked, "How do I access the cache?"

"Any member of the Well can access this cache. As such, you also have access to them all. You have to know where they are, however, in order to be able to use them." He walked with me towards the place where the ring of black robes had stood.

There on the ground was a stone in the street that bore a mark upon its surface. If I didn't know what to look for, I would have mistaken it for an odd pattern in the stone, or perhaps some dirt that was covering it. However, to my knowing eyes, I found the tiny image of a dark orb with eight wavy lines extending from it. It was the symbol of The Eternal Well. As I approached, it seemed to glow faintly, letting me know that I could but will the cache to be opened, and it would take me within.

"And where does the stone take us again?" I asked Grimoire.

"To a small hole in the universe. A place between here and the unseen world, small enough not to be detected, but not large enough for any real defenses," he explained.

I nodded, with a greater understanding in the dream than I had outside of it.

Grimoire took a breath. "Though, I suppose one could hide in there for a while, if they needed to. Time passes differently in these little nooks. However, I would strongly suggest never testing that for long. The presence of a soul within these places will make it easier to detect, by far."

Chapter 12

"Thank you, Grimoire. As usual your instruction has been invaluable," I said. My thoughts in the dream drifted off to some other purpose for a cache such as this. One larger and intensely different, but before I could finish the thought, I stirred from the dream.

"Are you coming, Wrack?" Brin asked.

I was alone in the cellar, and she was standing in the threshold of the secret door. Beyond it, I could hear the sounds of Tarissa talking to Avar, and the faint clamor of the Golden Swan above.

"Yeah. Sorry," I said, shaking off the memories. "Listen, I think I have an idea where we can go..." My words dropped as I made eye contact with Tomas.

He nodded at me, awkwardly, then stepped forward to close the door behind us. I saw his eyes dart downward to Ukumog and then away. My stomach was suddenly tied in knots.

"We have to get out of here quickly," I whispered to Brin. "The Juindars are still looking for us, and I think they spread word about your sword."

She looked down at Ukumog, as if she had forgotten that it was there. "Uzk."

Quickening our pace, we caught up with Tarissa, Avar, and Verif. From behind, we urged the group to move quicker through the crowd. Tarissa realized what was happening with a few glances and responded with a subtle nod. In seconds we were out on the street, and mere moments after that, we were in a side alley well

Flayed

away from the Golden Swan. Shortly after we were tucked away, we saw a patrol of guards headed in the direction of the tavern, with Marius Juindar in the lead.

"Someone sold us out," I said casually.

Tarissa sighed. "Swift did say that things were getting rough. Though I would prefer to think it wasn't one of my contacts that gave us up."

"Where are we going to go?" Avar asked. "Do we have any other allies in the city?"

"None that I would trust," Tarissa said. "All the contacts I had before will have become particularly mercenary with the threat of war looming over us, and the houses we made friends with while we were staying with Mavren have probably turned against him. We need to find somewhere to lay low."

"I might know of a place," I whispered.

"Exactly how do you know of a place?" Avar sounded frustrated.

"Avar," Tarissa scolded.

"I'm sorry, all this running around and secrecy is not my thing," Avar said with a sigh. "I am a little overwhelmed."

"Aww..." Tarissa kissed him on the temple.

"I had a vision, memory, thing. Anyway, in the vision, I saw The Eternal Well creating a magical caches here in Flay. If we can find one of those, we might be able to use it to hide in."

"Magical caches?" Verif asked, her eyes lit with curiosity.

I nodded. "Something about putting things in a pocket within the unseen world..."

"Is it safe?" Brin asked. "I mean, safe for people to be inside there?"

Again, I nodded. "Safe for short periods of time, at least."

Chapter 12

"Can't be any worse than remaining out in the open," Tarissa said quietly.

Brin chuckled. "Yeah. I don't relish the idea of running into the uzkin' Juindar brothers while all this gaak is going on."

"If that army is actually coming, it should hit anytime now," Tarissa reminded us.

"Will the cache work for waiting that out?" Avar asked. "The Baron's siege of the city could take weeks."

"If the Silver Lady is actually on our side, hopefully she will inspire The Doomed to quit pissing on each other and leave the rest of us well enough alone," Brin muttered and then stood up.

"I don't think that's very likely," Avar groaned.

"Where is your optimism, Avar?" Brin grinned at him. "Alright, Wrack, where the uzk is this cache?"

Searching the memory of the vision, I looked for clues about the location. In the memory I was standing behind a building, and I thought I saw an alley that could see the marketplace in the center of lower Flay. The way the shadows moved, I could tell it was on the east side of the city, and we were close to the wall of thorns. "East of the market, near the wall. That is all I remember. Hopefully, if I get close I will remember more."

Without another word, we began our winding journey through the unfriendly streets of the city just as the light of the sun woke up the inhabitants of Flay. Before we got close to the market, it was well into the day and the panic of the oncoming army had changed the electricity in the air. Common folk strode with purpose and fear through the street. As for the city guard, they seemed focused on what was happening outside the city, not particularly caring when children were shoved out of the path of urgently moving adults, or when the looting started.

Flayed

Some revenants were around the market, trying to control the looting of merchants' shops and carts, and they were merciless in their duty. We saw more than one corpse lying in the street on our way to the east side of the market. None of them wore the colors of The King, so I could only assume that the streets were lined with the murderous handiwork of the guards. This city of careful control was starting to unravel.

The sun was long set by the time we reached a spot that seemed familiar. "Over here!" I said without thinking, and immediately afterwards I worried that this place was familiar not because of my vision, but because of my adventure to the market with Tarissa the day before. The group of us moved behind a building that seemed uncommonly familiar, yet much had changed since my vision, and it caused me to doubt.

"What are we looking for?" Verif asked as she scanned the area.

"The stones in the street," I said. "One of them will have a mark on it. Like a dark orb with eight wavy rays emanating from it."

We all looked around, and after what seemed like forever, no one found anything.

"Maybe I am remembering the place incorrectly," I said, sheepishly.

Two buildings to the south a call from Verif came, "I found something!"

We all rushed over to where she stood, and there was indeed the stone I remembered from my dream. Symbol of the black sun and all, yet aged significantly from what I remembered.

"Well?" Verif asked, impatiently.

"This is it, I think," I said.

Chapter 12

As I got close to the stone, I saw the symbol glimmer, and two glowing eyes appeared in the middle of the orb, just as they had in Grimoire's necklace that first night in the Headless Mermaid. I took a breath and stepped forward. My hand reached for the stone, but I paused just before I touched it and said, "All of you should hold onto me."

My friends needed no other instruction, and they all grabbed onto my robes. Brin grabbed a handful of my backside, which gave me a surprising rush of adrenaline. She gave me a smile and a shrug, before I turned back to the stone.

The sounds of distant catapults firing, and then the crash of stone on stone reached us just as my finger touched the stone. A dim light burst forth from the stone, and we were taken away from the city of Flay.

The journey into the cache was an odd one. I found myself outside time and space, and the feeling of moving with great speed washed over me, yet I remained still. Even in this state where I was stretched between the city of Flay and wherever the magic of the stone was taking me, I found myself alone with images. Unlike my dreams of the past or visions of the future, I felt as if I were actually there, in that moment. Yet that moment made no sense.

The morning sun shone through the window in a small tenement flat. Gentle rays of light quietly warmed the floor inside the flat, and there in the pool of glowing sunlight was a tiny girl. Gwen looked up from the wooden blocks she was playing with and our eyes connected. She smiled a big generous smile, her eyes filled with laughter. She lifted her tiny body from the floor and once she was steady, she started running towards me. This moment filled me with so much joy that I forgot for a moment even who I was, or that this was not real. Time slowed, and each of her steps

Flayed

seemed to last for a lifetime. All the while I could hear her playful giggles. The moment stretched on and on, and when it seemed to completely be frozen in time with her eternally running towards me, I remembered who I was, and that I had watched her father die. The sorrow punched me in the throat, and my eyes immediately welled and their bounty began to fall from my face, yet they too became trapped in this one perfect moment. Yet, it wasn't perfect. It was not me that she was running towards, but a man who would never embrace her again. Doubt and fear took over my thoughts, and I lost myself to that bitter loneliness. I would never know the simple joy of my own child's laughter, for I was a dead and terrible thing.

Just as the sorrow reached its peak, I found myself in a small chamber. The air was stale and old, yet had the familiar scent of a well-tended library. My companions were also there. I was actually surprised to see them; the vision had been so compelling that I had to readjust to the reality of my situation. Quickly, I wiped away the tears that were leaking from my eyes. Avar turned away from the group to do the same thing, and it made me wonder if they had encountered the same vision. When I saw Brin's face, I knew that she had seen something remarkably different.

Her eyes were distant, and her mouth was bent into a harsh frown. This face contained the hopeless anger that bubbled up inside her whenever a conversation about her father went on too long. Verif also had a look of unpleasant shock hanging on her face. Tarissa, on the other hand, seemed to be the most unaffected by the experience. She was already scoping out the many shelves covered in all manner of books and knickknacks. The walls we could see were lined with wardrobes and more shelves. Ladders were generously spread around the space, which would be useful, as the shelves ran from floor to ceiling in this place. The shelves were

Chapter 12

easily sixteen feet high, if not taller. The aisles between shelves were extremely narrow as well. It seemed that whoever stocked this place was trying to make efficient use of the small chamber, and perhaps had gone a little overboard in doing so.

"Hello?" a voice called out from elsewhere in the chamber.

We all looked at each other to make sure that it was none of us that had made the call. Finding us all present and similarly bewildered, none of us responded.

"Hello? Is someone there?"

Again, we said nothing, and collectively we tried to make no noise.

The unseen person let loose a frustrated sigh and said, "Grimoire, you know I do not appreciate practical jokes." His voice was getting louder.

Unsure what to do we all froze in place, hoping he wouldn't see us as he passed the aisle we found ourselves in. This plan was, of course, folly. As he turned the corner and saw us all standing there, he stopped dead in his tracks.

He was a pale man, wearing the same black robes that all the members of The Eternal Well did, save one thing. He was wearing the same belt I once had. Ropes of black and red woven together with tiny silver skulls dangling from its knotted ends. Brin too noticed the rope, and before anyone could say a word she strode towards him. Ukumog greeted this new stranger with its usual *clink!*

"Who are you, and why are you wearing that belt?" Brin threatened.

"I–I–I… Um. Ah…" the stranger fumbled.

"I asked you a question," Brin said with quiet rage.

"Answer the lady…" Verif suggested, adding with a whisper, "…before she cuts your uzkin' head off."

Flayed

I could not help but smile at her morbid sense of humor at Brin's expense. Verif's face immediately brightened, seeing my smile. Our eyes locked for a moment, and I for the first time I saw her without the usual lust glistening in her eyes.

"If you make me ask you again, it will be after there are pieces of you scattered all over this place. Do you understand?" Brin's tone held only the thinnest of veils over the threat of violence that lay between her words.

The man raised his hands defensively, dropping the armful of books he was carrying. Brin nimbly stepped out of the way, but Ukumog was raised slightly as she did so. Brin was preparing to strike him.

"I'm no one. Just the one in charge of cataloguing all the artifacts in this storehouse. Really, I know nothing. Please don't hurt me!" he whined.

"Where did you get that belt?" Brin used Ukumog to lift one of the dangling tails of the belt tied around his waist.

"What? This? I didn't get the belt. It was brought here. I don't even know where it came from. I just liked it. Please don't kill me!" He answered her so rapidly that there were almost no pauses between his sentences.

"Where is Grimoire?" I asked from behind Brin.

"What?" the man cried out.

Stepping forward so the man could see me, I asked again, "Where is Grimoire?"

The man was dumbstruck. He seemed unable to speak or look away from me. Brin lost her patience waiting for him to answer, and used the bone pommel of Ukumog to knock some sense into him. The cracking noise that came from the collision

Chapter 12

sounded like she intended to hurt him, not just snap him out of his unspeaking state. Losing his footing, the man fell to his knees, and I stepped forward, motioning for Brin to cease her attack.

"Just tell me. Where is Grimoire? Were you expecting him?" I asked the man again.

His eyes were wide and filled with fear and awe. I could see my face reflected in the sheen of his eyes, and what I saw frightened me. A hooded dead man with ferocity in his face, and the threat of death surrounding every wrinkle. Quickly, I withdrew from him, not wanting to see the monster that I had temporarily forgotten lived in my skin.

There was a sudden shift in the air around us, like the passing of an unfelt breeze, then Verif said, "I'd say he was expecting him."

"Wrack? Brin? What are all of you doing here?" Grimoire's voice called down the aisle.

The man Brin had attacked scurried away and around the corner while our attentions were diverted towards Grimoire.

"You shouldn't be here," Grimoire shook his head in frustration. "All of you should have fled the city."

"Why should we have fled?" Brin's question was filled with hostility.

Grimoire sighed and waved his hand at the two members of The Eternal Well that flanked him. "Did you not understand my warning, Wrack?"

"That was a warning? Seems to me that you just said goodbye," I said.

A look of relief washed over his face. "Well then…" There was a pregnant pause while he scanned our faces, his face looked like it would erupt with words at any moment, then finally, he spoke again. "Here is the situation out there. The siege of Flay is

Flayed

already underway. The barrage of falling stones caused a riot on the southwest side of the city. Currently the Juindar brothers and many of the guard are trying to contain that mess. Meanwhile, The Baron's men are trying to simultaneously bash down the main gates on the south end of the wall and burn down the wall on the east side."

"Can the thicket burn?" Verif asked.

He chuckled. "If you had asked me that question yesterday, I would have said no. Today however... They have had some success with their endeavors. Enough to create a hole large enough for a single person to make their way in at a time."

"Holy uzk..." Brin muttered.

"Some of The Baron's men are already inside the walls. The force that burned the hole did so after the riots started, and my information says that the first few people through the hole were not wearing the customary black and red livery of The Baron. I can only imagine the kind of mayhem that they have planned for the city."

"That is why you came back, to collect things from here." I said.

"Indeed. There are some things in this place that we would rather not have buried. Gods only know what will happen if the keystone to the cache is destroyed." Grimoire's voice was grave.

The other members of The Eternal Well looked like they were looting the place. Each of them were rifling through the items on the shelves, obviously searching for specific things. The whining complaints of the caretaker could be heard over the sounds of the targeted looting, but no one was paying any attention to his prattling.

"You should, nay, you must leave," Grimoire said. "Do you have any more of Elaina's blood?"

Chapter 12

My mind immediately went to the vial of Gordo's blood that I had in my robes. As I shifted, I could also feel the jeweled scarab that Grimoire had given me, and I became uncomfortably silent.

"I still have one vial, yeah," Tarissa said.

"Good," said Grimoire. "Use it to leave, and pray that the army is not on the other side of the wall when you make your way out. Neither side is famous for taking prisoners."

"Where would we go?" Brin asked with a frustrated tone. When no one responded she continued, "We came here looking for Grumth, and got swept up into the nonsense politics of this city. I believed that we could make a difference, and now you are telling us to run away?"

Grimoire sighed, "Brin, I—"

"You? You what?" she interrupted him. "You didn't mean for all of this to happen? What sort of game were you and Mavren playing here, Grimoire?"

He listened to her with a stony face, waiting for her to stop. "The only game that matters. Trying to loose the grip that The Doomed have over this place."

"Well, it worked out great for Mavren," Verif scoffed.

Grimoire's bushy eyebrows nearly jumped off his face. "What happened to Mavren?"

"Before or after the fire?" Verif asked.

Grimoire's shoulders slumped. "Serena?"

"Dead," Brin said with accusation in her tone. "Darkweaver set a fire that killed Serena and a few of heads of households loyal to The King."

Grimoire's face fell, but he regained his composure. "Then what happened to Mavren?"

Flayed

"We hid in an old abandoned temple for a day, and he went mad. Kept insisting that he had to return to The King," Tarissa said.

Grimoire gave us a somber nod. "The pull of The King is powerful on those who serve him. Darion must have been calling Mavren back to him." With a deep sigh, he continued, "I hope that my old friend is alright. I fear for his mind and his soul."

"Well, he is far beyond our reach now. Nearly killed us all when he ran back to his master." Brin's voice was harsh and unforgiving.

Nodding, Grimoire said again, "You should leave as soon as you can."

A member of The Eternal Well whispered in Grimoire's ancient ear, and he nodded to them in response. "Can I speak to you for a moment, Wrack?"

"Sure." I shrugged at my friends, trying to express that I was as confused as the rest of them.

We walked to the opposite side of the room, and Grimoire moved us behind a great big bookshelf. With startling speed, Grimoire whirled around and grabbed my arms. He pulled my ear down to his face and whispered, "She isn't the one, Wrack. If you don't get them out of this city, they will all die here."

"What are you talking about?" I whispered as I tried to loose myself from his freakishly strong grip.

"Brin isn't the next prophet. It doesn't follow bloodlines, no matter what the foolish Shadow Hunters think. The Silver Lady picks her mouthpieces, and over the ages they have gotten further apart by time. Brin isn't the next."

Freeing myself from his iron hands, I recoiled and stared at him with confusion. My curiosity would not let me just walk away, however. "What the uzk are you talking about?" I whispered.

Chapter 12

"The bards who speak the words of hope from the Silver Lady. Brin's heart is too dark to be one of them. That is the one thing that all of the bards have had in common, a never ending ocean of hope. That and… well."

"Well, what?"

He sighed. "Things never end well for the bards. The price they pay for the promise of life in the arms of the queen of inspiration. There certainly isn't a seat in the Silver Forest waiting for you or I."

My brow furrowed, and without knowing exactly why, I was deeply offended by his last comment.

"Either way," he said with a quiet sigh. "Don't let her die here. Anyone as wild and dark as she deserves to die on her own terms. Not crushed between two armies wielding ancient forgotten grudges."

I wasn't sure what to say or do. All my encounters with Grimoire were puzzling, and this was the strangest of them all.

He nodded at me, and smiled. "Chin up, Alexander. We will see the other side of this little scuffle. We always do." Walking away from me he called out, "It is time, brothers and sisters. Let's depart this cache and hope it is not the last time our feet tread upon these stones. May the patrons of love and light guard this place with all the strength they can push through the darkened veil."

There was a rush of air, and suddenly we were alone in the cache.

"What the uzk was that all about?" Brin asked me once they were gone.

"Sounded like a prayer to me," Avar offered.

Brin shook her head. "Not that. I mean the private chat with Wrack," she scolded Avar. Then turning to me, she said, "What was all that?"

Flayed

"He really wants us to leave," I said, still dazed by the confusion burning its way through my thoughts.

Tarissa walked over to the exit sigil in the floor, the same black sun that was our entry. "I think we should go to the west side of the city. With the riots acting as a distraction, we should be able to slip out through the wall easily."

"Sounds dangerous," Avar said.

"Then let's do it." Verif's cat eyes flashed with excitement.

Brin scowled at us all. "Fine. Any suggestions on where we go?"

"Winterland?" Verif suggested.

"Let's figure that out when we get outside the walls," Tarissa said.

Avar nodded.

Shrugging, I said, "I go where Brin goes. Simple as that."

Through her sour mood, I saw that simple smile that I had grown to love. She reached for my hand, and once our palms met, and our fingers gripped the other hand tightly, she said, "Ok, Wrack. Take us the uzk out of here. This place is starting to creep me out."

I nodded and reached towards the sigil, hoping that I would escape this place without seeing the same thing as I did coming in here. With all my mind I focused on Brin's smile, and the warmth of her hand against my dead flesh. Silently, I gave a prayer to whatever gods might be out there. I just wanted to be away from all this death, decay and misery, and be with her, my dark-hearted warrior. Bard or not, I did not care.

Somehow, I felt that something benevolent had heard my wishful thinking, and we were whisked through time and space back to the streets of Flay.

CHAPTER 13

We appeared on the street with a *crack*, and I was disoriented for a moment, just as I had been when we went in. This time, there were no visions to torment or test me. It was as if I went to sleep in one place and woke up in another. However, our journey took us from a serene library to a city under siege.

The smell of burning things punched my nostrils and immediately I sprang into a defensive stance, letting go of Brin's hand. The rest of our group acted in a similar fashion, but in the street behind those buildings we were not in immediate danger.

"The west side of town, yeah?" Brin said more than asked.

Tarissa nodded. "Let's get out of here."

Quickly, but cautiously, we moved through the grid of streets towards the marketplace at the center. We passed hundreds of people with eyes filled with panic and fear. All of them were quickly rushing to and from destinations unknown. Some of the alleys that we travelled through contained a body of some poor human. Most were men, but there were some women, and even the rare child. We did not have time to inspect their wounds to discover the cause of death, but many of them looked like they were likely victims of circumstance, in the wrong place at the wrong time, perhaps in possession of something that another desperate soul thought they needed.

Flayed

I could not help but wonder what was going through their minds, all these panicked people. *Did they blame The King for this siege? Or had they placed the blame on some foreign enemy? What web of lies had The Doomed who sat upon their thrones used to ensnare the hopes and dreams of these people?* With so much beauty in this city, I could not escape the idea that the humans in this place were indeed filled with inspiration, but none that those ancient monsters could have given to them. Perhaps Avar's goddess, the patron of inspiration, had secretly found a way to sow the seeds of her gifts to the people here. Yet the fear that now came raining down on these people made them cast away their dreams, the veneer of society's charms stripped away from them, and the bestial nature of humankind floated to the surface. It saddened me that it was so easy for some to lose their empathy, their compassion, for that is truly what separates man from monster.

While each moment seemed to last forever, we arrived at the marketplace quickly. The entire place teemed with soldiers wearing the livery of The King. They watched every artery that led into the market, as was the giant statue of the crowned man. When my eyes landed on that gleaming structure, I chuckled.

"Odd," I thought to Murks. "Darion's vanity must me the thing keeping that statue in place. I doubt he continues to look that way."

Murks quietly agreed. "His Majesty was never known to be a humble man."

Another volley of rocks came screaming over the walls to the south. From our hiding place, we could hear the rocking arms of the catapults, and the sound that their ammunition made as they streaked through the dark sky above us. I felt helpless and paralyzed in the next few moments. We had no way of knowing if one of these

Chapter 13

stones would crash into us, or if wherever we moved to would be the unlucky target of the attack. The five of us just hunkered down between two buildings and waited for the sound of crashing stone.

The stones made impact, delivering shockwaves of their victory echoing through the night. One stone even crashed through the raven holding a crown that sat upon the statue in the center of the market, sending the massive bird bouncing through the tents and wagons gathered there in the marketplace. When the cacophony of destruction stopped, clouds of dust hung in the air, and a moment later the wails of the survivors began. Yelling started to cover some of the screams as people, both soldiers and civilians, began trying to save anyone they could from collapsed rubble.

Humans are interesting things. While this siege had devolved a few into selfish beasts who would kill a stranger for some base desire, others would selflessly charge into danger and strain themselves to help a stranger in need. Hard to predict what they would do. I wondered if that is why The Doomed felt it necessary to crush their spirits and remove their faith. *Were they easier to control when you could anticipate their actions?* Reducing them to their base instincts may give you more of an upper hand, but then again, it seems that they will always find a way to surprise you.

"Ok," Brin said. "We are not going to make it through the market with all these uzkin' soldiers here."

"We can make our way around to the north. There are plenty of alleyways along that route," Tarissa suggested.

"Yeah, we don't want to go to the southern part of the city if that is where the soldiers are massing to fight the possible invasion," Avar said.

Verif frowned. "The soldiers on the north side will be less distracted by the siege."

"And?" Avar asked.

Flayed

"And they will be looking for possible infiltrators through the breech that already happened," Verif said with some disdain.

"Well, Brin. Which way do we go?" I asked.

She looked at all of our faces for a moment, seeming to judge our reactions to the situation. "We go around the north side. Smaller numbers of guards might be on alert, but we can kill those uzkers if we have to." She nodded at us, and we all nodded in return.

We made our way through the dark streets of the city with relative ease. We had no time constraints, save the rising of the sun, and so we were vigilant with our movements, and the few guards we came across were easy to out maneuver.

As we came closer to the west side of town, a clamor came to our ears and grew louder with each step. My preternatural hearing picked it up first, I will admit, but I cast the noises aside as just another ambient change due to the war that loomed over the city. It was Verif who actually got the rest of us to take notice.

"Hey... hey, what is that noise? Is that combat? Within the walls?" she asked.

Brin stopped in her tracks, and then after a brief pause she changed her direction, heading towards the sound of clashing steel. Carried by our collective curiosity and worry, we all followed her without complaint.

Our path put us right next to the thorny wall that marked the edge of the city of Flay. No echo of the commotion reflected to our ears from the wall. Instead, it was filled with a comforting silence, like walking alongside a snow-covered hill. The sound was simply being absorbed. The racket of the city and dark thoughts of the events which I believed were about to play out before us were exhausting. The tired part of my soul wanted to get away from all this noise and misery. If I had been the one in possession of Elaina's blood, I cannot say for certain that I would have continued to follow

Chapter 13

Brin and the rest, instead insisting that we leave the city and leave the fates of the people here in their own hands. Our path would have taken a drastically different direction if that had happened.

We walked down an alley towards the sounds of the conflict. The light of torches glimmered in a stream of dark fluid that trickled through the cracks of the stone street past us, towards the thorny wall. I followed it and saw that we had stepped over it as we walked down the alley. At the end of its journey, where the stream of blood met the thorns, a single white flower bloomed, even in the cold of the winter. This unusual sight stopped me in my tracks, and I missed what happened next with my friends.

Shouts calling my name pushed their way through the haze of questions that had overcome my senses, and when I rushed to the end of the alley to discover my friends, I stepped out into a war. Soldiers wearing the livery of The King were hacking and chopping their way through a crowd of mostly-unarmed citizens of the city. Rage rushed through my blood, and a lump formed in my throat. Bodies in various states of dismemberment were strewn around this tiny corner of the city, and the street ran red with blood. There was a surge of energy near by, and the strange smell after a lightning strike. After this show of power, it was easy for me to find Verif, then Avar and Tarissa, and finally Brin and Ukumog. They had all charged into the fray in defense of these poor souls who were being slaughtered by the army of The King.

I lost my breath as memories flooded my mind of many poor souls being chewed to pieces at the base of a great tower while I watched from the woods nearby. The face of the ancient general who led the attack flashed through my mind, and I had to shake off the memory of fear. My friends had engaged these enemies

Flayed

who would kill the same people they were charged to protect, but this time I would not cling to the shadows and watch as my world crumbled. Not this time.

At my feet lay the body of a soldier whose head had been bashed in. I reached down and lifted up his sword, still dripping with the blood of his last victim. I wiped the blood off on the nameless soldier's tabard, cleansing the sword of its previous purpose and silently dedicating it to a new one. Once it was clean, I stood and looked again for my friends. Ukumog burned brightly in the light of a few scattered torches as it carved blue streaks through the air, resulting in a few guards losing their limbs. Brin's hair was flowing through the air like waves crashing into the shore. Verif stood in the back and held her hands up, controlling a shield of glimmering force that she used to protect the group's flank. Avar and Tarissa fought with their blades against the assembled force of guards at Brin's side.

The faces of the common people were filled with fear and awe. Many of them seemed confused about the appearance of these skilled warriors coming to their defense. Many took this opportunity to escape the conflict, others paused, but then joined in the fight. Then I heard it, the reason why they rejoined the fight: Brin was singing.

Her voice poked holes in the sound of the conflict, but I could hear enough to know it was her father's song, the forbidden song that told the people to throw off the chains of The Doomed who ruled over them.

"...we know their names." The chorus rang out over the crowd.

As the song hit me, my memories took hold of me, and I was no longer in Flay.

Chapter 13

"Come now, gents! You don't need to harass these good folk on this fine day!" Teague said to small crowd of leathery thugs.

"Teague..." I said from behind him. "This isn't our fight."

He turned and smiled at me with his green eyes flashing. "Of course it is our fight." Then he turned back to the thugs and waited for their answer.

The wagon the thugs were attempting to rob looked like it had two families in it. While their clothes did not speak of any wealth, the things they had strapped into the back looked well made.

"Bugger off!" hissed one of the thugs at Teague.

"Tsk tsk tsk," Teague responded, still with a smile on his face. "I bet that you lot haven't even asked them where they are going," he said to the thugs.

The would-be bandits looked bewildered.

"Where are you headed then?" Teague asked the burly man who held the wagon's reins.

"Uh. We're headed up to Marrowdale. They sent word that they needed a smith up there, and so my brother and I are bringing our families up that way to see if we can fill that need," the burly man said.

The thugs seemed unsure what to make of the situation, and from where I stood in the shadows, I wasn't sure that they had seen that Teague was alone. Their eyes did move from Teague to the wagon, and then to the strange sword that hung from Teague's belt. Ukumog responded to their inquisitive glares with a simmering blue malice.

Flayed

"See, gents? You wouldn't want to rob a village of their new smith, would ye?" Teague smiled at them. He then continued with a more serious tone in his voice, "Be on your way lads. There are no spoils to be made here tonight."

All eight of the angry brutes took a step towards us. The one in front scoffed at Teague, "Boys, some geezer wif a bizarre sword be tryin' to stop us from doin' owr jobs."

Grumbling came from the other men, and some of them made aggressive motions with their hands. Their scare tactics had no effect on Teague's demeanor. He still stood there defiantly.

The leader of the bandits took another step forward. Moonlight illuminated the tabard he was wearing. Emblazoned on the empty black field was the red skull of The Baron.

"Owr liege dunna like it whens we come back empty handed, geezer. Keep makin' a fuss, and wez gunna tax you next," the man said.

"I didn't want it to come to this, lads," Teague said, his voice filled with regret.

"Come to wot?"

With a familiar clink! Ukumog whirled into the space between the thug and Teague with its runes glowing brightly. "Last chance, my friends. Leave the family alone or I shall resort to the blade. Trust that I have no desire to shed blood this eve. It is you who is making this choice."

The leader of the thugs snarled at Teague. His hand drew the sword at his hip and he said, "First the geezer, boys. Den we collect Da Baron's taxes."

Chapter 13

From behind Teague, I watched the fight explode into action. At first they came at him one or two at a time, but Teague's mastery of the blade allowed him to keep them at bay easily. His strikes cut shallow wounds into the arms of his attackers. "Come now, friends. We needn't do this. Be smart and just let this one go."

His ability to turn their strikes aside only made them more angry. With snarling faces, they pressed down on him, trying to flank him on all sides. Teague gave ground and moved around his attackers, striking them with non-fatal blows to keep them all from pressing him at once.

"Friends," Teague urged, "there is no need for anyone to die tonight."

One of the thugs responded, "You iz gunna die, geeza." With that shout of intent, they charged forward and brought a cudgel down on Teague's wrist.

The Bard gave a quick howl of pain, and suddenly his posture changed. The charm vanished from his face and was replaced with cold rage. Ukumog reflected its wielder's change in demeanor, the runes glowing with intensity.

The shadows of the thugs began dancing in the blue light as Teague swung the black blade around with lethal accuracy. One after the other, these thugs ran forward to give their lives to the blade's hungry edge. In mere moments, their number was cut down to one.

Teague kicked the man in the chest, knocking him to the ground. Before the thug could recover, the Bard moved forward and put his boot on the man's throat.

"You tell your master that these woods are no longer his. The people here will not submit to his parasitic desires," Teague said, with a terrible coldness in his voice.

The man gasped for air under Teague's foot.

Flayed

"Nod if you understand me."

The man tried to nod, all the while trying to relieve some of the pressure that Teague was placing on his windpipe. When he was satisfied, Teague removed his boot and stepped back. Ukumog remained gripped in both of his hands and seemed eager to shed more blood. The faces of the family on the wagon behind Teague were filled with surprise. One of the two men was clutching his frightened wife while looking on with an open mouth. His wife opened her eyes and looked up at her husband, and seeing his mouth open, she pushed it closed with her forefinger. The thug climbed to his feet, trying to cough away the memory of Teague's boot and clutching a wound on his arm. "Who shoulds I tell Da Baron dis message is frum?"

"Teague of Shadow's End is who sends the message, friend." Teague paused for a moment. "I am sure that your master and I will meet soon enough."

Fear and confusion filled the thug's eyes, and after taking a moment to judge Teague's intentions, he hobbled off into the darkness.

Ukumog's grip over Teague's emotions faded, and he started humming a tune, pausing only briefly to say, "On your way, folks. I hear that Marrowdale is in desperate need for a smithy." He winked at them and strode towards my shadow within the moonlit forest.

Shaking off the vision, I came back to a street filled with conflict. The blue streaks of Ukumog's blade danced in the torchlight. Screams and shouts echoed through the night, but were met with a chorus of unskilled voices singing Teague's dirge of

Chapter 13

rebellion. His words of hope seemed to fuel the weary souls of these common folk, who were fighting for their lives, pressed between two titans: The Baron and The King.

Stones from unseen catapults streaked overhead and crashed into the city behind me as I caught my breath. The pounding march of hundreds of boots rang down the street towards my ears, and while I could not see the soldiers coming, I knew we were about to have more visitors. Urgently, I rushed into the crowd, holding only that sword I had claimed off the body of a fallen soldier.

"Brin!" I shouted at the crowd.

A peasant turned in my direction just as a gust of wind blew my hood back revealing my deathly guise. The woman's face was filled with panic, and she closed her eyes as she stabbed forward with her pitchfork. I was caught completely off guard, and the rusty prongs of the tool pressed through my flesh and punctured my innards. Two of the three prongs burned me with the pain of their entry, and the event knocked the wind from me.

The peasant woman who drove the sharp end of the tool through my gut screamed, and her whole body shook with fear. Unfortunately for me, this vibration made the piercing of my torso even more unpleasant, and the pain drove me to my knees. As I fell, she let go of the handle and backed away into the crowd of citizens wielding a wide assortment of weapons. The pain was worst when the handle hit the stone street, and I nearly blacked out.

"Is that one of the Eternal Well?" I heard someone from the crowd shout.

"He looks like a revenant!" another voice said.

I reached down and grabbed the handle of the pitch fork. The movement of the prongs inside of me caused even more pain, but I suddenly felt a surge of strength and power rushing through my veins. I pulled hard against the handle, trying to remove the rusty

Flayed

points from my insides, but it felt as if I might tear my intestines out along with it. The pain became too intense, and I stopped to catch my breath before trying again.

"He is pulling the fork out!" someone from the crowd yelled.

"Get him! Stop him before he can get back up!" someone else shouted.

I felt as if the entire crowd was about to descend on me and cut me to pieces, so I pulled again on the handle. The pain was just as intense as the first time, but I felt it move inside me a tiny bit before I fell over. Lying there on my side, I could feel the cold stone through my robes, and again I fought against slipping away into the darkness of unconsciousness. The sound of leather beating on stone rumbled in the distance, and I saw the line of peasants brace for more combat. All curiosity over my state was lost in an ocean of combat jitters. Again, I pulled on the pitchfork, twisting it a bit as I pulled. Rage and desperation fueled my attempt, and all the muscles in my body tensed, as if to lend their support no matter where they were located. With a final rush of pain, the prongs left my body, and I mustered all my strength to push the pitchfork away from me in defiance.

Boots stepped over and around me as they rushed the front line of citizens. I lay there motionless, lest they discover that I was not just another one of the many bodies that lay strewn around the streets.

"Together, men! Crush these rebels into the dust, where they belong!" a voice commanded from in front of me.

Opening my eyes, I caught glimpse of a man with short curly hair. He turned again to shout commands at the men around him, and I saw the paleness of his face. He was one of the revenants who kept the city under The King's control. Remaining still, I tried

Chapter 13

to study him more when I could glimpse him through the legs of his soldiers. The chainmail that dangled out from under his tabard was old and shredded. It carried the memory of countless fights. So, too, did the tabard that rode on top if it. The fabric was tattered, singed, and stained with the marks of all the death it had seen. My eyes then fell upon the chains that locked this curly-haired man into his livery and armor. They were many and thick, with numerous locks of various shape and size dangling from the links. Wrapped around his sword arm were loops of chain that looked so heavy he could have used them as a weapon all on their own.

I lost view of the curly-haired revenant because of the ranks of soldiers that came between us. I could tell by their continued press forward that the line of the citizens was failing rapidly. Lying there, I was not sure what I should do. The soldiers of the enemy surrounded me, but my friends and these innocent people were going to get crushed. The wounds in my abdomen healed, and with the pain gone, I could suddenly hear the song of rebellion rolling over the crowd. These people may be outnumbered and losing ground, but they had not yet lost hope. Nor should I.

Still gripping the stolen blade in my hand, I waited a moment more for the soldiers to settle around me, and then I stood. My rise was steady and slow, and the men around me moved away, uncertain what was about to happen. I have no doubt that the paleness of my flesh gave them pause, as they were used to the dead being their commanders. By the time I was to my feet, they had formed a wide circle around me, each of them prepared to defend themselves, but I could smell their fear.

My eyes scanned the ranks around me, looking for other revenants. I could see the back of the curly-haired one, and in the distance I could hear Marius' voice yelling commands. This tiny rebellion was more important than the siege, it seemed, for why else

Flayed

would The King divert his most powerful soldiers to deal with this internal threat. It was then that I knew Darion had no intention of just stopping this rebellion. He had send his army down here to kill every single person that had raised a weapon against him. He would crush these rebels out in the streets, even during a siege, just to assure his dominance over those who lived inside his prickly walls.

"Friend or foe?" one of the soldiers shouted at me.

My eyes gazed across the stern faces that stood against me. Each of them had fear and doubt hidden behind a veneer of discipline. I choked back the bloodlust that was growing in my heart, and like that vision of Teague, I tried to appeal to them. "Go back to the walls. Fighting off the siege is more important than these simple folk."

A few of the soldiers shifted their weight and looked for a cue from their companions, but none left. I sighed in frustration.

"Identify yourself!" one of the soldiers shouted.

"I am Wrack, and it appears I will be he who reluctantly sends you into the waiting arms of death." With that, the battle was on.

My weapon railed against sword and shield as I parried and attacked. Outnumbered as I was, I had no way to defend against them all, especially with only one sword in my hand. Over and over, I took deep wounds, wounds that healed as quickly as the steel was withdrawn from them. Fueled by my rage and the energy of the war going on around me, I also started granting mighty wounds to my opponents.

These mortal men were locked in a battle of attrition with a force that knew no loss. Each time I received a wound, it pushed me forward. Their wounds, however, were not so inspired. Body after body fell to the stone street as I whirled around in this arena of pain,

Chapter 13

walled by the ring of their shields. When one of them would fall, another soldier would step over their fallen comrade and replace them in the circle.

For a moment, it felt like this was an endless cycle. There always seemed to be more of them, and the pain of their strikes to my flesh were wearing on my strength. I needed to escape.

Over the crowd, I saw a blue streak of light dancing as it arced up and down. "Brin," I thought. "I must get to Brin." With this renewed focus, I concentrated my attacks on the soldiers between me and the light. The men behind me drove their blades into my flesh over and over as I brought the edge of my sword down like a relentless hammer. One step at a time, and through the pain, I dented the circle that was before me.

"Why will he not die!?" some of the soldiers behind me screamed. Their fear gave them pause, which slowed their attacks.

Cold air rushed in through the many slashes and cuts that the swords of my enemies had created in my clothing. Once again, I was wearing nothing but black tatters in the rough shape of a robe.

My sword came down upon the swords, shields, armor, and flesh of the soldiers who stood in my way. With each strike my anger grew, and with each step I could smell that their fear was deepening. Power rushed down my spine and flushed my hands with the biting cold of its embrace. I needn't look down to see that my limbs were now wreathed in black and purple energy. I could feel it lingering there, eager for me to unleash it upon these fools who would stand in my way. With this energy called up from the depths of my soul, I could not even feel the attempts of the soldiers around me to bring me down. The flesh that they sought to ruin was no longer like theirs; it was charged with the darkness of the universe, the power that exists between the stars, from where no human should dare to pull strength.

Flayed

My undead might grew with my power, and after three rage-filled blows my stolen sword broke in half when it met the helmet of a soldier that I had been showering with steel kisses. The broken blade tore through the metal of his brain cage and found lodgings inside the soft, warm place inside. As the soldier fell, I let go of the broken sword, and it remained lodged in his skull.

With a fist crowned in dark power I used my own knuckles as the next weapon in my arsenal. The dark power which surrounded them broke steel, wood, and bone, each strike also unleashing black lightning, which coruscated through the crowd, causing soldiers to drop to their knees in pain. Resorting to my unnatural power not only came easier to me, but also allowed me to clear the way much faster than the sword could have dreamed.

As I stepped through the line of soldiers, I came face to face with the civilians who had been fighting them. They looked ragged and tired, many of them fighting with wounds that would have caused their opponents to step back. Yet, they held their makeshift and stolen weapons fiercely in my direction.

"Here," I said, an inhuman echo present in my voice, "take the weapons of these fallen soldiers. Their armor, too, if you can. I will hold the line for a moment while you do."

The citizens took a moment to decide, but I picked up the bleeding bodies of fallen soldiers from the ground and tossed them gently in their direction to change their minds. They looked at me with astonishment as I turned around and began unleashing the power that was boiling out of my angry soul upon the hapless soldiers that surrounded me. Purple lightning flashed, burning men left and right. With a twist of my fingers, the shadows beneath their feet erupted into dark tendrils, entangling and strangling them.

Chapter 13

One palm open and towards the army which faced me, I pushed forward, and an unseen force moved through them like a charging bull, tossing bodies in every direction.

Chaos rippled through the ranks of soldiers near me. Many of those in the back turned and ran away from the scene, while others were frozen with panic. Unable to rally their shield-brethren, the rest held their position and braced for more attacks.

What they did not know is that these shows of force had taxed me. Great was the weariness of my soul, and having found relative safety, the anger in my soul began to wane. My show of force did allow me to change my tactic somewhat. I could just stand there and look menacing. My simple motions caused the line of soldiers before me to brace themselves for a magical assault.

Without a word, the citizens rejoined me at the line, now clad in the armor and weapons of fallen soldiers. I smiled at them, and despite their wounds, they seemed ready to continue fighting. I took a few steps forward, and the line of soldiers shrunk before me. A grin curled up on my face.

"Perhaps I have given these desperate souls a fighting chance after all," I thought to myself.

After collecting a few more swords and shields and tossing them to the citizens who stood at the line, I felt as if I had done what I could to help them, and with a silent nod, I moved past the line of citizens in my quest to follow the dancing blue light.

Shadows danced in the torchlight behind the line. The wind was unpredictable there, constantly changing in direction and intensity. It was odd, and added to my feeling that these humans were caught in the middle of a terrible storm. There in the flickering shadows, the casualties were tended to by those who would or could not fight. Briefly, I entertained the idea of using my blood to heal the wounds of those who were stacked up against the walls of the

Flayed

stone buildings. Blood ran liberally through the streets, and the sound of weeping men, women, and children could all be heard amidst the constant clash of steel.

"This suffering is the price of war," I muttered to myself. "Like a wildfire, it can start without warning and burn until there is nothing left but ashes and memory." These thoughts made me hate The Doomed lords of these lands even more than I already did. Fighting against my own sympathy, I refused to consider these humans to be lost causes or just faceless victims of circumstance. These were those who tried to remove the oppressive shackles of those who would try and contain them. Surely they must have known the price would be paid in blood.

Mindlessly, I navigated through the bloodshed and madness towards the dancing blue streak of light. I tuned out the sounds of misery and pain, for I knew that I should not stop to help them. My help would only bring more fear and sorrow. Luck was on my side during those few moments, for no one behind the line of the citizens stopped to consider why this one revenant was walking in their blind spot.

Halfway to my goal, I saw a volley of flaming arrows fly overhead. Most of them collided with stone, but one crashed through a window on the second floor of a nearby house. The haunting red glow of an unseen fire flickered in that window, and within moments the greedy tongues of flame were licking the window frame. Screams heralded the eruption of people from the building. Two large families, so it seemed, fled the building while carrying children and important possessions, then people started rushing back into the building. I assumed that it was to put the fire out, and while that might have been the intent of some of these people, others used the chaos to loot some easy-to-grab valuables. Men from the household shouted after a pair of men who had come

Chapter 13

out carrying silver candlesticks and had more goodies bundled up in their shirt. One young man from the house even chased after those thieves into the dark streets beyond my sight.

"Don't get involved," I told myself, trying to keep my eyes on Ukumog's dancing blue light. Murks squirmed uncomfortably in my pocket, and my next step was towards the burning building.

"What are you doing, Master?" Murks' voice was filled with concern.

"I'm not entirely sure, Murks. If these people need my help, I aim to help them," I replied.

Members of the displaced family looked over at me with surprise as I approached, but as the light hit my face, a woman who was holding a child screamed, and several others grabbed for anything that could be used as a weapon.

Holding my hand up I said, "Take it easy. I am here to help. What can I do?"

They relaxed a bit, but they continued to give me suspicious looks. The woman who had screamed gathered up the small children and took them away from me and the burning building. The pillar of fire spilling out through the broken window was growing by the second.

One of the men stepped forward. "Not sure there is much you can do. Whole place just went up so fast."

We stood there for a moment looking up at the fire. The raw elemental power of the flame was hypnotizing and terrifying.

"I'm going up there to see if I can put it out," I said without thinking. "I don't think I can save your home, but I can stop the fire from doing more damage."

The man just looked at me blankly and then nodded. I took that as all the permission I needed.

"What is Master's plan?" Murks asked.

Flayed

"I don't have one yet, Murks. We are going to go in there and just see what we can do."

If there is a telepathic version of a nervous swallow, I felt Murks do that.

The door to the house was standing wide open. Smoke poured upwards from the frame, and deep inside I could see the foreboding red glow of flames. At the threshold, I hesitated. I wasn't sure what I was doing, but my desire to help the people of Flay was so strong. I simply could not deny its pull on me. I took my last breath of fresh air before stepping through, into the inferno.

The air was hot and thick with smoke inside the house. The bottom floor was not yet bathed in flames, but the powerful glow that came from the stairs up to the second floor cast its angry light through the drifting clouds of smoke. From the outside, the home looked like it was made of stone, but the inside told a different story. The outer shell of the building was constructed of masonry stonework, but the inside was almost entirely wood. There were doorways leading off from the tiny entry room, and those ominous stairs that led up into the smoke. Without thinking, I skipped up the stairs into the mouth of the beast.

"Master, Murks is not sure about this. Master is not fires-proof!"

Ignoring the wise words of my tiny companion, I reached the landing at the top of the stairs and stopped. Before me was a dark wall of smoke. It churned in the air before me like a living thing slowly writhing, looking for escape. Through the haze, I could see the glow of the flames themselves devouring the guts of the house. The heat up on this floor was even more intense than the floor below and I thought that I even began to sweat. Not sure what to do, I just stood there and watched the flames crackle their way through the lives of the family that called this place home. I was

Chapter 13

amazed at the speed with which things that held such temporal and sentimental value were consumed by the unfeeling elemental force of the flames. So stunned was I that I didn't even realize I had been holding my breath this entire time until something bumped into me from behind.

Coughing, I spun around and came face to face with the young boy who had gone running after the thieves who had looted the house. He was tall and lanky, with dark curly hair. He held a scrap of cloth over his nose and mouth, and his eyes were freely flowing down his cheeks, leaving riverbeds through the soot on his face.

"Get the uzk out of our house!" he screamed.

Stone-faced, I just stared at this wild young boy who was so angered by a stranger in his home that he gave no concern for his own life. A cloud of smoke passed between the boy and me, and when it passed I saw his eyes grow wide.

"I am not here to rob you, boy. On the contrary, I came to see if there was anyone or anything I could save." Pausing, I looked at the ruin of the rooms around us. "As you can see, not much is left. You should get out of here before the fire gets further out of control."

His eyes narrowed with suspicious confusion. "What about you?"

"I am going to try and suffocate the flames." Even my voice was unsure how I would do that. "It is too late to save your things, but we have to stop the fire before it spreads."

The boy gave me one more stare before nodding and heading down the stairs.

"What are we going to do, Master?" Murks asked.

Flayed

A loud crash roared from beyond the wall of smoke, and air rushed through it. Stale hot air and embers washed over me, driving with it a billow of smoke down the stairs behind the boy.

"I dunno, Murks. Have any creative ideas?" I said, patting some flames out that had found their way to the hem of my robe.

The hemodan in my pocket went silent for a moment, searching for the answer. "No, Master. Murks has no ideas."

"Great," I said.

Feeling helpless, I tried to rattle my mind for the answer to this problem. It felt silly that I could wield my strange power to fend off the terrors that haunted this world, but I couldn't summon a force to put out a simple fire.

Just thinking about the cold darkness that was bound to my soul, my spine trembled with cold. The power shot through my limbs, and suddenly my hands were wrapped in dark power. But what was I to do with it?

In my panic, I irrationally considered that the cold power might work against the flames, then I quickly reminded myself that cold was not the actual opposite of flames.

"Fire requires fuel and air," I thought out loud. "What can these shadows that call when I beckon do? They aren't thick enough to smother the flames, nor can they deprive them of their fuel. What can I do?"

"Use this!" a voice from behind me said and I turned to see Avar standing behind me, a bucket filled with water in his hand.

I smiled and flexed my fingers, sending the dark power to the hidden vault deep within my soul from whence it came. I reached out and took the bucket from Avar, and tossed the water upon the fire. Another bucket found its way to my hands, and again, I showered the smoke and flames in water. Another and another

Chapter 13

bucket came up the stairs through Avar's hands, and each time we sent the empty buckets back the same way, but the fire was too much. The floor groaned and warped beneath my feet.

"Go down! The floor is going to collapse!" I shouted.

Our assembly line of buckets scrambled down and out the building. While we had lessened the flame's strength, we had not succeeded in stopping it from gorging its never-ending hunger upon the material things held inside this bank of human memories. I continued to toss bucket after bucket of water towards the house, hoping that the flood would eventually stop the flames.

Behind me the battle still simmered, but the intensity of the conflict had greatly diminished.

Curious, I asked Avar, "What happened? When I went inside, the army was pressing down hard."

Avar wiped the sweat from his brow, leaving a smear of ash upon his skin. "More catapult fire. I heard a horn blow from the direction of the main gate, and then more than half the soldiers marched in that direction. I think, maybe, that The Baron's army breached the wall."

Looking around, I could not see the blue streaks of Ukumog dancing on the field. "Brin and everyone alright?"

"They were when I last saw them," Avar said through his exhaustion, "But... that was some time ago."

I nodded. "Go find them. There isn't much more to be done here."

He sighed and looked over at the now homeless family. "Yeah, I suppose not," he said to me, then turned to face family who were all huddled together trying to comfort one another. "I'm sorry that this happened, but always remember: this pile of wood and stone is replaceable, none of you are." He smiled at them and then sprinted off towards the battle.

Flayed

I stood there silently watching the remains of the house slowly burn. After a time, the dark-haired boy came and stood next to me. Bravery filled his eyes and reminded me of the little boy from Yellow Liver, the first human soul to have been brave enough to show me kindness. My mind drifted off, wondering where that boy would be if we had gotten to The Ghoul's chamber in time to prevent his final meal. *How old would the boy be?* I had no doubt that he would have been a part of the city watch, if Captain Melanie would have let him.

These thoughts drifted through my mind like so many plumes of ephemeral smoke, and the cold fire of rage burned in my heart, yet I just stood there and watched the flames, never asking for this new brave boy's name.

Chapter 14

Day was breaking over the city of Flay. Hours had passed, and the fighting in our corner of the city had quieted, yet there were rallying horns in the direction of the marketplace. Our group did not wait to see what would happen next, however. Once the fighting ended, Brin made the decision that we should keep moving, lest the army of The King come back to that corner looking specifically for Ukumog or the rogue revenant.

We skulked through the back streets of the west side of the city and watched the sun rise. Brin was not yet ready to flee the city, a move that I admired. It seemed that the selfish motivation for revenge had been replaced by a desire to protect the innocent people of the city, at least for a time. We stopped behind a building not far from the market so that Tarissa could try and gather some intelligence on what the army was doing.

"You hear that?" Avar mumbled through a mouthful of dried meat.

I listened, but heard nothing that stood out as unusual. "Hear what?"

"Uzk," Brin said, a look of shock on her face. "The catapults have stopped firing."

"This is worse than I thought," Avar said.

Confused, I asked, "What do you mean?"

Flayed

Tarissa strode around the corner with urgency in her eyes. "We need to get the uzk out of the city," she said forcefully.

Avar stood up. "What happened?"

"Oh, gaak," Verif said. "They are organizing a search, aren't they? For us!"

Tarissa nodded. "I heard Lord Tiberion tell everyone assembled that the siege was going to cease until the blade of The Betrayer was in his possession."

"Well uzk." Brin threw her food to the ground. "We can't fight the entire uzkin' army. You're right, Tarissa. We need to get the uzk out of here."

"Go where?" Verif asked.

"Winterland or Yellow Liver, I imagine," Brin said. "Do we still have some of that magical blood?"

I patted myself instinctively and felt the vial of Gordo's blood I had in my pocket. The reminder of his death made me extremely sad.

"Here," Tarissa held up a vial. "I have one."

Avar's brow furrowed. "Didn't Elaina give us three vials? What happened to the other one?"

"Oh gaak!" Brin spat. "Gordo still had the third vial. That means they have it now. Gaak!"

"It isn't far to the wall," Tarissa said. "I suggest we get moving."

A roar came from the marketplace as every soldier in Flay shouted something unintelligible from this distance. Still, it sent a fright through my spine, causing me to jump a bit. A thundering of boots followed that echoed through the arteries of Flay as the soldiers rushed to do their work.

"We are too late," I thought to Murks, who was growing more and more afraid by the moment.

Chapter 14

Quickly, we gathered the things we had set aside while waiting for Tarissa and started running through the streets. The tide of soldiers was quicker than we had anticipated, however. Mere moments after we set off, they were already on our heels. Behind us, I heard a voice shouting. It wasn't a soldier. It was a woman shouting and pointing in our direction.

"They went that way!" she yelled to the soldiers in the street.

Whistles started blowing in some sort of code. Short bursts of sound mixed with longer wails of the air passing through steel. This was not like last time at the baths. This time they were not going to give up.

"WRACK!" a familiar voice shouted from up ahead. It was not any of my companions, but I knew it all the same. "WRACK! OVER HERE!" the voice shouted again.

Brin glanced over her shoulder at me, and I shrugged. With a dubious look on her face, she shifted direction towards the voice. Just as we turned the corner, I heard a grunt and a thud from behind. Looking back, I saw a soldier wearing The King's colors, with a dagger blade sticking out his back. Tarissa was at the other end of the dagger wearing a face made for war.

"Tarissa!" I shouted before I lost sight of them, then I said, "Brin, we are losing everyone else."

Brin did not slow. Instead she turned one more corner and stopped. It was so unexpected that I nearly ran into her from behind.

"Uzkin' David?" Brin shouted.

"David? What?" was all I could think to say.

Brin was right. David, the man I had carried from Yellow Liver to Sanctuary and to whom I had given my blood in order to save his life, was motioning from an open doorway for us to come in.

Flayed

"What the uzk are you doing here?" Brin shouted.

"Quick, get off the street!" David responded.

Trapped by my curiosity, I could not help but follow his invitation. Brin seemed likewise captivated by David's unexpected appearance and willfully walked into the doorway. Once we were inside, David closed and barred the door.

"Wait, we have friends still out on the street," I said.

David's face filled with alarm, and he moved to unbar the door, but his hands froze when a handful of armored men ran past the grime-covered windows near the door. Instead, he placed a finger to his lips and looked at us with stern eyes.

Forced into silence, I found my eyes drifting around the room. The house looked like it was abandoned and empty, save for a few scavenged supplies. The first floor seemed to have almost no interior walls, just support pillars and stairs that led to the second floor. It reminded me greatly of the house which had been consumed by the malicious flames of The King's army just hours before. Turning back to David and seeing no soldiers outside, I said, "David, what is all this? Why are you here in Flay?"

"I got in through the wall when some of The Baron's men breached it on the east side of the city," he whispered.

Brin shifted her stance, placing a hand on Ukumog's handle. "We heard something about agents from Skullspill getting inside the walls."

David nodded. "Of course, I am not really an agent from Skullspill, though I did convince some people that this siege needed to happen."

"You what?" Anger filled my throat.

Chapter 14

David shrugged. "It seemed to be the best way to give Yellow Liver a chance to grow strong enough to defend itself against The Baron when he decided to reclaim it. Pit the two powers against each other..."

"What about the people that get crushed between them?" I asked.

Brin motioned with her hands for me to lower my volume. "Quiet, Wrack."

"I can't save everyone," David said with a shrug.

He was right, we could not save everyone. Regardless of any actions taken to end the stagnation The Doomed had forced upon the world, people were going to suffer. Even if no one did anything, people were still suffering, still dying. David had at least taken some action, and I had to commend him for that.

"So you left Sanctuary to set all this in motion?" I asked.

David nodded. "I saw the war that was going on there, and I knew that there wasn't much I could offer, so I took a different tactic. If we can weaken the forces against us by pitting them against each other, we can bring them down to our level. We have to make this a fair fight."

Something about these words echoed in my mind, as if I had once said the exact same thing. *Had the idea for rebellion against The Doomed been brewing in my blood all this time, and David's exposure caused it to become his purpose? Surely the power in my veins could not change the will of others.*

"What about our friends in the street?" Brin said.

David's eyes fell to the floor. "I dunno. Things got really bad out there extremely fast."

Ignoring David's commentary, I sprinted up the stairs, hoping I could get a better vantage point so we could find them. I refused to believe that Avar, Tarissa, and Verif were simply lost to

Flayed

the ensuring madness in the street. Once up there, I moved quickly from window to window, trying to find my missing friends. Brin followed me, and the two of us scanned the grid of streets, but came away with no sight of them. All the passages between buildings seemed to be flooded with an ocean of green and white. The soldiers were even searching from house to house now, forcing their way into every home like a wave of tyranny washing over the city.

"It won't be long before they find us here," Brin said.

David remained silent. Nervously, his eyes twitched around the building, searching for some solution to hide us from the creeping doom lurking in the street. If David came up with a brilliant idea, he didn't act on it, nor did he give any verbal cue. The three of us sat in the quiet of each other's company, watching and waiting for the storm to come.

Brin remained perched where she could see the flow of soldiers in the street, David quietly paced, and I sat upon the floor. My thoughts kept going in circles and they were centered on one simple question: *how did we get to this point?*

It seemed that not long ago Brin and the rest of our company were engaged in an intrigue within the highest ranks of the city, one that smelled of rebellion and righteousness. My mind kept coming back to that meeting with Lord Darkweaver and was focused on how one meeting could throw all our plans and personal desires into this death spiral. Without a fairly significant stroke of luck, it seemed that our tiny company of rebels would be swept away by the tide of green and white, the city washed clean of our influence, only to allow The Doomed to use their very souls as fuel for a pointless and ceaseless war.

Chapter 14

A loud banging nearly battered down the front door of the building. "In the name of His Majesty, Darion Kalindir, we have come to search this house for unlawful invaders. Please open your door and allow us entry, or we will let ourselves inside," a voice from outside shouted.

"This is it," I thought. "The moment where the tide turns for us or against us."

"What do you mean, this house is empty?" the same voice shouted again. There was a pause before the loud voice continued, "Well, if no one lives here, we don't need permission! 'Course, we didn't need permission in the first place."

A round of laughter came from the front of the building.

David's eyes got huge, as if he just had realized something important. "The floorboards in the pantry are loose," he whispered. "Enough room in the space below for one of us, at least."

We all looked at each other, none of us being willing to hide in the hole.

"We should hide Ukumog down there," Brin said. "That is what they are really after."

David nodded in agreement, and before I said a word, the two of them were headed down the stairs. My worry that our movement in the house would make the soldiers more urgent in their search went unsaid, because even thinking of the words made me feel a bit of a coward. David and Brin made it to the bottom of the stairs before the door came crashing open, showering the open room with splinters of wood and shards of stone.

The surprise immediately charged my body with energy. I felt the cold of my dark power race down my spine and embrace my hands in its loving malice. Brin rolled away from the shattered door and came up in a fighting stance, clutching Ukumog in both hands. David shielded his face and ran into the back of the building away

Flayed

from the soldiers who began storming through the open doorway, their swords already drawn. I watched in terror as five soldiers entered the room within seconds, and through the grime-covered windows, I could see countless others waiting to come in.

Memories flashed through my mind in that moment. Mostly they were the simple times, those quiet moments when Brin shared her secret smile with me. The time we wrestled over something foolish on the hill outside Marrowdale also made an appearance. The softness of her lips when she kissed me in the sewers right before Gordo died, filled me with fire. It was a torrent of happy thoughts, all of which I shared with the woman who was facing down unbeatable odds.

I recalled a conversation from some time ago. Words I spoke to Brin back in the Forest of Shadows, years ago, cut through the mists of memory. "We will do this together."

That oath, frankly stated, was a sincere promise from me to her, and it was the star by which I navigated the seas of indecision. Here, in this moment most dire, my loyalty would not waiver. If we were to lose here, in this moment, we would do it side by side.

The air crackled around me as I descended the last few steps to the floor. Malice lived in my eyes as I waited for these soldiers to do their master's bidding. For the briefest of eternities, we all stood there waiting for someone else to act.

"The revenant is here! Call Lord Juindar!" a voice shouted from beyond the doorway.

Another voice called back, "Which one!?"

"Both of them!" the first voice replied.

"Uzk," Brin spat, the fire in her eyes nearly scorching the hesitating soldiers.

"Get them, you dogs!" a voice called from the back.

Chapter 14

The soldiers facing the two of us flexed their grips on their swords, and then, yelling in unison, charged at Brin and me.

A storm of steel erupted in the open room. Not having a weapon myself, I dodged the first attack by one of the soldiers, then grabbed his arm and with a swift motion, disarmed him. His bones cracked under the twisting pressure my maneuver placed upon his attacking appendage, and he fell back, grasping his sword arm behind his shield.

Two soldiers stepped forward to cover their fellow's retreat. They lunged at me in unison, careful not to extend their attacking arms into my dangerous grip. Parrying their attacks, I stepped to the side, putting their backs towards Brin. Even though she had her own enemies to deal with, Ukumog could not miss an opportunity to rip through armor, flesh, and bone. With a flash of Ukumog's hateful runes, one of the two facing me fell to the floor with a fountain of red.

My remaining opponent glanced with fear at his fallen friend, and hesitated to attack me. Capitalizing on his fear, I put my stolen sword through his face. I was unable to wrest the sword from the sticky contents of the dead soldier's head before the two fallen warriors were replaced by three. Behind them, soldiers were shouting and trying to push their way into the fray.

Brin was holding her own, but the soldiers leaping over their fallen comrades kept causing her to give ground. I counted at least five fallen bodies on her side of the room. Ukumog sang with each swing, parry, and hit. The bare floor inside the abandoned home was quickly flooding with a pool of viscous red, yet our small victories still gave us no method to escape this deathtrap. More swords slashed at me, and I dodged all but one. The tip of that sword caught me in the side and cut deeply. Had I been a mortal man, the wound would have been disabling, if not entirely fatal.

Flayed

The pain did come, and worsened as the grinning soldier twisted his sword to pull it from my undead flesh. As the steel, drenched in my black blood, retreated from the wound, I felt the tickle of my body immediately repairing the wound. Bolstered by this rush of my immortality, I grabbed the retreating blade with my bare hands, and with a quick twist of my wrist the blade snapped in half. The soldiers were all wide-eyed at the broken blade and the dark power which retreated from my hand back up my sleeve.

The three of them looked at me with bewilderment and refused to push forward, even with the waves of soldiers pressing on their backs.

"You can just run away, you know," I said.

They paused to consider my suggestion, but the shouts of their commanders from behind spurred them on, and they again pressed the attack. As soon as they stepped forward, I lifted the broken blade over my head, with point towards the enemy. The tip of that blade came down with inhuman force upon the shield of the first soldier who stepped towards me. The blade, charged with dark power and propelled by my undead strength, punctured the shield that was between the soldier and me and slid through the hole it therefore created. The room filled with a terrible grinding sound as the sword screeched its way through the shield and through the armored chest of the warrior. I felt the blade catch his flesh and shatter his bones. With one final gasp, he fell lifelessly to the floor. Drops of black blood dripped off my fingers to mix with the red tide beneath my feet. Again, the painful tickle ran through my fingers as the wounds in my hand stitched themselves back together.

A column of soldiers pressed on Brin, pushing her into the back room where David had fled, out of my line of sight. Panic shot through my body, and the chill of my dark energy burned me through to the bone. Murks stirred in his secret pocket and crawled

Chapter 14

out of the neck of my robe and onto my shoulder. The soldiers before me took a half-step back as the hemodan emerged, sweat dripping from their helmets.

Murks leapt onto the floor with a tiny splash, right where my blood had fallen. The tide of blood began flowing directly into his little form, and he began to grow in size.

Spurred on by the ranks behind them, the soldiers attacked again. I dodged one blade and punched the other soldier in the face when his shield dropped, causing him to stumble backwards into the ranks pressing him forward.

"HEMOSTRANGULATA!" Murks screamed.

I felt a tug on something deep inside me, pulling in Murks' direction. Suddenly, the massive carpet of blood under our feet began to bubble, as if it were starting to boil.

One of the soldiers swung his sword down at Murks, who jumped to the side and shot a spray of blood back at the soldier. Murks' fluid repost splashed the visor of their helmet, some of the blood finding its way inside.

The other soldiers around us showered me with the edges of their blades, trying to deliver their steel to my flesh. Focusing on evasion, I was able to step, duck, and roll out of the way. The latter move put space between myself and the oncoming horde of warriors, but put them between Murks and me. There was no time to lament my instinctual actions, as the soldiers did not cease their assault.

A cry from Brin burst from behind the stairs, filling me with a flash of rage. I pushed aside the next blade to come in my direction, and grabbed the soldier by the throat. My teeth pressed against each other to the point of cracking as I channeled my anger through my extended arm, easily crushing the throat of the grappled soldier. His armor and bones snapped and cracked as my

Flayed

titanic grip continued, until I held a crushed stump in my hand, and his severed body collapsed beneath me, save for his head, which oozed blood and remained wrapped within the handful of chain armor that I gripped in my fingers.

Bubbles of boiling blood that covered a majority of the floor made the terrain seem alive. From the other side of the soldiers, I heard Murks scream again, "HEMOANIMATIA! HEMOSTRANGULATA!"

Another barbed tug tore at my soul, and the dark power which coursed through me bled unseen into the world. Immediately, the blood on the floor reached its bubbling peak. Millions of bubbles roared the release of their air into the room, filling the space with a dampening white noise. With no warning, sinuous and thorny tendrils of red shot up from the surface of the blood and writhed around the soldiers in the room. Screams floated over the roar of boiling blood, as the tendrils began to squeeze and tear the lives of the armored men and women away from them.

Murks, now tall enough to come up to my waist, weaved his way out from the maze of dying soldiers to return by my side. There was a moment of peace in the house, though I knew that the worst was about to come. It was almost as if I could feel the power of the revenants that were amassing outside the door. Being careful not to get my robes caught in Murks' bloody garden of violent vines, I moved around to the back of the house. There, three soldiers still faced off against Brin, who had been backed into a corner. I grabbed a sword from the dead grip of an entangled soldier and planted it directly into the back of one of the three who had caged Brin. Distracted by this unexpected attack, the other two soldiers fell quickly to Ukumog's swift strikes.

"I had all three of them," Brin said, even before the last one had fallen to the floor.

Chapter 14

Nodding, I said, "Where did David go?"

She shrugged, still breathing heavily from fighting. "Under the floor of the pantry, I assume."

A section of the supports looked like it would be the natural place for a pantry. I took one step towards it and then stopped. The world shifted somehow, and the fountain of power that had always been both my bane and my gift felt as if it had been shut off.

"What is it?" Brin asked, still catching her breath.

"They're outside," I said, without really thinking.

"Who is outside?" Brin asked.

Her question was answered, but not by me. The sound of blades and boots clearing a path into the magical garden of death of Murks' creation filled the house. The vines of blood sat motionless, wrapped around their victims. The red upon the floor had ceased its boiling and now lay silent. We could hear them clearly as they hacked and kicked their way through the fallen.

"Tiberion, when we doth find Alexander, let me be the one to kill him," Marius shouted.

"Brother, why is it that thou be such a shameless hound for meaningless glory?" Tiberion responded, his voice filled with ancient mirth.

This gory scene was nothing to them. These fallen soldiers were but crushed bugs whilst in service to their uncaring lord. Their voices sounded gleeful while they hacked through the corpses of soldiers.

"Because glory doth make the man, brother!" Marius yelled. "Pray that once we finally meet our match, and are sent to the grave, that our glorious story be all that is left behind. Thy story will be one of blind duty and most boring honor. Whereas I will be a glorious hero... or perhaps an insidious villain. I care not, as long as I am someone worthy of tales everlasting."

Flayed

"Thou dost sometimes disgust me, brother," Tiberion responded without humor in his voice.

"Yea, this putrid world does likewise disgust me, yet we are here," Marius said.

A spray of blood spurted in our direction, and one of the vines collapsed taking with it the body wrapped in its coils. Through the hole in the forest of blood I saw them, the revenants. Marius stepped through first, staring at us both with a sadistic grin. His brother, Tiberion, followed shortly after. Tiberion's curly hair was wet with blood, but I recognized him immediately as the same revenant who had been leading the soldiers the night before. There were more undead faces beyond the gap in the vines, but they lingered in the shadows with glowing eyes smoldering.

Marius rolled his shoulders and tossed his head back and forth, displaying his eagerness to fight us both. "Thou escaped me once, little girl." He stared at Brin with malice gleaming in his eyes. "It shall not happen again."

"I needn't have to remind thee, Marius, His Majesty wants these knaves both alive," Tiberion said sternly, then over his shoulder, he said, "Bring us the rods, lads. It seems that we shall need them after all."

Marius chuckled.

The speed with which they pounced upon us was something I could not perceive. Quite literally, one moment Marius was responding to Tiberion's command, and the next moment I had Tiberion's sword impaled in my shoulder. I had not yet even felt the pain of the attack before I heard the familiar ring of Ukumog's black steel against Marius' hammering strike, Brin had been able to deflect the strike with ease. For a moment, I felt relieved, then the pain pulsed and I looked back at my attacker. With his lips pulled up and away from his ancient teeth in a terrible grimace, Lord

Chapter 14

Tiberion of house Juindar, Champion of His Majesty King Darion Kalindir, attempted to paralyze me with pain by slowly twisting his sword, causing shockwaves of misery through my system. For a moment, his plan was working perfectly, but he had apparently not seen Murks.

Through my connection with the hemodan, I felt anger wash over him, and a cloud of malice formed around a determined plan of action. Tiberion howled in pain and withdrew the sword, knocking me to the ground. I opened my eyes and saw that Murks had buried his head into Tiberion's leg and seemed to be drinking deeply of the revenant's ancient blood. With a swift motion, the champion's sword swung low, and sliced off one of Murks arms. The limb was dry and looked like a scabby twig before it hit the ground. Murks did not emanate any feelings of pain or fear, and I watched as his arm regrew as quickly as it had been severed. Tiberion shook his leg, trying to get Murks off, but the hemodan held fast and continued to feast on Tiberion's reserve of blood.

I bounced up to my feet, and moved to help Brin against Marius while Tiberion was distracted by Murks' attack. Ukumog's runes burned brightly as it arced down onto Marius' shield, nearly cleaving it in two. Brin's grunts were almost feral, and for a moment it seemed that Ukumog was the one directing her arms to move, not the other way around. With no weapon in hand, I did the only thing I could think of and charged Marius with my arms wide, hoping to grapple him. Much to my surprise, my haphazard plan worked, and my shoulder collided with his shield. At the last moment, he drove his sword down into my torso, leaving his body open for Brin to attack him. I felt the cold blood escaping the brutal wound that she had scored as I pushed him away and then to the floor.

Flayed

Keeping him pinned beneath me, I sat upon his shield, but he still had his sword arm free, and he used the pommel of his blade over and over on my face. I had no chance to reply with my own barrage of attacks, for his strength was mighty, and each time I felt my skull crack under his blows only to heal just before the next was delivered. There we were, with me pinning him to the ground, and both of our undead gifts keeping us locked within this repeating stalemate. Brin never came to aid me against Marius, and so after what seemed like a lifetime's worth of skull cracking blows to the face, I finally got the sense to duck away from his attack.

My face was inches from his deathly guise, which was filled with violent hatred. In his eyes I could see an endless fury, like a storm that had no end. He continued to strike me and try to push me off of him, but I was able to hold him down. Something in his eyes looked strange to me, however. The reflection on his glassy orbs was wrong. While I should have seen the images of the light around him, I instead saw the hollow face of a shriveled and dead man looking back at me. Upon this withered head there was a mighty crown made of dusty gold ravens.

"Darion!" I shouted at the tiny image in Marius' eyes.

A sudden and unearthly rage rushed down my arms, and I mindlessly gripped Marius' armor, tabard, and chains in my powerful grip. "Darion! This will not end here!" I screamed again.

The image of The Ghostly King silently laughed at my futile attempt to deny him his power. My blood boiled, my hands twisted and clenched, and then there was a powerful *snap*. When I looked down at my grip, I held a broken lock in my fist, a lock that was as ancient as The Cursing lay crushed and broken in my hand. I looked at it with a powerful awe, and beneath me, Marius ceased his struggle.

Chapter 14

I looked down and saw the face of a man I felt I once knew. The hatred and vicious desire to kill all who opposed his master was missing, and without that corruption, he looked familiar. Stunned as I was, I was powerless when he pushed me off of him and then stood up. There was recognition in his eyes, along with fear and disgust, then his face twisted again, and he screamed with pain. The pommel of his sword found its way directly to his own forehead, bashing it over and over again.

"What didst thou do to Marius!?" Tiberion screamed, and with a great force he kicked Brin with the flat of his foot, pushing her away from him as if she were made of nothing but straw.

The crushed lock had turned to a pile of ancient rust in the palm of my hand, and as Tiberion turned his rage towards me, I threw the dust in his eyes. He reeled back and screamed, while I rushed to Brin's side. I found her battered, but not out of the fight.

"Brin, are you alright?" I asked, all the while wondering if I should give her some of my blood.

She grimaced through the blood and grime on her face. "Where is that uzkin' son of a whore? I will kick him until he has no uzkin' teeth."

I smiled. "Marius has fled the field."

The sound of boots beating the wooden floor hit my ears, then a numbness washed over me. Shaking and screaming, I rolled to the floor. My ears were filled with a terrible deadness, and my sight was blurred. Motions and echoes from the room told me that Brin had gotten back to her feet and continued to fight, but she was facing more than just Tiberion. I tried to speak, but my mouth seemed like a strange puzzle that I hadn't yet solved. Motion blurred over me and my eyes struggled to focus. I heard Brin scream and it sent shocks through my bones. I tried to call forth my dark power, but it did not respond to my desperate need.

Flayed

The cotton faded from my ears and I could hear Tiberion mocking me with laughter. "Alexander. What has happened to thee? Wracked with misery? Seems rather apt that it would end in this way. His Majesty doth desire a word with thee, however. Before thou art planted in the ground... for good."

The blur cleared for a moment, and I saw four soldiers with dead faces all celebrating with their ancient commander. In his gloved hand he held, not a sword, but a rod of roughly hammered black iron. The end of it came to a wickedly barbed point, which made it look like some demented fire poker. I knew immediately what it was; one of the rods of Nekarsli. Quickly I looked over at Brin, who lay motionless upon the bloody floor.

Tiberion didn't give me enough time to even call out her name before he plunged the stinger of the rod into my heart. The rending of my flesh and bones at the barbed edge of that twisted iron was unlike any pain I remembered. My soul felt emptied at its puncturing kiss, and that terrifying oblivion soon swallowed me whole.

There was no dream, no vision that visited me in that abyss. I returned to the darkness that I knew back in that shallow hole by the foul waterfall. Emptiness was my only companion, and while I could not truly perceive the passage of time, I felt the weight of eternal solitude press upon me like a mountain of shameful loneliness. But then, there was a beat. Like that of a tiny drum, but closer than any instrument could ever be. The beat came from deep inside me. Then another came, and another. My heart stirred in the miserable darkness, and the magic of my undead life began to pulse through me once again. After one thousand and one beats, my mind finally stirred me back to the world.

Chapter 14

I awoke in a roughly-made iron cage with the sounds of thousands of voices howling in my direction. My mind was still muddled from the dark and empty place it had been after the rod struck me. Upon my face was a cool mesh of wire attached to vicious hooks that were dug into my flesh, a ssligari mask, one like they had put on Verif when they captured her.

The beaten iron of my prison was dark and ugly. Its misshapen form stood at distinct contrast to the craftsmanship I had seen all over Flay. Reflexively, I rolled up to my knees and shook the cage door, which faced away from the shouting crowd. No luck. While I could rattle the cage, the locks held the gate to my freedom fastly in place. The cage itself was fastened to a stone platform, and I recognized it immediately as the stage which stood prominently in the market square of Flay. It was night, and in every direction from the stage spread an ocean of angry screaming faces.

It was then I heard a slight groan to my left, and I noticed another cage. Inside lay the beaten body of Brin. Panic overtook my mind, and my rage rattled the cage again. Even my fury was not enough to escape this metal trap. Yet I saw no third cage, and I could not help but wonder what had happened to David.

Booming laughter rolled over me and I turned to see Rimmul's pale face mocking my attempts to find freedom. "Father! He thinks he can escape!" he said to an empty throne that sat at the far end of the platform. The mocking laughter moved through crowd in waves, as Rimmul's comment incited the crowd to follow his lead.

Disgust filled my soul, hatred burned my skin, and rage locked my jaw in place. My mind reached out for aid, not from Murks, but from Ukumog. I wanted to feel the power that I had felt when I held its handle in that sanctum under Yellow Liver. My

Flayed

misery recalled the rush of dark pleasure I felt when I cut The Ghoul, Palig, in half with one mighty swing. The flaring runes of the blade roared through my mind like a mad bear howling for escape.

"Yes, father," I heard Rimmul whisper, and he motioned towards some servants, beckoning them forward and pointing towards the crowd. Each servant rushed forth with a goblet made of silver. The goblet was unusually wide, almost like a bowl with a handle on the base of it, and off to one side stood a sharp spike. From where I was, I could not make out all the details, but every inch of these goblets was intricately carved with the regal craftsmanship I had recalled from my memories of Darion's court. The servants went forth, into the crowd, and immediately people pushed forward to puncture their flesh upon the spikes and then drain some of their blood into the chalices.

"Oh uzk," I muttered to no one. In my rage, I shook my cage again and roared with frustration. My attempts to break the locks, bend the cage, or make any progress to escape at all was completely fruitless.

A desperate gasping sound came from Brin's cage as she woke from her forced slumber. I watched as she repeated my same attempts at escape from her cage. "It is no use," I said with despair, "they have sealed us in tight."

"UZZZZZZZZK!" Brin railed against her cage. When she was out of breath, she leaned back against the poorly-shaped metal lattice that held her tight, and I saw the hope leave her eyes. "So what now? They enslave us?"

While my lips remained silent, I knew that The King would not risk sparing our lives. He meant to make an example of both of us. Before I could wallow in that misery, I tried to shake the thoughts from my head.

Chapter 14

The servants with the blood scampered back from the crowd, and I took a moment to take in more of our surroundings. Our cages were off to one side of the stage. The market had been specifically set up for this display of The King's almighty power. The noble houses, or at least what was left of them, were all noticeably in attendance. A sea of the common people in every single direction raised their arms and voices, cursing we who were trapped by their beloved King. The throne was drenched in layers of white and green silks. Dozens of banners floated over our heads, one for each of the great houses of Flay, and above all others, the banner of The King himself.

"He is here," I muttered in Brin's direction, then began scanning the stage. My eyes twisted and tingled as I switched between my normal and dark vision, but something wasn't right, I couldn't use my gifts. Not only had they placed a mask of ssligari on me, but these cages were enchanted like the Rods of Nekarsli, as Murks called them. Somehow it seemed to be cutting off the source of my magic. I was without the very power that had cursed me since I awoke at just the time I needed its dark gifts the most. My fingers found the hooks of the mask and started to pull them free, but they were drilled into the bones of my face. My attempts resulted in nothing more than a great deal of pain.

"PEOPLE OF FLAY! I GIVE UNTO THEE THOSE THAT WOULD MURDER YOUR KING!" Rimmul's arms were lifted in celebration, his white mane of hair shaking with glorious victory. His voice rose above the roaring crowd, and when he motioned towards us, the sound from the masses was deafening. The Prince then turned away from the crowd and waved to Tiberion, who marched with purpose to the stage. Behind the revenant were two other soldiers, one of whom was carrying something bulky hidden below a black velvet blanket. This object was thick in the

Flayed

middle and thin on each end, but much wider than the soldier. My mind raced at the thought of what terror lived beneath that velvet curtain.

When they reached Rimmul, the Tiberion and the other soldier flanked the bearer and all three faced the masses. So filled with curiosity, I found myself clutching the bars of my cage with my face close enough that I had no bars blocking my view, yet my soul was filled with hopeless dread.

Rimmul held his hands up and a hush fell over the crowd. "Good citizens! These foul assassins have brought unto us a most precious gift indeed!"

Brin stood up in her cage and grasped the bars tightly. She started whispering, "Uzk. No, no, no, NO, NO!" and ended with a yell that caused all eyes to turn to her.

The Prince flashed his fangs at Brin with a malicious smile before turning back to the crowd. "People of Flay! Your Majesty! I give you, THE SWORD OF THE BETRAYER!"

Tiberion tore the velvet blanket away to reveal the glowing blade lying upon a dark green pillow. The soldier tiled the pillow downwards to show the black rectangular blade to the audience. Ukumog's runes blazed like tiny blue suns as it sat helplessly upon the pillow. Even at this distance, I could feel the sword's rage.

The crowd answered this revelation with shocked silence which then erupted into the roar of approval.

"NO! NO! NO! YOU UZKIN' BASTARDS!" Brin screamed and tried to shake and kick her way to freedom, but the roar of the crowd drown her protest in a wave of zealous celebration.

This was it, I feared. *Was this how our journey together would end?* We had not even come close to avenging the murder of Brin's father, and these Doomed souls still sat upon their cursed thrones. I could not help but wonder if the screaming masses

Chapter 14

assembled there understood what was happening before them. Surely there were some who had been touched by the songs of the Bard. Perhaps there was some valiant souls out there who would carry on our fight after we were gone. While Ukumog had not worked to kill the revenants here in Flay, somehow I knew it could be my end, for I did not have the magical chains and locks that the others did. The finality of it struck me deep, but at my moment of great despair, I could not simply give up. Gordo wouldn't have wanted that. In my mind's eye, I could still see his brutalized body hanging from that pole, not ten feet from where we were imprisoned now. I could not lose Brin without a fight, nor could I shamefully dishonor the memory of my fallen friend. So, I started humming. I did not know the words to the song, but I knew the tune.

As the roar of the crowd quieted, Brin could hear my song, and she sang the words. She nodded at me, as tears streamed down her cheeks. As the celebration of the masses became quieter still, our song softly lifted out of the zealotry, and soon, the words floated powerfully, filling the air.

Flayed

"Shadows rise and shadows fall
One shadow forged to kill them all
From haughty tower
To sunken grave

We know their names

Hungry for each other's strength
Tearing, ripping at the length
Of destiny's cruel desire
Throw off your chains

We know their names

With fire bright and purpose bold
They'll feel the pain of sins so old
Their thrones will burn
Our names they'll learn

Throw off your chains

Curses can be broken
Torments undone
And in their joyous passing
Unsung tunes will be sung

THROW OFF YOUR CHAINS!

WE KNOW THEIR NAMES!"

With tears streaming down her face, Brin's haunting voice danced over the crowd. Even Rimmul seemed entranced by the melody until her voice cracked on the final line. As Brin took a

Chapter 14

moment to collect herself, The Prince rushed over to her cage and slammed it so hard with his fist that I thought I heard it break.

"SILENCE! Thou dost dare to sing that seditious song!" he roared.

Brin laughed. "What's the matter? Scared of a little girl, blood-sucker?" Growing bold, she motioned to Tiberion and said, "Why don't you give me back my sword, and I will teach you all a UZKIN' LESSON!" Rage overtook her words and she roared with white knuckled fists shaking the dented door of her cage.

The fire filled Rimmul's glassy eyes. "Thou shalt be the one who is taught a lesson, traitor!" He strode over to Ukumog and grasp the red leather wrapped bone handle.

"NO!" Brin and I screamed in unison, both of us reaching through the gaps in our cage for the same handle that Rimmul now gripped firmly.

A bolt of lightning shot down from the sky and struck Rimmul's sword hand. The scream that burst from him sounded like it was two voices instead of one, and one of the two was not human. The bolt bounced from Rimmul's hand to the blade of Ukumog itself, then again to the cages that held Brin and I prisoner. Ukumog clattered to the stone stage and The Prince's sword arm cast smoke up from its burned hand. He grabbed his right wrist with his left hand and sucked air into his lungs through his teeth. "Bring me the tribute!" he screamed at some nameless attendants.

A goblet, similar to the ones from the crowd, was brought forward from the side as Rimmul grinned evilly at Brin and me. Brin was entirely focused on trying to reach Ukumog through her cage, even though it was clearly out of reach.

"Brin!" I said, intending to tell her how I felt, before it was too late.

Flayed

Her gaze met mine, but blue light from Ukumog reflected eerily in her eyes. It scared me enough that I backed away from her and collided with the other side of the cage. Something stung the back of my neck, and when I turned around one of Rimmul's servants was walking away from me. Touching my neck, my hand came back covered in my blood. "My wounds aren't healing," I whispered. Then I turned to Brin, "My wounds aren't healing!"

She just shook the cage and roared, ignoring me.

"Citizens! Thy tribute and the tribute of these traitors shall fill me with such unearthly power, that I will conquer this horrible blade!" Rimmul shouted, holding one of the wide silver goblets over his head.

The crowd went berserk in their worship of The King's mighty son. People off to the side of the stage began rending their clothes and tried to push through the soldiers guarding the stage, all screaming for The Prince to devour their very souls. One of the hooded servants who had been collecting blood for the masters of Flay came over to our cages, and with masterful subtlety tossed a key into both of our cells, then stood off to the side, waiting.

Brin was so focused on the sword that she hadn't noticed, but when Tiberion came and took the sword away, the spell over her mind was broken. I was already quickly trying to get the key into the lock while everyone's attention was grabbed by The Prince's display of vampiric feasting.

"Brin, there is a key in your cage. Open it and let's get out of here," I said quietly.

"A key? From where?" She felt around the floor until she found it.

Without looking at our savior I said, "From that nice masked servant over there."

Chapter 14

My lock clicked, and I felt the door loose, but I held it shut, waiting for Brin. She stumbled with the key, wiping tears out of eyes that kept darting over towards Ukumog and The Prince.

"Focus on the lock, Brin," I urged. "We have to get out of here."

"Not without my father's sword," she growled through her teeth.

My heart was racing. Every possible outcome of us attempting to collect Ukumog that I could conceive ended in Brin's death or worse.

"If we escape, he will have to come after us. It will be easier to kill him on grounds we choose than here in the middle of his fanatical army."

She glared at me, but I saw the odds of the situation sink into her mind. Then there was a click, and her door came open.

I looked over at Rimmul who had nearly finished slurping the cup of blood and realized. "It is now or never, Brin."

"Uzk," she said. With a sigh, "I found it once, I suppose. Can't keep fighting if I am dead."

With that, we both pushed open our doors and bolted off the stage, following the servant who was now pushing people out of the way, clearing a path for us.

The crowd was so stunned that we were all the way through the collected mob before they actually realized what was going on. When we neared the end of the thick body of the collected masses, a sharp sickness gurgled in my gut. A wave of nausea washed over me, and I felt as if I would empty my guts right there on the street. The crowd gave a triumphant cheer, and I looked over my shoulder to see Rimmul holding Ukumog triumphantly over his head.

Flayed

Some forgotten lore that was buried inside my mind told me that Rimmul using the blade should not be possible. That Ukumog was warded against The Doomed wielding it. This was wrong. Completely wrong.

Fighting through my sickness, I stumbled after Brin and the hooded servant, who were still sprinting through the crowd. We reached the silent shores beyond the sea of zealous humanity to find nearly-empty streets. The servant tore the mask and hooded robe off and threw them in the street, yet I was surprised at the person that was revealed.

"My name is Moriv," he said, quickly sweeping his curled mustache to either side of his mouth and giving Brin a slight bow. "Your friends and I conspired to free you. Come, they are waiting for us."

Moriv's face seemed familiar to me, yet I was not sure if he could be trusted. Brin and I shrugged at each other, recognizing that we had little choice but to follow this strange new friend.

Zigging and zagging through the grid-like streets of Flay, we ended up in a section of the lower city that I had never seen before. The buildings here were pushed much closer together, and new houses were built in what were once alleyways between other buildings. Once in this cramped part of the city, Moriv walked with purpose up to a specific door and greeted it with an unusual knock. While he waited for a response, he wiggled his eyebrows at Brin, making her giggle.

After a moment, the door opened, and Tarissa was standing there. She gasped with surprise and disbelief then rushed forward and closed her arms around Brin with a sigh of relief.

"Oh gods, it's really you," she said.

Chapter 14

Avar appeared in the doorway before Tarissa finished embracing Brin and gave a slight cough, then disappeared back into the building.

"We should probably get off the street," Moriv awkwardly suggested.

Brin and Tarissa broke their connection, both of them wiping away emotional tears, and then we escaped the street into that tiny building.

Everyone was there. Avar had a cloud of worry hanging over him, Tarissa was more emotional that I had ever seen her, and Verif gave me a genuine look of surprise before coming to stand by my side. David's eyes were filled with relief, and Murks immediately ran towards me and nested within the hidden pocket of my robes.

After an exchange of hugs and tears, Tarissa spoke. "We were really worried the plan would not work."

Verif scoffed, "You and Avar were worried. Moriv and I knew it would work." She smiled at me, and her body language told me that she wanted to reach out and hold my hand.

Brin suddenly looked suspicious. "How exactly did you meet Moriv?" she asked our collected friends.

"I was stalking you," Moriv interjected before anyone else could speak. "I was sent here by the Great Pyramid in Shatter. The ancients told me to find those who would fight against The Doomed. Once I heard the criers here in Flay talk about the woman with the strange sword, I knew it had to be you."

With this acknowledgement from Moriv, I remembered seeing his face when Tarissa and I took our journey away from the temple beneath the castle. His was the dark face I saw in the tavern during our flight back to the temple. However, my reflection was disturbed by Verif.

Flayed

"We need to get moving. When that crowd disperses, they will no doubt be howling for blood," she said.

Brin nodded, and the next thing I knew, we were back in the streets heading for a section of the outer wall. Haunting whispers drifted through my mind with a voice that was not my own, but I could not hear them well enough to grasp their meaning, and due to their distraction, I could barely pay attention to the conversations that were happening on our way to the wall. In what seemed like a mere instant, we had reached a section of the thorny outer wall, and I watched as Tarissa dripped Elaina's blood upon the thorns and commanded them to open for us.

Still distracted by the whispering voices, I followed close behind my chattering friends, unable to pay attention to what they were talking about. Once the wall began closing behind us, I found my mind in a different place altogether.

"Lord Mavren Ruthrom!" a ghostly form sitting upon the silk drenched throne called out. The crown upon his head was a shimmering collection of raven's wings. It was The King himself, Darion Kalindir, who now looked down on The Rotting One. Mavren was bound in chains and was kneeling before The King. His head was hung to the ground.

Mavren's voice was filled with sorrow and disappointment, "Yes, your Majesty."

"Ye kneel before us accused of heinous acts of treason. What words will defend these accusations?" The King asked with righteous fury.

Chapter 14

Beside the silk throne stood Rimmul with Ukumog gripped tightly in his hand. The blade's runes were erupting with blazing protest, and Rimmul's sword arm seemed to vibrate with pain, but he held the bone handle of the sword with a ferocious grip. His face was filled with a zealous glee that only partially veiled the intense discomfort that the sword was causing him.

"Your Majesty, I am but your humble servant. I live to do thy will," Mavren wept, his rotten tears falling to the stone dais.

"Lies, Your Majesty." Prince Darkweaver stepped up beside the throne. "He set an ambush for us, all with the intent of undermining your authority."

The King paused, absorbing Gelraan's words before leaning down towards Mavren. A cold hatred was stretched across his ghostly face. "Why dost thou weep, brother? Is thy regret for sins committed against us so great?" When Mavren said nothing, The King sighed. "Very well. These tears are enough evidence of thy guilt."

A wave of cheering flowed out from the stage to the opposite shores of the crowd. The blind lust for blood over crimes committed against their lord was startling. Darion stood from his throne and floated to the edge of the stage, and after taking a gulp of blood from one of the tribute chalices, rose his hands into the air, silencing the audience.

Before The King could say a word, I could see Darkweaver sneer at Mavren, and then he shared a nod with Prince Rimmul. Their conspiracy was evident in that moment, yet The King had his back to them and did not see.

"Loyal subjects!" The King's unearthly voice echoed over the silent mob. "We thank you for bearing witness this day. While our mighty guardsmen seek the escaped prisoners, we shall deal with a supremely important matter."

Flayed

Captivated by their liege, the crowd remained deathly silent. The noise of steel armor shifting occasionally filled the void of sound, and my ears could hear Rimmul fighting to remain calm for the pain that shot through him.

The King floated towards Mavren, until he was looming over the kneeling Doomed. His face was tight with merciless glee. His translucent eyes betrayed his joy that this moment had finally come.

"MAVREN RUTHROM! I, DARION KALINDIR, SUPREME LORD OF THE EMPIRE OF RAVENSHROUD, SENTENCE THEE TO DEATH UNENDING! BY THE STRIKE OF OUR SON'S BLADE, THOU SHALT DISAPPEAR INTO THE VOID AND THY TRAITOROUS SOUL NEVER FIND PEACE!" The King's voice boomed across the entire marketplace and seemed to cascade beyond, echoing into the very bones of the world itself.

With his face still pointed at the ground, Mavren calmly replied. "Never in all my days would I have assumed you to be one to break the ancient covenant, Darion."

Darion fumed, "We are above such petty ancient magics. The world kneels at our command. We are *omnipotent*!"

Mavren gave a wheezing chuckle. "That isn't your son's blade, and without it, you are powerless to take my miserable life."

Glaring eyes from The King's ghostly visage shot invisible daggers at Mavren.

Mavren weakly continued, "But your mindless followers don't know that. What good are these sheep if they know nothing? Are they simply food to feed your lust to feel whole again?"

"Art thou quite finished?" The King scolded.

Chapter 14

"Do you think your son has forgotten who wields the power to end ancient lives, Darion? Has his ambition faded with time?"

"Hrumph," The King scoffed and turned to see the greedy eyes of Gelraan Darkweaver staring at him. Without averting his gaze from the foreign prince, he said, "RIMMUL, OUR BELOVED SON! EXECUTE THIS FOUL TRAITOR!"

The crowd erupted with maddening howl, worshiping The King's absolute power over life and death. Broken chants proclaiming The King's god-like might, even over the other immortals, could be heard drowning in the sea of insane celebration that flooded the city of Flay.

Buried in the sound of the crowd, Mavren's words were only heard by the three Doomed which sought his destruction. "That sword is not yours. It will be reclaimed by its true master, and he will see your end."

The Vampire had bloodlust in his eyes as he walked towards Mavren with his fangs bared. His sword arm was vibrating, and with each step the blue runes upon Ukumog's surface grew more intense. Rimmul's struggle to command the blade was evident to my unique perspective, but invisible to the massive crowd that continued to celebrate this ominous moment.

When Ukumog was clasped tightly in both of Rimmul's hands and lifted over his head, the crowd again exploded with bloodthirsty howls of jubilation. The sword seemed to be made of blue stars shining from a pillar of darkness as it vibrated in Rimmul's hands.

"Remember this, for one day it shall be you in my place," Mavren wheezed up at Rimmul.

Flayed

Anger flashed through The Vampire's face, and with a mighty roar, he brought the blade downward. The vibrating edge collided with the side of Mavren's skull and moved downward through his putrid flesh, slicing diagonally through his head and throat, and severing his left arm from his body. His severed bits splattered their way across the stage and into the crowd. The remainder of his body still knelt for a breath, and then the spasms of death toppled it to the ground. For another breath, the body lay still there, and then dark energy came surging out of his wounds and rushed towards Rimmul. The Prince lifted Ukumog to try and deflect the tendrils of power. The power moved like a striking snake and suddenly was wrapped around the glowing blade in Rimmul's hands. He pulled against the dark tendrils, attempting to free Ukumog from their grip, but his attempts were in vain.

The writhing darkness quickly began to disappear, almost as if the blade was consuming their mass. Darion and Gelraan were helpless as Rimmul shook violently with his eyes rolled back into this head while Ukumog drank its fill of the dark power. The crowd continued to cheer the might of their dark masters, blind to the reality that was displayed before them.

When Ukumog finished absorbing all the dark power, Rimmul staggered to remain standing. The ordeal had completely unsettled him, but it was not quite over yet. After one more breath, Ukumog shot itself upward, to the limit of Rimmul's limbs, and flashed with blue light. A crash of thunder so loud that it caused windows to shatter and people to go tumbling was released from the blade, and black lightning shot into the sky. Finally, the blade went silent, and Rimmul collapsed to the stage.

Chapter 15

Mindlessly, I crawled through the tunnel along with my friends while the vision dominated my thoughts. Somehow I knew that the events I saw in my mind were happening simultaneously as we were pulling ourselves through the wet, root-covered earth. We reached the other side, with David going out first to make sure that any of The Baron's men were distracted. In the haze of the vision, I barely noticed when David said goodbye to all of us. It wasn't until we reached the nearby forest that I thought to ask, "What happened to David?"

"He said he needed to return to Skullspill," Verif told me. "Something about meeting up with Mariano."

"That low-life Mariano certainly has his greasy fingers in a lot of pies," Tarissa chuckled.

I went to speak, but was interrupted by a loud bang that seemed to come from my bones.

The next thing I knew, I was lying face down on the ground and my blood felt like it was boiling. Many hands reached out to lift me from the dirt, but I heard the discharge of static zap anyone who brought their flesh too close. Stunned, it took me a moment, but I was able to climb back to my feet. My ears were ringing from the explosion, and I could not hear what my companions were discussing, but the look of panic was evident in their faces.

Flayed

"What happened?" I asked, but could not even hear myself speak.

Brin mouthed at me, but I couldn't hear her, and so I shrugged and pointed at my ears. She threw up her hands in frustration and started arguing with Verif.

Murks crawled from my robes and up to my shoulder. I could feel the confusion lingering in his thoughts. There was a sharp pain from deep inside my ear, where Murks had apparently stuck one of his tiny arms and suddenly I could hear from that side again.

"What happened?" I asked again.

"Can you uzkin' hear me now?" Brin replied.

"On this side I can."

Murks crawled from one of my shoulders to the other around the back of my neck and began poking me in the other ear.

"We don't know what happened," Brin said. "It was like you were struck by lightning or something."

The vision I had just seen flashed before my eyes. Black lightning had left Ukumog after Mavren had been slain. *Had the blade sent me the power it absorbed?* My thoughts spiraled into unanswerable questions that I dared not utter.

"Are you ok?" Verif asked.

"I think so," I lied, blood still simmering beneath my pale skin.

"We should keep moving," Moriv said.

Brin nodded, and within moments we were back to fighting through the dark woods on our way to who knows where.

Chapter 15

Hours passed, and I was still lost in my thoughts. Moriv seemed to fall right into Gordo's old place at the front of our group, yet he made Brin laugh more than Gordo used to. She was always smiling at him, but I was too addled to really get a sense of this new member of our little band of rebels.

"Are you really ok?" Verif asked, her voice sounding more genuine than ever.

"I think so," again I lied, trying to hide the trouble in my mind.

"We need to get that mask off of you." When I didn't respond, she gave me a tight lipped smile. "If you ever need anything..." Her hand touched mine gently, sending a bolt of warmth through my body, then she took it away.

I stared at the dark mane of Brin's curls bounce as she walked, talked, and laughed with Moriv. Everything seemed upside down and sideways. I had no answers, only more questions, and I felt as if the person most important to me was walking farther and farther away with each step we took.

When night fell we searched for a while, seeking a good spot to make camp. We were not far from the armies of The Baron, so we had to be sure that they would not see a fire through the needly trees of the forest. Once camped, everyone went through their usual tasks. Brin and Moriv went hunting, Avar and Tarissa cooked, and Verif cleaned. A wasteland of emotion set me apart from the rest of my companions. While I was there physically, my mind and my feelings were lost in some unseen void. It was like I was locked in some battle with myself that even I could not really perceive. They chattered for hours, and eventually I found myself to be the lone soul awake, looking up at dark sky through scattered branches.

Flayed

The moon shed no light on that night, and even the stars seemed dull and distant. Murks tried to talk to me through our link, but I ignored him. My sulking over something yet unknown was more important than anything my hemodan had to say. Endlessly, I seemed to wrestle with questions I could not completely form, and in the darkest part of the night, I tore the ssligari mask from my face.

Metal shredded, bone shattered, and leather ripped. Moments later, I held the accursed thing in my hands. A surge of power rushed through me, renewing my flesh and bones. In my rage, I pulled on the sides of the mask with all my undead strength. Links in the mesh popped and burst as I tore it like paper. Triumphant, I reveled in the destruction of the tools of my enemy.

Almost instantly, the world seemed more vibrant. However, the novelty of the brighter stars and lovely smell of the trees faded quickly. I fell back into the malaise of the dread that loomed over my spirit. This despair was quite like what I had seen in Mavren's eyes when anyone mentioned his tormented wife. *Had I become as lost as he was? Without Ukumog, did we stand a chance against these foul immortals?*

I had no answer for these lingering questions. The terror that the blade Ukumog had often made me feel, I now found in the lack of its presence. *Would we even try to move against the dominating powers of the world? Or would we vanish into the hordes of those who ignore or celebrate these dark lords? Was Ukumog the only thing keeping us at odds with them? If this were true, then who were we really?*

Then I asked myself a question that only others had asked me in earnest. *Who the uzk am I?* No answer came immediately.

Chapter 15

The following morning we made our way back to the road. The sounds of the siege engines had resumed behind us. Flay was again under attack by The Baron's men. We stood there on the road, watching the smoke rise from the walled city. It was both beautiful and terrible at once.

The smell of amber came to my nose as Brin walked up beside me. Her hand found mine as she came close to me. "I'm worried about you, ya know. You haven't seemed like yourself. Are you alright?" she asked.

I wanted to answer her, but instead I received the answer to my own question.

Darkness. Then rising from the fog of the dream came the sound of a hammer beating against something metal, but not metal. With each crash came a pulsing of purple light. Sparks burst into the air with each flash, causing showers of cascading tiny blue fires. Louder and louder the pounding became, crushing the distance between me and the dream, until it was like I was actually there.

In my right hand, I held the hammer. A thing made of stone and bone, yet somehow formed into a powerful tool. The anvil upon which my thunderous blows fell was a black rectangle, perfectly formed from the shape of the dark room. There was no light, save for the purple fire which burned down the length of the glowing blade that I expelled my wrath into. With each attack upon the glowing surface, I howled with a burning rage and as my anger met the air, it fueled the form I was shaping, slowly giving it mass and letting it take shape. Blinking away the tears of hopeless frustration, I tried to find solace as I emptied everything I hated into that terrible thing which I was making.

Flayed

Opening my eyes, I found myself somewhere else. Somewhere I had been many times before. It was a busy tavern, but everything moved slowly in the dream. Across the room, I saw a young man walking towards my table with haste, his hands gripping four mugs of beer that tipped forth a few drops of their bounty as he pushed through the crowd. He smiled at me as he approached, his green eyes brimming with charm. Here I was again, in the belly of the Headless Mermaid in Yellow Liver. This time, it was Brin's father that brought me drinks at what seemed like precisely the same table where I had started my journey with Brin.

"I'm Teague," he said, handing me one of the mugs as he sat with me.

My lips took a sip from the brim of the mug, and after I swallowed the foul brew, I cleared my throat. "I know who you are, Teague. That is why I sought you out." My tone was darker than I was used to, and filled with confident purpose.

"What did you say your name was?" Teague asked between gulps from his mug.

"Wrack," I said. "I've heard some of your music, friend. Very fascinating work. What gives you inspiration?"

"Thank you." Teague smiled. "From wherever I can get inspiration, I suppose. Mostly I just sing what is in my heart."

"And if I were to look into your heart, what would I find there?" My voice was cold and unfeeling. I felt as if I were inside the mind of an inhuman predator, and Teague was my chosen prey.

Teague took another swing of his beer and responded with blatant confidence, "Hope."

The sound of rattling chains came to my ears from far away, and before I could say anything else, I was whisked from that familiar place in Yellow Liver.

Chapter 15

The air was strange and unearthly. The space around me was charged with a power that made me think I was not in the world, but somewhere else. Everywhere I looked, I could see the threads of creation weaving every surface of everything. Here they formed a dark chamber, lit by a single brazier. I warmed my dead hands in the heat of the fire and watched the magically-created flames dance over coals nested in a bed of iron. While the fire did give off heat, there would never be any need to replace its fuel. Nothing about this place was real, not in the same sense as the world outside. This place was entirely crafted and controlled by me. I was the only god in this dark corner of the universe.

The chains rattled again, and a deep moan came from my prisoner. He was a hulking thing, misshapen and grotesque. Massive arms grew from his wide shoulders, and a few more sprouted from random places on his exposed torso, each of these appendages ending in clawed hands all writhing with the eager desire to cause pain. His head was malformed and twisted, and the proportions of his features were all wrong, making him look almost as if he had been sewn together from multiple people, but I knew this was not the case. Tugging at the chains that forced him to stand with his arms spread wide, he roared with frustration.

I enjoyed watching him struggle. With each growl or moan, it reminded me how clever I was to have captured him in the first place. None of the others had even cared about the countless humans this monster had torn to pieces. They let him wreak his havoc upon the people that these kings and barons were supposed to protect. I alone was strong enough and smart enough to bring this beast to heel. His howls were simply a celebration of my divine glory, and I intended to savor every moment of it.

"You killed him?" the gravelly voice of The Baron asked me.

Flayed

They surrounded me, The Doomed. We stood in a great chamber, lavish decorations hung upon the walls, and the ceiling was covered in a great mural of dragons of every color bound together into the great divine circle. Tapestries told the stories of the gods and the creation of the world. Gleaming figures stood between the mortals of the world, all clamoring for spoils and blessings, and a great and giant beast that lay sleeping in the void above the gods.

The men who were doomed stood in a circle, all of them facing me. Lucien, Andoleth, Darion, Rimmul, Palig, Mavren, and Gelraan were there, yet I knew that there were others of their number that were missing. Their faces were filled with displeasure and disappointment, and some of them wore the pallor of a deathly guise.

"Alexander, thou may not go around murdering our subjects of thy own volition, especially when are they members of the sacred circle. We are bound together by a holy oath. Thou hast broken the circle, young wizard," Darion, he who would be called Emperor, said to me.

"How would you punish him, my lord?" a voice came slithering to my ears. Se'Naat glided up beside The King. "Alexander is bound into the circle, just as all of you."

Darion looked displeased.

Andoleth, wearing his macabre armor, glared at me. His desire to carve me into little pieces nearly burst forth through the anger in his eyes.

Palig whispered sinister things into Andoleth's ear, and the warlord nodded in response.

I tried to bend my hearing so that I could hear what Palig was saying, but alas, I could not quite make it out.

"I'm sorry," I said. "I thought we had taken an oath to protect the world from things which would seek to destroy it.

Chapter 15

All but Lucien looked at me with unforgiving eyes.

"Frondius had become a mindless monster. He had to be stopped." Confidence filled my voice, and I felt my back straighten.

Only Lucien's eyes held any understanding, and yet, he walked away without saying a word, abandoning me to the judgement of these bloodthirsty fools.

"It seems that the commander has the right idea," Gelraan scoffed and departed the circle of judgement.

Those who remained looked at me with murderous intent, but I knew that they would not dare attack me here. Not in this holy place. Silently, I stood my ground, and eventually they left me alone in that empty temple. I closed my eyes and thanked the gods, then found comfort that I had not been forced to use my knife.

When I opened my eyes, I was back in the chamber with the beast. His chains rattled with the last remnants of his defiance.

My eyes focused on the beast's distorted face as I walked towards him. He growled with the remainder of his energy, like an animal fighting for survival with his last breath. My hand reached out and I felt my fingers wrap themselves around the handle of a dagger. There was a sinister smirk in my throat, and I choked it back so I could savor the intensity of this moment.

"Shh. Shh. Shh. It is alright. The pain will all be ended soon. Tonight, you will be released from this place, from this torment." My promises were all lies. I didn't want to release him. I wanted to drink the juice of his misery. Nervously, I rolled the handle of that dagger around in my hand, making sure to keep it hidden from The Abomination. Slowly, I made my approach, ducking under some of the chains which held his limbs stretched into place. The room was round, but seemed to have no walls. Chains ran off into the darkness that hugged the room, and the brazier burned serenely, casting dancing shadows behind the beast.

Flayed

He struggled in vain to keep his eyes on me as I walked around him. When I slipped from his view, I could sense his fear growing more intense. Like a beast come for the slaughter, he felt resigned to his fate. He knew that this was the end, even before my knife slipped into the back of his throat. Wet gurgles escaped his flesh as his black blood flooded out of his wound. With my blade deep inside his body, I could feel the pumping of his unnatural heart.

I closed my eyes and listened to the beat of his dying pulse for a moment. It was beautiful. I wanted my soul to be one with his so that I could feel it depart, like standing in the rain for the final moments of the storm. Deeper I dug my knife, and I heard him grunt as its sharp edge sliced its way through more of his soft flesh.

"Not as dead as once we seemed," I whispered to the beast.

Instincts drove me to place my empty hand on the other side of his neck. Even in the moment, I was confused by this strange and unbidden inspiration, but I followed it. My right hand was covered in the flowing river of blood, and my other embraced the flesh of his neck, and something strange happened. I felt my power grasp the fabric of his soul.

A wind of fire blew through my spirit, and I saw into the eyes of the universe itself. The sun, moon, and stars all made sense for that instant, and I saw their predator, the dark force which hid between the stars, lurking, stalking, and waiting for the right moment to pounce. Not even the endless force which had given rebirth to our universe countless times knew about this danger. These things were the terrors that sat upon the edge of oblivion, and they waited to devour all the worlds, both seen, unseen, and even the great curtain that separates our worlds from the gods.

Chapter 15

Fear gripped me, and I wondered if these great and twisted beasts were looking back at me through this terrifying view that I had of their own hearts. Suddenly, I felt my own pulse match the heartbeat that I heard echoing through this space between the stars. This black blood I spilled was theirs, The Abomination was their handiwork, yet he had been created by my own hand. *Did this mean that I was nothing more than a tool for these unspeakable horrors?* I railed at the thought of it.

His soul began to be pulled away and pulled apart. The pulse of the dark things grew even greater as they anticipated the grand feast. I watched with unseen eyes as thousands of hideous tentacles reached forth from a dimension unknown to mortal men and shredded The Abomination's soul before my magical sight.

I refused to let this once-kind man fall prey to these cosmic predators, so I dug the fingers of my left hand into his flesh until my nails struck bone. My grip became like that of an unholy vice, and I felt his bones break like twigs under my might. Power surged through me unlike I had ever felt. Magic greater and deeper than even The Cursing was surging through my flesh and my soul. In that moment, I became a devourer of souls, an eater of life, and I was elated as I felt the pulse of power, for I was denying them. They were the true parasites upon the fates of men, and I swore a secret oath as The Abomination's power surged through me, that I would be their undoing.

Blinking away the tears that were forming in my eyes ended up blinking me away too.

Suddenly, I was looking down at the face of a man whom I cradled in my arms. His face was filled with pain and sorrow, yet his brilliant green eyes still held a glimmer of joy. Teague was dying in my arms.

Flayed

Dust covered his skin, making him look older than I knew he was. Blood was splattered and streaked across his face and down his torso. His doublet, once the actual image of color and beauty, was now ragged, dirty, and torn. Blood soaked his torso, and I suddenly felt his warmth running over us both as the river of his life poured forth from the wound in his gut. My head stopped turning, but I could feel the unmistakeable leather wrappings of Ukumog in my hand. I knew that it was the dark blade that had split open my dearest friend, and I began to weep. Grey tears dropped from my face onto his dusty doublet, and I was without words.

"Wrack, my friend. It seems that our journey has come to a rather abrupt end," he struggled to say through the pain. "I fear that I won't be much of an able companion shortly," he chuckled, gurgling up some blood.

In my arms, I felt his body shiver from the pain that his wounds charged him for his humor. The temperature of his body spiked upwards, and I felt helpless. I knew that all my power, and even my blood, could not undo the wounds that Ukumog had done to him.

"Why are you the one who is crying?" he asked me. "It is I who will never see my daughter again, you selfish bastard." His smile beamed through the blood and dust.

For a moment, his humor overwhelmed my sense of regret. A pulse of warmth travelled down Ukumog, and I felt the rush of power shoot through me from the hand I had upon the handle. Stillness filled my heart, and I knew that the sword was drinking his soul, stealing it from his body. The sword was devouring my friend.

"I have to remove the blade, Teague. If I don't, Ukumog will slurp away your soul, and there will be nothing left of you to return to your beloved mistress," I said.

Chapter 15

He nodded and clenched his jaw, waiting for the burst of pain to run its course. Gently, I set his head upon the ground, and stood up. Ukumog pulsed with malice and hunger as I put both my hands upon its handle, then with one swift tug, I pulled it free from Teague's fallen body.

Blood erupted from the terrible wound and then began flowing freely. Time slowed as I tossed Ukumog to the ground and leapt upon Teague's wound, trying to put pressure on it to stop the bleeding. Wet blood pulsed through my dusty fingers, and I only succeeded in slowing the flow a bit. Teague lay there, in a pool of moonlight, looking up at the night sky.

"Funny, innit?" he asked. "How things start, and how they end? I suppose I always knew it would end this way, my friend. It is the part we play in this damnable theatre called life." He laughed again, causing him to cough up a lungful of blood.

I said nothing, still holding onto both hope and his wound. Silently, I wished for a different outcome, but deep down, I knew that this was the end.

"Wrack. We had a bit of fun, didn't we?" He smiled at me with bloody teeth. "Can I ask you a favor, friend?"

Tears burst from my eyes and fell onto the backs of my bloody hands. "Anything, Teague."

"When you aren't busy killin' The Baron or The King, would you mind checking in on my wife and daughter? Seems I won't be around to make sure that Brinny grows up strong and brave, like her old man," he said, coughing up more blood.

Guilt flooded my mind, I blamed myself for this brilliant man being here in an ocean of his own blood. I struggled through the lump in my throat to offer a hollow promise, "I will."

Flayed

He smiled one last time, and then set his head down and lifted his eyes again to the night sky. "Beautiful..." he said to no one, and then stopped moving. The blood had stopped pushing its way through my fingers, and his body rapidly began to cool. My only friend was gone.

I sat back from his body and cried. Tears came freely, and my face hurt from the sorrow. I was stricken by this pain for hours. The well of my grief was deeper than I could have ever imagined. While I sat there, a cold wind blew in, and brought with it a dusting flurry of snow. The tears on my face began to chill my flesh and bite me as they left my eyes. Teague's blood I wiped away onto my dirty robes, and my freezing tears onto my sleeve. With cold hatred in my heart I turned and saw Ukumog glowing dimly in the darkness. No part of me wanted to touch this foul enemy that had taken away my only friend. Instead, I roared in frustration and sorrow. My voice was amplified by my dark power, and its intensity echoed down the road. I hoped that all The Doomed could hear my rage and feel my misery. For soon I would bring it to bear against them.

My sobs within the dream carried me somewhere else. In the deep darkness of my unholy forge, I stepped back and marveled at my handiwork. There, on the featureless black anvil, lay a blade in the shape of a long rectangle. Its edges gleamed with sharp malice, and the dark surface of its flat side seemed to be the eternal depth of the universe itself.

"Two more steps," I said to no one.

Using my left hand, I tore off the flesh of my own forefinger exposing the bone beneath. The rush from the pain sustained me as I sent my dark power through the links of my finger, and with its sharp tip I began to carve into the surface of the blade.

Chapter 15

Days went by with no rest, as I carved the detail of each symbol into the flat surface until fifteen symbols were engraved with power, pain, and anger on each side. When all the runes were complete, they took on a faint blue glow.

Clutching the pain in my hand, I spoke again to no one, "Last step. Every sword needs a handle."

Digging the fingers of my left hand into my right shoulder, I pulled and pulled. First there was the snap as the shoulder dislocated, then began the terrible rending of skin and muscle. Black blood flowed through the tears in my skin as they appeared, yet I continued pulling. In my head I remembered the mocking laughter of The King and The Baron as they sealed me away in this tomb, as they called it. They called me The Betrayer, because I had dared to do what they would not. It was they who had corrupted the sacred oath that made us all the eternal protectors of the world. They who had turned our blessing into a curse, and through them that the world itself was doomed. Through my pain, my anger, and my sacrifice they would all meet their end.

Righteous thoughts gave me a burning courage, and it was with that extra strength that I was able to complete the job. With a sickening snap, my right arm came off my body. I threw the lifeless limb upon the anvil. From my stump of a shoulder, a shower of dark blood sprayed the room, some of it spattering upon the blade. Before my eyes, the blood somehow etched another symbol into the base of the blade: a sun with eight rays. For a brief moment, the rays glowed with a silver light, and my black blood gathered into the spot of the sun itself, making the symbol complete. A black sun with silver rays. Deep within the blood, I could see my own reflection. The anger in my eyes glowed with an intense fire, and the face that looked back at me looked more like a monster than a man.

Flayed

All the events of my life had led to this specific moment. Should my soul be damned so that I might save the world from those corrupted monsters who wished to consume it, I would go unflinching into the darkness, but I would see light returned to the world, no matter the cost. This was the fate I chose for myself, and I did so gladly.

Pain shot through me again, as my right arm began to regenerate. The shock of it was so immense that it knocked me to the cold stone floor. Hours seemed to pass as my shoulder gave birth to a new arm. When I was whole again, I began stripping the flesh from the limb which lay lifeless upon the altar of fabrication. The meat I burned in the purple flames of my magical forge. The skin I magically manipulated, using my own blood, and turned into long strips of red leather. The bone from my upper arm I fused to the blade as it lay upon the anvil, leaving the ball of my old shoulder as the pommel. Carefully, I wrapped the leather around the handle, returning my flesh to the bone.

"The blade is not yet finished, my boy." The voice of my long dead grandfather echoed through the chamber. "The final spell must be cast, and then a name must be given."

I grabbed the bowl of ashes from the anvil, and began sprinkling them down the length of the blade. As they reached the purple flames, they erupted into golden fire, and with each burst of light, the runes upon the sword flared to life underneath them. I did this three times for each side of the blade, murmuring words so magical and so arcane that they sounded like nothing but formless noise through the vision.

When I was done, I reached for the handle of the sword, and lifted it before me as if the darkness held those the sword was crafted to destroy. "I, Alexander of The Great Tower name thee Ukumog, the final voice."

Chapter 15

Power rushed through the chamber like a hurricane, and in its torrent, I was lost.

I returned to the world with a euphoric rush. Now it all made sense. All the visions, the reactions of every creature I had met up to that point. The final pieces had fallen into place. I was one of them. More than that, I was the most reviled member of their accursed number. In my heart, I suppose I always knew, and at my realization, I felt Murks fall into despair. This secret that he had guarded me against had unlocked itself all on its own.

There was a weight lifted, in that moment, where my curiosity was abated because I finally had found some truth. I was indeed a monster, perhaps the worst monster of them all. It was by my hand that The Curse corrupted the world and infested everything around me, and by that same hand that the terrifying sword had been crafted. The macabre handle was indeed a relic of my bones fused with a dark blade forged of my own emotions made real. Yet with all of these realizations, I finally breathed easier.

Brin turned and looked at me as my steps slowed. I gave her a warm smile and took her hand. Behind me, the city of Flay vanished beyond the tree-covered rolling hills. I gave it one more look before letting it pass out of my sight. In my thoughts, I said a quiet farewell to Mavren, who had been my unknown ally for all these years. *In my previous life, how did I miss his matched desire to destroy The Curse that lay upon all of us? I must have been stupid to not see that.*

After a day of travel, my old friends, plus this new traveller, took refuge in the wilderness to rest and eat. I watched them consume their meal and make their small talk, but I was still lost

Flayed

in my own thoughts. Trying to piece together a timeline of events from my shattered memories, I knew the sum of their parts, but the pieces still did not make sense. The future would undoubtedly have more things to show me from the past. I dared not share my new epiphany with anyone, especially Brin, for I had really no idea how they might react. Yet, I knew that not saying anything would eventually catch me in trouble when the truth was revealed, but this was a risk I felt was worth taking.

While all my friends were asleep, I never had time alone, as this new companion, Moriv, insisted that more than one of us stay on watch. I spent my time studying this stranger. There was obviously something deeper to his interest in our group than what he stated, yet I sensed a great conflict in him. The looks he gave Brin were the same that I knew I had once given her.

The smile that Brin often shared with me seemed to happen less frequently. She spent a great deal of time talking with Moriv as the two of them guided us towards his homeland. It gave me the distance and time to think. *What did it mean to be me? What did I want?*

Of course there was this mysterious legend of The Betrayer, how he turned on the other Doomed. I could not help but wonder, *how had he betrayed them?*

"He killed them, Master," Murks silently responded to my thoughts. "First it was one known as The Abomination, a poor man turned into a monster. The Betrayer imprisoned him and then found a way to end his torment."

A storm of memories rushed through my thoughts. I saw that twisted monstrosity lost in rage and destruction, but also I saw a meek man who only wanted to till the dirt of his land. Instead, he was gifted with a curse that caused him to destroy the villages of the people he was meant to protect. The magic of The Cursing

Chapter 15

turned against him. Then I saw a doorway, sealed with a gemstone key, that would transport me into a space that I controlled. It was that place where I was like unto a god that I turned it into a prison to hold the monstrous beast. That stream of thoughts had shown me how he was bound inside that dark place, and how I spent countless time torturing him. My work on him was not malicious, at least not at first. My goal of ending his torment, even if that meant his death, was plainly clear at the start, but then it seemed that I started to relish his misery. It sickened me. This person that I had become after The Cursing was someone I would never wish to be. He was darker than anything I had seen up to this point, worse than any of The Doomed that I had met. While he still looked human and alive, his soul was lost to the darkness.

Then I saw it again, his death. I remembered standing there, looking upon the lifeless corpse of The Abomination as his bubbling blood pooled into an ocean upon the floor, and I was disappointed. His scream, his death throes were not enough for me. I wanted more of this sadistic evil, I needed to kill more of them simply to feed the dark hunger I had for their suffering. My skin crawled at the knowledge that these were *my* thoughts, *my* desires. Not some fictional creature whom I could cast aside as a fairy tale or hearsay. I knew it to be true.

"Are you alright?" Moriv asked. We had been on watch together that night, and I had abruptly stood up.

I could not impart my dark history to this stranger, but I needed to step away. To walk under the night sky alone for a moment. To let the physical actions of my body push away the personal horrors that I had dredged out of the murky river of my past.

"I just need a little air," I said. Not waiting for a response, I walked out of the camp.

Flayed

Dire worry filled my mind as I roamed through the thick forest. I took small steps and avoided treacherous terrain, all while walking in a wide circle around the camp. I never let the tiny fire that warmed the bodies of the people I cared about out of my sight. I just could not reconcile my own fall from grace. Just as my frustration at a past I could not change reached its peak, and I felt like screaming, I walked into an open grove.

Moonlight, pure as liquid silver, poured into the serene opening within the trees. Instantly, I forgot about my troubles, and my eyes looked upwards into the starry heavens above. The moon hung low in the sky, and with my naked eye, I could make out some of the cracks and mountains on its surface. It had never seemed so brilliant or so bright. Its silvery light fell upon the earth and everything living seemed to be nourished by its kiss. The trees seemed to almost glimmer in the light, as if made of silver themselves. A peace washed over me that I had never known before. All conflict, frustration, and sorrow were brushed aside, and my very soul was lifted up.

There, in the middle of the grove was an impossibly beautiful woman. So graceful in her movements, so magical in the way the silver light reflected off her glimmering gown. She petted a small rabbit that sat passively in her lap, and then with a whimsical giggle, she let it free. Brushing her dark hair back over her shoulder, I saw her impossibly perfect face. She smiled at me. It was a smile filled with love. There was no malice or lustful greed. It was pure and true, and it shook me to my core.

Frozen in her gaze, I feared that my life would be pulled out through my eyes just trying to comprehend her indescribable beauty.

Chapter 15

"All these troubles, they too shall pass. Lift up your chin, Alexander," the woman said with a musical tone. "We know your road is hard, but if you give up, who else will lift up your burden?"

There were no words. My mind was overwhelmed by the beauty that was before me.

She smiled again, seemingly amused by my silence. "You are not alone, Alexander. Do not give up hope."

I blinked and a breeze passed over me. The woman was gone, as if she had never been there. The light from the moon did not glow as brightly, nor did the grove seem as lovely as it had before. My desperate burden returned, but this time I felt more prepared to carry the heavy weight.

"Did you just see a woman?" I asked Murks.

"What woman, Master?"

My eyes blinked, trying to shake the dust from my mind. "I may be going mad, Murks."

"Murks knows, Master. But Master cannot give up. There are many people who would suffer if not for you, Master."

"I know, Murks. I'm just not sure I am ready for whatever lies ahead." My feet started taking me back towards the camp.

"Murks knows you are ready, Master."

Knowing that at least this little creature, admittedly made of my own blood, understood what troubled me made my burden seem a tiny bit lighter. For that, I was immensely grateful.